Donald R. Burleson

Wait for the Thunder

Stories for a Stormy Night

Hippocampus Press

New York

Acknowledgements: See p. 299

Published by Hippocampus Press
P.O. Box 641, New York, NY 10156.
http://www.hippocampuspress.com

Cover art by Thomas S. Brown
Cover design by Barbara Briggs Silbert.
Hippocampus Press logo designed by Anastasia Damianakos.

First Edition
1 3 5 7 9 8 6 4 2
ISBN13: 978-0-9814888-1-3

For Chuck Harrell—

here's to sixty-plus years of friendship

Contents

Wait for the Thunder

Tumbleweeds

The desert sky, blue and vast and bright, lay like a warm hand over the town. Baking in the blaze of late afternoon, the one paved road came in from the chaparral country like a weary traveler looking for a place to rest, but found the town too small to stay and visit, and traveled on, rolling back out into limitless New Mexico desertland and vanishing in a dazzle of blistering light.

It wasn't much of a town, but to Jed Wilton it was the whole world, as it was to Homer Mills, Jed's friend for more years than anyone could remember. Sitting on the rickety porch steps of Trujillo's General Store, Jed and Homer smoked cheap tobacco in grimy corncob pipes and surveyed their world.

Across the dusty road, the boy who worked at the gas station tipped a chair back in the shade and dozed, leaving the gas pumps to stand sentry duty in the broiling sun. There hadn't been a car by in recent memory.

"Sure is hot," Homer said.

Time passed. Across the way, a gray cone of flies gathered, swirled in the shimmering heat, and dispersed, melting away like the remnants of a dream. Somewhere off in the distance, beyond the town, a jackrabbit scampered through a grizzle of sagebrush, leaving a wake of dust. In a moment the dust settled, and it was like an evaporation of dream-dust, as if nothing had happened, nothing had really moved, ever, in all of time. In any case it had been a long, long time since Jed and Homer had shot jackrabbits together.

"Sure is," Jed said.

"Sure is what?" Homer asked.

"Hot," Jed replied, scratching. "You said it was hot."

"I did?" Homer asked. "Yeah, maybe I did." He tamped fresh tobacco into the blackened stump of his pipe with a scrawny thumb and struck a match and sent tendrils of gray smoke out on the air, floating

11

like gossamer, then scattering away when a gust of wind roared in from the desert, pushing the heat ahead of it. Seemingly from nowhere, a huge tumbleweed rolled across the sandy plain behind the gas station, fetched up against a barbed wire fence, and huddled there until the wind shifted and sent it on its way again.

"You ever wonder about 'em?" Jed asked, refilling his own pipe and lighting it.

"Wonder about who?" Homer asked, squinting, rubbing dust from his eyes.

"Not who. What. Them tumbleweeds."

Homer pushed his greasy old bill-cap back a notch on his head and wiped at rivulets of sweat. "Tumbleweeds. What's there to wonder about? They catch along the fences and the sheep ranchers have to clear 'em away."

"No," Jed said, "I mean, where do they come from?"

"Well hell, if that's all that's bothering you," Homer said. "The plant dies, wind snaps her off at the stem, and she goes tumbling away." He spat into the dust. "Nothing mysterious about that."

"Okay," Jed said, "but did you ever see them plants alive and still in the ground? I mean, what kind of plant is it, what does it look like, before it's a tumbleweed?" The wind rose a little, and three or four tumbleweeds, smaller than the one before, scuttered along the street like some boisterous gaggle of schoolchildren out jaywalking.

"Can't say as I ever worried much about it," Homer said, puffing his pipe.

They fell silent, watching, listening to the wind whisper up the lonely street. Jed's pipe, neglected, went out, and he relit it and smoked it thoughtfully. After a long while Homer spoke up again, as if no time had elapsed.

"It's like worrying about where we go after we die," he said. "Where do we go? Maybe we go to heaven and play a harp. Maybe we go to Vegas and play the slot machines. Maybe we don't go noplace. Drive a man daffy thinking about it, so why bother? Leave it to them religion people to figure it all out, is what I say."

They fell silent again. The wind, persistent, moaned about the parched eaves of the old building, searching, probing. Inside, through the dilapidated screen door, they could hear Juan Trujillo humming a song to himself, something in Spanish.

"Still, it sure does seem odd," Jed said after a while. "We don't really know much of anything about them. What are they, where do they come from, where are they going?"

"Huh," Homer snorted, knocking dottle out of his pipe on the edge of his shoe. "They're gnarly ugly damn weeds, they come from where the wind's blowing from, and they're going to where the wind's blowing to. There. The problem doctor has solved all your problems neat and proper, so you don't have nothing left to worry about. Course, there's the little matter of my fee. That'll be fifty dollars."

"Funny man," Jed said. "C'mon, it's going on dinnertime over to Miss Walker's."

The two of them, wheezing, struggled to their feet like a wobbly pair of cranes. Everybody, Jed thought, everybody thinks they're a damn comedian. Can't talk to some people about anything serious. Same old Homer, he reflected—wouldn't ever change if he lived to be a hundred and ten. Even his walk was the same, if a little slower, after all these years—reeling forward, pausing, then reeling forward again, like a series of false starts. Following Homer up the street in the direction of the boarding house, Jed had to admit he liked the old fart.

The next afternoon, or maybe it was the afternoon after that—one day looked pretty much like another—they were sitting on the steps at Trujillo's again, smoking their pipes, drowsing. Across the way, the boy at the gas station might have been some strange growth that had accreted there like a barnacle; he was still asleep in the tipped-back chair, might have been asleep there forever for all a person could tell.

Chief of Police Hawkins strolled up to Trujillo's and paused, surveying the two occupants of the porch steps.

"This is the only building in town that's got gargoyles," he said.

"Morning, Chief," Homer said, gesturing with his pipe.

"You two old boys practically live on these steps," Hawkins said, grinning and shaking his head.

"Everybody's gotta be somewhere," Jed said.

"I reckon so," Hawkins laughed, going on up the steps between the two old men and opening the screen door. "Don't go getting in any trouble, now."

"Chief, if we was young enough to go getting in any trouble," Homer said over his shoulder, "we wouldn't be here."

They could hear Hawkins chatting with Juan Trujillo inside, soft voices that floated out on the air and faded away.

"So you still worried about them tumbleweeds?" Homer asked Jed, smacking at his pipe and spitting a brown wad of phlegm into the dust.

"Funny," Jed said, "that you said what you did. I mean, about it being like worrying about where we go after we die."

"Here we go again," Homer said, "the philosophers at work. Where do you think we go?"

Jed puffed his pipe, stared out into the white glare of the desert, shook his head. "How do I know? Don't nobody know that. I don't care what them Sunday school teachers say, ain't nobody ever come back from the other side to tell us about it, so how do we know? Answer is, we don't. We don't know diddly-squat. But I just keep thinking."

The wind crept up, warm and dry, gathered a little strength, and explored the creaking rafters of the building behind them. Down the road leading in from the desert, a little group of ragged shapes bumbled along in the wind like odd sea animals that had forgotten that this hadn't been a sea bottom for millions of years.

"I just keep thinking," Jed said again, "about them tumbleweeds."

Homer said nothing in reply, and it was the reply Jed had expected. Homer was a very special old man, but he wasn't made for deep questions like this.

Chief Hawkins came out of the store carrying a paper bag and paused to look back at the two loungers. "You fellows take it easy now." Then he was off up the street and gone.

Later on, Geraldine Kelly, who played piano at the church, walked by and waved and continued on her way somewhere.

No one had any way of knowing that this was the last afternoon anyone would see Homer and Jed on these rickety old wooden steps together.

That night Miss Walker served fried chicken, mashed potatoes, and black-eyed peas for dinner at the boarding house, and by ten o'clock Jed and Homer had both gone up to their rooms to turn in. But lying alone in his little room, eyes wide in the dark, Homer couldn't sleep.

Something he couldn't quite grasp kept running around the back of his mind, something furtive and unaccountable, like a spider, or like—

He was up in the dark, pulling his trousers and shirt back on and slipping his feet into his shoes, and sneaking down the stairwell and across the lightless parlor and out into the desert night.

He waited till he was down the road from the house before he lit his pipe. There were only a few other houses on this street, mostly quiet and dark now, their windows dulled in sleep. He walked to the end of the street, took a turn, and meandered down an alley toward the edge of town. Why he was out here he couldn't have said. Looking for something? Just trying to sort out his thoughts? He didn't know. Probably some damn fool nonsense that that old cuss Jed had planted in his head with all his silly talk. Jed was his dearest friend, but he could be a bit of a pest sometimes. Anyway, Homer thought, here I am, out in the night alone for no good reason, like a crazy man.

He came to the end of the alley, where the town essentially ended too. Behind him, houses slept side by side, exhausted from the heat of the day. Before him, beyond the limits of town, a dark endless void of desertland stretched away into the night like the unreverberant emptiness between galaxies. Overhead, the sky, black and cloudless, was frosted with icy stars. Somewhere in the night, a coyote howled, a mournful sound that drifted on the sable air and was lost.

Homer stood for a moment, at a loss himself, then turned left along the caliche sideroad, heading toward the main road through town. He still wondered why he was out here at this hour. Maybe he just needed to clear his head, get some fresh air, get good and tired so that he'd sleep when he got back to bed. Making his way along the silent street, he tended to trudge forward, pause, trudge forward. Jed would tease him about that sometimes. And as if in response to this thought about Jed, the wind came up a little from the sandy plains, sighing, playing among the yucca and chamisa and sage, riffling the range grass like fingers through hair. And with the wind—

Farther down, an indistinct mass was moving across the road. Even in the uncertain light, Homer knew that it was a little group of tumbleweeds herded along by the husky breath of wind that sighed among the nearby telephone wires and raised warm, subtle touches of dust from the desert plains, wind that prodded the eternal tumbleweeds on, on, on, from places unknown to other places unknown.

Well. He had walked just about far enough anyway, time to turn around and get back home. As he turned to retrace his steps, he noticed that the tumbleweeds out in the dark in the direction he had been heading were veering in their course, altering their path to edge toward him.

So the wind had shifted. Nothing unusual about that; the wind shifted from one second to the next out here.

By the time he got back to the point where he had emerged from the alley, the tumbleweeds had rolled closer, and there appeared to be more of them now. But they were still perhaps fifty or sixty feet away, and anyhow, why should he care? They had brambles on them, but he'd never heard of anybody getting mauled by tumbleweeds. He turned down the alley and continued on his way.

And when the tumbleweeds reached the mouth of the alley, they turned too. And came into the alley behind him.

Now this was a bit strange, he reflected, shuffling on up the alley, looking back from time to time. He didn't understand why they would come up the alley like that, when he could see, back out on the caliche road, that the dust there continued to blow more or less in the direction it had been blowing; the wind itself didn't seem to be coming through the alley, which was sheltered by fences. There was a streetlamp out in front of one row of houses somewhere, but it cast only a wan and half-hearted illumination back here. Still, he could see the tumbleweeds, perhaps twenty-five or thirty of them now, bumbling their way up the alley, drawing closer. At times they would rattle and scratch their way along the back fences, rebounding, scraping, breaking clear, then they would advance along the middle of the alley, unobstructed. Getting closer all the time.

He stopped in his tracks, wheeled all the way around, and faced the tumbleweeds.

They stopped too. Others, new ones, rolled up to them from behind and stopped. After a moment, they all began edging forward, rustling along the dry ground. Then they came on again, at their natural speed, threatening to cover the intervening space in perhaps only a few seconds if Homer remained still.

This was ridiculous. He faced back around in the direction he had been walking, up the alley. Ahead, there was a recess in one of the back fences where someone had parked a car just off the alleyway, and he headed for the spot, resolving to dodge in there and get out of the path of the tumbleweeds, avoid them, let them tumble on by and be gone. He reached the spot where the fenceline turned inward toward a lightless back yard and where the car was parked, and he turned the corner of the fence and entered the recess. There was room here, despite the car, and he leaned against the rough boards of the fence and started catching his breath.

And the tumbleweeds came into the recess.

"Damn." Pushing himself away from the fence, he started angling around toward the front end of the car, deeper into the recess, but the tumbleweeds, rolling forward, followed him. Some of them bunched up in the rear, as if waiting to round the corner and come in. It was hard to see over the ones in front, but there might altogether have been thirty or forty of them now.

"Damn," he said again, appalled at how empty and powerless his voice sounded on the night air against the dry burring of the tumbleweeds as they came pressing on. They were larger than he had thought, as well as more numerous, but there was room for most of them in here. He rounded the front of the parked car, only to find that one fender was closer to the fence than the other, so that the space between the car and the fence tapered off to nothing. The tumbleweeds, rasping forward as if under their own volition, came around the front end of the car too, closing him in altogether.

And in a moment they were upon him.

Jed sat on the porch steps at Trujillo's, smoking. After a world of weeping, his face was dry of tears now, dry with a million desert days, dry and crumpled with loneliness. The boy across the way slumbered in his chair as always. Jed wondered idly if he ever woke up. If he ever would wake up.

Homer certainly never would wake up. The coroner who had come over from Santa Rosa said it was probably a wild animal attack of some kind, bobcat maybe. How conveniently they explained away the end of a man's life. Death by bobcat. Homer, Jed suspected, would have laughed at that one himself. But Homer was in a box, and the box was in the ground. At least it had been a pretty nice little funeral.

The folks at the boarding house had all come, of course, and Jed thought someone had sung "Amazing Grace," but he remembered surprisingly little of the ceremony.

Now, today and tomorrow and the next day and the next day, this was going to be the time for remembering. Remembering a friendship stretching back—how many years?—sixty, seventy? He and Homer had talked about it, more than once over the years, and neither could even remember when they had first met.

But Jed thought he knew how they would meet again.

Because the wind was rising now, whispering through the dry boards of the general store, feeling its way into corners, feeling its inexorable way into Jed's old bones. And ahead of the wind, driven like a deranged herd of scruffy sheep, came the tumbleweeds.

Just passing through, for now.

Just passing through, but one of them, rather larger than the others, had a way of lurching forward, pausing, lurching forward again, even when its companions simply rolled continuously on.

Where do we go, Homer had asked, when we die?

Where do we go, Jed had wondered, when we die?

Where do we go, whom do we see again, on the other side? With whom, with what old companions in the undying heat of desert days and nights, do we hunt?

One-Night Strand

It wasn't much of a motel. Eric had started forming that opinion while edging the Toyota off the highway and onto the bumpy drive in front of the office, where a neon sign proclaimed "VACANCY" in sputtering yellow hesitancies as if laboring under the ravages of some strange electrical disease. The opinion grew a little stronger while he was checking in, under the ministrations of a sallow desk clerk whose breath conjured up impressions of beer-vomit and unwashed dentures. And the opinion grew stronger still when Eric saw his room, number 18, where he suspected he was not to be the only guest, not if you counted tiny ones with more than two legs. But maybe it wasn't that bad, maybe he was just tired. A quick look around revealed dinginess but no obvious vermin, and the plumbing did seem to work, minimally.

At any rate, it was dark, and he had to get off the road and get some sleep. This certainly wasn't one of those places with key-cards and free coffee and color TV, but it was going to have to do for tonight.

Room 18 at least had the virtue of being at the end of a row of rooms, with number 17 on the right but with nothing on the left but an open field stretching off into the night. Not that noisy neighbors would have been a problem anyway, he thought, surveying the place as he closed up the car and took his single bag to the door; there were only a few other cars here and there, down the way, and it was already pretty late. It appeared that nobody was in number 17, next door, and that was fine with him. He was going to be sleeping like a mummy as soon as his head hit the pillow.

But he didn't sleep. Lying on the spongy bed, he found himself wide-eyed in the dark. It was going to be one of those nights when he was paradoxically too tired to sleep. And it seemed a waste, when he had all this quiet around him, no noise from outside at all except a distant swish of passing highway traffic, and nobody in the room next door.

The thought was scarcely formed when a quick wash of headlights filtered through the drawn blinds, scattering a wild profusion of jittery shadows. Someone had pulled up in front of number 17 and shut off the engine. For a few seconds it was so quiet then that he could hear the low tick-tick-tick of the engine cooling. Then the opening of a car door, then other sounds: laughter, footsteps, a car door closing, someone fumbling with a key at the door of number 17, muttering, more footsteps, laughter again, a man's voice, then apparently a female voice, a chittering sort of giggle that Eric found somehow disquieting.

He had to get up and have a look.

Prying the edge of the blinds back an inch or two, he peered out. A dim bulb somewhere nearby cast a faint illumination on the scene. There next to the Toyota was a rusty-looking blue Dodge Colt, its front doors both hanging open, making it look like some giant insect. A tall, cadaverously thin man in a wrinkled light gray suit was standing next to the car door on the passenger side and appeared to be struggling to lift something out of the front seat, something large and lumpy under a blanket. Whatever it was, when the man got clear of the car with it, it seemed to poke angularly up into the blanket in places, and made Eric think vaguely of several bottles of champagne sticking up out of a large tub, as if anyone would bother to conceal such a thing under a blanket, especially at this hour and in a dump like this. That odd, chittering laughter came again, from somewhere, and Eric surmised that the mystery woman must already be inside the room. He just hoped they didn't make noise all night, but maybe that was hoping for too much.

As he watched, the thin man disappeared into Room 17 with his odd burden. Through the adjoining wall there filtered more mumbling and more laughter, his in a muffled bass, hers in that high staccato chirp that he found so uncomfortable. Momentarily the thin man reappeared, returning to the car and fumbling in the back seat for something. He went around slamming car doors and came stumbling back toward the motel room carrying a second burden even stranger than the first. Eric, watching from the dark of his room, blinked and tried to see more clearly in the wan light.

Mr. Bones, as Eric had decided to call him, was clutching a double armload of women's high-heeled shoes, maybe half a dozen pairs. They were all white, gaudy with sequins, and seemed to have holes cut in the soles, leaving just the toe and the spiky heel on each shoe, and a rim or outline of what would have been the sole. Mr. Bones dropped a few of the shoes on the pavement and bent over, wheezing and mumbling, to gather them up. Was this going to be how he got his thrills, then? Watching his companion for the evening change shoes repeatedly? The world was becoming a peculiar place to live. Well—let them do whatever they wanted, as long as they were reasonably quiet about it.

But of course there was no chance of that. Lying back in bed, he listened in the dark, and his anger grew.

Through the thin intervening wall, sounds kept coming. He writhed in the bedsheets, trying to get comfortable, trying to ignore the sounds. Muffled talking, muttering, laughing, now his deep and hollow voice, now her insane piping and chirping, now the bedsprings groaning. Eric put a pillow over his head, but that was intolerable; he felt as if he couldn't breathe. It was hot now, and muggy, and he was more uncomfortable by the minute.

Through the wall, the sounds would swell from time to time into a medley of murmuring gruffness and chittering giggles. Suddenly there came a succession of sounds not just through but along the wall, a frenzied clack-clack-clack-clack-clack-clack-clack-clack that sounded, for God's sakes, like high-heeled shoes on the opposite side of the wall. Was *that* it, then? Did Mr. Bones get his jollies watching her put a pair of the shoes on her hands and clack them in a noisy path across the wall? Were people, even these days, really crazy enough and rude enough to do things like that in a motel where other people were trying to sleep? Thoughtless bastards!

A near-quiet had fallen, over there, broken only by a sort of dry rustling like bedsheets. Maybe they were tired, ready for some sleep themselves. But the sounds came crashing through again to shatter the silence—gruff bass mumblings, protestations of bedsprings, the high, mindless chittering laughter and, without warning, another round of shoe-clatterings across the wall, so many and so fast that Eric figured they must *both* be up doing it this time. He'd heard of some strange ways of getting aroused, but this was a new one, and one he wished he hadn't discovered, at least not at this juncture in his life.

Silence fell again, and Eric lay rigid in his rumpled sheets, waiting.

Nothing, nothing for a long while. Then a low suggestion of whispering and quiet laughing, and unplaceable *other* sounds, strange arid sounds like the rustling and crackling of dry grass. A voice came through, gruff and low-timbred.

"Mm, that's good. Another strand. Oh, yeah. Tie me good and tight."

Eric sighed in the dark. Bondage, yet? Tying him to the goddamn bed. What else?

As if in reply, the sounds swelled out into a riot of shouting, thumping, giggling, with the clatter of shoes again in an invisible arc across the wall. "Oh, g'haaaa—oh! Uh!" It sounded like a man in pain, but then there was no surprise in that, considering the source, Eric reflected. "H-hh-uuuh! Uh!" A sound like gurgling in the throat, and more of that idiotic chirping laughter, more thumping, more shoes across the wall, this time in a wider arc that seemed to go off the adjoining wall and fade onto the other walls of number 17, as if the lunatic woman were "running" the shoes clear around the room, and all the while no letup on the muttering and gurgling and chirping.

Eric was up on his feet, furious. If these inconsiderate sons of bitches thought they were going to go at this all night, they were going to have to reconsider their plans, and that was a pure fact. Pulling his trousers on, he made for the door.

Outside, the sounds were of course even louder. Eric had his fist poised over number 17, ready to knock, but thought: hmm, who knows what kind of loony-bin types we're really talking about here? The kind, perhaps, that would pick up a gun and blow you away, right through the door? Maybe he'd better check things out. Surprisingly, the blinds in number 17 were open, and he bent to look in, cupping his hands around his eyes to block out the reflection of the light behind him.

There was a low lamp on in the room, in fact, across on the far wall, and it served to lend a little illumination to objects in there, but it still took him a minute to understand what he was looking at.

In the uncertain light the bed looked rather like a large spool of thread, with wrappings of some fibrous matter in sticky-looking strands around a moving lump in the middle, a lump with a protruding head that bobbed and brayed with laughter. The threads were wound loose, actually, because Eric could see patches of the thin, naked body of Mr. Bones, and indeed the groin area had been left clear.

She was there, all right, all of her, bigger than Mr. Bones, her head down between his legs, her own angular legs and arms splayed out to clutch the sides of the mattress. Only it wasn't really arms and legs—it was just legs. Eric must have made some involuntary sound at the window, because suddenly her body turned, without relinquishing her multiple hold on the bed. As it came around, the shiny, bulbous abdomen scattered a silky froth on the air above the bed, and the face jerked toward him. Its unthinkable arachnid contours were smeared with lurid splashes of lipstick and rouge—obscene red markings that folded and refolded as the nightmare mouth continued to work, sucking the air. Eric froze at the window, and the myriad clustered little eyes seemed to pierce him, seemed to pin him to the night like a bug on velvet.

But she was up off the bed now, moving, making her way across the left-hand wall again, toward the window, chirping and chittering as she came. Eric had overestimated the supply of gaudy white high-heeled shoes; there were exactly four pairs, and she was wearing them all. As she came clattering around, he caught a glimpse of the bed, where the head in the silky wrappings lifted a thin, bemused face that grinned as if in vague drunken approval.

It was the high heels reaching the window that broke Eric's trance. And broke the window as she came trundling through, fiddling her legs over the sill, dropping two or three sequin-spangled high-heeled shoes off onto the cement. One sinewy leg actually touched his face before he could move away. Recoiling, he scrambled blindly and collided with the front end of his car, frantic not to have her touch him again. She plopped heavily to the ground and came after him.

He had a frantic sensation of dodging a hideous flurry of movement that seemed to come at him from everywhere, a deranged sensation of running around the car to find that she had scuttered under it to meet him as he fumbled the car door open. By the time his head began to clear a little, he could only infer that he had managed to get inside the car, and that his keys must have been in his pants pockets, because he was driving headlong into the night somewhere, not looking back at all, and trying not to think.

But some furtive corner of his mind kept remembering all the tiny bound bundles he'd ever seen suspended jittering in spiderwebs, tragic little scenarios in dusty corners of garages and toolsheds and attics, and he thought of Mr. Bones, and gave the Toyota some more gas.

Hopscotch

It was a ghoulish-looking place.

Flaunting its decay in a wash of toadstool-colored moonlight, it was the very picture of urban death, this rotting brickpile at the corner of Jespersen Avenue and Sixteenth Street. Where the warm lights of cosy apartments had once shown through their drawn shades like mellow eyes contemplating the night, the glow that bespoke life had long since departed, and the beetling face of the building had caved in, folding its dark eyes appallingly down and under, like collapsed sockets in a miasma of bone. Above what was left of an ancient door frame, the numbers 4022 tottered meaninglessly, and somehow that was the worst of all: that such squalor could have an address. She found it hard to believe, now, that life had once flourished here.

But, she reflected with an involuntary sigh, it had.

This whole part of the city was pretty much in ruins: a vastness of dark jutting shapes, remnants of vacant windows and half-collapsed walls and toothlike shells of buildings stretching away into the night in every direction, a ghost town in a dream, with only a flicker here and there of electric light in the distance, or the muted echo of distant traffic, to suggest that this was any real city at all, and not just a sprawling mass of corruption lying half embalmed under a shroud of sky. Off in the distance an ululation of wind sprang up, whistling, touching gaping rows of windows like the stops of some grotesque flute. Now, as she watched, even the few scattered lights were blinking out as if in despair, yielding to darkness. It was ineffably sad. But this corner was the most dismal, probably because she so especially remembered it the way it used to be.

This was what was left, then, of the old neighborhood.

Maybe it wasn't even safe now to linger on the street at night in such a place as this. Despite the attempts of the wan moon to dispel the darkness, the scene was mostly given over to shadow; the only streetlamps, sputtering yellow excrescences on the ends of scrawny goosenecks, were too far away to be of much use. And didn't many of these old buildings attract derelicts, winos, drug addicts? On her way here she had seen furtive figures crouched in dusky corners. But somehow these decrepit edifices at Jespersen and Sixteenth looked devoid of all forms of life, like cadavers forsaken even by the worms.

She was an anachronism now, standing here, seeing the place again after all these years. It has crumbled and died, she thought, yet here I am, come to see it; I have crumbled somewhat too, but I haven't died—I'm like the oldest family fossil, haunting the funeral home and witnessing, wraithlike, the last rites of others, myself surviving to stand owlish and half apologetic beside their remains.

Strange, that the place made her feel this way. She was only sixty-seven, and sixty-seven wasn't old. It just seemed so very long ago, now, that she had been skinny little Linda Sanchez here, all pigtails and braces and scraped knees and eyes aglow with childhood spirit and love of life. Now she was skinny retired accountant Linda Sanchez, the survivor: mousy hair instead of pigtails, false teeth instead of braces, arthritis instead of scraped knees, thick glasses instead of bright young eyes, and a repository of fading memories instead of love.

Somewhere, as if in choral response to this thought, a crowd of young people laughed faintly in the distance and the sound swirled around some corner and was gone. Here, on the old corner of Jespersen and Sixteenth, though, there was no one but her, and she had never felt so alone. Why, why in God's name had she come? Why had she gotten off the bus over on Ninth Street instead of just riding it home? She had lived across town for decades without ever really wanting to return here, and she should have known that it would be depressing here, where nothing remained of her faraway youth, and only urban blight showed its diseased face to the moon.

But was it true that nothing whatever remained?

She turned to her left and walked slowly away from the corner, past the shapeless wreck that had once been her apartment building—Mom, Dad, Lucy, Carlos, the birthday parties, the Christmas mornings, the joys, the sorrows—and stopped in front of the space between that building and what remained of the building next door, now a heap of slag and unaccountable cables lolling half in, half out of the debris like the entrails of some great fallen beast. Between the buildings, a narrow alleyway (irregular and ragged even in those far-off days and flanked by staggering walls of smoke-grimed brick), an oddly crooked, cheerless alleyway had retreated from the sidewalk into realms of increasing mystery, a fissure from dim light to brooding darkness, dead-ending some thirty feet back at a windowless wall, the rear of a building that faced onto Keating Avenue.

And something remained of the old alley. It was more ragged than ever now, with scatterings of crumbled brick on either side, toward the back. Or as far back as she could see, anyway; at best, the moonlight only put tentative fingers part way down the shattered walls to cast a wan patina of light on the pavement back in there; and now scudding black clouds were obscuring the moon from time to time, leaving the alley sometimes utterly black, sometimes half illumined like some bizarre Victorian lantern show. She thought she could just make out, in the darkness at the end of the alley, a tangle of trash and weeds thicker and wilder-looking than the mess of dirty newspapers and soggy cardboard and broken bottles that she remembered always seeing there as a child. It was as if the detritus had gathered back there like some ancient mass of phlegm at the base of a throat that had never quite succeeded in coughing it all up.

She stood on the deserted sidewalk looking at the spot. It fascinated her that despite the passing of so many years the general contours of the old alley remained, a not terribly changed relic of former times. And a reminder.

Of Marnie Blake.

God, she hadn't thought of her for years.

Little Marnie Blake, with her chalky face incongruously framed in crow-black shoulder-length hair, and with pale blue eyes shining out of that face like the beckoning luminescent eyes of a store-window doll. Little Marnie from upstairs, with her peculiar talk and her odd way of seeming to know a great many arcane things. She was always rather like a gypsy child, with some unplaceable sense of strange heritage about her, as if the exotic flavor of far-flung places and nameless caravan nights lingered in her bearing in a way that one couldn't quite fathom.

Little Marnie Blake, who had taught them all about hopscotch.

Pale-faced, ethereal little Marnie, who had died horribly.

Horribly, on the very spot where all of them, all the neighborhood kids, had played the game.

Linda wondered if the hopscotch diagram could possibly still be there—and, adjusting her glasses on her nose and peering into the near-darkness of the alley, she saw to her astonishment that indeed it was.

Mere chalk of course would long since have faded away to nothing over the years, but this hopscotch tableau had been laid down in white paint—Marnie had painted it herself—and there it was, fainter now but discernible, emblazoned on the dirty cement like some ancient inscription over which an archaeologist might pause and nod. Imagine: still there, after all this time, that long, narrow configuration of numbered squares and rectangles that looked, Linda thought now, like a scaly, sickly white tongue lying flat in the bottom of a mouth.

The sight of it disturbed her enough to make her shudder and draw the collar of her coat tighter against the chilly air. Something about the scene was distinctly unsavory in its associations, but when she tried to pin down the source of this impression, she couldn't tell, in the sluiceway of her long-neglected memories, whether it was what she remembered of playing hopscotch here or what she remembered of Marnie herself that bothered her more; the two currents of memory were commingled, neither one completely coherent without reference to the other.

Dark-haired and pasty-faced Little Marnie Blake had at times been solemn in a way that perhaps would have seemed comic to an adult, but only seemed sobering, and at times a little unsettling, to other children. Down on hands and knees, painstakingly outlining the hopscotch pattern on the pavement, starting five or six feet inside the alleyway and extending it back into the gloomy shadows of the canyonlike walls, she might spare you a look over her shoulder while daubing white paint with her brush. "Don't you know hopscotch is a very *old* game?" she would ask. "Roman kids played it thousands of years ago."

Linda remembered a boy from down the hall, Kevin she thought his name was, asking, "You mean the Romans, like feeding the Christians to the lions and all that? How do *you* know what they did millions of years ago?"

"Thousands," Marnie said. "I know 'cause I read it in a book. And even before the Romans, people played hopscotch. A long long long long time ago."

"You're crazy," one of Kevin's brothers said.

"She is not," little Mollie from across the hall retorted. "You're just jealous 'cause a girl knows stuff you don't."

And so it went, the usual badinage of childhood—but it was really more than that. There was something about Marnie and her peculiar talk, and something about the avidity with which she played hop-scotch, that made you wonder. It wasn't just avidity—she played the game with a sort of religious fervor, as if she were propitiating some vile god who might come for you in a roiling black cloud one day if you slighted him. When she was hopping her way through the num-bered spaces she seemed desperate not to make a mistake, and at times the expression on her face would approach a kind of frenzy, as if she were teetering not near the edges of hopscotch squares but on the edge of some frightful abyss.

But now that Linda thought about it a little longer, she felt that a large part of what was bothering her about these memories was the long-suppressed recollection of her own turns at hopscotch, a recollec-tion all the more disturbing because time had rendered it vague with-out making it less ominous.

In those childhood days she had been lithe, clever, quick on her feet, and having played hopscotch plenty of times before on the school grounds and elsewhere, she at first approached the numbered spaces in the dim alleyway with a swagger of confidence. But there was some-thing odd about the way it worked, there in the alley.

She couldn't quite think what it was, but she recalled that some-how when she would start to hop through the squares, it would seem okay when she started but would be different after she got going, dif-ferent in some peculiar way that, once moving, she couldn't do any-thing about. She always ended up feeling trapped, tricked, betrayed. What was it? How had it been different from what she expected? She couldn't remember exactly.

What she did remember was one particular time when she had finished and sat down just inside the alleyway with her back to the wall of
her building, and Marnie had sat next to her and leaned close to her face
and said, with great solemnity, "You almost slipped, you know." Linda
had been so astonished at the earnestness of this remark that she hadn't
known what to say. But after a moment's reflection Marnie had added:
"But then I guess it doesn't matter that much with you. I'm the one."

Linda had shaken her head in puzzlement. "What do you mean,
you're the one?"

Marnie had looked at her almost pityingly, like a much older person trying to explain something inexplicable to a child. "I'm—just the
one. The one chosen." And that was all she would say.

Linda couldn't be sure, now, how long it was after that, before—
God! she shuddered again, remembering more vividly—before whatever happened happened.

One morning she had heard a lot of crying and shouting upstairs,
and in the stairwells and outside. People were milling around in great
consternation, and the police came, and someone upstairs was sobbing. In those days adults didn't take children greatly into their confidence, and it was left to Linda's own ingenuity to ferret out and piece
together what had happened, mostly from the talk among the kids on
the street. She gathered that one of the people in the building, a man
who lived down the hall from Linda's folks on the first floor, had
found poor little Marnie Blake disemboweled and scattered in the alley.

Or at any rate had found as much of her as hadn't apparently been
eaten.

The police would call it a vicious and senseless killing, possibly
even an act of cannibalism, perpetrated by some homicidal maniac of
whom they could find no trace. So far as Linda knew, no one was ever
charged with the crime.

She stepped into the alley now and stood looking at the spot
where she had sat, those many years ago, beside doomed little Marnie.
There on the cracked and dirty pavement she noticed a bottle-cap, not
a relic from those early days, surely, but suggestive nonetheless.

On an impulse she picked it up, turned it a moment in her fingers,
and tossed it onto the square that was still legibly numbered 1.

Now that she stood a little closer she saw that all the squares and rectangles still bore their old numbers, touchingly now, in Marnie's childhood scrawl: side-by-side squares 1 and 2 in front, then a rectangular bar numbered 3, then side-by-side squares 4 and 5, then rectangular bar 6, then side-by-side squares 7 and 8. This was one of countless existing variants on the game of hopscotch, but it was the one she knew from her youth on these streets.

But *did* she still know how it worked?

Again on an unreflective impulse she drew a breath, steadied herself as best she could, and hopped with her right foot onto square 2. It hurt a little, bringing her weight down on the ankle, but somehow she had to do this, and ignoring the pain she hopped again, planting the same foot in the long block 3. Could she really still do it? She doubted it; the smart thing would be to give it up, step aside, take one reminiscing look around, and start for home. But now she remembered how the game was supposed to go, and she sprang forward again, onto both feet this time, left foot in square 4, right foot in square 5. It was incredible, how the memories came flooding back! This was the point where you were sort of able to catch your breath and regain your balance because you could land on both feet.

But, she remembered now with great clarity, this was also the point where you felt things start to change.

From squares 4 and 5 you were supposed to hop on your right foot into block 6, then—this had been the tricky part, even for a child—hop and *twist* onto side-by-side squares 7 and 8 so that you landed backwards with your right foot in 7 and your left foot in 8; and then hop back out in reverse: left foot in 6, land on both feet (left in 5, right in 4), left foot in 3 and then next in 2, and you would bend and pick up the bottle-cap on the way out.

But in the middle, straddling squares 4 and 5 on the way in, she found it changing again, as always.

Somehow when you were in motion the whole tableau seemed *longer* than it was supposed to be. Even as a child she had thought that it was because of the confusing repetition of patterns in the blocks, the similarity of the wide block 3 followed by 4-and-5 and the wide block 6 followed by 7-and-8. It just seemed difficult to think exactly where you were in the process, and even now it was the same—she should only have one wide block and two side-by-side squares ahead of her, but there appeared to be more than that. It was as if the eye couldn't quite come to terms with what was really there, because it looked as if the alternations of numbered blocks stretched nearly to the back of the alley, where now as always an uncouth clutter of dirty newspaper and pale weeds tangled with themselves just beyond the light, a light which kept fading and revivifying with the whims of the clouds that tried to block out the moon.

The pattern couldn't really be different, of course. Maybe it had seemed so to a child, and maybe even an arthritic adult foolish enough to be doing this in intermittent moonlight in an urban wasteland might be gulled into imagining odd things. It was confusing, too, to have her own wavering and indistinct moonlight-shadow projected out at an angle onto the squares before her. She resolved to prove to herself what nonsense it all was, and took a breath and sprang onto her right foot, into block 6, wincing again as she landed on an ankle that was far, far more brittle than that of the little girl Linda who used to play here.

And now came the hard part: she would have to spring off from her right foot and turn her body around and come down backwards with both feet in 7 and 8. But when she sprang, she had barely enough time to register that she mustn't twist after all—that this was to be another straight side-by-side landing, with the twist-point farther ahead somewhere beyond another long bar. There was only supposed to be one straight landing, though, and she must have been confused, thinking that she had already done it and that this could be a second one. She canceled the twist and came down still facing into the alley, with her feet covering two numbers. Ahead, with the moonlight failing again, she couldn't quite make out the number in the next long bar or in the small squares beyond. She must still be about to proceed to bar 6, though she could have sworn she'd already done that. She hopped onto her right foot, nearly toppling over but managing to keep her balance. Now the tricky part: the twist onto squares 7 and 8, finally.

But no, that wasn't right. Flailing her arms to keep standing on her foot, which was really beginning to hurt now, she squinted into the receding alley and found still more of the diagram ahead of her than should be there. Beyond, the clutter of weeds and paper at the end of the alley loomed a little closer than before, and some stray breath of wind seemed to be stirring it, making shreds of newspaper look like little tentacles in the pallid light. The end of the diagram had to be coming up next, and she was *not* going to let this get the better of her.

Hopping again, she came down with both feet in the next side-by-side squares, whose numbers she couldn't guess at now, as confused as she was. But yes, now this was right. Or sort of right. The cloud cover lifted, and in the brighter moonglow she could see that the bar ahead was number 6, and the adjacent squares beyond were 7 and 8. The only thing was, she had the feeling that it had taken her too long, had taken too great a toll on her aching right ankle, to get here. Why she was doing this at all she couldn't have explained; somehow she just had to, had to go through it and get it *right* and snatch up the bottlecap at the end.

She sprang once more onto her right foot, crying out a little this time when she landed on it in bar 6, and, without giving herself time to hesitate—or without giving the tableau time to change again?—she jumped, did her best to twist around and, considerably surprised at herself, landed on both feet more or less in blocks 7 and 8, facing back out toward the street. She had caught only a glimpse, while turning in the air, of the confusion of weedy rubble just beyond the end of the diagram, and it could only have been the strain of the whole undertaking that made it seem to her as if some of the shredded and filthy newspaper there was disentangling itself from the encroaching weeds and starting to move. In a way, it was comforting to be facing the alley entrance again.

But now something really was wrong. Dreadfully wrong. Wrong in something like the way it used to be when she had been a child, but even worse.

The sidewalk, the street out there looked too far away, much farther than she could have come to get here. The diagram that stretched back toward the healthier light at the entrance to the alleyway was far, far too long, with too many squares. It had to be a trick of the light. Even when she had imagined, hopping across the tableau to get here, that she had landed too many times, there couldn't have been *that* many squares.

In any sane world she should simply have been able to laugh, step off the diagram altogether, walk back out to the street, and leave. But she understood perfectly well now that this little world that she had re-entered was not a sane world, and that to get back, she had to hop through the diagram, as she had had to when she was a girl.

Added to this reflection was the realization now that something was audibly, unmistakably stirring behind her in the back of the alley.

With a sudden sense of urgency she hopped onto her left foot—thank heaven at least it wasn't her throbbing right foot again—and landed in what could only be bar 6. Filaments of sooty cloud were covering and uncovering the moon, and she couldn't read the numbers clearly. Balancing on her left foot, she sprang again, coming down on both feet in what must be squares 4 and 5; even standing this way, her right foot was still in pain. Logically only one long bar and the final two adjacent squares should remain, but that was what troubled her: that a good many bars and squares, like the segments of some nightmare tapeworm, seemed to stretch themselves into the distance between her and the salvation of the sidewalk beyond the alley entrance. There couldn't be that far to go. But there was, and it needed to be quickly too, because something was coming up close behind her. She could hear it, an odd blend of dry paperlike rustling and a sticky-suction sound; and now she could *smell* it as well, a foetor like something grown mushy and phosphorescent in a cellar.

She hopped onto her left foot again, coming down in the next long bar, but there were many other squares ahead, impossibly many others, and her left foot was already starting to hurt. Choking back a sob, she sprang again and landed on both feet, her legs nearly buckling under her this time. In the act of hopping again, she cast a glance behind her and nearly swooned at what she saw.

Something was coming, all right, something ragged and twitching and leprous-white, something that seemed to be trying to get a shape.

But in front of it was another presence, advancing toward her as well, itself pursued, apparently, by what had risen out of the back of the alley. And this other presence, half-transparent like a gathering of bubbles, had the shape of a child.

A child with feverish blue eyes shining out of a bone-white face limned in wildly tossing locks of raven hair.

The child came on silently, terribly, and motioned to her to go on, go on, go *on*.

Linda, blinking away tears now, completed her spring and came down on both feet, barely managing to remain upright. She didn't dare look around again, but hopped once more onto her left foot, which, throbbing now, came very close this time to snapping under her. Behind, a gurgling kind of sound kept coming nearer, together with a sense of something like altered pressure in the air, a small but insistent pushing behind her. She sucked a breath into her lungs and sprang again, landing on both feet, and immediately jumped off again, coming down hard on her left foot, which raged with pain now. Howling, she sprang forward yet again, and another time, and another and another and another, until the agony was almost unbearable.

But at length, heaven be praised! only one more long bar—number 3—and the final adjacent blocks, where the bottle-cap glinted dully in the moonlight. She cast one rapid glance behind her, a big mistake, because her mind wouldn't accept whatever was there, and that in a way was worse; maybe she could have endured whatever it was, if she could really have looked at it. But as it was, her mind registered only an appalling mass of white putrefaction lurching along behind the smaller shape that kept coming, the translucent little-girl shape whose face desperately implored her now, wide-mouthed but silent, to keep moving.

Linda hopped once more onto her left foot and screamed outright at the outrage of pain that shot up her leg, but she managed to spring one last time into the final squares, and bent with a groan and tried to pick up the bottle-cap but missed it—missed it!—before hurling herself out of the diagram.

In her forward momentum she whirled around then to face the alley again, in time to see a childish shape hopping ahead of the thing that came behind it. Even now, little Marnie was faithful to the demands of the tableau, coming down first on one foot, then two, then one, as the seething near-shapelessness welled up nearly upon her. But if she still moved through the eternal ritual with meticulous care it wasn't to save herself—because Linda understood now that Marnie, who popped like a soap bubble and vanished when she hit the stronger light, had been in no danger at all. Her time for being in danger was long since over, and as the pursuer came on through the vanishing apparition and bulged across the remaining space, it was all too clear that someone else was the chosen one now.

Jigsaw

Out of chaos, a face.

At least the dim suggestion of a face—vague, remote, formative, like something undecided, something not yet born.

Propped against the back of a wrought-iron candleholder in the center of the kitchen table, the face, the face as it should look, peers at Esther Lillibridge across the table like a presumptuous dinner guest who has leaned too close, her features large and imposing. The picture on the cardboard boxtop represents a section of a painting by Modigliani, showing a tubular neck barely supporting the narrow, tilting head of a young woman, delicate, pretty in a strange kind of way, with a face out of which pupilless blue-green almond eyes float blankly beside a long sloping nose overshadowing small rosebud lips. Hers is a creamy-peach face above which the auburn hair is pulled up and fastened into a bun. Enlarged to allow inclusion of only thin crescents of pale green background, the face fills nearly the whole scene with its wan suggestion of a smile, a smile made more indeterminate by the fact that the background is nearly the same color as the blank eyes and seems to show through them, as if the eyes were holes in a fragile paper mask; overall, the woman is oddly intriguing. This is the figure, so clearly detailed in the picture, that so problematically struggles, against all odds, to show through its jumble of chaos on the tabletop, where frenzied hundreds of tiny fragments lie in disarray, the job barely begun.

Twenty-five hundred fragments, to be exact—this is one of the so-called "grand jigsaws," terribly difficult, a supreme challenge even to so seasoned and expert a puzzleworker as Esther. The pieces are tiny, tedious, maddeningly alike; they pose a problem that may well take weeks.

But then what is that to Esther Lillibridge? She has plenty of time, if little else. Is it odd of her, perhaps, to presume that she has plenty of time, at eighty-six? She thinks not; indeed, for her, time has largely ceased to exist as a concern; she never worries about it one way or the other, except to reflect, now and then, that the less one thinks about time, the less it is a problem. It runs backwards as well as forwards anyway, when one has so many memories. But in any case she has a great deal to think about as it is, with this puzzle, and no time to fret about time. If the puzzle takes a month, two months, a year, well—the pleasure is in the journey, after all, not in the arrival.

She will prevail, of course; the drably papered walls of her simple apartment are bedecked with preserved triumphs over past puzzles, glued down and framed, frozen in time like subdued and mummified rows of trophies, dried-out and brittle spoils of the hunt. These puzzles, these once opaque problems, have long since succumbed; Esther survives them.

But in all her many years she has never begun such a puzzle as this.

The near end of the kitchen table is cleared away, stays cleared away most of the time, her usual workspace; and a few ragged pieces of the puzzle are in place, staggering around a drunken square, the border, which of course one always assembles first. This large border is like a stage with the curtain going up, a vacuous, pregnant space in which one can scarcely imagine what is about to happen. Within, Esther has merely put down a few disconnected pieces that may, just may, belong somewhere in the vicinity, due to their coloring or, in rare cases, their patterning, their fragmented resemblance to some feature of the desired picture. But most of the pieces are still in the box, yet to be sorted by color or pattern, and Esther realizes that the large face, consuming virtually the whole picture on the boxtop, will possess broad, bewildering expanses of unbroken peach-flesh, relieved only by exceedingly gradual gradations in color, gradations only discernible to a sharp eye—the faint suggestion of shadow near the nose, the very slightly darker cheeks near the edges of the oval face and at certain places about the eyes. It will be difficult.

Difficult, yes, but *that*, Esther has to admit to herself, is not the subtle and peculiar something that is troubling her.

"It isn't healthy, you know." Claire Woodbury, from down on the third floor, fusses over needlework and sniffs her eternal disapproval, no different today than any other time, glaring at Esther from the far side of the table. Her pinched face, hanging above the cardboard Modigliani image, seems to have a beard, but this is only the cardboard woman's bun. "Not healthy, and not normal. A person spending all her time putting together silly puzzles. You weren't always like this."

"Like what, Claire?" Esther asks absently. Somewhere there is a piece that should belong near the center of the lower lip, but she can't find it.

"You aren't listening to me at all." Claire has drawn her arms up and crossed them, and is pouting. At length she says, "You and I used to go to concerts. I still go. But *you*—I don't think you ever stir out of that chair."

"Yes, I do," Esther says wearily. She seemed to recall this conversation from another of Claire's always unannounced visits. Anyway, what does Claire know about life, when she is only seventy-three? These young people always think they know everything. "I get my meals, I tidy up the place."

"Ho!" Claire's eyes widen out of a nest of creases like small bright birds wriggling awake. "Tidy up, do you." She runs her hand along the ledge beside the rolltop desk, her fingers coming away bloated with dust. As this circumstance seems to speak for itself, she says no more on the subject.

"I like my puzzles," Esther says, wondering why she bothers to defend herself, and searching, still, for the missing piece of ochre lip. Ah, there it is. But no, when she tries to fit it onto the meager structure already laid down, it only *almost* fits, its tiny tabs feeling not quite right, its contours leaving tiny crooked spaces where no spaces should be, where the fit should be tight, but is not. The eternal frustration—a piece either fits or it doesn't; almost doesn't count. Where *is* that other piece?

At some point she notices that there is no one at the opposite end of the table. Claire must have left. Then again, poor Claire has been gone for over a year. Esther simply resurrects her in the mind at times, for someone to argue with.

Today has been cloudy-gray, and the late-October evening has come with a gentle rain beyond the window, a soft blurring that makes the garish vertical neon sign on the smoke-grimed hotel façade across the street look like something in a dream. H TEL, it proclaims, sputtering and sizzling, its articulation oddly impaired. The effect of the neon illumination filtering through Esther's rain-spattered windowpanes is to spread a surreal dappling of light and dark through the room, in particular half lighting the fragmented chaos of the jigsaw puzzle on the table, adding a bizarre chiaroscuro to Modigliani's already strange craft, in such a way as to make it unclear, on first glance, which ragged splotches of dim light are peach-flesh puzzle pieces and which are merely random patches of lighter tabletop amid regions of dark. One could try to pick up pieces that aren't even there. Esther snaps on an overhead light, sending the rain-projected shadows fleeing, and stands looking over her puzzle, which is still only barely begun but evincing some tendency now for the enigmatic young woman's face to begin showing itself.

Esther rubs her temples and sighs. What is it about this puzzle, this face, that bothers her?

She sits down, scoots her chair up a little closer to the table, and starts to work again, sifting the pieces, scanning the problem with a wary eye. At this point, the portion of the face assembled so far is rather bizarre in its outlines, since it consists primarily of part of the jaw, most of the mouth, part of the nose, and most of the woman's left eye, augmented by scattered pieces laid down roughly in position but not actually fitted into the puzzle, mostly pieces of peach-colored cheek or forehead. In this fragmented view there is something almost cadaverous about the visage, the partial face, but that, Esther reflects, is not so strange. Naturally it looks odd, this half-coherence, this ragged outline; she has seen such effects before.

Though not exactly like this either.

This is different, because—suddenly she realizes it—the face that is beginning to emerge on the tabletop seems to look a little different from the picture on the propped-up box lid.

Now, that would be downright unfair, and well-nigh unprecedented, Esther thinks, annoyed. They have to give you an accurate picture, a true representation of what the assembled puzzle will look like; they have to give you that.

But this, this is odd. In the picture on the cardboard box, the woman's expression combines a faint smile with a certain rarefied sort of wistfulness; altogether it is an expression or mingling of expressions that one would find engaging. Yet in the jagged half-face beginning to appear amid the jumbled pieces on the table, the expression is subtly different. Maybe, Esther thinks, it's only because so much of the face is still missing, maybe the fragments that are in place don't really carry all of the true expression.

They seem to carry, instead, an expression that looks vaguely mocking.

Getting up and turning off the light to let the wash of rain-speckled neon light from the window play upon the tabletop again, Esther looks at the emerging face in that light, thinking that that may make a difference. And it does.

In this uncertain light, the effect is heightened.

Esther makes a desultory attempt to put a few more pieces in place, but it is late, she is tired; she leaves the puzzle as it is and goes to bed.

Thinking of what Claire Woodbury would say about the need to get out and around, Esther washes her breakfast dishes, resists the urge to work on the jigsaw puzzle, gets her overcoat and hat, and heads out the door and into the musty stairwell, where it is five flights down to the street. Out in the open air, which is crisply cold this morning, she pulls her collar close to her throat and walks to the park. She spends the morning on a bench there, watching comical fat pigeons trundle about on the sidewalk, then she walks farther downtown to Manny's Diner and has lunch at the counter, a ham and cheese sandwich on rye with a big mug of coffee. Somehow with the chatter of other customers all about her, the Modigliani face seems distant and unreal. Esther leaves the diner, spends the afternoon at the library browsing newspapers and magazines, and doesn't get back to her apartment building until dark. Invigorated by her day out on the town, her first in a long time, she barely notices the rigor of the long climb up the dimly lit stairwell, and is only a little winded when she reaches the fifth floor and fumbles with her key in the lock. The day has done her good; she feels refreshed, clear of mind.

The feeling changes when the door glides open to the maw of darkness that is her apartment.

Something in the air here is different. But of course it is; even the air of the city, out on the streets, is fresher than these stuffy old rooms.

Still, that's not it. She stands half in the doorway, listening.

Because she has the most peculiar feeling that someone is in the apartment. It's nothing she can place, this impression, just a feeling, a certain charge in the air.

Of course the door has been locked. But even five floors up there is always the fire escape, the windows. She inclines her head a little more into the room, listens closely.

Nothing. Quiet in there. But is it, perhaps, the quiet of *someone,* someone trying not to make any noise? That feeling is still very strong, that somebody is in there, in there in the dark.

Reaching around the jamb, she expects a hand to close upon hers, but she flicks the light switch without mishap. Everything looks normal so far. There is still that feeling, a cold little sensation catching at her throat. But she steps into the room, closes and locks the door, hangs her coat on the rack, and moves quietly through the front room toward the kitchen, realizing that she is walking quietly not to cover up—*other* sounds. On her way, she glances into the bedroom, sees only what she should see: bed neatly made and unwrinkled, nightstand, dresser, lamp. She steps into the kitchen and switches on the overhead light. The windows are still closed, untampered with. Nothing out of the ordinary here.

Nothing with the possible exception of the jigsaw puzzle, which she has felt right along is a bit out of the ordinary.

The face, still one-eyed and ragged, tries to stare up at her in its fragmentation. In its jutting outline, the impression is still cadaverous, but gobbets of flesh are slowly being added, not taken away, making a cadaver in reverse. Esther pulls up her chair, sits, and fiddles with the puzzle a little, fitting two pieces of cheek near a slightly darker region, the edge of the nose. With one more piece, the mouth is complete. Most of the nose is in place. There is still the other almond-shaped eye, and she works on sifting through the box and finding the pieces for that. One by one they emerge and she fits them together, making a sort of island precariously attached to the nose, an island with an eye. By eleven o'clock the face has both its eyes in place, though they float in patches of peach-colored cheek in a way that makes them resemble a cartoon-character robber's mask perched over the nose. There is nothing humorous in this impression, though. Now that both eyes are looking up out of the tabletop, they subtly work together with the contour of the ochre lips to convey more of the face's expression.

And it is undeniable now that the expression of the face emerging in the tabletop is not the same as in the picture on the box.

In the green eyes, blank as they are, there is something unpleasant, something that Esther cannot quite make out, a vague something that makes the pursed rosebud lips, the mouth, seem—but the impression is unplaceable.

It is late, and Esther is glad not to work on the puzzle any more tonight.

"You *will* keep doing that, and me telling you it's unhealthy." Claire's ghost has shown up for midmorning coffee and criticism. She peers at Esther from across the table, shaking her head. "Never saw anyone so—"

"But I did get out, Claire. Yesterday. I went to the park, and later to the library."

Claire sniffs in her characteristic way. "But of course you wouldn't think of asking your old friend along."

Esther smiles. "I would have, Claire, but I left so early, you'd still have been asleep." Asleep indeed: across town, under the sod.

"Hmph." Claire stirs imaginary coffee. "I don't think you went out at all." She gets up, walks around the table to scrutinize both the puzzle itself and the picture on the box lid, and gestures with her coffee cup. "I think you're the one's that's painted on cardboard and stuck in a stuffy old apartment. And is this what you're so avid about? Why, that's not even a good picture."

"It's Modigliani. You know, the Italian artist, turn of the century," Esther says.

"No," Claire says, "I mean, the picture they gave you to go by isn't even a good picture."

Esther knows she meant that, and reflects: *she* notices it too. Claire goes back and sits down and finishes her coffee, and the two do not talk much more after that. Claire seems nervous and at some point, Esther notices later, has left. Esther hopes she hasn't been rude to her friend, even in the imagination, but the puzzle preoccupies her. It seems more comfortable to work on it in daylight. Abandoning, for now, the rest of the face proper, Esther is concentrating on fitting together some of the chin and neck, that long, rubbery-looking neck so typical of Modigliani, that tubular neck on which the head sits at a quizzical tilt. Somehow it is more desirable today to work on this part, rather than on the enigmatic face. By early afternoon most of the neck is in place, together with most of the shaded outline of the chin.

And the old impression is beginning to grow again, that there is something wrong with the whole expression of the face. Something wrong, decidedly.

Esther decides to go out for a late lunch at the diner. Afterward, she stays out longer than she has planned, walking around the park, strolling down some nearby streets, windowshopping and—she finally realizes—making excuses not to go home. But the darkening sky has grown grumbly with clouds, and it looks as if the rain may start before she can get back. She has no umbrella and walks back in something of a hurry, getting to her building just as the first fat drops are beginning to fall.

Up at her apartment door, fitting the key in the lock, she again has a kind of presentiment, but scoffs this time—she has been through this before, there is no one in her apartment.

No one, she thinks when she is back in her kitchen with the light on, no one but this woman. The woman in the puzzle.

She remembers feeling, early on, that the expression in the face seemed vaguely mocking; the impression is stronger now, in the blank green almond eyes tilting in the face, the slyly puckered lips, the long sloping nose, the head tilting atop the long, thin neck. Everything seems to combine in a sort of alchemy, yielding the face that looks up out of the tabletop with a faint suggestion of a smile, a smile that is not pleasant. Esther turns the light off, and as before the sensation heightens. Outside, the thunder grumbles, and the rain, heavier now, sends ripples of wavering neon light from across the way to wash across the table, the face.

In this pale and blotchy light, the face suddenly looks almost sinister.

Esther walks out of the kitchen, goes and gets ready for bed. But before going to bed she stands for a moment, in the dark, at the kitchen doorway, and realizes that she is listening. A curious little touch of fear has wormed its way into the base of her spine. This is foolish, of course. There is nothing she can possibly be listening for.

Nothing except that faint, faint raspiness, that dry and airy sound somewhere there in the dark: a suggestion of someone breathing, breathing, in there where no one could possibly be.

After a while it grows even fainter, and stops; or becomes so quiet as to be inaudible, and then the silence in the apartment is maddening.

After a nearly sleepless night Esther sits over her morning coffee, hair in her face, eyes puffy, and reflects once more that Claire's old philosophy is eminently right, that one has to get out and around, not just out for a sandwich, but really out. Maybe a trip somewhere, a vacation. She can't afford to take a real trip anywhere, of course, but that does not remove the need. This apartment, these rooms—this room—must be getting on her nerves.

Well—she knows one place she can go today.

By ten o'clock she is standing in Mulhany's, the department store uptown where she buys her jigsaw puzzles. She has the Modigliani box lid with her.

"Well," the young man waiting on her says, "I can't say I ever really thought about it before. I mean, I always just assumed the picture on the box was a good picture of the puzzle. Of course it could be a *little* different, I guess; you know, the colors, the way it's reproduced or something." He takes the box lid and looks at the printing on the top, the sides. "But you know, that's funny."

"What's funny?" Esther asks.

"Well, this brand. We don't sell puzzles of this brand. In fact, to tell you the truth I've never even heard of it. You sure you bought it here?"

"Well, yes, I did, I buy all my puzzles here."

"Huh. I guess the distributor or somebody mixed it in with these others by mistake. If it's—do you want your money back?"

"No," Esther says, "I'll keep the puzzle. It's nearly put together."

She walks around town, having dinner out, browsing unseeingly in bookstores, putting off her return home, but finally she has to go. The poor weather will not lift; it has drizzled off and on for most of the afternoon, and again as the sky shrouds over with darkness there is a black hint of heavier rain, and when it begins to fall it is tinged, though too early in the season, with sleet. Esther barely makes it home in time.

In the kitchen she stands over the puzzle, somehow too keyed up to sit, not bothering to put on the light. Behind her, the rain and sleet worry with long nervous fingers at the windowpanes, and again a wash of sickly-pale neon light struggles through the trickling rain to illumine, in half-hearted fashion as if scarcely willing even to try to clarify, the face of the woman in the tabletop, whose now ghostly features sit tilting atop a tubular neck that has come to look almost serpentine. As before, it is difficult to distinguish between blotches of light and genuine pieces of the puzzle, but not many loose pieces remain. Esther's fingers fidget among them, sorting them, finding them, fitting them in, and in no time the last one, a ragged chunk of light green background flanking the face, slips into place. Esther, tired now and eager to sit after all, fumbles with a hand behind her and drags her chair forward and sits at the table and looks at the completed puzzle.

She feels, this time, no exultation, no sense of triumph over a difficult problem. The scenario forbids so simple or wholesome a response, for the face—there is no denying it—is most certainly not the face in the picture on the box, but a twisted caricature of that face, a sardonic parody of that face. It is superficially the same picture, the same woman, in essential details, but somehow the nose, the high forehead, the cheeks look pasty, bloated, unhealthy, to the extent that they somewhat change the shape of the face, and the expression is one almost redolent of the triumph that Esther should have earned the right herself to feel. The real shock is that the woman in the tabletop looks—alive. Alive and not well disposed, not pleasant, not friendly. Suddenly, to Esther, the effect is ghastly, unbearable, and she pushes the chair back and stands up and leans over the table on her outstretched arms, one hand planted on each side of the puzzle. Despite her repugnance, or perhaps because of it, she looks deeply into the face of the woman in the table, searches that darkly compelling countenance for some understanding of what, if anything, it means. Abruptly she is aware that the rim of greenish background around the woman's head is like the surface of some brackish pool, green with phosphorescent rot, an undulating pool in which the head, on its rubbery neck, floats like some pale and puffy flower. It is as if the tabletop itself is not a solid surface, but rather the opening to some well or pit, out of which a tilting face now raises itself, oddly staring. Esther, mesmerized, perspiring, can only watch, can only feel the skin on her own face tighten with fear, can only feel her own eyes bulge. Surely to God, if there is mercy in heaven, the face, the head in the tabletop does not really move. Outside, the thunder rumbles, the icy rain whispers more insistently against the glass, the neon light wafts its leprous radiance through the troubled air to wash across an almond-eyed visage that either changes in the imagination only or changes so very, very gradually that it seems like imagination.

But slowly, slowly, dear God so slowly but so surely, the rosebud lips draw apart, the mouth opens. The head ever so excruciatingly slowly tilts even farther on its side, and yes, the mouth opens, smiling, to reveal two shocking rows of thin yellow teeth. Esther is under the impression that the mouth is also screaming, because someone is, and some corner of her mind registers a suspicion that it is she who is screaming. But she can think only of the face, whose eyes, like vacuous slits in a paper mask, seem mockingly to flaunt their very emptiness.

Suddenly, other senses are assaulted—there is the ragged sound of breathing, and Esther feels a press of warm and sickly air against her cheek, a rush of breath that reeks with a repellent sweetness that sends her backing away, choking. Somehow, flailing her arms, she finds her way out of the kitchen and into the front room, while from behind her there comes a vile medley of sounds, like the sounds of someone clambering up, muttering and wet and slimy, out of a pond onto dry ground. By now Esther's eyes have filled to brimming, so that she only vaguely sees someone push by her in the dark.

Returning to the kitchen, wiping her eyes and wondering why they have been watering, she snaps on the overhead light and peers at the table, where the pieces of a jigsaw puzzle lie in disarray, the randomly scattered pieces of a puzzle she has not yet begun to solve. Good heavens, it has been a strange evening, somehow. Her hair has partly come down, and she stops to fasten it back up into a bun before turning to the puzzle again. Craning her neck to see the picture on the box, she notes that it is the face of an elderly woman, and for some reason she feels uncomfortable about this puzzle. It is, for one thing, an unfamiliar brand, even though she bought it at Mulhany's as usual.

Country Living

The house at the end of Blackwell Lane was so ragged and colorless, its timbers so wheezing with dust, its stark clapboards so long unpainted, that it appeared to have grown there, sprouting like some dark, hunch-shouldered toadstool out of the very woods that crept under its rotting eaves. Dim and gaunt, it stood back from the lane in shadow, and one could have walked past it without seeing it. Not that anyone walked here, anyone but Jill. The lane led nowhere, and no one else lived within half a mile. A few crumbling cellarholes, down toward the point where the lane branched off from the main road, gave evidence that other houses had once stood here, but that must have been ages ago, and even then the somber structure at the end of the lane could have had no near neighbors.

Jill Swinburne loved the house because it rather reminded her of herself, in its solitude, its detachment, its eloquent silence. Like the house, she was a loner, self-sufficient, defiant, unconcerned with the passing pageant, the commonplaces of life. She and the house were eminently suitable companions. She had everything she needed here. Downstairs she had a simple but adequate kitchen, a living room, a front bedroom, a dingy little bathroom, and, off the kitchen, a large back room fitted up as a laboratory. Upstairs she had two more bedrooms, musty but serviceable—one of them sparsely furnished as a little sitting room—and another tiny bathroom, as well as an alcove that she had converted into a kitchenette. Yes, she had it all—space, quiet, a good place to work, even a barren little patch of ground beneath the thinner trees behind the house.

A place to bury her mistakes.

Well, only two mistakes so far. She couldn't help it if the Williams girl's reaction to the injections had turned toxic. She suspected some undetected allergic syndrome, but in any case experimentation always had its risks. The girl was only a drifter anyway, and who would miss her? And the wino Jill had picked up in town—no problem there either, but she should have known that a high blood alcohol level might prove to be an unmanageable extra variable. At least the old man had died quickly and quietly, not like the girl with her paroxysms and her high, gurgling screams.

Jill looked out over their featureless graves from the kitchen window, then sat back down with her coffee. She might have been able to save these experimental subjects at the university, where the lab facilities were more extensive. But then *they* wouldn't have allowed her to use human subjects in the first place. Ah, the university. God. It was a relief, being free of it for now, free to work on her own out here in the country, alone, no prying eyes, nobody to report to. Those pompous asses had cramped her style. *Look here, you think you're ready to do research in muscle and tissue relaxants,* Professor Higgins had intoned, glaring down at her through those bottle-bottom bifocals, *and you're not even passing your first-year graduate courses. So as chairman of your committee I'm sorry to have to inform you—* Ha. A year or two working out here should do it. Then she'd go back, ready to sail through her courses, and possessing enough research to write a thesis that would knock the wind out of those arrogant, tradition-bound swine.

Sipping the last of her coffee, she fingered the scrap of newspaper she had cut out this morning, relishing the feel of her own words, however mundane. *Upstairs apartment for rent. Quiet and pleasant country living.* She smiled at herself in the reflection in the kettle.

Anything for science.

But in the meantime, knowing she could scarcely afford to lose another experimental subject, she needed to be sure the new reagent was safe for injection. The titrations required to produce it had taken weeks, and now extensive tests were under way with the mice. Checking the clipboards on the animal cages, she once again cast her glance about her and felt how much in her element she really was.

For her, the setting imparted a kind of romantic thrill to it all. With its bleak and shabbily papered walls, the room itself had always contrasted sharply with the chemical apparatus filling it, and she felt like what she knew she was, a brave pioneer pushing at the outer bounds of knowledge, laboring unseen in her obscure corner, building a new world to come. Ultimately the implications would be spectacular. Convinced that the human aging process itself was largely a function of cell and tissue elasticity, she knew in her heart that once that problem could be properly addressed, human aging could be slowed, perhaps deferred indefinitely. And it was going to happen here, in this humble and unlikely room where the musty wallpaper ran with stains from a leaky roof and the ancient radiators clanked and rattled and the brittle floorboards creaked and the windows were bleary with a century of staring at the dark tangle of woods beyond the panes.

"How are we doing this morning, Number Seven?" She held the mouse lightly by the scruff of the neck and inspected him. "Looking good, fellow." The muscles and tissues were soft, elastic, more so than yesterday. She drew a little blood and placed the animal back on its bed of newspaper confetti in the cage, noting the changes on the clipboard, placing the blood sample in the hopper for testing, and proceeding to the next cage. Female subject this time, the usual tests to run on hormonal balance and other factors. Again, the animal showed signs of progress in its tissue responses. Yes, looking good.

Today the mice, tomorrow the—

"Worley. John Worley's the name. I'm a writer and I need someplace quiet. This sounds like the kind of arrangement I've been looking for," he said, standing below her on the rickety porch steps. "Could I see it?"

"Certainly. Come right in." She led him through the living room and up the stairwell. "My name's Jill Swinburne," she said over her shoulder as she reached the landing at the top, where a little hallway ran left and right with the bedroom opening off it at the left end. Inside, connecting doors led to the other rooms. "I think you'll like the apartment." She took him through the bedroom, pointing out the windows facing onto the woods. "You wouldn't have a lot of sun in here, but anyway, it's very private." Leading him through the inner door from the bedroom, she showed him the sitting room—"You could use this as an office!"—and the little bathroom and the kitchenette. "I think you'll agree the price is right. I mean, compared with those apartments in town."

"Oh, yes," he said. "I've already looked at those. Besides, they're noisy, and it seems to be really quiet here."

She sized him up. About forty, maybe forty-five. Slender, seemed to be in good health, but with the usual incipient signs of tissue change appropriate to the age group. He would do nicely.

Worley proved to be an unobtrusive renter. He worked in his rooms a great deal, making only occasional trips to town when he had things to mail, and she only glimpsed him on the stairs from time to time. His route in and out of the house only took him through the front hall, nowhere near the laboratory, and he kept very much to his own affairs, never asking her, in their brief conversations, anything about herself. In the ensuing days she was able to work her way quickly through the primary tests on the mice, and had now begun the next run of tests, on the guinea pigs this time. She knew that she really needed to run tests on a chimp, but her funds were running low, and she was going to have to do her best, in preparing human dosages of the new reagent, to make the right computations transitionally from guinea pig to man without benefit of the extra data she might have garnered from a subject of intermediate metabolism and physiognomy. It would work out all right. She had confidence in her abilities as a scientist. And there were going to be some red faces back at the university when all this came out in her thesis! Who could tell?—a Nobel Prize might not be out of the question.

She examined the third guinea pig in her series for tissue elasticity and scribbled notes on the clipboard, replacing the animal in its bed of confetti, pleased with her progress. Soon it was going to be time.

"Do you drink coffee, Mr. Worley?" She had met him in the front hall as he was heading down the stairs with an armful of manila envelopes.

He shifted his load of mail from one hand to the other and smiled. "Do I drink coffee? I practically live on the stuff. Why do you ask?"

She took her hands from behind her back and handed him a large glass jar filled with instant coffee. "It's instant, but—"

He took the jar, clearly pleased. "I'm not fussy about that. Just as long as it's not decaffeinated."

"No, no," she said, returning his smile. "It's real coffee. But it's a flavored import. I know some people don't care for that sort of thing. I got several jars of it for Christmas last year and I can't drink that much of it, it keeps me awake at night. So if you can use it—"

He slid the jar into his jacket pocket. "I appreciate it. I need the caffeine, and my own coffee tastes like shoe polish most of the time. May the gods of wakeful nights bless you."

She sat in the overstuffed armchair in the living room and went back over her dosage calculations. At the level of saturation of the reagent, and assuming one and a half to two teaspoons per cup, and estimating the number of cups per day—well, everything seemed well within experimentally acceptable bounds.

In a day or two she might be able to note some effects. Meanwhile she would continue follow-up tests on the mice and the guinea pigs. The mice were further along in the treatments, and she thought she could even detect a slight suggestion of tissue quality aging-reversal in a couple of them. Exciting thought.

John Worley was about twenty years her senior. She found herself wondering what he had been like when he was younger. It was just an idle thought. She wasn't *all* scientist, sometimes. Detachment and objectivity were fine, but you had to dream a little too.

"Mr. Worley?" He had started down the porch steps, evidently on his way to town. She had been puttering in the front yard with the potted plants, rather thinking he might come down.

"Good morning," he said. "Please call me John."

She eyed him. "I was just thinking, John, you look—I don't know, different somehow. I don't mean to pry, but are you feeling all right?"

"Never felt better," he said. "As a matter of fact, it's odd, I mean considering how hard I've been pushing to get my writing projects done, but somehow I feel more relaxed now than I've felt in a long time. I used to have a lot of tension, you know, sore neck muscles, tight in the shoulders, but all that seems to be going away. Even with all the coffee I'm drinking, and it's delicious, by the way. Unusual flavor. But yeah, I'm feeling good. Must be the country living, as your ad in the paper said."

She nodded. "There's a lot to be said for not living in town. Turn around and take your jacket off for a minute, would you mind? My sister used to be a masseuse, and she's taught me some of it." She massaged his shoulders briefly. "You do feel pretty relaxed. Stop down from time to time and I'll give you a shoulder rub if you'd like."

He nodded, looking a little surprised. "Might just do that."

The next day, she caught him before he went up the stairs, and took him into her living room. "Sit down here." He did so, slipping the jacket off, and she stood behind him and massaged his shoulders. Sure enough, the tissues were notably more elastic than yesterday. "You are getting looser in the shoulders. That's good. A person ought to relax."

"I do feel good," he said. "Almost too good. I'm so relaxed I'm not sure I want to work today. But I have to. Deadlines. Hey, you know, you're good at this massage business. You don't mind doing it?"

"Not in the least."

After he had gone upstairs, she made some notes on his clipboard.

The next day, she began to see that something was wrong.

Around midmorning John came down the stairs looking puzzled. Jill was just coming in from the porch and met him in the front hall. "Hi, John. Anything wrong?"

He shook his head. "No, not really. I don't know, I just feel kind of funny."

"Did you sleep all right?"

"Oh yeah, in fact I got up late. There's just something—"

She took him by the arm and led him into the living room and sat him down, pulling his jacket off. Rubbing his shoulders, she was astonished at the elasticity in the muscles. But she needed to be sure. "Let's do this right. Why don't you take your shirt off?" She helped him slip his shirt and undershirt off, then massaged his shoulders again.

What was this?

She was fascinated by the texture of his flesh. Not only were the muscles looser than she could readily have believed, but the skin had a slippery, waxy quality to it that was unlike anything she had ever seen. The flesh gave the impression of being moist, even oily, without actually being so. Now that the light was better than it had been in the hall, she saw that even his face had an odd, almost glistening look when he turned his head to look at her. Somehow the flesh of his back put her in mind of the texture of tofu. It wasn't an unpleasant sensation exactly. In fact, she found it strangely erotic, somehow, and she must have managed, in touching his bare back, to convey that sensation through her fingers, because now he was turning toward her with a new look in his eyes.

But in bed, even when they kissed, and when they caressed, and when she pressed her body to his, it was no good. She knew why, of course, even if he did not. It wasn't his fault, certainly. She held him, comforted him, looked into his eyes. "Another time," she said, kissing him again. "We'll be together another time." And once he was upstairs and the rush of passion was over, and once she had time to think, she knew that something had started to go amiss.

In the lab, she examined the animal specimens closely, one after another. With furred creatures it was trickier to tell, but she now thought that in the mice and the guinea pigs the epidermal and musculature processes were going too far. The muscles and the skin felt much looser than she would have expected, and watching the animals in their cages she noted a wobbly motion when they walked, as if their legs wouldn't support them. She took a few blood samples, smeared the slides, and spent a fruitless hour staring into the microscope. Later when she picked up a mouse to examine the rims of its eyes for signs of anemia, a good deal of the animal's fur came off in her hand.

But of course the volume of blood was tiny compared to the human circulatory system. John wouldn't be in any danger, surely.

In any case, what was she to say to him? Don't drink the coffee, I've been experimenting on you? Then again, she could say precisely that. Come clean, risk his response, think first of his safety. But she knew she wouldn't do that.

The experiment had to run its course. She had to know. Had to know how it was going to come out.

By midmorning the next day the animal cages were replete with things Jill didn't want to contemplate, and John Worley had not come downstairs.

She had been checking the mice and the guinea pigs with a growing sense of dismay. The animals could no longer stand on their legs at all. When she picked up one of the mice, it felt like a handful of spaghetti. Hands beginning to tremble, she went over her clipboards, her notes, her computations, checking everything. And the next time she held one of the mice in her hand, it squished between her fingers, all pulpy and liquescent. She placed the animal on the tabletop and it continued to melt, its eyes running down into a puddle beneath where the head had been.

Oh God.

She ran through the house, stopping at the bottom of the stairs. "John?" Her voice in the stairwell sounded flat, dead, ineffectual. "John!"

From upstairs, only vague sounds.

She went up and stood outside his door. "John. Are you all right?" She tried the door, but it was locked.

A gurgling voice sounded faintly from within the room. "Suhhhh."

"What?" She pressed her ear to the door.

"Suhhh—shick." The -*k* was a nauseating, thick liquid kind of sound. "Wery shick."

She slammed the flat of her hand on the door. "Let me in."

The response was appalling. "Hu-hhh! N-no. Can't cuh—can't cuh hin."

Why couldn't he pronounce anything that required using his lips? She bolted back down the stairs, rummaged through a drawer in the kitchen, and returned with a key. But when she pushed through the door, she wished she hadn't.

He was sprawled on the floor, wearing only a pair of trousers. His chest, his arms, his head, his feet—his whole body was a nightmare. Spluttering, he flailed an arm at her. "Huhhh—heh—hev—hev we. Hev we, whor God's shake."

But those were the last words he was able to speak. Like the mouse, he was collapsing, puddling down into a mass of cheesy miasma that her mind almost refused to register. She saw his blearily blind eyes float apart, saw the mouth widen and the teeth float away, and the next thing she was conscious of was wandering the grounds outside, muttering to herself. The ancient house, its austere window-eyes possessed of unspeakable secrets now, looked down upon her like some reproachful elder, judging her, finding her culpable.

Enough of that. Getting something of a grip on her nerves, she faltered up the porch steps and entered the house and stood in the front hall, trying to think. She knew what she had to do.

Dragging a large tarpaulin up from the basement, she partly pushed, partly scooped John Worley's decomposing body onto the tarp and pulled the whole squishy burden one ghastly step at a time down the stairwell, some deranged corner of her mind chattering *Jack and Jill went down the hill to fetch a pail of horror.*

Digging in the rocky soil out back, she found herself blubbering like a child, and she didn't know whether it was because of her failure as a scientist or—well, she had lost her objectivity over John, and that was bad science too. She dropped his jellylike mass into the hole, filling the grave in and tamping the soil down with the shovel. As if to comment upon the occasion, a mournful wind riffled through the pines, touching Jill's face like a corpse-hand. She returned to the house, whiled away the day and the evening, and slept fitfully.

For some days she passed the time reading languidly, walking up and down the cheerless lane, and in general trying not to dwell upon what had happened. But she knew that sooner or later she had to go back into the lab. When she finally did, she discovered something else.

In her distraction she had left the dead and dying rodents in their cages, and by now their remains, little more than viscous lumps when she had last seen them, were putrescent to the point where the smell was nearly too much for her. But that wasn't all.

In trying to remove the animal remains, she found that the effects of their dissolution had apparently extended to their surroundings, for the confetti in which they had lain was now a thick, mucoid soup spread upon the bottoms of the cages. In fact, the chemical processes she had set in motion must have been even more bizarre than she had imagined, because the cages themselves seemed to be starting to decay now, insinuating a slow-moving gray ooze over the tabletop.

Somehow the sight of it, bringing back a flood of frightful memories and impressions, was more than she could bear. Storming through the house, she ran out the back door, down the steps, and across to the graves, across to where John Worley lay interred because of her. Choking back a sob, she flung herself upon the barely perceptible mound that marked his resting place. "John, John, what have I—"

But instead of colliding with unyielding soil, she sank into the grave, into a pool of brown foam that once was dirt and stone. Descending into the froth, she found her own words coming back to her—*We'll be together another time*—and the thought outweighed even the panic of suffocation as she settled down and down and down into the mire of her bridal bed, until the foamy earth, bubbling and putrid, took on the quality of foamy flesh and bone.

Sheep-Eye

What Jud Willis found, deep in the desertlands of New Mexico, wasn't anything he had gone there to find.

He hadn't intended to stop in the Territory of New Mexico at all, in fact. California was the Promised Land at the far, far end of the trail—California and its beckoning fields of gold, its lofty dreams of wealth and the carefree life.

Naturally, that had been the dream, back in Boston three years ago. That had even been the dream a year ago in Missouri, when he had joined the caravan and hit the trail, once again trading the comforts of a warm bed for the uncertainties of the open country. He had seen the same dream in a thousand faces, and wondered if it glowed with the same avidity in his own.

But those wearying months on the Santa Fe Trail had been enough to dim the glow in any face. Before the horses and mules and wagons had pushed very far into the yellow prairie expanses of western Kansas, where the only trees were gnarled and furtive-looking cottonwoods and the only roof the limitless sky and the only sounds the sounds of the caravan—long before he and his companions had crossed into New Mexico, Jud Willis had come to feel that California was receding to a more distant realm every day, not drawing closer. Even when the terrain changed, and waving fields of prairie grass became infinite seas of sand and pungent sagebrush, and the plains of Kansas became the mountain-ringed valleys and canyonlands of New Mexico Territory, the image of California seemed to fade like a dream that flickers and passes into oblivion when the sleeper wakes. And Jud Willis had awakened to the realization that he was not going to California.

He supposed the change of heart had come sometime back up the trail, not long after the caravan had entered the Territory. Crouching beside the wagons with his traveling companions and making coffee over the fire, he had tried to look into his own mind, tried to examine his motives, his real wishes. What did he really want? He hadn't been sure. Still wasn't sure.

What he *hadn't* wanted was more weeks or months on the trail with a caravan. True, he had grown to like the people he was with, the familiar faces, the familiar voices—but he needed to be on his own. Sometimes when the group had pressed onward, he had wanted to stay longer, or take a different route, or proceed more quickly, or more slowly.

Alone now, he could do things his way. Not that he had any particular plan, but that was part of it—he needed to be free to have no plan.

Watering his horse now at one of the little streams that trickled down cold and clear from the foothills, he surveyed the scene around him. The rocky hills sloped gently down to a sandy plain dotted with mesquite and spiky-headed yucca and spectral armies of cholla cactus stretching away westward to meet the crimson remnants of a setting sun. Somewhere in the distance, a hawk fell across the sky like a meteor. Suddenly Jud felt very alone.

When he had left the caravan at the banks of the Pecos River, many days' ride north of here, the others had tried to talk him into going on with them, but even then the group was splitting up, some heading on to Santa Fe and beyond, some leaving the caravan to make their way northward, seeking the gold fields of Colorado. Jud himself had ridden into Santa Fe to gather supplies, returned to the caravan camp to bid the others goodbye, and saddled back up and followed the river south.

And while the ensuing three weeks in the New Mexico desert hadn't done much to clarify his reasons for leaving the caravan, he had no real regrets at this point. He had done a little prospecting in the streams after he left the rivercourse to ride southwest. Panning for gold, he had found none, which was about what he expected. But this was more than compensated for, he felt, by the splendor of the landscape itself, which seemed a world away from the political turmoil of Santa Fe, and a universe away from the streets of Boston. The land was gold enough. It was a dreamworld, this sun-dazzled sea of sand and rock and cactus under a dizzying dome of turquoise-colored sky. It was beautiful, but if you didn't keep your wits about you, it could kill you.

Somehow its beauty was laced through with a certain . . . darker quality.

As if to underscore these thoughts, a dry burring sound came up from nearby. Some yards away, its mottled colors blending with the colors of the sandy ground, a prairie rattler coiled itself in the shadows at the base of a yucca and sounded its warning. After a while the snake uncoiled and sidled away. Jud really didn't mind these creatures. You just had to keep your eyes and ears open, and give the snake a little room.

No, something was strange, and a little disquieting, about this place, but it wasn't rattlesnakes.

Looking to the west, away from the foothills behind him, he thought the impression had something to do with the low, rocky hill that rose from the land some four or five hundred yards ahead, its craggy form obscure in the red-orange blaze of the sunset. The sight of the hill gave him a creepy sort of feeling, as if there were something about it that he should know, but did not.

He climbed back into the saddle and pointed his horse in the direction of the hill. Maybe the way to dispel this odd feeling was just to ride over and have a look.

Up close, the hill was a dark rockpile jutting sharply from the desert floor, too steep on this side to give access. Jud made his way around to the western end, where a more gradual slope presented itself. There was even a rough, narrow footpath leading up among the rocks, and Jud hitched his horse to a mesquite and began to climb the hill, his shadow long and thin ahead of him on the path.

His impression of strangeness grew rather than diminished now that he was here. The stone surfaces were covered with odd patterns and etchings, sometimes densely crowded together, sometimes isolated. Here a stone bore the figures of primitive hunters, there another stone showed circular patterns like swirled disks, there another stone was covered with zigzag lines. The figures on the stones must have numbered in the hundreds. They were no doubt the work of ancient peoples; even a newcomer like Jud knew that Indian tribes had been on this land for hundreds, maybe thousands of years. He had seen Indian pueblo settlements farther north, and occasional little groups of Indians along the way south, interspersed with Mexican ranches and desert farms. This land had been part of Mexico until recently, and part of Spain before that, but it was the Indians who were truly *old* in the land, and these etchings in the rock only served to remind him of that.

The footpath gradually rose among the angular outcroppings of rock, and after half an hour he came to the end of the path, where it ran blind up against a natural wall of stone. He retraced his steps, and by the time he was halfway back it was getting dark, so that the figures on the rocks were immersed in shadow.

Even so, he noticed now, to his right and several yards off the path, a curious figure he hadn't seen on the way up. He stepped across to get a closer look.

The stone in question stood somewhat taller than Jud, and contained one large etching, a full-size stick-figure man that somehow made Jud's flesh crawl to look at it. The arms, legs, and trunk were long, thin, almost willowy, but it was the head that was striking. Like the rest of the body, it was etched in thin outline, a circle enclosing a rudimentary face turned sideways so that only one eye was showing. Or maybe the face was looking frontward, and *had* only one eye.

It was the huge eye that Jud couldn't stop looking at.

It wasn't etched into the stone like the rest. Rather, a natural bump about the size of a fist rose from the general level of the stone face, and the ancient artist had used the protuberance for the eye. The effect was chilling, somehow, as the eye seemed to look at you with a bleary kind of insistence. Jud shuddered and turned away and stepped back toward the main path.

And ran headlong into someone.

He gasped for breath, his heart pounding. "God! Who the devil are you?"

Now that he had a chance to look, he saw that it was two white-haired old men. One was Mexican, one was Indian. While the Indian just stood and watched, the Mexican nodded to him and spoke in a dry, cracked voice.

"*Ese dibujo,*" he said, motioning toward the strange figure on the stone, "*se llama Ojo de Oveja.*"

Jud had picked up a little Spanish along the way, but he couldn't follow this. He shrugged. "I'm afraid I don't—"

"*Ojo de Oveja,*" the Mexican repeated, nodding toward the stone figure again. "*Ojo de Oveja.*"

Jud opened his mouth to try to say, again, that he didn't understand, when the old Indian spoke up.

"Sheep-Eye," he said.

Jud blinked at him. "What?"

The Indian looked away, not toward the stone but away into the gathering night, then looked back at him. "Sheep-Eye. The people call Old Sheep-Eye. Always been here. People afraid. Sheep-Eye have great power. Walk on the wind."

"I see," Jud said, though he didn't.

"*Es leyenda que se ha contado desde hace muchos siglos,*" the old Mexican said, but Jud didn't understand. He thought perhaps it was just as well.

"We go," the Indian said. Jud wondered whether he meant all three of them, but the two old men started back down the path and didn't seem to object to his not following them.

"*Buenas noches,*" the Mexican called back to him.

"*Buenas noches,*" Jud replied. That much Spanish, at least, he could manage. In a moment the two men had been swallowed by the night. A waning half moon had risen, but it showed no one but himself.

And the figure on the stone, barely visible from the footpath. Jud glared at the thing. "Sheep-Eye. What nonsense."

But there was something in the blind-looking stare of that great bloated eye that almost made the words stick in his throat.

When he had faltered his way back down the hill to his horse, he went riding off in search of a good spot to bed down for the night. Some distance to the southwest of the rocky hill he passed a little adobe house shrouded in shadow, its battered wooden door closed against the night, its tiny windows lightless. He wondered if anyone lived there. In any case he was going to spend the night the way he now spent all his nights, under the open sky.

Farther along, he chose a spot suitably flat and free of snakeholes, and made a small fire and spread his bedding on the ground beside it, tethering the horse nearby. A light breeze had sprung up, making spikes of yucca wave eerily in the moonlight like seas of tentacles. Even with the brightness of the moon, the black vault of sky was crusted over with a million stars. One didn't see a sky like this back in

Boston. He ate a strip of beef jerky, drank some water from his canteen, rolled himself into his bedding, and slept.

And woke.

What on earth was that?

Some sound, some sound off in the night somewhere beyond the feeble glow of the campfire.

He sat up and listened. The wind had risen a little now, so it was hard to tell—

There it was again, a wispy, windy kind of sound, not like the wind exactly, but like something *with* the wind. He heard the horse whinny once, nervously.

Then the whole impression was gone, and the wind dwindled, barely stirring the fire's dying embers. Silence reigned, broken only by the far-off cry of a coyote. Jud lay back and stared at the star-frosted dome overhead until the light of a new day crept across the heavens.

He breakfasted on dried beef and coffee and repacked his saddlebags and rode off toward the southwest, heading in that direction till midday, seeing nothing but open prairie. But he changed his mind and turned the horse around and rode all the way back to the little adobe house, not knowing why he did so. He reached the house just as the sun was going down.

This time there were signs of life. Behind the house, which was little more than a dilapidated hut of cracked adobe, a Mexican woman was washing clothing in a little stream. Evidently she hadn't heard him ride up. He hitched the horse to a small tree near the front door and stepped around to the right side of the house and called to the woman.

"*¿Señora?*"

The woman was clearly startled, dropping her wash into the stream and fishing it out before turning to face him. "*¿Señor?*"

Now what? he thought. "I—I was passing through and saw your house—"

The woman smiled wanly and shook her head.

"You don't speak—" Jud said. "*¿No habla inglés?*"

The woman placed the wash on a stone and stepped closer, wiping her hands on her dress. She was simply but cleanly attired, and rather pretty, evidently a decade younger than himself, perhaps twenty-five or so. "*No,*" she said, "*no hablo inglés.*"

He stood at a loss, trying to think of something to say, when a sound came from inside the house. It was the thin crying of a baby, clearly audible as the door was open.

The woman started toward the door. *"Mi niña,"* she said. When she stepped through the door, she motioned for him to follow, and he did, having to stoop to get through.

The place was only one room, with crude furnishings—a small wooden table, two rickety chairs, and a kind of wicker crib ensconced in a shadowy corner. The glass panes in the windows were so small and so dusty that they admitted very little light, but he could see that the mother bent over the crib, took up the baby in a ragged blanket, rocked it until it was quiet again, and placed it back in the crib. Turning to Jud, she said, *"Tiene usted hambre?"*

Jud made a helpless gesture with his hands. "I'm sorry, I don't—" The woman touched her fingers to her mouth and pointed to him, questioningly. He nodded. "Hungry, you mean. Yes. *Sí.* But I couldn't ask you to—"

However, the woman was out the door. He followed her out and watched as she built a little fire in a sandy pit between the house and the stream. She was soon cooking a kind of vegetable stew in an ancient-looking iron pot. At length they were back inside, seated across the table from each other, having their dinner.

The woman smiled at him from time to time but seemed ill at ease, often glancing at the windows, where the night had fallen and was re-lieved only by a little oil lamp on the table where they were finishing their meal. Once he felt emboldened to take the woman's hand in his, but she gently pulled the hand away, averting her eyes. Outside, a wind had come up, and she half rose to go and close the door, but Jud got up and closed it for her, sliding the rusty bolt.

Sitting back down, he pointed to her, rummaging in his mind for the right words in Spanish. *"¿Cómo se llama—?"*

"Lucinda," she said. *"¿Usted?"*

"That's a pretty name," Jud offered, hoping that she might some-how understand. "My name is Jud."

She seemed to turn the name over in her mouth. "Chood."

"Right." He had to ask something else now. There should logically have been someone else here. "Where is your—" He fished for the words. *"¿Dónde está su—?"* What was the word for *husband?*

But before either of them could say anything more, a kind of slithering seemed to pass over the outside of the house, moving from the front door to a side window. Lucinda's face was now a mask of fear, and Jud jumped up and ran to the window, having no idea what he was supposed to do.

He had little time to consider the matter, because a kind of face, emerging from the blackness of the night, framed itself in the window, looking in. If it was really a face, it was one Jud had seen before. Drawn like a smoke-ring against the dark, bobbing and undulating, it leaned against the window opening but was too big to break through. Jud could just see a neck and a pair of arms, flailing and jittering. The figure withdrew itself from view almost before Jud could notice that the face had only an appalling hole where its great single eye might have been.

He turned to see the apparition reappear at the opposite window, scrabbling at the frame with its wiry hands and pressing its eyeless visage against the window. Lucinda only buried her face in her hands, wailing.

Now a second voice joined her. The baby was awake again, its thin gurgling little voice swelling into a chorus of crying as the wispy thing outside the house moved around to the front and began scratching and thumping at the door. Lucinda rose from the table and went to see to the baby, looking over her shoulder in terror at the sounds coming from outside the door. But mercifully these sounds ceased, and a kind of rustling whisper ensued, as if something were moving itself across the sand, away from the house. It was only now that Jud noticed that the horse, tethered near the front door, had been neighing and snorting pitiably.

Jud turned to see Lucinda pick the baby up again, wrapping the blanket tight around it. He stepped closer to see if the baby was all right, but Lucinda turned away with it, rocking it in her arms, crooning some lullaby in soft Spanish tones.

Suddenly the whole horror of the situation seized his mind like a vise, and later he would barely remember bolting out of the house, unhitching his horse, and riding away into the night. That much would remain a blur in his mind. What would burn itself more indelibly into his memory was what he saw when he stopped.

Riding at full gallop, he was managing well enough to point the horse away from cactus and mesquite and snakeholes, until the moon went momentarily behind a cloud. The sudden darkness was so disturbing to his senses that he pulled the horse up to a halt, and instinctively turned and looked behind him as the moon came back out.

It was there, all right, old Sheep-Eye following him at a distance but coming closer, that unthinkable stick-figure, its limbs like pencil strokes on the night, its eyeless head nodding. Eyeless, because when it had come down off the rock, it had left that part behind, in the stone.

The thing whispered forward a few paces, the spindly legs bowing and straightening and closing the distance without quite touching the ground, the wire-thin arms reaching, reaching. It stopped, turned a blind face more squarely toward him, and sniffed the air. Catching his scent, it came rushing toward him like a vapor.

He rode furiously, desperately, scarcely daring to breathe or to blink his eyes or to think how close the thing might be. He seemed to ride forever. In the end, he outran the pursuer, and all the next day and night he would lie prostrate with exhaustion in a dry arroyo far, far to the west, visited by the great spidery shape only in his nightmares. He now had time for reflection, and his thoughts kept going back to Lucinda. By all rights, he should have felt like a cad for running away and leaving her, but he had had his reasons.

Because what would haunt his dreams even more hideously than the dreadful thing itself was that *other* glimpse he had had of the gaping eyeless face. It had been bad enough, the way he had seen it first. But it was worse, seeing that ghastly contour not in stone, nor in the mad night air, but on the tiny pink face of Lucinda's baby.

Tummerwunky

Greyport, Massachusetts, according to legend, derived its name from the fact that when early sailors rounded the jutting rocky face of Cape Ann and caught sight of the port settlement to the north, it resembled a brittle shell of gray fungus growing on the shoreline, its severe stone façades and gaunt wood-frame houses turning somber faces to the sea.

These impressions of the town persisted into modern times and were by no means lost on Emily McMullen, who had an eye for detail and a sense of the poetic, even when the poetry was somewhat on the dark side. She had felt, upon first seeing the town, as if there were something about it that were not quite real. But it had better be real, as she was going to live there.

And nothing was going to diminish her excitement about finally realizing her dream. An antiquarian at heart, she had always wanted to have a seventeenth-century New England house, and now she owned one. And why not? She was at a point in her life when she should be doing something precisely like this for herself. She was divorced, her son and daughter were grown and living far away, and her investments had treated her generously enough so that while she was not what she would call wealthy, she had enough independence of means to do as she pleased, at least for a while, and within reason. And buying Belham House was well within reason.

Holding a bag of groceries and shivering a little in the October evening breeze, she stood across Belham Lane and looked at the time-darkened three-story house, whose decks of ancient diamond-paned windows regarded the quiet byway like the many eyes of a spider. The structure, wreathed in ponderous oaks and separated by hundreds of yards on either side from its nearest neighbors, was gaunt, much taller than it was wide, and altogether too large a place for her alone, but that was unimportant; she was happy to have bought the house. It was a thrill to reflect that it was over three hundred years old, yet in reasonably good condition, since over the years its sale to various parties had involved some restoration.

No edifice could ever stand as long as this one had without acquiring a reputation, and she had heard it said, around town, that odd things had happened in the house. Strange people had lived there, and something, folks said, was thought to live in the cellar.

Preposterous, of course. True, in the few days she had been here she had noticed that the cellar smelled unwholesome, but she would take care of that in time. She walked across the street and up the steps to the door. Belham House was her home now, foolish stories or no.

After dinner she relaxed in an easy chair with a volume of Hawthorne. A light breeze whispered around the eaves. Being surrounded by dark wood panels and lattice windows and vast expanses of bookshelves made her warm and cosy in the mellow cone of light from her lamp, and she felt at peace with the world.

Except that lingering thoughts of the cellar skittered like waterbugs across her mind.

Cellars in most of these old houses were dank and unpleasant, she knew. So far, she had made only one visit down there, to see the furnace, a crusty fossil she would have to replace eventually. She had found the odor oddly composite, a medley of unplaceable impressions. The memory of these impressions now was displacing Hawthorne in competition for her attention, and it was no good trying to ignore it. Setting her book on the endtable, she made her way through to the kitchen, where the door to the cellar stood beside the pantry.

The rickety wooden steps led down into darkness, until she pulled the cord and switched on the hanging bulb, but even then the light was so feeble that her shadow, staggering out ahead of her, was scarcely more defined than the gloom into which it descended.

She stood on the dirt floor, a cheerless expanse of soil relieved only by the antediluvian furnace gurgling in a far corner, and overlooked by a lone cellar window so grimy that it admitted only a wan suggestion of moonlight. She could just make out, around the edges of the dirt floor, a suggestion of badly decomposed cement that vanished as it got out one or two feet from the walls; it was as if the whole floor had at one time been covered in a thin layer that had later entirely crumbled away in the middle, though Emily failed to see what sense that would make.

No question about it, the odor here was vaguely repellent in a manner unlike anything she had known before, and, smelling it, she found herself reluctant to breathe deeply. At the very least she was going to have to spread some lime around down here.

But she wondered if that would even do any good. The dirt here was, on first glance, coarsely uneven, rather as if someone had dug it all up, not bothering to pack it back down smoothly. Yet on further inspection she thought there was an almost porous quality to the dirt too, and she was unsure whether she merely imagined that it felt spongy underfoot. As an added impression, the air down here was humid in a way that made one feel as if the earth itself were exhaling a moist and malodorous breath.

Suddenly she felt that she would rather be back upstairs.

She was halfway up the creaking wooden steps when she had the odd notion that the air had slightly thickened, with a subtle shift in pressure that somehow made the hair on the back of her neck bristle. Mentally chiding herself for being a credulous fool, she actually wheeled around on the steps and looked back down at the cellar floor, knocking the lightbulb into gentle motion as she turned, so that the pallid light sent shadows twitching among the clods of earth. Surely it was the uncertain light that made her almost think the cellar floor had been changing in some way that it had ceased doing when she turned to look. In any event, when she climbed the remaining stairs and closed the door to the cellar, she was glad to be back in the kitchen, breathing wholesome air.

The young man at the supermarket checkout eyed the address on her check. "Belham Lane. You live in Belham House?"

"Yes, I do. Why do you ask?"

The lad seemed eager not to appear to have meant to offend her. "Oh, nothing, except that—nothing."

She had to chuckle. "I know, I know. People tell stories about the place."

He looked embarrassed to have brought the subject up. "Well—you know, the person you ought to talk to is old Miss Trent at the library."

"Why?" Emily asked.

"She's the expert on all that stuff. Helped write the history of Greyport a few years ago. She's a walking encyclopedia. I bet there's nothing about your house she doesn't know."

Emily smiled. "Well, thank you. I might just go and see her." In truth she doubted that she would, but the fellow was only trying to be helpful.

After dinner that night she settled into her chair again with her companion Nathaniel Hawthorne, and with no intention, this time, of being distracted by thoughts of the cellar.

Again, it was a cosy evening. She felt snug and content, ensconced in her little island of lamplight. The wind gave the old house an occasional creak, but this only added to her sense of comfort.

Sometime during the evening, though, she began to suspect that there was something she was missing, something just eluding her senses. She sat very still and listened, but she could hear nothing but the gentle soughing of the wind around the windows and beneath the eaves. Nothing but the wind and—

Something else.

Listening, she wished the wind would settle for a moment so that she could hear whatever else there was to hear. The impression lay just below her perceptions, more like a nagging thought in her mind than a real sensation within her hearing. But no—it was a real sound after all.

Closing her book, she strained to hear, and now she thought the sound was a curious kind of low crunching, like coarse paper being crushed. There seemed to be no way to tell where it was coming from. At times it almost came to resemble a kind of faint scrabbling, like claws upon wood. Clearly, she was tired, and her mind was playing tricks. But maybe she had better go and look.

Opening the cellar door, she stood in the kitchen and peered purposelessly down the stairway, seeing nothing more than blackness but feeling unwilling to reach in and pull the string to turn on the light. She had the sudden and overwhelming impression that some density, some heaviness of the stinking, humid air had gathered just behind the door, clustering at the top of the now invisible stairs but drawing back, sinking back into the gloom below, when she opened the door. There was a lingering suggestion of sound as well, as if something had been scratching and shifting around, down there in the dark, but now hastened to be quiet.

She closed the door and stood for a few moments longer in the kitchen, telling herself that it was all nonsense. Her nerves were beginning to get the best of her, that was all.

But she slept poorly that night, seeing an unclear succession of shapes ascend the cellar stairs before she awoke altogether and lay waiting for the dawn.

Shirley Trent, Research Librarian, was a sharp-eyed, birdlike little woman of perhaps seventy-five years. Her manner belied her rather severe appearance, because she smiled and laughed rather easily, though her overall bearing still exhibited, in quiet lineaments, the character of a serious scholar. Her office walls, enfolding her tiny room at the rear of the Greyport Public Library, were festooned with diplomas, awards, certificates, and honorific photographs of the estimable woman in company with various notables. Looking across her cluttered desk like some eccentric magistrate, she eyed Emily with an expression that mingled curiosity with gentle concern. "So you want to know about Belham House."

Emily shifted in her chair and slipped her coat off. "Well, if I'm going to live in it, I'd better know something about its history. I don't mean to take up a lot of your time—"

"Stuff and nonsense," Miss Trent said. "Ask anyone who knows me, and they'll tell you I'd rather talk about Greyport history than eat or sleep. But the history of Belham House isn't a pretty story."

"If you'd rather not—"

"Oh, no, I don't mind. I have a strong enough stomach if you have."

Emily raised an eyebrow. "Is it going to require one?"

"You decide," Miss Trent said, and began. "The house was built in 1675 by Silas Wade Belham, a vile and unprincipled man who was only twenty-two at the time. Silas was a wealthy merchant who made his money in shipping, sometimes dealing in goods it was best not to inquire about too openly. He swindled a fellow merchant-trader out of the land on which he was to build the house, a chap named Ephraim Smith. Sounds a little like *The House of the Seven Gables*, doesn't it? I've often wondered whether Hawthorne ever knew of Belham House. Anyway, not long after the house was finished, Ephraim came to the door in a drunken fit one night. They argued, and according to onlookers who dared to tell tales but not to pursue the matter legally, Silas killed Ephraim and chopped the body up and buried the pieces in the cellar." Miss Trent related this in a matter-of-fact manner that suggested that while she found the tale unpleasant, she had no real squeamishness about telling it.

"I'm beginning to see what you mean," Emily said. "Pieces. My cellar."

"It gets better. Or worse. Rumors began to go around that Silas, if he had ever had any mental health, was losing it, because when he was drinking he would tell anyone who would listen that what was in the ground in his cellar didn't seem to want to stay buried. More than once, he said, he took a shovel and went down there and put things down again that shouldn't have been moving around at all."

"He must have been crazy," Emily said, realizing how inane this sounded; of *course* the fellow had been crazy. How could a sane person even think such things? But Miss Trent was continuing with her account.

"Even in those Puritan times, or maybe especially in those times, Silas's wealth and influence kept him safe from prosecution. He lived on in the house, and around 1689 a son was born to him. Nobody ever knew who the mother was, probably some slave girl Silas raped and later murdered. Jeremiah Belham, the child was called, and he inherited the house in 1710 when Silas died. Jeremiah married an Elizabeth Wilkins in 1713. She had fled from Salem in 1692 at the age of twelve, and some said it was for good reasons. People in the neighborhood claimed the two held eerie rites of some kind in the house. By now the cellar was a thoroughly unclean place whose dirt floor was riddled with wormy-looking holes. Some claimed it was alive with something that lived in those holes."

"This is getting—" Emily began, but Miss Trent went on.

"In 1714, twins were born to Jeremiah and Elizabeth. One girl, Sarah, and one boy, Joshua. As a child of three or four, Sarah was wayward and ill-behaved. I don't know how to say this with any delicacy. The parents strangled Sarah, in front of her brother, and sometime later they ate the body."

Emily blinked. "You can't be serious."

"I wish I were not," Miss Trent said simply. "From what we can figure, they left the girl's corpse lying about for several days before they, ah, decided to partake. You can imagine. It made them deathly ill, and they went down to the cellar to be sick. All over the cellar floor. Sank into those holes. Joshua, witnessing all this, had his mind unhinged and was never the same again. His father Jeremiah was something of a gadabout, I meant to mention, and likely as not Joshua had congenital syphilis."

"Nice family," Emily said, not knowing what else to say.

"Elizabeth died in 1741 and Jeremiah remarried in 1742, an out-of-town girl named Anna Blake. They began to treat Joshua, now twenty-eight, with contempt, and one night, from what can be guessed, he'd had enough of it, and killed them both; nobody ever saw them again, anyway. Joshua lived on in the house alone, increasingly deranged. One legend has it that using some of his parents' black arts, he managed to raise and—well, reassemble—his dead sister from the ground, down in that cellar, long enough to have a child by her."

"Surely to God," Emily said, beginning to feel exasperated, "you don't believe that."

"I've learned," Miss Trent said, "to keep an open mind. In any case, a child was indeed born to Joshua in 1744. Her name, with all the apologies I can personally offer to Mr. Shakespeare, was Juliet. She was seldom seen outside the house, but townspeople said she was hideously deformed. Her face and head were bloated and spongy—"

Emily, not able to help herself, thought of the porous dirt in the cellar.

"—and people said her teeth just seemed to float in her mouth like—I'm trying to think how someone once put it—like corn floating in a pink sauce."

Emily winced. "I'm glad I've already had my lunch."

"On rare occasions," Miss Trent said, "when people saw the girl, the way she looked, they scarcely expected her to live long, but she grew up, living in the house with her father Joshua. He disappeared at some point, and she was alone in the house, till 1771 anyway, when she started consorting with a strange sailor named Bradford Morwell, a scurvy-ridden halfwit who could barely talk and who actually seemed to enjoy Juliet's ugliness. They started having numerous children, who had the misfortune to look a great deal like their mother and to have the mentality of their father. It was about the time the children were four or five years old when stronger rumors starting going around that there was something living in that porous, stinking earth in the cellar. The kids didn't mix much with normal folks, but when they did, they said something called Tummerwunky lived under the house, and their mother told them it would get them if they didn't watch out. They said they were afraid to go to sleep because it would feed on them."

Emily felt as if her head were spinning. "My house," she said. "It sounds idiotic. I mean, the cellar smells bad, but that's no—"

"From this time on, the history of the house and its occupants becomes unclear," Miss Trent said, "and all the more so with the turmoil of the American Revolution. Somewhere along the way Juliet and Bradford disappeared. There is a school of thought to the effect that the children killed them and ate them. It was also said that these children interbred, producing more children, creatures even more repellent than Juliet had been. Generally they kept themselves out of sight, but the common understanding was that some of them were barely human. The house fairly teemed with an unwholesome life."

"The real estate folks don't always tell you everything," Emily said.

"I dare say they don't," Miss Trent replied. "Anyway, by the early 1800s the 'family' in Belham House was thinning out. Not surprisingly, perhaps."

"Yes, if they were that inbred," Emily offered, "it would probably be no wonder they didn't live very long. And the place must have been filthy beyond belief, making it even less likely any of them would survive. Or are you suggesting there really was some other reason they were dying off?"

Miss Trent smiled wryly. "You have a fertile mind. Whatever happened to the rest, one girl named Martha did survive, only mildly simpleminded and not quite so repulsive as the rest. Some halfway decent genes back there someplace I guess. In 1806 she married a man named Chester Bartleman, and in 1807 they moved away to New Haven, Connecticut. We don't know too much about them. By 1835 they had passed on, but there was a grown son named Frederick. Here in Greyport, Belham House was empty and went up for sale. Frederick Bartleman, hearing of this, bought the house and moved to Greyport."

"But why would he have wanted to live in the house?"

Miss Trent shrugged. "He was fascinated by the legends attached to it. I think he only half believed them, actually. He heard them from his mother, after all, and she was a bit strange in the head. He and his wife, Ruth I think her name was, moved into the house in 1836. At first they seemed all right. Mentally, I mean. But people always seemed to change when they lived too long in Belham House. Anyway, after a while they started having children, two boys and two girls. Except for being rather unattractive, the kids seemed all right too, at first."

"And then?"

"Well, they were school age in the late 1840s, early 1850s. Their teachers and their classmates said they came to school looking increasingly—well, looking sort of haunted."

"By—?"

"Whatever it really was, the other schoolchildren had a taunting little rhyme about it. Some of them probably still know it to this day. It goes—let me think—

> "'Tummerwunky, Tummerwunky, hiding in the gloom,
> When he starts a-movin', it will mean your doom.
> Up out of the shadows, up the cellar stairs,
> Creeping up behind you, better say your prayers.'"

Emily shook her head. "Children have such a way of expressing things sometimes."

"Don't they?" Miss Trent looked thoughtful. "The Bartleman kids gradually stopped coming to school. Nobody minded too much, because they looked terrible when they did come. Pale, emaciated, sickly. The parents were seen less and less often in public, too. I think it was about this time that some townspeople began to say that if you crept up close to Belham House and put your ear to the ground, you could hear an odd sound in the earth, a sort of crunching, shifting, slithering sound. And—well, I hate to tell you this."

Emily shook her head again. "Why? We've come this far. Go on."

"Intending just to check on the family, Reverend Williams of the

First Congregationalist Church in High Street went to visit one day and found—horror. The place was an indescribable charnel-house. Madness had set in. There was blood all over the house, and worse. Reverend Williams found Frederick Bartleman down in the cellar, vomiting blood and gibbering and laughing to himself. It appeared he had killed and eaten his family. He denied it, in an incoherent and babbling kind of way. Kept saying something else did it, said he wasn't alone in the house even with his wife and children gone. That was in 1854. They took him to an asylum, and he died screaming there the next year."

Emily took a deep breath, feeling exhausted by all this. "And the house?"

"It sat empty for many years. Or presumably empty. Maybe it really *was* empty. People said they couldn't hear those strange sounds in the earth near the house any more. Maybe whatever lived in the ground needed to have people in the house, and maybe when they were gone, it died."

"Or slept," Emily said.

Miss Trent eyed her oddly. "As I said, you have a fertile mind. Don't let it run away with you. I don't want to make you afraid to go home! As I said, the house has been empty a great deal since that time. In 1877 a family moved in and tried to live in it but soon gave it up, and wouldn't tell anybody why. Neighborhood children made a regular legend of the house, saying that shadows moved around in the place even when it was empty. Tenants tried to live there, from time to time, throughout the 1880s and 1890s and into the early twentieth century, as late as 1927 I believe, but they never stayed long. In 1928 a small importing company bought the house and tried to turn it into a retail outlet for their imports, and at first everything seemed normal. Even with the Depression going on, they sold teakwood from Japan, clothing from China, chess sets from India, all that sort of thing. But then—"

Emily was almost reluctant to ask. "They turned weird in the head?"

"You might say that. Gradually they took to importing and selling peculiar merchandise, things sometimes of doubtful legality. People lodged complaints about them, and the Commonwealth of Massachu-

setts revoked their business license in 1935. When investigators came
they found some of the company staff half dead, half mad, caked with
blood, crouching around some peculiar altar they had built in the cellar. It was as if they were worshipping something. Heaven knows what.
There were company employees missing, unaccounted for, people who
never did turn up. When the surviving people were prosecuted, federal
authorities came to the house, and some of them claimed they could
hear sounds in the ground while they were taking the altar away and
searching for contraband. They poured concrete in the cellar to try to
cover up the stench down there. After that, more tenants came and
went every few years, and then the house was used for storage from
1973 to 1992, but eventually a lot of the things stored there were
found to have a terrible odor, and strange molds growing on them. After that the place sat empty again, an eternal listing with the real estate
agents. Till you bought it."

"Right," Emily said. "I always did have an eye for bargains."

She thought the librarian's stories would make her uneasy living in the
house, make her unable to sleep, make her think about moving out.
But none of these things seemed to be happening. By late October,
with her visit with Miss Trent three weeks behind her, she was beginning to wonder why she had even momentarily been frightened by
what she had heard, however bizarre. Nothing out of the ordinary had
happened to her, anyway. Evenings, when she sat writing letters or
reading or doing crossword puzzles, she sometimes found herself
pausing to listen, but there was nothing.

Nothing definite, anyway. Occasionally, she would think she
sensed some subliminal vibration, some minute alteration of pressure
in the air too attenuated to quite amount to a sound; but she knew this
was fanciful. Listening carefully, she would realize there was nothing to
hear, and that the recounted history of the house had had more effect
on her nerves than she had acknowledged. It was foolish, anyway, to
imagine that a house, however sordid its history, could be haunted by
something that lived in the soil beneath it.

Something that had grown there from some residual aura of murder and perversion, something that nurtured itself on blood and may-
hem and madness.

Something, she hastened to tell herself, that might have a place in some gothic novel scribbled for the gullible, but had no place in the world of sanity and light.

It was all rubbish. This was just a creaky old house, nothing more, nothing less. She was sure of that. Everything was going to be all right.

It was on an evening in mid-November that she discovered what a mistaken notion that was.

The New England autumn had for some days been making its bleak transition to early winter, the evening wind growing more mournful and sometimes spattering the ancient windows of Belham House with cold rain and flakes of prophetic snow, harbingers of the wintry months to come. Choosing a volume of T. S. Eliot, Emily settled deeper into the plushness of her chair the more insistently the wind played among the darkened eaves with its burden of rain and snow. She was just reading the lines

> *At the first turning of the second stair*
> *I turned and saw below*
> *The same shape twisted on the banister*
> *Under the vapour in the fetid air . . .*

when she heard it. Or felt it. She wasn't sure which. Perhaps both.

Suddenly she felt not cosy in her island-cone of lamplight, but very profoundly alone with the sound she thought she had heard, the impression some corner of her mind had felt.

She sat very still, not even breathing. Listening. Listening.

There it was again. She could swear she felt the vibrations now, not just heard them. From below.

She struggled to understand what sort of sound it was, a curious hybridity of impressions. It put her in mind of something crunching, yet at the same time, in a sickly kind of way, it sounded—wet—like something purulent and squishy with decay. She tried to tell herself that this was her own morbid fancy, but the truth was, there was something about the sound, some half-understood quality, that sent a spike of cold fear down her spine. Maybe the sound would go away.

But it refused to do that. If anything, it became more terribly distinct as she listened. Louder. Closer.

Tummerwunky, Tummerwunky, hiding in the gloom . . .

The thought was as irrepressible as it was unwanted. Dropping her book, she walked quietly toward the kitchen. Toward the cellar door. She had to see.

When he starts a-movin', it will mean your doom . . .

The rhyme would no more go away than the dismal moaning of the wind, or the unspeakable whisper of that other sound. Had something indeed started "a-movin'" down there? She was prepared to open that door and look down the cellar stairs.

What she was less prepared for was seeing, when she stepped into the kitchen and switched on the light, that the cellar door was already open.

Up out of the shadows, up the cellar stairs . . .

But it was too late for that, too late to think about looking down the cellar stairs to see if something was coming up, because it already had.

Creeping up behind you, better say your prayers.

Only it was in stark reality before her, not behind her, and she was not inclined to think it could be prayed away.

For a moment the unreality of it, the sheer fantasy of what was wedging itself through the doorway, paralyzed her. The eye would accept it, but the brain would not. Its writhing mass called up no familiar categories in the mind, no psychologically comfortable precedent. It was just what it was, a sinewy nightmare of thin, glistening strings, curling and wriggling and reaching, filling the doorway, pouring onto the kitchen floor in almost liquid fashion like some foul half-digested soup that the cellar spewed forth. A ropy strand of its substance whipped out and actually touched her on the cheek, feeling revoltingly damp and soft and rotten, as if one might sink one's hand into its mushy shapelessness. The sensation of its touching her face snapped her out of her inaction, and a paroxysm of panic and loathing surged through her. Only now realizing that a choking stench had filled the air, she tried to scream but only gagged, and turned and ran just as the thing was bulging across the kitchen toward her.

She barely made it through the connecting doorway into the parlor before it was at the doorway itself, jittering and groping in the air, shooting long stringy tentacles out into the room and advancing with a sound that had no place in anyone's parlor, anyone's life, anyone's world. She did scream now, but it was a response she could ill afford, because it was going to take every ounce of her energy to move fast enough and smart enough to stay alive. An image suddenly filled her mind, and all she could think of was those hideous wet threads snaking their way into her nose, her mouth, insinuating themselves into her flesh. The thought had the effect of sharpening her fear with an edge of defiance. There was no way the filthy thing was ever going to touch her again.

But it was flowing into the room and across the floor with terrifying swiftness, and in another moment it would be upon her. Doing the only thing she could think of, she shoved the easy chair into its path, and it fastened upon the padding, penetrating and shredding it in an instant. This took just long enough for Emily to pull the front door open and burst through the screen door, out onto the front porch. She didn't realize, until she had clambered down the steps and out onto the half-frozen lawn, that she had unconsciously pulled her overcoat off the rack on her way out the door. Blinking snowflakes from her eyes, she slipped the coat on and looked back toward the house.

The thing from the cellar now filled the door frame she had just come through, and as she watched it, it filled the second-story windows as well, and, after a few moments, the third-story windows. It moiled repulsively in the flickering lights from the windows, before the lights went out altogether. She stood staring at the house, unable to move.

But at length she regained enough presence of mind to rummage in her coat pockets, where she found a credit card and an assortment of pens and scraps of paper, but no car keys. Those were in her purse, and her purse was in the house. Unimaginable, to go back in there for any reason. The immediate necessity was to find shelter, but she knew no one in town well enough to impose on them, especially with a tale like this. There was only the motel two miles north of here, and she would have to walk.

Barely aware of the darkened streets, the howl of the wind, the huddled houses with their windows curtained against the night, the solitary streetlamps leaning over her like thin-necked urchins, she walked through the thickening snow until a sputtering neon sign ahead proclaimed what she wanted to see: *Greyport Inn.* And: *Vacancy.* She needed to get warm, to rest, to calm down, to have time to think. She would need to call someone, but right now she was too tired, too cold, too bewildered to know who.

The young man at the desk in the lobby processed her credit card and eyed her curiously. "Are you all right?"

She nodded, busying her hands with unbuttoning her overcoat to try to keep him from seeing that she was trembling. Melting snow puddled around her feet. "I—yes, I'm okay. I had some trouble. My car. Had to walk. I just need a good night's sleep so I can—you know, see to things, in the morning."

"Nasty night for walking," the clerk said, shaking his head. "Anyway, you've come to the right place. Room 203, just take the stairs there and it's on your right. Complimentary coffee and doughnuts in the breakfast room from six-thirty to nine-thirty."

Up in her room, she thought that a quiet space and a warm bed had never felt so welcome, so good, even though her heart was still pounding. Her mind was so overloaded with what had happened that she simply couldn't think about it any more. Tomorrow would be soon enough for that. She didn't think the thing from the cellar would venture outside the house; there had been nothing in the librarian's account to suggest that it ever had. Nevertheless, she knew she would have to tell someone about all this, probably the police. Then again, how could she expect them to believe that something lived in the wormy earth beneath her house, something born out of a history of murder, incest, cannibalism, necrophilia? They would have to see it for themselves. But maybe by morning the thing would have crept back down its wormholes in the cellar, and they would think she was insane. She wasn't so sure herself; maybe she was.

But however that might be, she had to try to sleep now. She pulled the bedcovers tight around her throat and closed her eyes.

And opened them again, in the dark of the room.

What was that?

It hadn't been a sound exactly, not like in the house, yet there had been something uncomfortably familiar about it. Also, she realized, she had simultaneously felt as well as heard something, a curious little pain like a twinge of neuralgia in her head. She had no aspirin with her, but no matter; she was so exhausted that a bit of headache was scarcely going to keep her awake. She closed her eyes again and settled her head into the comforting softness of the pillow.

And listened, in spite of herself.

And not in vain either, because there it was again.

Just a subtle little suggestion of pain, and a sound. A sound somehow both dry and wet, like a stalk of celery being crushed or chewed. Once years ago when she was having a tooth pulled and the dentist was twisting the root of the tooth with his instrument, she had heard a sound like that in her head. And this new sound, dreadfully familiar now, was coming from inside her head too.

With that realization came a crescendo of pain, and she understood all too well. As something bristled within her head and began to come out in a spray of sticky wetness, she had just time enough to recall what the librarian had said—*You have a fertile mind*—and to reflect, sadly, that in fertile ground, things are bound to take root and grow.

A Student of Geometry

"Erica."

The voice was distant, disembodied, irrelevant.

"Erica?"

Nearer now, but still of no interest to her. Who was it? She didn't really care.

"Erica Miller! Would you please answer the question?"

Now it was Mr. Kelly's imperious math-teacher voice, a ship of sound cutting through a fog of daydream. She forced herself into focus.

"I'm sorry, Mr. Kelly. What was the question again?"

The rolled-up eyes, the shaking of the head. "I *said*, why then is angle ACB an acute angle?" He was pointing to the chalkboard, where a triangle had its parts labeled with letters of the alphabet and had one of its sides extended out like an antenna.

She blinked at the diagram. "I—uh—because—well, because it's—it's—"

"Never mind, Erica. It's obvious that you're unprepared, as usual. You were supposed to be ready with this proof for today's class. Or am I mistaken? I did assign this theorem, didn't I? Last time? Unless it was all just a very vivid hallucination on my part. Ronald?"

The boy in front of her had had his hand up. "Angle ACB is acute because, ah, its complement ACD is greater than the remote interior angle CBA, and CBA is greater than ACB because that was given, so ACD is greater than its complement ACB, and that makes ACB an acute angle."

To Erica all this was outlandish gibberish. Mr. Kelly, though, was nodding his approval. "But why is ACD greater than CBA? Remember, you have to justify all the steps in your reasoning."

The boy replied, "ACD is greater than CBA by the Exterior Angle Theorem."

Mr. Kelly nodded again. "That's right. I'm happy to see that *some* of you are prepared."

But Erica, sliding back into the fuzzy comfort of her own formless thoughts, barely heard this.

"I'm glad Mr. Kelly asked you to stop by and see me, Erica. I've been wanting a chance to chat with you. Please sit down."

This was Miss Fletcher, the counselor, not much older than the students she counseled. She had a habit of arranging her hands with palms down and fingers laced together to make a kind of saddle in which she rested her chin when she talked. Her head movements and bright, close-set eyes always put Erica in mind of a nervous little bird.

"Mr. Kelly tells me you're having a hard time in his geometry class. Now, I don't think, and he doesn't think either, that it's because you can't do it. Your aptitude scores are very high. You're doing okay in most of your other courses. Let's see—you've even got a solid B average going in English. But Mr. Kelly says you seem to be preoccupied in his class. Sort of daydreaming."

"Mm," Erica said, shrugging. "I guess so."

"What do you think about, at those times?"

Erica mulled this over, and was rather surprised at her own answer. "Nothing, really."

The birdlike face puckered in good-natured skepticism. "Oh, come on, now, surely there's something. A boyfriend maybe?"

"Don't have one." The truth was, she didn't even have any particularly close girlfriends; people seemed to drift away from her after a while.

"Problems of some kind? Something that's worrying you?"

Erica considered this for a moment. "No, not really. I mean, nothing in particular. I just think. Not about anything. I'm always just—thinking."

Miss Fletcher smiled. "Well, doesn't that seem a little strange, thinking without thinking *about* something? What's it like? Do you see pictures in your mind, pictures of some place maybe, somewhere you'd rather be?"

"No, it's not like that," Erica said. "It's—I just sort of let my mind go blank, like. It feels, well, it feels good not to be—connected, like. Not to have to bother with things."

Miss Fletcher looked thoughtful. "I think we all feel that way some-times, Erica. I know I do. There are times I'd just like to snuggle down somewhere and hide, and pull my dreams in around me cozy like a blan-ket. But I've got my job to do, and so do you. We're coming up to the end of a reporting period pretty soon. You're going to have to try to pay atten-tion and put more effort into your work. Do you think you can do that?"

"I'll try."

But when grades came out for the marking period, there was the inevi-table ugly scene at home. She tried to retreat behind the cloudy buffer of her private thoughts, but Dad's face kept peering through.

"An F in geometry? You're perfectly capable of doing better than that, and you know it. You got a B in English. You got C's in history and Spanish and economics. C's are nothing to brag about, but they're passing. What's with this F in geometry?"

"I—don't know."

"Well, I think I do. Look at the comments your teacher wrote here. You daydream in class. Daydream! I've noticed it around here, too, more and more lately. I think you do it all the time and only get passing grades in most of your subjects because they're easy for you and you don't have to put in much effort. But geometry's different. You've got to think about that, don't you, and you're too—too some-thing. Too lazy, is my bet."

"I'm sorry, Dad." She had to say something. She hadn't been lis-tening very closely, so this seemed like a safe thing to say. "Sorry."

"Sorry isn't going to get it, young lady. Buckling down and *studying* is what's going to get it."

"Your dad's right, dear." The other face, Mom's, pushed itself into the sanctity of her thoughts, alongside Dad's scowl. "You're going to have to work at it. What if you decide you want to go to college? With these grades you may not even be able to get in. We only want what's best for you."

"I'll try harder, Mom." Anything, anything to get them to leave her alone.

"Erica."

Was he talking to her?

"Erica!" Mr. Kelly's face, a mask of annoyance, swam into her awareness.

"Yes?"

"What is an isosceles triangle?"

She figured there was no use trying to cover up. "I don't know."

Mr. Kelly stood for a moment looking at his shoes. "Erica?"

"Yes?"

"Would you have the kindness to turn to page 77 in your book?"

"Yes, sir." She rustled through the pages.

"Now please read to us. The definition at the bottom of the page."

She peered at the print nestled at the bottom of page 77 and cleared her throat. "Uh, definition: an isosceles triangle is a triangle having two sides."

A muffled titter of laughter went around the room, and she could tell from Mr. Kelly's face that he rather wanted to laugh too. She didn't mind. What did it matter, really?

"Erica, have you ever seen a triangle with only two sides? I suspect Euclid would come back from the grave for such a sight. Please read the *whole* definition. It requires turning the page."

"Definition," she read. "An isosceles triangle is a triangle having two sides"—turning the page—"of equal length."

"That's a little more like it," Mr. Kelly said. Some people in the class laughed again, and the lesson went on.

But it had been a magic moment for her.

At home, up in her room, she lolled across her bed and pulled the geometry book out of her bookbag. A magic moment, and only she had known it.

Somehow in that strange moment, like a sort of epiphany, the whole nature of the thing had come clear to her. There wasn't anything difficult about it at all. Now it was just a matter of doing a little catching up. She flipped back to the first chapter and began reading: axioms, definitions, theorems, proofs.

It wasn't alien to her any more. When she put the book aside and pulled a blanket over her and snapped off the light, it was nearly three in the morning.

That was a Wednesday morning. That afternoon Mr. Kelly was out sick, and the substitute teacher, passing along Mr. Kelly's assignment, just gave them the extra hour to study. Erica's classmates spent the time various ways; she spent hers reading geometry. Not reading the English and history assignments she had fallen behind on; there was only one thing for her now.

Thursday was spent similarly, but Friday afternoon Mr. Kelly was back, with a vengeance. He was evidently eager to see with what diligence the class had worked on the assignment he had given.

"Now class, listen carefully, and think. The Alternate Interior Angle Theorem says that if two lines are crossed by a transversal that makes congruent alternate interior angles, then the two lines are parallel. What does the converse of this theorem say, and to what is it equivalent?"

Erica had her hand in the air like a shot. Mr. Kelly was visibly taken aback. "Ah—*Erica?*"

"The converse says that if two *parallel* lines are crossed by a transversal then the alternate interior angles are congruent, and this is equivalent to Euclid's Parallel Postulate."

Mr. Kelly looked a little as if he had been kicked in the stomach. "Uh. Ah! Y-yes. Yes! That's exactly right. Very good!"

Several students were eyeing her with a species of surprise that clearly bordered upon outright awe. She paid little attention to this, however, and little attention even to Mr. Kelly's startled praise. Such things weren't important now.

"Erica, hello, it's good to have you stop in again. Please sit down." Miss Fletcher flashed her best young-counselor smile. "Some things have, er, changed since I saw you last, and we should talk."

Erica parted the mists only slightly, regarded Miss Fletcher's bird-like face nestled on interlocked fingers, and began a mental retreat. Miss Fletcher seemed to sense this, though, and went out of her way, with a raising of the voice, to call her back.

"I've heard such fascinating reports from Mr. Kelly about your progress in geometry!" she effervesced. "He says you're at the top of the class. He's amazed—and pleased, needless to say. But how about your other classes?"

"Mm," Erica intoned, noncommittally.

"I have reports from your other teachers that you—well, that you're daydreaming. In their classes. Now, Erica, I was a student once, just like you, and not so long ago either, and I know what it's like trying to juggle all those courses. And I think it's wonderful how you've caught on to geometry. But you do need to try to find a balance between that and your other studies. I really think it's all in how you allocate your time, don't you?"

Erica nodded and smiled, sensing that that was an appropriate response to whatever she had just been asked.

It was a time of tremendous awakening, in its own way. Those blank cloudy screens of formless thought, those cottony layers that she had been so accustomed to gathering about herself in her mind, were blank screens no longer.

They were alive with the beautiful vistas of geometry.

As everything else receded into irrelevance, the new vision grew into an almost painful clarity.

Mr. Kelly gradually cut down on calling on her in class, probably because it seemed unfair for her to be answering all the questions alone, day after day. But she speculated on this motivation, and on the situation itself, only from a distance. There was so much now that wasn't worth thinking about.

She emerged into partial focus in her English class as Mrs. Riley emoted and gesticulated, discussing—what? Who cared? Some poem, something. What fascinated Erica was the geometry. Not the book geometry, but the geometry around her.

Planes intersected at various angles to form the shiny surfaces of desks, which in turn sprouted students: odd configurations of cylinders, ellipsoids, cones, irregular shapes that yet had their curious regularities. The windows of the classroom were a symphony of latticed design, nets of parallel lines catching the light in infinitely interesting patterns. Mrs. Riley herself, up at the front of the room, was a moving study in intersecting solids, with her cylindrical legs and arms, her spheroidal head. The English-teacher voice went on, extolling the virtues of heaven only knew what, and Erica wished that she could *see* the sound, follow the sinuous graph of its geometric structure. The very clock on the wall was more interesting for its geometry than for its power to say that the class was nearly over, and when the bell rang, she got up and went out only because she felt vaguely herded along by the others. But it was all right—out in the hall, and in her next class, and later in the streets and at home, there would always be further delights.

"I just don't know, Erica. I just don't know what to make of you." Dad's reddened face was nearly circular, lips pinched up in an expression somewhat more complex than mere annoyance this time. "It's the damnedest thing I ever saw. An A in geometry. That's great, don't get me wrong. But down from a B to a D in English? And D's in everything else? You're not even going to get out of high school at this rate, much less into college. What happened?"

She felt herself shrug, barely able to muster the interest in these matters necessary for doing so. "Don't know."

Mom's face floated into view, distantly. "It's good that you're doing so well in the one class, but we didn't mean for you to neglect everything else. Your father is right to be upset."

But such exchanges meant less and less to her as the days went by, and she had only a vague awareness that by the time the spring term was drawing to a close, there had been several counseling sessions, sometimes with Miss Fletcher, sometimes with teachers too, and sometimes with Mom or Dad, in various combinations. It was all like a movie that someone in another room was watching, with the sound coming vaguely, meaninglessly through the wall—for her, a wall of surroundment by private thoughts, thoughts no longer passive and blank but dynamic, writhing, alive.

She had begun to notice more and more detail in the geometric configurations around her. In class (if that was where she was—she could seldom be sure, and scarcely cared to know) the clusters of shape and color surrounding her were only vaguely understood to be people, classmates, teachers. More importantly, they were wedges of space, color, angles, planes, curved surfaces, elongations, truncations, endlessly variegated forms that flowed with a visual music that at times nearly moved her to tears. Beneath all this, there was always a sort of subtext, a sort of drama unfolding, if one cared to watch: a drama of words and expected responses, of humanity and its comic relations, its pointless concerns. But this she could ignore easily enough.

She was remotely aware that nasty scenes were acting themselves out at home. Like distant thunder, there seemed to be shouting, pleading, threats. On occasion, she would allow herself to be distracted from her true concerns, enough to see what was going on in that absurd human drama that drifted like clotted sewage beneath the real essence of things.

". . . end of the school year, and you're about to fail four subjects out of five! One A and four F's, now that's going to look just beautiful." Maybe you plan to make a career out of being a junior in high school." Dad was in rare form this time, if one cared to make such comparisons. His neck protruded cylindrically from his collar, his mouth worked in an oddly compelling bewilderment of geometric foldings and refoldings.

". . . and if you *don't* get your act together, you're going to make it all up in summer school, and you're going to spend every damned day and every damned night at those books. No movies, no music, no TV, no nothing." Was this the same occasion, or a different time? She wasn't sure, but then it didn't matter. Anyway, it was funny to hear this—as if movies or television as such meant anything to her, when their real fascinations could be seen in the shifting shapes and patterns to be found in the pageant that was everything around her. And music, did he say? Music was for the eye.

On some other occasion, probably later—who cared, whether time flowed forwards or backwards?—her impression, beyond the spatial attractions, was that someone's face, Mom's she supposed, hovered nearby, and was saying something, but apparently not to her. Something like, "Not now, Charles, not when you've been drinking—" But the voice was cut off by a thunderclap of sound and pain, and she pieced together for herself the awareness that a hand had slapped her, one tubular object (some corner of her mind whispered) impacting with another; she felt her bedspread beneath her, and supposed that she had fallen back onto the bed. Later sometime she was alone, and mustered

enough interest in the absurdity of her surroundings, her physical situation, to focus upon her own face in the mirror, a face now bruised red-
dish-blue on one side. Somewhere, she thought she could hear crying,
and wondered if it was her own, but it didn't seem to be. She contem-
plated the geometric contours of her bruise, and smiled.

In the underflow of uninteresting events there were apparently further
nasty scenes, more unpleasantness. Very little bothered her, actually,
but these scenes were starting to, if only because the voices were becoming louder and more insistent, the faces more truculent; the effect
increasingly was to draw her away from the altar of her own thoughts.
More and more, she was finding it difficult to maintain her mental distance from the squalid and senseless things going on about her, and
difficult to forgive the distraction, the interruption of her usually joy-
ous meditations. The metaphor for this attempted distance between
her and the so-called real world was of course a wall, itself a geometric
entity, and when they broke through that wall, even momentarily, they
were tampering with a sacred structure.

When it was, that her smoldering anger came out as action—
ironically, reluctantly, the playing of a part, herself, in the ridiculous
human drama—when it was, she couldn't have said, because she didn't
know when anything was, and didn't care. But at some point there was
a sensation of exceedingly interesting geometric patternings, more than
in anything she had seen before. The struggling, the scuffling, the
screaming—all this she effortlessly ignored now, in light of the sheer
fascination of the visible. A beautifully curved silver shape—a resplen-
dent blade, gradually flowering into a crimson bloom of streaking
metal—rose and fell in delicious arcs. Moving shapes changed, bloom-
ing in crimson flowers themselves, lying still. She only idly understood,
or cared to understand, that the reason why two particularly condensed
areas of geometric intensity appeared to be wide-eyed faces turned
upward, was because in that ridiculous other world they were precisely
that. Somewhere in this complex space, at the end of the mile-long
jointed object that was her right arm, a hand flexed and the silver blade
fell away, twirling through angles of inexpressible loveliness.

And at some other time, later as she supposed (though it didn't
matter, this foolishness which they called time), she began a series of

especially profound contemplations of her surroundings. Parallel cylinders ran across the high, bright square of sunlight that was the one window of her room: iron-colored vertical cylinders beyond which the light cavorted in patterns of untold variegation. Behind the delectably patterned gray expanse of her walls, voices sometimes seemed to moan, but this was of no importance, any more than the words issuing from the round faces that sometimes appeared and disappeared amid the overall swirl of angles and surfaces. And though the scene around her did not materially change, it presented ever-fresh realms of reflection, day after day, year after year, to her charmed apprehension. Laughing, she rejoiced in the private inner spaces of her mind, and crooked one arm a little in its rough white sleeve, and watched the angles change.

Fwoo

For Nancy Lee Johnson, in memoriam

Nancy Lyman had a monster living under her bed.

Or in corners of the room where furtive shadows gathered, or in the closet when the door was open a crack so that something could look slyly out from the darkness there. Somewhere, watching her, waiting for its chance, something lived in her bedroom. Always had.

Well, in truth, not quite always. For a time it had faded into the uncertain landscape of the barely-remembered. But after many years' absence, it was back. And somehow its return made the passage of those many years seem unnaturally quick, in the troubled waters of her memory.

She hadn't actually seen it, at least not clearly; but she knew that it was back.

When she had been a little girl, the thing had been there, watching, always. When she had grown older, it had receded, like some noxious tide on the shoreline of her perceptions, and her false sense of security had let her tell herself that the thing had never been real, had vanished like a puff of air when her mind, her emotions grew older, so that she saw the world not through the febrile eyes of a nervous child but through the prosaic eyes of a busy young woman who had no time for monsters.

She had seldom thought of the thing during her young adulthood, her middle years, her later years with Tom and the children. It was, after all, only a typical infantile fantasy, a typical nightmare of childhood. When you thought about it, there was something almost laughably trite about the very idea, a monster under the bed, a goblin in the closet, a lurker in the shadows.

But with her own children off and gone, and with Tom dead now, the terrors of her youth were gradually reasserting themselves. Maybe they had never really been absent, but only ignored, repressed by a blasé pseudo-sophistication of the mind. Maybe she had been kidding herself all these comfortable and complacent years.

Maybe the thing had never really tired of watching her. Maybe she just hadn't noticed.

She folded her evening paper decisively, as if putting away these haunting notions as well, and surveyed the living room. It was cosy here on the sofa, in this warm wash of lamplight, and she disliked the thought of getting up and going to bed. Well, she hadn't finished her milk, and that was a ready-made reason to linger. Sipping from her glass, she thought of those far-off days, when a highstrung little pig-tailed girl had been so afraid of—

Fwoo.

That's what her grandfather had called it. Sometimes, he had told her in his mock-horrific tones like some old-time radio announcer, *sometimes you'll hear it call its name when everybody else just thinks it's the wind outside the window at night. But* you *know that it's saying* Fwoo, Fwooooooo, *and you know that it's talking to nobody but you.*

Nancy got up and carried her glass to the kitchen sink, and headed for the bedroom. Her mom would always get mad at Gramps for subjecting her to such stories. Nancy paused in front of the mirror over the dresser beside her bed, and her mother's face, alive again, seemed to stare back in place of her own now wrinkled visage. "Dad, why *do* you insist on telling her such things? It's going to give her nightmares." Had she spoken aloud just now, mimicking her mother's oft-repeated complaint, or was this the dry, lifeless voice of memory? She didn't know, and she guessed that it really didn't matter.

When she was in bed with the lights off and with the top of the sheet pulled up to her chin, she felt that those intervening decades had never happened, that she was still the frightened little wide-eyed girl who had listened to her grandfather's creepy tales in spite of everything. What was it Gramps had said about the name . . .?

Sometimes when it moves under your bed, or turns over, slowly, like some great dusty insect in the dark, or scuttles across the carpet just below where you can see, it makes a dry sound: ffffffw—, as if it wants to tell you its name, but it's teasing you, not saying it right out.

Of course, a lot of things sound like that, so you can't ever be sure, can you? Sometimes it doesn't finish saying its name, and sometimes after it starts saying it, off there somewhere in the shadows of your room, the wind picks up and finishes it, outside your window: *Ffffffwooooooooooooo,* and you're glad, at least, that it seems to be outside after all, and maybe can't get in. But sometimes when you pull the covers up, it starts sounding like that: *fffffw——,* and you wonder. . . .

She shuddered, now, to remember what he had said next.

When you pull the covers up, he had said, and it makes that quick dry sound, you try to tell yourself that maybe it's not the thing after all. Maybe everything is all right.

But maybe not. And then if it ever finishes saying its name, right there in the dark and lonely room with you . . .

And she remembered, now, the horror she had felt as a child, reaching down and pulling the blanket up, and hearing that terrible, sibilant rustle, and fearing that the thing would finish saying its name.

She realized, with this rush of memory, that she hadn't pulled up her blanket now.

She leaned forward, her head just slightly off the pillow, and groped into the darkness near her knees, and found the top of the covers, and pulled them up.

Ffffffw——.

And, after some uneasy reflections, she slept.

And woke in a more practical state of mind.

Enough was enough. Why should a woman over seventy worry about the idiotic phantasms of childhood?

She spent the day cleaning the house and paid particular attention to the bedroom, where in the calm light of day everything was normal. No matter how different everything might look at night, this familiar scene offered nothing to disturb the mind right now: the bed, the dresser, the wicker chair, the low table decorated with her milk-glass bowl and antique Hull vases. How could any of this ever look threatening?

But in the evening, reading again in that snug cone of lamplight on the sofa and sipping a cup of herbal tea, she dreaded going to bed. She was sleepy and hadn't intended to stay up very late, but maybe she'd start reading that new novel tonight after all, and have another cup of tea. She told herself that she wasn't just making excuses, that she needed no reasons to read some more if she wanted.

But in her heart she knew better, and it was with an uneasy sigh that, only a few pages into the novel, she finally gave it up and rose from the sofa and switched off the lamp and started getting ready for bed.

Predictably, from all too much experience, nothing in the bedroom looked the same after she was in bed, the sheet tucked under her chin. Strange objects loomed about her in the shadows. Beyond the windowpanes, out in the night, a forlorn little wind moaned at the window like some strange little beast wanting to be let in. She felt jittery about reaching down in the dark and pulling the covers up. She found herself wondering, and not for the first time, why she didn't just pull all the bedclothes up to start with, and not have to grope for them in the dark. But it was her habit, had always been, to pull just the sheet up at first, and later the blanket. And besides, to pull all the covers up to start with, as she easily could—wouldn't that be a concession to her fears, a somehow shameful concession that she was unwilling to make? No, she wasn't altering her habit for some foolish fantasy.

But, reaching down in the dark, she thought: how foolish is it? What if there's really something . . .

Pausing, her arm out from under the sheet, vulnerable, she looked around the room, feeling the darkness almost palpably close around her face like some oppressive mantle. Out there in the dark, the vague outline of the low table was somehow disturbing. Or was the source of the impression what was *on* the table? What could that low, dusky shape be, if not her milk-glass bowl? Nothing but overwrought nerves could have suggested that it moved craftily, or even slid off the table altogether. No, it was still there, had to still be there, and still just a bowl. How could it be otherwise?

And how could there be anything on the dresser, any low, flat shape, a shape that wasn't there before, as if something (from the table?) had slithered up there like some obscene, flat sea-creature in a sea of darkness. . . . She rubbed her eyes. Certainly not; there was nothing on the dresser, could be nothing on the dresser, nothing but what belonged there. When she blinked, the disturbing impression seemed to recede, though something of the feeling remained.

But she couldn't let herself dwell on those feelings. Swallowing, taking a deep breath and letting it out slowly, she flexed her fingers and reached down into the dark and pulled the blanket halfway up.

Fffffw—

She froze, listening, thinking about the sound, trying not to think about the sound but thinking about it anyway.

Nothing, silence. Just a sad little moaning of the wind at the window.

Her eyes, a little more accustomed to the dark now, surveyed what she could see of the dim, shadowy outlines in the room. Low table, wicker chair, dresser. All normal. Nothing on the low table, nothing on the dresser but what should be there. How could she have imagined that some low, flat, lurking shape—

But no more of this. The blanket needed to come the rest of the way up. She flexed her hands again, and pulled.

Ffffffffwooooo.

It had to be the wind, of course, that last bit of sound. But in any case there was a problem. A blanket shouldn't cling, shouldn't fasten itself to you like some great sea-bottom nightmare. But it did, and she realized, with a sense of irony that almost made her laugh out loud, that she had pulled up not the blanket, but the thing itself.

Down in the Mouth

"April is the cruellest month . . ."
—T. S. Eliot, *The Waste Land*

It was the third week in April, the eighty-second April of his life, when Haskell Wells found out that he wasn't alone on the farm.

Even for upstate Vermont, this was a bit late for a snowfall. And if it hadn't been for the two or three inches that lay like a cottony blanket on the ground for most of a day before melting, he probably would never have noticed anything out of the ordinary at all.

That morning, with the fresh snow on the ground from overnight and with the last few flakes settling out of an ashen sky, he booted up and pulled on his dirty old parka and his knit cap and strolled out, Candy following along at his heels. The dog was seldom out of his sight, and with Becky gone these past two years, Haskell had to admit to himself that the dog was welcome company.

Lighting a corncob pipe, the old man leaned on a fencepost and surveyed his land. How many years had it been since he'd actually farmed this land instead of just living on it? Even the last several years Becky had been alive, he had pretty well retired. His eyes hadn't been any too good even then, and his limbs had felt brittle and unwilling, and still did. Puffing a gray eddy of smoke out onto the air like a floating spiderweb, he strained his eyes to look across to the machine shed, where pieces of farm machinery stood idle like hulking dinosaurs, their metal bones flaking, their eyes dull. Across the way, animal pens stood abandoned, the wind blowing gentle white brushstrokes across them. Out at the boundaries of his land, shabby fences stretched away into the distance, thin and ragged armies marching single-file. Almost on the horizon, an old stone fence crawled along the whitened ground, a segmented gray worm with its eyeless head lost in the faraway stretch of pines. As always out here, it was quiet, maybe too quiet—he was miles from any neighbor, and he seldom even saw the mail truck any more. He sniffed the air and puffed out another volley of smoke. Candy was nosing about in the snow, tail wagging; nothing else stirred.

Haskell finished his pipe, knocked the rest of the ash out, and headed back toward the house. The dog ran ahead with a sharp little bark, but veered to the side before reaching the battered door, and ran to a spot in the snow some several yards from the house, between the house and the toolshed. She nuzzled her snout into the snow, lifted her face to his, and barked again.

"I know, old girl. It's gettin' to be spring, spite of this crazy white stuff. You can smell the groundhogs and the moles. There'll be a day for huntin', you just got to be patient." He opened the storm door, and the dog followed him in. He'd left water to boil for coffee, and it was bubbling. Instant coffee it was, now; the real stuff was just too much trouble. How had he and Becky ever managed all the chores, he wondered, back when the farm was alive and active? He didn't have any too much energy to spare these days.

It was well past middle of the morning by the time he had had his second cup of coffee and thumbed through the latest farm catalogs. Why he still bothered to look at them he couldn't really fathom; he guessed it was just an unwillingness to give up old habits, maybe. Anyhow, it was something to do. He ambled into the kitchen and looked out the window. The sky was still overcast, though maybe a bit brighter than before. He glanced out across the fields, then scanned the ground nearer the house and saw that, as he'd expected, the snow was already starting to melt. It was around forty-five degrees, according to the thermometer hanging just outside the window. That was the way with these late-season snowfalls, here and gone in the same day. It was just as well, too; there had been more than enough snow this winter for him.

He was about to turn and go back into the front room when he noticed it.

Several yards out from the house, toward the shed, just about where Candy had been nosing around, there was a spot on the ground where the snow was almost completely melted. Funny, that it would melt faster there than anywhere else, when there weren't any pipes or anything there under the ground that could be producing heat.

He scratched his chin and decided that it called for a look. Lighting his pipe and pulling on his parka and cap and boots again despite the warming day, he whistled to Candy and went out the door.

The dog ran out eagerly, kicking up powdery little sprays of dry snow, and stood nuzzling what little there was left of the snow at the spot Haskell had been looking at from the window. The old man bent down and brushed a place on the ground bare and flattened the calloused palm of his hand out on the sod.

And stood up, blinking.

Damned if it didn't feel a little warm there. Or was it his imagination?

He tried again, feeling the ground with his hand, and still thought it seemed to hold a vague little warmth that really had no reason he could think of to be there. When he had withdrawn his hand again, Candy sniffed the spot and barked. There was something, Haskell thought, a trifle nervous-sounding in the tone of that bark, but then the dog always had been a bit squirrelly.

"C'mon, old girl, gettin' on toward lunch time. We'll have ourselves a bite to eat and then come out for another look, what do you say?"

When he opened the creaking old door to the toolshed around two that afternoon and peered in, it came to him again how everything on the place had come down to idleness and disrepair. The dilapidated door was nearly off at one hinge, and the inside of the shed was a sorry mess of spiderwebs and dust. There had been a time when he would have thought such conditions shameful on a farm. But that had been a long time ago. These days he was lucky if he could just keep his own body running. He fumbled among the neglected tangle of tools in the dusk of the shed, brought out a shovel, backed out—watching not to bump his head on the door frame—and shut the door with a wheeze of dust. Candy was at his feet, tail wagging in anticipation of some new adventure.

"Let's go have us a look, how about it?"

He stood over the place on the ground where the snow was completely gone now, in contrast with the dusting of white that was still visible everywhere else. The spot was some four feet or so in diameter, and remarkably circular. Looking at it made him feel somehow foolish, as if there were something fundamental about his land, his own door-yard, that he ought to know but didn't. He tried the ground with the shovel. The ground everywhere was pretty well thawed by now and ought to yield. Sure enough, he turned over the first shovelful of gritty sod with no particular trouble, dumping it to one side in a tumble of dirt and pebbles. Damned soil always was rocky, and no helping it. He started digging in earnest, wondering what he was looking for. Candy watched from nearby, shifting nervously. Whatever it was down there in that soil, he might be eighty-two but he wasn't too old to have a look-see for himself, thank *you*.

He dug the circular spot out all around, down to just a depth of six inches or so, and leaned on the handle of his shovel. Despite the crisp coolness of the day, he was sweating, and he wiped a gruff hand across his forehead and started digging again.

That was when he smelled it.

At about the same moment when the odor wafted up out of the ground to him, the dog whined and began angling off toward the house. Haskell paused with the shovel and sniffed. The smell was un-placeable—oddly, a little like creosote, a little like something rotten, meat gone bad or something. But not quite like those things either. All he knew for sure was that it was the most disgusting thing he had ever smelled in his life. He slowed in his digging.

Did he really want to uncover whatever this was?

Maybe it was toxic or something. The thought sent a little thrill of anger through his frame; if somebody had let some kind of poisons leach into his land, he'd damned well have their heads on a platter. But how could that be, when he was miles from anybody out here? Never any trouble like that before. Sure, it was one thing if you had land right next door to a chemical plant or something, but out here what could it be? Trying not to breathe the stuff too deeply, he kept digging. By now Candy was curled up over on the step by the kitchen door, looking very uncomfortable.

Haskell had gotten down maybe another three or four inches with the shovel when he saw something.

Scraping a little more dirt away, he leaned closer and peered into the shallow hole. It looked as if he had uncovered a little bit of something, something gray and soft.

And unless he was very much mistaken, something slightly moving.

With a grunt he stepped back a pace, bringing the shovel back with him and out of the hole. "What in—" Again he leaned a little over to look. It was hard to tell what he was looking at. Whatever it was, it still had a coating of dirt on it, and he gingerly slipped the shovel blade forward and scraped at the surface, drawing the dirt away. Whatever was beneath the dirt was soft, almost gelatinous, and seemed to quiver. The odor swelled out now in an almost unbearable wave, and he shrank back, spitting, feeling as if there was something unclean in his nostrils and mouth. Scooping up a shovelful of loose dirt, he covered the thing again and tossed the shovel to one side and walked to the house, where Candy still waited with eyes full of what he could have sworn was fear.

"Let's go in, girl. Whatever that stuff is, it can wait awhile. I'm tired, and I got to think."

Somehow the rest of the day indoors seemed to slip by faster than usual, and he realized, having his supper, that he'd been thinking, musing, woolgathering, all afternoon, about one thing and another. Nowadays his thoughts seemed to wander sometimes, and it wasn't uncommon, when he was sitting in the front room on the sofa, for him to nod off. That was the way the day had gone.

But his thoughts had kept coming back to the matter of what was out there in the ground.

Again a number of times he had found himself speculating whether some sort of foul chemicals or something had leached into the ground, but always he ended up discounting it as very unlikely, out here. The thing had him puzzled, for sure. The cloud-muffled sun was just setting when he began to think that he'd better go out and have another look, and he cursed himself for not stirring sooner; there wouldn't be much daylight left now, especially as overcast as the sky still was. Nevertheless, he had to do it. Whistling for Candy, who hung her head and looked decidedly unexcited about going along, he pulled on his parka and boots and cap again and went out, letting the storm door slam dustily behind him.

He realized, walking over to the hole he had dug, that he'd been afraid, all day, of coming back out here, and that now what he was afraid of was letting it get completely dark before he had another look. Why he felt that way, he couldn't say, but he had to have that look by daylight. Somehow, he didn't fancy peeking down into the hole at night with a flashlight. Somehow, he didn't fancy being out here beside the hole after dark at all. He stopped at the edge of the digging and looked down.

Things weren't quite the way he had left them, here.

Just inside the circular rim of the digging it looked as if another, smaller circle had pressed up an inch or two, ridgelike, out of the ground, though he couldn't really see anything through the dirt. The impression he had was that it was like a ringworm, a very large ringworm, pushing up, festering up on the ground in the base of the shallow hole. Retrieving the shovel, he carefully scraped the blade along the surface of the round ridge, dislodging the little dirt remaining, revealing more gray surface beneath. What he saw was a ring, some yard or more in diameter, of soft, gray stuff that looked dull, phlegmlike in the failing light. Now the odor emanated forth again, and he tried not to breathe it in.

"I don't know what the devil's going on here, but Haskell Wells ain't a man to be trifled with," he muttered as much to himself as to the dog cowering behind him. "Let's just see."

He began shoveling dirt out from the middle of the raised ring. It was hard going, because he had to lean and push the shovel blade in at a shallow angle; he didn't particularly feel like stepping into the ring to dig. Little by little, turning his head around to breathe cleaner air as he went, he hollowed out a spot two feet or so deep, a cuplike cavity inside the ring. There wasn't a lot of light now, but he could see that the inner edges of the ring went down into the ground at least as far as he had dug, and showed no signs of ending. Whenever his shovel touched the gray stuff, he felt a jellylike quiver that made his stomach want to lurch. He stopped, standing off a couple of feet, leaning on the shovel and catching his breath.

And the gray ring unmistakably began to move.

"God a-mighty." He straightened up and, without thinking, picked up the shovel with one hand on the top of the handle and one hand halfway down, holding it defensively, like a weapon. He peered through the gathering gloom at the thing in the shallow hole.

The gray ring undulated, rippled, slightly but undeniably. And without warning, the dirt down in the bottom of the cuplike declivity within collapsed with a sucking sound, and Haskell Wells found himself looking down a gray, dark funnel that looked like the inside of a throat. In some half-hysterical, illogical kind of way, it put him in mind of looking down the throat of a baby bird, a baby bird grown large and craning skyward to be fed, though the thing really didn't look that way at all. At the surface, uncomfortably near his feet, the dull gray ring—the mouth—moved with a kind of semiliquid smack, a sound that made him think of the quivering of packing-fat around a canned ham. The stench that belched up into the air now was ghastly, unthinkable. At some point he must have dropped the shovel and made for the house. In any case, the next thing he knew he was inside, in the front room, on the sofa, having a hard time breathing, the dog curled beside him on the cushions and very clearly trembling with fear.

He had to clear his thoughts. All the windows in the room had the shades still drawn back and were squares of black where the night looked in. The only light was the dim little bulb over the sink in the kitchen, its pale glow filtering through to the front room to outline hulking furniture shapes in the dusk. How long had he been sitting here? He didn't remember coming back in the house. Didn't remember at all.

Had he locked the door on his way in?

Struggling to his feet, he went around and pulled down all the shades, shutting out the dark. He went to the kitchen and rattled the doorknob; the door was locked. On an impulse, he reached up and switched off the little bulb over the sink, leaving himself in complete darkness. This made him feel better, somehow, made him feel less—visible. He pulled the curtain back from the kitchen window and peered out into the night. There was only a wan sifting of moonlight through the clouds, and he could see nothing but a faint suggestion of the angular forms of his outbuildings across the way.

And—the unclear suggestion, closer, of something else, something dark against the blacker dark of night, something that couldn't very well be the tool shed or the machine shed or any other outbuilding, because it seemed to be too close to the house. Something in the dooryard.

Something large.

Something that moved.

Something that, in the *way* it moved, made his bowels feel like ice.

Baby bird, his mind babbled, childlike; baby bird, baby bird come to feed. But the shape moving out there was no baby bird, no kind of bird. Whatever was sliding its bulky blackness against the black of night out there didn't really have any shape at all as far as he could see. Drawing a raspy breath and rubbing his eyes, he leaned to the windowpane again and peered out.

Nothing.

He snorted. "Well, hell, of course there ain't nothin' there. What'd you expect, you crazy old goat?" He thought about the icy feeling he had felt in his bowels, and shook his head. "Goin' senile, Haskell." He chuckled drily. "God's sakes, you dig up a little patch of some goo in the ground, and first thing, you start thinkin'—"

There had been a sound.

His voice had nearly drowned it out of his own ears, but there had been a sound, around at the other side of the house, at the front door. He noticed only vaguely that the dog had yelped softly, off there in the living room. He started to make his way in that direction and stumbled over a chair, and realized he would have to have some light, though somehow he didn't want to turn on any lights in the house. Fishing a flashlight out of the kitchen drawer, he reached the living room in time to see the dog disappearing behind the sofa, tail between her legs. And in time to hear the sound again.

It was like a soft, puffy kind of pushing, a pushing against the front door from the outside, like something large and soft, something insistent, pressing its form against the wood. The sound ceased, then suddenly came again, more emphatic, more insistent, pressing, pushing. The wooden panels in the door creaked, kept creaking until the sound let up again. Haskell listened. Quiet. He played the light from the flashlight around the surface of the door. All quiet.

Then without warning the pushing at the door returned with such force that the creaking, this time, sounded like splintering. In the jumpy beam from the flashlight he could see a jagged crack open up across two of the door panels, and even as he registered this, a fist-sized piece of the wood came loose, falling with a clatter to the floor. The crack branched into a network of cracks, and part of another panel snapped loose and fell. He felt glued to the floor, unable to move, able only to watch, and to register an atrocious odor that was finding its way through the splintering door.

The pushing stopped.

Trembling, his hands shaking so hard that the light jittered and danced over the door and adjacent wall, he listened.

Nothing.

Slowly, he raised a hand to wipe sweat off his brow and out of his eyes. "Jesus." Carefully, he leaned back onto one arm of the sofa and sat, easing his weight slowly and quietly down, never taking his eyes off the door, through which jagged blotches of night blackness stared. He exhaled, still trembling. "Jesus."

And then it was back.

It was as if something unthinkably immense and heavy, something tired of being kept back, pressed its bulk against the door with a suddenness and a determination and a completeness that was not to be resisted. The door, shattering into several large pieces and ripping off its hinges, fell into the room, casting insanely angled shadows on the wall as it fell.

Behind it, in the doorway, was a solid mass of gray matter, shapeless, or so large that the old man could not see its shape in the door frame. It mattered little, either way, because the thing was squeezing its way into the room, like some foul, thick liquid squeezing out of a tube.

"Christ our Lord." The old man dropped the flashlight, edging back toward the other door, the door that led from the living room to the bedroom. Once in there, if he could make it, he could close the door and push something against it from the inside, and maybe keep the thing out.

As he not so much ran as fell into the bedroom, he was conscious of something moving beneath his feet, between his legs, and realized that it was Candy, darting into the lightless room with him. In the crazily misdirected light of the dropped flashlight he had had one nightmare glimpse over his shoulder on his way into the bedroom, one panic look back into the room from which he fled. That glimpse had shown him something large and glistening, something heavy-looking but moving in almost a liquid manner, something bulging across the room to find him. Part of the thing had seemed to pucker out into a mouth, and now as he worked to close the bedroom door against a mass that was already beginning to press against it, his mind chittered insanely again: baby bird, baby bird from the nest, baby baby bird come to feed.

With a desperate expending of strength he closed the door all the way and snapped the bolt and looked wildly around. The windowshade across the room was up, and the clouds must have thinned a little, because a pale suggestion of moonlight was filtering into the room. It wasn't much to see by; he could only barely make out the shape of the bureau near the door. He had to move the bureau, had to set it against the door. Even as he began to drag at the bureau with his hands, the wood in the door began creaking and groaning with the weight that was being squeezed against it from the other side.

He shifted the bureau a little, and the picture of Becky fell face-down amid a general rattling and clattering. But it was no use; the bureau was too heavy, he didn't have the strength to move it. A sob found its way out of his throat, then an inarticulate curse. Not fair! Damn it to hell, not fair! He was too *old!* Even as he thought this, the wood in the door began to splinter inward, and the abominable odor came through to him, choking him.

He wheeled toward the wan square of window across the room, and realized something very important. Thank heaven—there was neither a storm window nor a screen in the window. He had started, a couple of days ago before the snow when it was deceptively warm, to go around and take the storm windows off and replace them with screens, but had gotten no farther than this window and the one in the bathroom. He had taken the storm window off in this room, but hadn't put the screen on. He hurried across the room to the window, striking his knee painfully on the edge of the bedstead as he went. As soon as he had the window up, the dog bolted through it with a bark, and he knew that he had to follow. In another second or two, the thing out there behind the door would be in the room, maybe was in the room already. He leaned out the window, his belly pressed into the sill, and swung one leg over, and half turned himself, and brought up the other leg, and heard the door across the room shatter and fall inward.

"Please, God."

He rolled outward and let go, and fell sideways onto the sloping metal surface of the rusty bulkhead below the window, sliding to the ground with a moan of pain, the wind knocked out of his lungs. "Please, God. Please." Even as he pushed himself to a half-standing position he could see, in the sickly paleness of the moonlight, something gray and wet-looking outlined in the bedroom window from which he had just dropped. The thing was already there, already at the window and pressing against the opening, oozing out, coming for him.

He was halfway to the toolshed before he even consciously knew he was moving, hobbling painfully on his bruised leg, wheezing for breath. Somewhere behind him in the night, he knew, the foul grayness was coming, coming for him, its obscene mouth puckering, sucking, writhing. "Baby bird," he said to himself, under his breath, over and over. "Baby bird." The bad leg buckled under him, and he fell in the dirt with a groan of despair.

Something wet touched his cheek, and he screamed. But it was Candy, Candy licking his face and whining pitifully. Craning his neck, he could see a movement near the bulkhead behind him, and he struggled to his feet and stumbled toward the toolshed, the dog running on ahead to the door, where it stopped and ran in fitful little circles, yelping. He made it to the shed and pulled the door open and lurched inside, the dog following. Barely aware that he had banged his head on the top of the door frame, he reached out and pulled the door closed, and had two realizations in that moment. One was that the thing was already at the shed, its foul bulk quivering in the dim light, its surface pinched into an open mouth. The other was that he had forgotten that the shed door was in poor repair, hanging almost loose at the upper hinge. With a cry, he backed away from the door into the dusty interior of the shed, bending his head beneath the low roof and feeling a warm trickle of blood down his cheek. The thing out there was at the door, pressing, gurgling, squeezing itself into the shed where he was hopelessly trapped. Some corner of his mind registered the fact that the dog was barking, and that its barking sounded deranged with fear. He himself was muttering, muttering, with no idea what he was saying. The door groaned inward at a slant, completely off at the top hinge, nearly off at the bottom one. It was over. There was nowhere to go. He was as far back into the shed as he could get, and it was over. He flailed his hands and cried out.

"Not fair! I'm just an old man! Damn you! Just a tired old man!"

His right hand banged against something familiar in the dark. It was a metal can, and it sloshed when he nudged it. Gasoline. He pulled at the container with both hands and fumbled it open. The pale patch of light that had been at the door was blotted out now, and though he could see nothing at all, he knew that the thing was in the door, in the shed, bulging forward. With the last of his strength, he emptied gasoline toward the thing, not knowing if he was reaching it. He made three or four passes in the foul air with the container, hearing a liquid *smack* each time. The air was unbreathable now in the shed; it was all gasoline fumes, and that other odor, that odor like creosote and rotten meat mingled. Digging a packet of matches out of his pocket, the old man struck one and caught only a glimpse of the gray horror that had squeezed part of its mass through the door. He tossed the match and tried to turn his face away, pressing his bloody cheek against the rough wood of the back wall. With a frightful *whoosh,* the air was alight, burning.

There was a deafening commotion, a raging that shook the entire shed, a crackling sound like fat frying, a stench that overpowered even the smell of gasoline and smoke. All this the old man's mind took in, in an instant, before darkness gathered in his brain. All this, and the odd momentary memory of Becky's picture falling face-down on the bureau, and the fleeting thought: thank God she didn't live to see this. And then only quiet.

He and Becky were strolling along the edge of the stream up beyond the north pasture, where the aroma of spring blossoms was afloat in the air. He took her hand, and they kissed, and she said, "See how clear and pretty the water is." The spring gurgled as if in invitation, and he knelt down and drank from the sparkling water, letting it play in cool abandon on his cheek. And the world knitted itself prosaically back together, and he was awake.

The wetness on his cheek was the dog, again, licking, whining, wanting him back. Even opening his eyes was painful, but nothing like the pain it took to sit up and look around.

Apparently it was morning. He squinted into the light. The front half of the shed was pretty well burned away, and out in the hazy light, beyond where the door had been, there was a charred mess on the ground, still faintly smoking; or was that the morning fog curling around the black patch on the ground? He raised an arm to his face, and saw that the sleeve of his wool shirt was burned nearly off, and that the flesh of his arm was seared. He didn't feel the pain until he saw the burns, and felt them only in a groggy kind of way now. He wondered if he was in shock. He ran rough fingers over his face, which felt crusty, raw, maybe burned. Beside him on the floor of the shed, Candy gave an interrogative little yip. He looked down at her. Her fur was singed along the back, but she seemed to be all right otherwise. Slowly, with a symphony of pain playing up and down his frame, he pushed himself to his feet and stumbled out into the light. He didn't want to look at the blackened pool on the ground, and shuffled past it, and around to the kitchen door and into the house. The dog followed, giving the patch in the dirt a wide berth. Haskell put down a dish of food for the dog, and, for the first time he could remember, poured himself a large glass of whiskey at the hour of nine in the morning.

The rest of the day passed in something of a mental fog. The old man had a second drink, then must have napped, sitting at the kitchen table. He hadn't wanted to go into the front room, where there was evidence of things not pleasant to remember just now. He knew the front door was off, the house open to the breeze, which chilled him; he had wrapped a blanket around himself, and slept sitting up. He was awake again, off and on, but lacked the energy to move around. By the time he felt ready to stir himself and get something to eat, it was morning again.

With Candy trailing at his heels, he walked around the far reaches of his land, smoking his pipe, trying not to think. Spring was really on the way now; the air, though still showing a certain crispness, was pleasant, and the sky had cleared. The scrub maples and birches were beginning to bud, and the world looked amazingly normal. He puffed his pipe and looked back across toward the farmhouse and sheds. They looked amazingly normal, too; he couldn't see the front of the house from here, with its ruined door. He'd have to fix it, sooner or later. Or call somebody to help him fix it. Who? He wasn't really close to anybody now, had pretty well outlived all his old friends. He hadn't even wanted to call the police in town or anybody to report—what had happened. What would he tell them? What good would it do? He rubbed his forearm, where the burned skin was rather painful, and motioned to the dog and began shuffling back across the land toward the house.

As he went, he felt that there was something—not quite the same; something subtly changed, something odd. But he wasn't going to dwell on morbid or unpleasant things. Strangely, he felt, on the way back across the pastures, almost a new energy, an increase in the springiness of his step, that made no real sense, under the circumstances. He was soon back at the house, where he had a quick nap but was soon back up again fidgeting around with some lumber outside and planning how he was going to put together at least a makeshift door for the front room.

But while he worked, the odd feeling came back, the feeling that there was something subtly different.

Late in the afternoon, he walked back out to the northwest boundary of his property again, following the stone fence along, trying to clear his mind, to get a grip on what was bothering him now. Not that he didn't have a right to feel edgy, considering what he had been through, which he was still trying not to dwell on. Still, something, something different. A feeling that there was something he ought to notice.

And a feeling that he didn't really want to notice it, was afraid to notice it.

He walked back down to the house, across the fields, his pace increasing as he went. Candy ran along beside him, looking surprised, he thought, at how fast they were getting back to the house.

It happened just after sunset.

He had been napping on the sofa, his blanket wrapped around him to ward off the coming chill of evening that seeped in at the ruined door, where he had only managed to prop up some plywood for the time being. And he had been dreaming some peculiar dreams, indistinct images of panic and confusion out of which he could draw no clear impression as he woke and tried to remember. His stomach seemed to grumble mightily as he came awake, and he wondered if he had eaten any supper. He couldn't remember. He got up and went into the kitchen and, for some impulsive reason he didn't care to examine, looked out the window, toward the horizon, where the sun had left a lingering flower of crimson.

Something—different.

Something wrong.

Even as things began to happen, he was figuring it out.

The horizon. Something about—

The grumble beneath him now wasn't his stomach, and probably hadn't been his stomach the first time, when waking up he thought it was. The ground was rumbling, and in a flash of terrible understanding, he knew, he knew what was going to happen.

He knew why, in spite of his ordeal and his fatigue, he had walked with a new-found spring in his step, earlier in the day, coming back to the house. Back down to the house. Because it was literally that. The ground, to a small and barely noticeable degree, had had a new slant downward. He knew too, now, what the most recent impression was. Out there at the limit of his vision, where the sun had set, the horizon—the horizon was wrong.

It was too high, because he was too low.

And even as the ground began now to churn and shift and sink, and as everything began to tilt and fall as if in a maelstrom with the collapsing house at the center, even as this happened he understood, and hearing the piteous yelping of the dog, wondered if maybe she understood too. In the last moments Haskell Wells possessed in which to ponder anything at all, he thought again: baby bird, baby bird, mouth open and hungry. Not birdlike at all, but you had to think of it that way. Baby bird, his mind prattled.

But he had invaded the nest, had killed baby bird.

This, now, with her own mouth open nearly from horizon to horizon, was mama bird.

Crayons

Crazy Sally leans across the table and runs a palsied hand through my hair. "You heard what Loach said. You'd better stay inside the lines."

I push her hand away and go on coloring with the big blue crayon. How am I supposed to draw anything right, with Crazy Sally shaking the table? The crayons are rolling around all over, and some of them spill off onto the floor and Chuckles picks one up, the big yellow one, and all the time he's laughing that *huh-HYUK huh-HYUK huh-HYUK* cretinous laugh of his. I grab the crayon back from him. How am I supposed to draw anything, with these people around? I switch to the yellow crayon and go on scribbling, and not all inside the lines either, I don't care what Loach says.

Anyway, it isn't Loach today, it's Miss Winkle. *She* doesn't care whether I stay inside the lines or not.

"Do you?" I ask her.

She fusses with the collar on her nice crisp starched uniform and blinks her eyes at me the way she always does. "Do I what, Claude?" she asks.

There I go again, I thought I asked her the whole thing out loud. I guess I just thought part of it. "Nothing," I tell her, and she just smiles and guides Chuckles to a chair by the wall, and it's *Huh-HYUK huh-HYUK huh-HYUK* all the way over there. What a moron.

"Whatcha drawing?"

"Yeah, whatcha drawing, Claude?"

It's Rose and Dirty Luke this time. Dirty Luke runs a hand up Rose's leg, under her gown, but Miss Winkle comes back over and slaps his hand away, and he nurses the hand and looks at her like she's knocked him down or something.

"I said, whatcha drawing?" Rose asks again. I don't think she even noticed that Dirty Luke ran a hand up her leg a minute ago. He's standing by the window now, feeling himself.

"It's a face," I tell her.

She looks at the paper, scrunches her nose up all disapproving-like. "Not much of a face," she says. "I mean, one eye is yellow and the other is blue, and you've colored all outside the lines. I'm glad *my* face doesn't look like that." She wanders off, muttering.

Well, Rose, I'd like to tell you, your own face has seen better days. But she can't help that, I guess. Damn. There they go again, ragging me about coloring outside the lines.

"Hey Claude, don't you ever draw nothing but faces?" It's Dirty Luke, back from the window. He still has one hand down the front of his pants.

"No," I tell him. "I like drawing faces."

"Who's it supposed to be?"

"Nobody in particular," I tell him.

"Hey, why don't you draw *him!*" Dirty Luke says, pulling that guy they call Boogers up to the table and putting an arm around him. He should have let Boogers walk on by. "Why don't you draw *him!*" Dirty Luke says again. Wasn't once enough?

I take a minute to think about it. "Because I don't have a crayon the right color for that stuff hanging out of his nose."

"Huh-HYUK huh-HYUK huh-HYUK! Stuff hanging out of his nose!" Chuckles exclaims from nearby, and wanders away somewhere, still laughing.

Dirty Luke gives Boogers an appraising look and sends him on his way. Boogers shuffles off to one side, runs a hand across his nose, pulls it away making a bridge of snot, and licks his fingers. Dirty Luke watches him expressionlessly for a moment and then turns back to me. "Then why don't you draw Loach?"

I pause and look up just long enough to see Crazy Sally coming up behind Luke. "Draw Loach!" she says, and repeats it sing-song. "Draw Loach, draw Loach."

"Yeah," I tell them, "maybe I will."

"Better stay inside the lines," Sally says, and both of them walk away. Dirty Luke has one hand on her butt and the other in his pants. Miss Winkle follows them, but I don't bother to watch what happens. I'm busy.

"Got a cigarette? Got a cigarette?"

I don't have to look up from my work to know that it's Hurl. That's what they call him, because of that yellow drool he's always got crusted around the corners of his mouth. I think some puke comes up in his mouth from time to time. Certainly doesn't do much for his breath.

"Got a cigarette?"

"I heard you the first time," I tell him. "And the second time." I hand the poor bastard a cigarette from my pack, even though I'm almost out of them.

Hurl pops the cigarette into his mouth, where it jitters up and down, jerky motion like one of those old silent movies. Hurl nudges me. "Got a light?"

God, you could tell him a million times and he'd never remember. "You know they don't let me have matches, any more than they let you. Go ask Miss Winkle."

But no, it's Loach today, fat ugly Loach. Here he comes now. His face is so red and puffy-looking you'd think he'd keel over one of these days. Just tip right on over on his porky ugly face. I think he'd start rotting before he hit the floor. Hurl goes up to him. "Got a light?"

Loach looks him over, the way you'd look at an animal in a pen. "Didn't your mother ever tell you them things is bad for your health?"

Hurl's mouth spreads into a big grin, and a river of thick chunky stuff runs down the front of his shirt. "My mother's dead."

"Yeah, I know," Loach says, "and I wonder just how *that* came about."

"Don't wanna talk about it," Hurl says. "Just gimme a light."

Loach digs into his uniform pocket and pulls out a lighter. "What do you say?"

Hurl blinks at him. "Uh—please."

Loach cups a hand over one ear. "What was that? I can't hear you."

"Please, Loach."

"Okay." Loach flicks the lighter and a little flame springs up. He holds the flame close to Hurl's cigarette tip but not quite close enough to light it. Hurl is puffing away at the unlit cigarette, trying to maneuver it into the flame. Every time he moves, Loach shifts the lighter away. Clearly frustrated, Hurl puffs harder and steadies the cigarette with both hands and tries to guide it into the flame, but Loach evades him. God, I hate watching this. Hurl couldn't help what he did, to get him thrown into this place. Poor son of a bitch is crazy, that's all. Finally, he's just about to steer the tip of the cigarette into the flame, when Loach snaps the cover down on the lighter. He grins his typical fat ugly beefy-faced grin.

"Oops. Too bad. All out of lighter fluid."

Hurl looks crushed, the cigarette now hanging loose in his mouth. "Aw, Loach, c'mon, it ain't out of fluid."

"Sorry," Loach says, and pushes him away. Loach comes over to where I'm sitting, where I'm always sitting. I have crayons scattered all over the tabletop, and I'm scribbling away. I try to ignore Loach, but he bumps the table with his leg, making me zig a long red unsightly thick line across the page.

"Sorry," he says again, sneering. "Didn't mean to mess up your masterpiece, Claude. Don't tell me you're drawing another face."

"Okay," I reply. "I won't tell you."

"He is, he is, he is," Crazy Sally is chanting, drawing up a chair beside me. "He *is* drawing another face. And just look at that!" She points at the thick red line, the one that Loach made me do. "I *told* him you said to stay inside the lines."

Loach gives out a nasty laugh. "I'm glad to see my words of wisdom have some effect on you idiots even when I'm not on the ward."

Chuckles comes up now, chewing on a candy bar. "Dirty Luke and her told him he oughta draw *you*, Loach, huh-HYUK huh-HYUK."

Loach seems to be thinking this over. "Yeah, okay. Why don't you draw me, Claude? What do you say? It'll give me something to show my nieces and nephews. Give 'em a laugh."

I tear the ruined page off the tablet to uncover a fresh sheet of paper. I take up one of these big clutzy crayons in my hand, feeling discouraged already. These things are an inch through the middle, and even the points are so thick that it's almost impossible to draw anything with them. Even regular little crayons would be an improvement. I look up at Loach. "Couldn't I have some colored pencils?"

Loach's eyes grow as large as they ever get, which isn't very. "Give you colored pencils? You know you ain't allowed to have anything sharp."

"Hey," I say to him, "this isn't Hurl you're talking to here, this time."

"Don't matter," he says. "You know the rules."

He's right, of course; I do know the rules, and one of them is that none of the inmates are allowed to handle sharp objects. Not even pencils. Whatever I do, I'm going to have to do with these bit clumsy crayons.

"All right," I tell Loach, "I'll try to draw you."

I start with a plump oval for the shape of the face and add two close-set little circles for the outline of the eyes.

"Hey," Loach protests, "my face ain't that fat, and my eyes ain't that little. Them look like pig eyes."

"I'm just getting started," I tell him. Off across the room, Chuckles is bellowing, "Pig eyes huh-HYUK huh-HYUK, pig eyes huh-HYUK huh-HYUK, pig eyes huh-HYUK huh-HYUK," until Loach silences him with an angry look. I notice out of the corner of my eye that Boogers and Rose are standing nearby. Rose is solemnly watching her companion pick his nose.

"Well," Loach says, turning back to glare at me, "you'd better do this right. Make my eyes the right color, and stay inside the lines."

I take a close look at his eyes, then survey the huge crayons scattered across the table. "The only blue I have is too dark," I tell him. "Your eyes are light blue." Very light, I could add, for a pig.

"You're not wheedling any pencils out of me," Loach says, "so forget it. Work with what you've got."

"I'll work on it," I reply. "I'll have it for you to look at tomorrow."

"I don't have a shift tomorrow," he says. "I won't be back on the ward till day after tomorrow."

"Whatever," I reply, waving him away. He looks at me for a minute as if he's going to say something else, then shrugs and walks away, and I see him off in the distance giving Rose and Boogers and Dirty Luke a bad time.

                              *   *   *

"Let me see how it's coming along," Miss Winkle says, looking over my shoulder. "Sally says you're working on a picture of Mr. Loach."

I glance back at her and shrug. "Well, yeah, but I've started over a bunch of times. What do you think?"

She squints down at my drawing, or at what I've got done of my drawing. I can tell she doesn't much like it, and is trying to think of something nice to say about it. Hurl and Dirty Luke show up and save her the trouble. Hurl points at the paper and kind of snorts, sending a spew of drool out in the air. "Face looks like a pig," he says.

"It *is* a pig," Dirty Luke says. "It's Loach."

"Now boys," Miss Winkle protests, "that's not very nice."

"That Loach wouldn't give me a light," Hurl says.

"Eyes are too dark," Dirty Luke says, tapping the paper with a grimy forefinger.

"I told him I didn't have the right shade of blue," I say, more or less directing my remark to Miss Winkle.

"Well," she says, "don't worry about it. I think it's good. He'll like it okay."

But he doesn't.

Standing over the table, glaring down at me with that ruddy smoldering kind of expression of his, he grabs the paper up and gawks at it. This is the same picture Miss Winkle looked at yesterday. I think it was yesterday.

"Christ, Claude, I was going to show this to my nieces and nephews to give 'em a good laugh," Loach says, "but it ain't even good for a laugh. I wouldn't wipe my ass with this."

I look up at him. "What's wrong with it? Miss Winkle liked it." Behind Loach I can see a little crowd gathering, as Boogers and Rose and Dirty Luke and Hurl and Chuckles and Crazy Sally wander over from various directions. Miss Winkle is down at the other end of the room, too; it isn't her shift, but sometimes they have her come in to help with medications.

Loach, apparently unconcerned that his antics are drawing a crowd, waves the picture in my face. I stand up and confront him. He rattles the paper in the air. "You did this to make me look bad," he splutters, more ruddy-faced than ever, his ugly little eyes flashing. "What do you have to say for yourself? Answer me. I said, you did this just to make me look bad."

"Sorry you don't like it," I reply. Off behind Loach, Chuckles starts up in a shrill voice: "Look bad, huh-HYUK, look bad huh-HYUK."

Loach tosses the picture on the table, where several of those big awkward crayons loll to one side and another. "Fix it. Get the eyes right this time." He sits down at the table and stares at me.

Get the eyes right this time. Well, somehow that's all it takes, hearing him say that. I grab one thick crayon in one hand and one in the other, and go to work.

It's all over in a few seconds. These big crayons don't have a very sharp point, and it's not easy, doing what needs to be done. Loach struggles a little, but I'm pretty strong, and I get it done. His face is *really* red now, in any case. Chuckles is beside himself—"huh-HYUK huh-HYUK huh-HYUK huh-HYUK huh-HYUK"—and Boogers gets so excited he snots himself all down the front. Hurl takes one look and blows chunks into the air like a geyser, and Crazy Sally and Rose and Dirty Luke just stand there looking amazed. Now Miss Winkle comes running over, shrieking and crying and flailing her arms. I really don't know what all the excitement is about. With the butt-ends of those crayons just showing, one in each socket, I think it looks pretty good, even though it makes one eye green and the other one brown. It was tough, pushing them all the way in, but like I said, it looks pretty good—and this time I did stay inside the lines.

The Weeping Woman of White Crow

Luana-Maria Trujillo had always vaguely suspected that one day she would meet La Llorona. It was sheer craziness, of course, to think it. The Weeping Woman simply did not exist; she was a folk figure who had a way of creeping into hearthside tales told from Phoenix to Albuquerque, from the adobe-visaged westside neighborhoods of Santa Fe to the bleak desert plains here in West Texas—but the legendary Weeping Woman was only that: a timeless motif for storytellers. In the clear, rational light of the mind, Luana-Maria knew this, that in reality there could be no such phantasmal figure, no gossamer wraith haunting the dry arroyos and canals of the American Southwest, no lithe ghost-woman wailing plaintively in the night for her lost children. But at the same time, in the shadow-places of her heart, Luana-Maria somehow knew, paradoxically but equally well, that she was going to meet La Llorona—somehow, sometime. It was a feeling, an insane, logic-denying sensation, but a feeling of such long standing that she could scarcely remember a time when she had been without it.

For now, though, there were more practical considerations. Jack would be home from the oilfields by eight; it was after seven now, and here she was, still walking around downtown. White Crow at this time of day seemed like the final stage-set of a play on which the curtain was run down for the night. Stores closed early here in this little border town, their fronts blinking in meaningless dim neon sputters to each other across Main Street like sleepy passengers nodding noncommitally across the aisle of a bus. These glass-eyed passengers were going nowhere, though. Not much happened in White Crow even in daylight, and by this time of evening, with the late October sky turning a somber turquoise and the light wind from the desert taking on an edge of sage-scented coolness, she was very nearly the only person in sight on Main Street.

Buttoning her jacket, she walked down Camino Lejo, a side street. She was angling toward home; it was only half a mile or so, their little house on the edge of town, and she would still be there ahead of Jack, getting dinner ready. Jack would cup his gruff laborer's hands around his coffee mug, and they would have their meal, comfortable with each other out of long habit but finding little to talk about, little to share. He would be weary to the bone, and would mumble some things about how a pump broke or the pickup wouldn't start or someone ("Could've been me") got hurt on the rig. And she would listen quietly, and maybe mention something about her own day, uneventful as it must sound to him, and they would watch television and go to bed. And she would wonder whether she could ever tell him, tell hard-working, unimaginative Jack, about things like—

Like the present moment.

She had stopped in the middle of the little bridge where Camino Lejo emerged from its surroundment of low buildings into more open space and passed over the irrigation canal, whose sloping concrete contours stretched into the gathering gloom, left and right, as if the street had sprouted long gray wings. There was no water in the ditch now, just a patina of wind-blown sand and an occasional stirring of tumbleweed.

And the sound.

She held her breath, listening. From off somewhere on the left, there it was again—a low, keening sort of sound, like someone crying. Or was it the moaning of the wind, whose movements could some-times invade the spaces between the buildings behind her, and sound like wailing?

But now there were other sounds, not the wind, but familiar sounds that the wind carried. Ahead and to the left, perhaps a quarter of a mile off, stood the port-of-entry plaza, with the little twin town of Cuervo Blanco on the other side, in Mexico, offering a vague electric glow to the gathering night. Faint music floated across: guitars, accor-dions, soft Spanish voices. This wasn't a bustling border place like Ciudad Acuña far to the east or Ciudad Juárez far to the northwest— just a sleepy little town across the Rio Grande from White Crow, just a wan interlude of light before the southward desert became the moun-tains of the Sierra Mulato, purple sunset waves in an ocean of sand and rock. In the foreground of this panorama, the mariachi melodies from Cuervo Blanco scattered now on the wind.

And left only that chilling howl that rose up close behind her.

She wheeled, gasping. To her right a low scuttling movement raked the night with whining. A dark face turned toward her, but it was only a ragged child pedaling a rusty little bicycle, its unoiled metals leaving a sharp *scree-e-e* on the air as the child rounded a corner in the dark and was gone.

She let out a breath that she hadn't realized she had been holding in, and stood for a moment looking across toward Cuervo Blanco, looking into Mexico, where Papá lay under distant soil, and where Mamá still lived, not in Cuervo Blanco but in another dusty little village far, far south. Gentle, sad-faced Mamá. The Rio Grande was only a shallow stream here, but it marked the orbit of another world.

Luana-Maria thought of the Weeping Woman, and reflected that at times she felt a little like weeping, herself.

Lying in the dark, her eyes wide, with Jack snoring beside her, she thought about things. About their moving out here from Bernalillo, New Mexico, sixteen years before, so that Jack could find work; about their life together, its featureless sort of stability, its quiet sameness now that the kids were grown and living far away ("I know, Mom, I always mean to write").

And she thought about the legends—not only the stories of La Llorona, which were told here too, as they had been back in New Mexico, but the other, more local stories. Somehow she had the feeling that these tales ought to be connected, though no one ever came right out and said they were.

Both towns—White Crow on the Texas side, Cuervo Blanco on the Mexico side—had derived their names, according to local history, from a fabulous bird that had been seen since early times: an ornithological improbability, a large pure-white crow. In recent times it seemed that no one you could find had actually seen the bird, though everyone seemed to have heard of someone's having seen it, a mote of elusive white light winging its way across a violet desert sky. Among families that had always lived here, there was generally some shadowy, long-departed relative, a great-grandmother perhaps, who had seen the white crow. Even today a sighting was occasionally mentioned, though most often by overly imaginative or temperamental people whose objectivity was questionable: mystics or artists or drunks. What the white crow meant, no one could say for sure. Legend had it that the Conquistadores had seen the bird much farther south, centuries before, and had taken it for a holy sign, at which the Indians must have smiled quietly, investing the bird with their own timeless understandings. In any case, the white crow at one time had been common knowledge to every schoolchild hereabouts, though nowadays such adherence to local folklore was falling away.

La Llorona stories existed here also, but these too seemed to be fading as time went on. Luana-Maria had once mentioned the Weeping Woman to a group of children at a birthday party and had elicited only blank stares.

People were forgetting. Perhaps she should forget too, perhaps she should turn her mind to more mundane things and let legends lie. But she knew she couldn't.

Jack had gotten an early phone call from the field office, an unusual event for a Saturday morning. He'd listened, mumbled something about coming out, and hung up. Now, over breakfast, he was explaining. Luana-Maria listened with her usual sense of semi-detachment; she knew the oilfields were dangerous places to work, and she didn't like to think about Jack's job too much. This morning it was something about some kind of mechanical problem that had arisen, and rather than let it wait, they wanted him to take a ride out there and help out with whatever needed doing. It wouldn't take long, Jack said, and: "Why don't you come along?"

She was taken by surprise. "Me?" He'd never suggested such a thing before, nor had she.

"Sure. It'll do you good to get out and get some air. You wouldn't have to come up to the rig or anything, you could just wait for me in the pickup, bring a magazine or something. I won't be but half an hour."

Soon they were headed north out of town, bumping along a dusty and only crudely paved road that quickly gave way to one not paved at all. If you drove far enough in this direction you would eventually come to Pecos, Texas, and be in civilization, as Jack sometimes put it; but this was a long way from Pecos, or from anywhere in particular. Out here, headed into the oilfields, what the traveler saw was miles and miles of open desert, seemingly limitless vistas of chaparral country populated only by sagebrush, mesquite, cactus, and rattlesnakes, with drilling rigs at intervals rearing their angular heads like giant grasshoppers. It was desolate, but Luana-Maria loved it—more, she suspected, than Jack did, though he seldom grew very expansive about his feelings. She found it hard to feel justified in faulting him for this, actually, because she realized that she herself was growing more and more introspective, becoming less and less inclined to feel that she could really share her most important thoughts—not, in her case, because she wanted to conceal them, but rather because she didn't really understand them herself.

Several miles north of the town limits, they passed a land feature that she felt oddly inclined to stare at as they went by, though she certainly had seen similar things enough times before. It was the opening of a large arroyo, a U-shaped dry gully perhaps eight feet wide and ten feet deep that went zigzagging its tortuous path away from the road out into the countryside, an erosive crack in the parched ground, a sandy-bottomed conduit that would be bone-dry until a sudden rainstorm somewhere up country sent a torrent of water down its lengths, sloshing up its sandy sides, only to subside again and leave the arroyo much as before, though possibly a little wider as the water further eroded the sides. Arroyos like this were seen all over the region, of course, and Luana-Maria found it difficult to think what it was about the sight of this one that so intrigued her.

"They call that one Arroyo Largo on all the topo maps," Jack was saying when they had driven past. "It's miles and miles long. The roustabouts out in the field tell some funny stories about it."

"Oh?"

"Yeah. You start walking in one of those things, the bigger ones, I mean, like this one, and you can walk for hours. Well, what some guy out on the rig was telling me was that his dad started walking one time in Arroyo Largo, started early in the day and walked and walked and walked, till after it was dark. He said—well, this is nuts, but like I said, it's just a story. He said he came out in Mexico, somewhere down below Cuervo Blanco."

"But," Luana-Maria said, "that's—I mean, there's the river."

"I know," Jack said, swerving to avoid a large rock in the road. "The Rio Grande. The arroyo couldn't cross it; I mean, you couldn't really walk through there and come out on the other side. There *is* another big arroyo on the other side, on the maps, but you can see they're not connected. The guy's dad sounded kind of crazy anyway. Especially when he kept saying—"

"Saying what?"

"Well, later on, even years later, he kept saying something like, 'And that's not all, but I won't say what else.' Like there was something too weird even to talk about."

Luana-Maria glanced behind, wishing she could still see the entrance to Arroyo Largo through the dust that swirled in the wake of the pickup. "What else? You said they tell a lot of strange stories."

"Oh, well," he said, "if you listened to some of that stuff too much you'd end up a little daffy. One old fellow I met out in the field said he walked into Arroyo Largo one night when he was younger, and guessed he got lost in there or something, twisting and turning, but couldn't remember much of anything about it later. Said he'd gone in about ten at night, and the next thing he knew it was dawn and he was walking back out. I figure he probably had a bottle with him, fell asleep in there somewhere. You can't ever tell, with some of these guys."

"No, I guess not," she said. She was very wrapped up in her own thoughts for the rest of the day, and slept fitfully that night and rose the next morning from a sense of bizarre dreams she couldn't quite recall.

Around the middle of November, Jack had to go to Dallas for a week. Luana-Maria kissed him goodbye in the driveway and watched him leave in a company car. Then she had the house, the pickup, her thoughts, had them all to herself.

Maybe too much so, because she found herself restless, immersed in vague but somehow unsettling thoughts as she puttered about the house or strolled through the streets.

What was bothering her?

She thought she knew, but kept pushing the thought out of her mind. Still, she thought she knew.

It was something she had to do, and by the third night alone she found that she couldn't distract herself any longer with books or housework or inane television shows.

And she found herself driving the pickup north into the desert, almost without having consciously thought about doing that at all. When she started out, the sun had just been setting in a riot of crimson in the west, and by the time she was pulling off the road and shutting the engine down, night had fallen and the air was getting chilly—that crisp, dry chill that only a desert night can bring.

Buttoning her jacket, she stepped into the yawning mouth of Arroyo Largo and began walking its sandy course. The dry bed of the arroyo was dotted with scruffy little creosote bushes and sagebrush, and she had to watch her step; it wouldn't do to twist an ankle out here, or step on a rattler. She strained her eyes to see ahead of her; there was a gibbous moon above, but it cast only a faint light into the depths of the wash, and she felt silly for not having brought a flashlight.

It was deep enough in here that she couldn't see over the arroyo's sides, which were jagged surfaces of coarse sand mingled with twisted weeds and mesquite and cedar roots, and although the main course of the wash was wide and fairly clear, she occasionally found herself starting into a dead end where only lifeless pits of shadow waited, and she would have to backtrack and redirect herself. When she was fifty yards or so in, she could no longer see the road: not so much because it was dark, but because the winding and twisting of the arroyo had already cut it off from view. She wished she had seen Arroyo Largo, the whole thing, on one of those maps Jack had talked about; she really had no idea where or how far it might lead. Why she was here at all, she couldn't really say, but now that she was, she could only walk on.

Because what would really seem foolish right now would be for her to turn around, walk back out to the road, and just get into the pickup and drive back to town. That would be the sanest thing she could do, but also the most unthinkable.

The arroyo wound on and on with a mind-numbing sort of sameness: pebbly dry stream-bed underfoot, jagged and crumbling walls of sand high on either side, sometimes one side utterly dark and the other feebly illumined by moonlight, depending on which way the arroyo zigged or zagged. After an hour or so—had it been longer? how far had she walked in here? three miles? four?—she was getting very tired, but she had to go on. She couldn't have said exactly why, when it appeared now that the oilfield stories were just stories—that the arroyo was only an uncommonly protracted dry wash that no doubt just tapered down and ended somewhere up ahead. But she had to see.

Stopping for a moment, she listened to night sounds: the wind up on the desert floor, whispering drily among the mesquites; soft insect scurryings; the faint, distant *hoo-hoo* of an owl.

And something else. Something from some region ahead of her, not up on the level ground but *in the arroyo:* a faint, unplaceable sound.

Something that was gradually resolving itself into a kind of moaning, low and formless, and frightful.

She had always wondered whether the hair on the back of one's neck could really stand up. It could, and was doing it now.

Her feet seemed rooted like inert plants in the sand, but—proceeding only because she was afraid to turn around and run, imagining, if she did so, what might come upon her from behind, overtaking her—she forced herself to move forward, slowly, listening. A stronger wind had sprung up now, whistling through the length of the arroyo and carrying, as it seemed to her troubled senses, a suggestion of mariachi music, so that she couldn't be sure about the other sound. But then there it was again, ahead somewhere in the shadows, a melancholy keening that sent cold little quills of fear feathering their way up her spine. As she advanced toward the sound, she found the arroyo seemingly to be taking a turn to the right; but when she made the turn she discovered that she was standing within one of those dead-end declivities in the arroyo wall, a sable space where wells of shadow gathered.

And out of that depth of darkness, something was moving toward her.

It came floating across the sand like something sustained, weightless, on the wan moonlight, something pale and ghostly, yet undeniably present and real. It appeared to be a woman, tall and lithe, a willowy figure arrayed in white, though there was a quality about it that refused to register clearly on the eye, on the mind. Luana-Maria, frantic now to get away, stumbled and fell back onto the hard sand, and when she looked up, the spectral figure in white was nearly upon her, the thin white-robed arms held out before her, the mouth open in a dismal and ululant nightmare of wailing. Luana-Maria scuttered backwards on the sand and was up and running, and the crying followed her. *Crying,* some corner of her mind whispered, *crying for her lost children.*

Luana-Maria, losing a shoe in the sand, darted through the half-dark, half-moonlit corridors of the arroyo, but realized in an instant that she was disoriented, lost, trapped. The twistings and meanderings of the arroyo were so labyrinthine that she had no notion which way to run, which way it was to the road, the pickup. She took what appeared to be a promising turn, but ended up in another sandy cul-de-sac, a jagged blind in the arroyo wall, a space from which she saw, wheeling around, that there was no escape now, for the wide-eyed figure in white, its face alive with shrieking, had entered behind her.

Sobbing now, Luana-Maria dropped to her knees on the crusty bed of the wash and simply looked up at La Llorona, not knowing what else to do.

For a moment, an interminable moment frozen in time, the gossamer figure in white just stood above her, wailing, extending her arms. Even through tears Luana-Maria could see that the pale moonlight worked its desert magic upon the creature most strangely, because somehow the extended arms did not seem to terminate exactly in hands, and the face had contours that were impossible to understand. Then, quite suddenly, the creature began to revolve in a slow and graceful sort of pirouette in the moonlight, trailing her white robes—or were they robes?—behind her as she turned.

And as she came slowly back around, everything changed.

The quality of the wailing seemed to soften into a sort of cooing, and when the face reappeared, the wan light made it look as if it were not a woman's face at all, but rather something with unaccountable angular projections and sharp shadows. Luana-Maria got up off her knees and stood before the creature, because in a moment of stunning epiphany she understood everything, and wondered why she had been afraid. She knew now what the story of the lost children really meant, and she entered the transition, the absorption, with joy. The moon-glossed beak now projected from between her own timeless eyes, and she felt her other shoe come off.

*   *   *

The white crow moved on powerful wings through the night, high above the desert. She flew in wide happy circles in the light of the moon, passing back and forth over the dark river—a very real river, a very imaginary boundary—and winged her way south into the true vastness of the desert. She moved with gladness, for it was seldom that she recovered, into herself, even briefly, any of her lost children: these poor, wandering creatures who walked through strange mundane lives in strange earthbound bodies and did not remember who and what they really were.

Spider Willie

Randall Weaver was not a well man.

The moaning of a cold Vermont wind seemed to agree all too readily. *Not well, not well,* it murmured around the eaves, flinging quick dry whispers of snow against the clapboards. *Not well-l-l-l.*

Faltering down the stairs on his cane, Randall realized that he really couldn't even say what was wrong. It was what some people might call a general malaise, perhaps. Not unusual, at his age, but disquieting nonetheless.

At the bottom of the stairs he stood at a loss. Why had he come down?

A picture of Doc Morgan took form before his eyes. *Only thing wrong with you, Randall,* the doctor was saying, *is you're getting older.* It was true, of course; he couldn't very well expect to feel as spry now as he had nineteen years ago when he'd retired. Still, he resented the subtle encroachments of time upon him. He simply wanted to feel the way he always had. Was that asking so much?

The doctor's face faded with Randall's finally remembering why he had come downstairs: to have his dinner. He hung his cane on the newel post; he only needed it, so far, for getting up and down the stairs. And that, at least, was encouraging, he mused, hobbling off to the kitchen.

Putting together a ham and cheese sandwich, he looked out the window at the bleak gray-white scene beyond the panes. By now the snow was tapering to great buoyant flakes that fluttered down like moths for a time and gradually ceased. Off in the distance, other houses stood like dim angular ghosts blanketed all around in white, their lawns forgotten and unimaginable beneath the cold dead hand of winter. There must be two feet of snow on the ground, maybe two and a half, Randall thought.

He sat chewing his sandwich, washing it down with coffee, and re-flecting that there was nothing wrong with his appetite at any rate. Cleaning up the dishes, he slipped his glasses on and looked out the window again and pondered the nature of a slightly elevated clump of snow some distance out from the house. What was that? Had he left the wheelbarrow or a lawn chair or some other item out in the snow? He didn't think so. One thing was for sure, he wasn't going out there to find out. The metallic clanking of the radiators sounded cosy and warm, and he wasn't going anyplace.

Except back upstairs.

On his way back through the living room he paused at the book-case and puzzled over the titles, finally picking out a volume of Haw-thorne. Taking his cane off the post, he made his way up the stairs, stopping in the middle to catch his breath. And there it was again, that vague sensation of discomfort, unease.

What was it? *Where* was it? He took a deep breath, held it in, let it out. His lungs, his chest felt okay. His heart wasn't doing anything out of the ordinary, so far as he could tell. His stomach didn't hurt. Still, there was something wrong.

Upstairs in the chair by the bedroom window, he tried to read, but even the stark imagery of "Ethan Brand" wasn't holding his attention. He found himself first staring absently out the window, then leaning closer to gaze down at the spot in the snow that he had looked at be-fore, down in the kitchen. From this new angle it wasn't just a white-on-white mound elevated slightly above the general level, but some-thing rather different.

There was a suggestion of something darker, something more solid than the crystalline sameness of the snow. It was as if the snow had *almost* buried something, leaving a vague dark portion peeking through.

He tried to remember what was there, what should have been there. The spot itself was perhaps fifteen feet out from the side of the house; beyond it, the back fence stretched along the edge of the prop-erty, its wooden slats standing stoically frozen in snow and ice. Some-thing—the spot in the snow corresponded to something, but he couldn't think what it was. Then too the daylight, what little there had been, was waning fast, and soon the snow was gray with impending night. He pulled down the shade and went back to "Ethan Brand," and woke up when the book fell from his hand.

Later in the night he lay in bed with his eyes wide open in the dark, trying to remember a scrap of dream that floated just at the edge of his grasp, then scuttered away beyond recall. What had it been? He dimly remembered something like a chant or a rhyme, some unclear phantom impression that danced away, tantalizing, unreachable.

Over breakfast he looked out across the brightening snow and found the mysterious mound uncommunicative. Surprisingly, the morning clouds had broken, and the sun had come out to cast a cold, clear brilliance over limitless vistas of snow and winter-blasted trees, dappling the landscape with sharp black shadows. The sun on the snow was so bright that he had to avert his eyes.

Maybe we've finally broken the back of winter, his mom would have said, countless years ago. By now Randall had seen even more Vermont winters than his mother ever lived to see, though, and he knew that a good many raw and blustery weeks still lay ahead.

Nevertheless, it was cheering to see the sun, even if it was only going to crawl through a short arc from southeast to southwest and set again. Randall actually thought he felt a little better this morning, at least until he was sitting on the sofa in the parlor, trying again to remember the dream. The vague discomfort seemed to slip back into his frame then, and he wondered if it was connected in any way with his elusive nocturnal vision. But how could it be? Dreams never meant anything, and anyway he couldn't remember this one.

Yet something did come back to him now, suddenly: his mother's and father's faces, in the dream, smiling, teasing. Randall himself was a child again, and his dad and mom stood over him after tucking him into bed and—

—and repeated the old childhood rhyme to him.

Good heavens, he hadn't thought about that for years, long incalculable years.

Dad and Mom would say the thing, grinning in good-natured fun, poking him lightly in the ribs to emphasize the rhythm of the words.

How did it go? Some of the words swam back to him now across murky currents of time.

Spider Willie, Spider Willie . . .

Ta ta-*da* ta-*da*. Something, something, something—he couldn't quite remember the rest of it.

Maybe it was just as well.

He puttered around the house for a while, had his lunch, then curled up on the sofa for an afternoon nap.

When he got up, he took his cane and started up the stairs, but something big and heavy followed him up, scratching up along the outside of the house, keeping pace with him. When Randall stopped part of the way up and turned and wheezed down the stairs again, the thing beyond the wall turned too and scrabbled back down alongside him. And when Randall got to the bottom of the stairs and stood panting beside the window there, something unthinkable, something nightmarish beyond words came crashing through the window to fasten itself upon him.

He sprang off the sofa and was standing on shaky legs, mopping his brow, before he was fully awake.

God, what brought *that* on?

He hadn't had a dream that terrifying in years. Maybe not in his whole life.

It was late afternoon by now, but upon going to the kitchen and looking out the window, he could still see the odd mound out in the yard, a raised place in the snow. What *was* it about that spot? It didn't look like anything from here.

From the bedroom window it might be different now.

He took his cane and climbed the stairs, grumbling and muttering. What sense did it make, letting his peace of mind be unsettled by—by what? By nothing at all. His head ached a little, and it seemed to him now that that could be the source of the vague unease he had felt: his head, his sinuses maybe.

Looking down from the bedroom window, he did see something a little different this time.

The sun had been out all day, and even though the temperature probably hadn't gone much above thirty-five degrees, the snow had started melting. He could see the back fence, beyond the mound, with the top crust of snow drawn a little away from the wooden slats like gums receding from a row of teeth. But it was the mound itself that drew his attention.

The slight lowering of the snow had left the top of the mound looking a little altered. Where there had been only a small dark spot before, now a number of long, stringy shadow-shapes seemed to radiate from a common point. Whatever it was, it was still mostly covered in snow, with only a dim outline revealed.

But so what? Why did he keep dwelling on it?

Because he found himself entertaining the impression that the obscure shape in the snow was somehow connected to the equally obscure discomfort that he had been feeling.

"Horsefeathers and nonsense," he mumbled, a little startled at the sound of his own voice. "Randall Weaver, you're a batty old fool." He'd been living alone in this house far too long. Why hadn't he moved to a retirement community in Florida?

On his way back down the stairs he realized that he remembered a little more of the old childhood rhyme now. He pushed the thought away, but it bobbed stubbornly to the surface.

Spider Willie, Spider Willie,
Creeping in the night. . . .

He must be losing his mind, thinking about such things. Imagine worrying about a silly piece of juvenile lore that he hadn't thought about since he was four or five years old. He heated up a frozen dinner in the microwave and made some coffee. It was too dark now to see much out the kitchen window, and he drew the shade down with a certain sense of relief. His head hurt a little. Must be sinus congestion. He took some pills and went upstairs to bed.

When he awoke sometime in the middle of the night and got up to go to the bathroom, something was moving around outside in the yard, below the window, something that scuttered in the snow.

He drew the shade up and squinted out into the night.

A blurred shape was indeed moving across the top of the snow. In the pallid light from the nearest streetlamp, which was a pretty long distance away, the thing cast jagged and spasmodic shadows as it tumbled across the yard and fetched up against a corner in the fence. It hung there, gray and twitching, but even in this uncertain light Randall could see now that it was a scrap of newspaper driven across the snow by the wind, which came in from the north as there was no fence on that side to shelter the yard.

The wind had blown away a little more of the snow from around the mounded spot, too, and now what had looked like short segments of largely unexposed thin ropy shapes were more exposed, and looked like footlong tongues. One of them had been uncovered to the end, so that it lay atop the snow crust, tethered only on the still-covered center. The others were only slightly more exposed than before, like long fingers visible only around the middle joint.

Who was he kidding? These dark, narrow appendages didn't look all that much like tongues or fingers.

They looked like the legs of a spider. An uncannily large spider.

"Preposterous," he snorted, glaring defiantly at the mound below. The wind came up again, moaning about the eaves and scattering snow, obscuring his view of the yard. He pulled down the shade. When he was back in bed he stared at the darkness and realized that the pills hadn't helped; his head still ached, even more than before.

But he must have slept in spite of this, for he opened his eyes to a midmorning brilliance of light projected upon the drawn shade. It was going to be another sunny day.

He had only coffee for breakfast, and avoided looking at the snowy scene beyond the windowpanes. After a while, though, he couldn't resist, and glanced at the mound. The wind had banked snow up in a different way now, partly obscuring what had before been uncovered. From this angle it didn't look like anything at all.

His head still ached dully, and he took some more pills and settled himself on the sofa in the parlor and flipped through a magazine.

And realized that now he remembered the whole thing.

The rhyme, from when he was little.

What had brought it back? He must have recalled it last night in his sleep, in his dreams. Its singsong idiocy rang in his head now, unwelcome.

Spider Willie, Spider Willie,
Creeping in the night,
Spider Willie, Spider Willie,
Give you a bite.
Creep into the bedroom,
Creep up on the bed,
Creep up on the pillowcase
And bite you in the head.

And they would tickle him in the ribs and all three would laugh. It was great fun, at the time, but he wondered if he hadn't been a little afraid; he couldn't remember. He supposed his folks had meant well, but across the prism of the intervening years the rhyme seemed like a pretty bizarre thing to have repeated to a child.

Putting a hand to his aching brow, he thought about the words, the loathsome imagery. Spiders. Ugh—he had always found the damned things appalling, with their bloated venom sacs and their nasty fiddling little legs.

He tried to put these notions out of his mind. Odd, after all these multitudinous years, to be thinking about such things, recalling them in such tedious detail. It was all nonsense, of course, and he spent the morning straightening up the parlor and sorting through accumulations of magazines and catalogs and bagging up a considerable quantity of trash, which he set out on the porch. Later he'd have to shovel the snow off the walk so that he could take the trashbags all the way out to the street. For now, he had some lunch and went upstairs for a nap.

And awoke from dreams that he somehow felt he was fortunate not to be able to remember. The ache in his head was growing worse, and neither aspirin nor sinus pills seemed to help. Gazing out the bedroom window to try to take his mind off his discomfort, he found himself looking at the oddly mounded configuration in the snow again. The wind had left it looking somewhat changed, but viewed from above it still had the aspect of a central mass radiating a sprawling bunch of legs. He even thought he could count eight of them, though the whole thing was still part under, part out of the snow, and confusing to the eye. Besides, his temples ached, and it was hard to think.

He had only a bowl of soup for supper, as he really wasn't very hungry. He took more pills for his headache, hoping against hope that they would ease the pain, and he went upstairs to bed.

And woke around three in the morning with a dreadful insight.

He lay in the pitiless dark, trying to deny the grim realization that had invaded his consciousness. It couldn't be true, couldn't be true. He would just go back to sleep, forget it, immerse himself in dream. He was immensely tired, so tired that sleep should have overtaken him readily. But every time his eyelids grew heavy, the terrible new knowledge would rush back to jolt him rudely awake again. He knew now. He knew.

There was something growing in his skull.

In his brain.

And he knew, of course, what it was.

The old chant sounded in his mind, unbidden.

> *Spider Willie, Spider Willie,*
> *Creeping in the night. . . .*

Quietly, subtly it had come from whatever regions might spawn such things. It had come looking for him.

> *Spider Willie, Spider Willie,*
> *Give you a bite.*

He could see it in his mind's eye, working its way to him through the distance, the darkness.

> *Creep into the bedroom,*
> *Creep up on the bed. . . .*

He had known it in childhood, and he knew it now—one was safe nowhere.

> *Creep up on the pillowcase*
> *And bite you in the head.*

This last part was metaphorical, of course. If only the menace had been just a spider bite. But how? How had it got into his brain to lay its foul eggs?

The thought, in the middle of the night in the dark, was one that paralyzed him with terror. He was afraid to move his head on the pillow, afraid—that he would *feel* the thing inside him.

But he did push himself up off the bed, wincing in anticipation of new pain. He switched on the lamp, giddy from the throbbing in his head, and ran the shade up and tried to look out at the snow. The windowpanes showed him only the reflection of his own anxious face, however, and he was obliged to shut the light off again in order to see out. When he did, the object below was clearer in outline than ever before, with most of its legs freed from the snow. He knew that it was going to become even clearer, even more definite in form. And he knew something else now too, with hideous certainty.

He knew that somehow, in some insane and unthinkable way, the emerging sight of the thing in the snow was helping to grow the spider in his brain.

The mother (*creep into the bedroom, creep up on the bed*) must have crawled into his ear. Yes, that was how it must have been. Randall had seen a picture once of the inner ear, with its passages meandering deep, deep inside the head; wasn't there a way, down in there, for something to get into your brain? He was sure there was.

But once the egg hatched and the spider started to grow, Randall had been *feeding* it—feeding it with his thoughts, nourishing it with the vision of the emerging spider in the snow. Thoughts always blossomed and grew in the brain, and with every new contemplation of the spider-shape below the window, the *real* spider had grown a little more and a little more, until now—

How big, how big was it now? Dear God, how big?

He cried out, clutching his skull, and fell across the bed. He must have swooned, because when he opened his eyes painfully to the light, it was late afternoon.

He stumbled into the bathroom and leaned over the basin and gazed bleary-eyed into the mirror. The ache in his head was monumental now, but even that wasn't as bad as his new knowledge, the knowledge of what lived embedded in his brain. Pondering his reflection in the glass, he tried to see if anything *looked* different yet, but he couldn't tell. If anyone saw him now, would they know? Could they tell?

He made a miserable attempt to eat a bowl of soup and drink a cup of coffee, but both soup and coffee ended up cold on the table, while Randall stared out the kitchen window at the snowy mound. Even from this angle now, and in the gathering dark, the object in the receding snow looked damnably like an obscenely large spider, and he had gazed at it for quite some time before he realized what he was doing—a dreadful access of new pain brought him to his senses too late. He was feeding it again!

Howling in agony, he hobbled to the staircase and took his cane and labored up the stairs. Leaning into the bathroom mirror again, he felt around his head with trembling fingers, finding what he was looking for before he was even consciously aware he was looking for it.

Just at the left temple, he felt a smooth bump, and around behind his left ear, another. Running his fingers around into his hair on the back of his head, he encountered another bump, then another and another. On around behind his right ear he found another, and at his right temple yet another. Finally he found the one he should have noticed first, roughly in the middle of his forehead. The bumps were barely perceptible, but his fingers found them, read them like Braille.

Eight of them.

Pushing out, the thing was pushing out with its abominable legs, all the way around.

Shrieking, whether in pain or horror he couldn't have said, he found himself back in the bedroom, looking out the window. It had started to snow again out there, but not fast enough to cover the shape that the wind had largely uncovered; most of the long wispy legs wriggled, shifted, flailed in the wind, and he could feel the real ones in his brain respond, pressing his temples, his forehead, his scalp.

But it wasn't just the legs now. He could feel the pressure of *eyes*, eyes behind his own eyes, pushing out. It was a sickening sensation, this bulging of the eyes under the insistence of the remorseless thing that obtruded upon them from behind. He put a hand over his eyes and could *feel* them bulging half out of their sockets. The pain in his skull swelled to a nearly unbearable level, and when he instinctively tried to close his eyes, he found that he could not do so. His eyelids would no longer cover them.

Wailing, he pressed his face into the window with nearly enough force to break the glass, and stared out at the waning day, whose last fugitive rays of light were perturbed with flickers of falling snow. Beneath the eddy of swirling flakes, the spider-shape was all uncovered by the wind now, the long tapered appendages lolling and flexing in all directions, the brown center lying squat and ugly in the snow. The legs flexed again, down there, and the ghastly thing in Randall's head flexed too, and he was certain that the harsh sinewy legs had torn free at last, coming all the way through, and he was sure that the horridly multifaceted eyes behind his own had protruded all the way out, dividing his vision. The splash of warm wetness on his cheeks could only be blood. He pitched forward onto the bed, clutching his head in both hands, praying for the pressure in his skull to subside.

But he knew that the thing down there in the snow had decided—that his thoughts had nourished the monstrous shape in his skull, nourished it and swelled it to lethal proportions. Churning its way through the gray matter of Randall's brain, Spider Willie was being reborn, pushing and wriggling his way out into the light. Randall thought he could see them now, at the periphery of his bleary vision—the spider's protruding legs, jittering and writhing.

Then, quite suddenly, he remembered something.

He released his throbbing head long enough to push himself up off the bed and stumble to the window. He knew now what the thing was, down there in the snow.

Still flailing its tonguelike legs in the cold wind, it sat atop the snow as if it had a right to be there.

And in a way it had, because Randall had left it out there in the yard before the snows of winter had come. The legs were not legs but leaves, and the darker center was not a fat brown spider-belly after all, but a brown ceramic pot. He had left the spider plant in its pot atop a little plastic stand, and the snow had covered stand, pot, and plant alike, later gradually receding to show, in stages, the long wilted leaves whose arachnid appearance gave the plant its name.

But spider plant or not, it had grown the frightful thing in Randall's head. Spider Willie had come home, true to the old rhyme, creeping in the night, for what could creep more inexorably than thought itself? Falling back upon the bed, Randall clutched his head again, finding its contours familiar, and when he drew his hands away, they were wet not with blood but with tears. He understood then that the spider had grown not in his brain but in his mind. But with this simple realization, as the newborn snow of a winter's night came whispering down, his weary heart had stopped.

Jack O'Lantern Jack

The seven or eight shots of bourbon Jack had already imbibed, one after another at the bar, emboldened him to say, "How about it, Vinnie?
I'll carve you another pumpkin for one more drink."

But Vinnie, the bartender, was less than excited about this propo-
sition, and Vinnie wasn't generally a man to mince words. "We ain't
got any more. And in case you hadn't noticed, it ain't Halloween any
more, Jack." He polished a glass and set it in place beside its partner in
the mirror. "It's about time them jack-o'-lanterns came down anyway.
They're beginning to rot."

"Yeah," a man down the bar said, holding his beer mug up in af-
firmation, "that one's starting to remind me of my mother-in-law." He
pointed to a pumpkin-face beside the register. The eyes and the corners of the mouth were beginning to sag.

Jack drained the last drop from his glass. "Fine thing," he said, half
to himself. "Didn't I carve you the best damn jack-o'-lanterns you ever
saw? Ain't another place in town decked out like this."

"Yeah, yeah," Vinnie said. One orange face grinned from the other
end of the bar, another from a shelf over the mirror, others from various places about the room, like some assemblage of strangely cheerful
goblins. "You carve a wicked pumpkin, okay."

"One pumpkin, one drink," Jack grumbled. "That was the deal."

"And come Halloween next year, I'll make you the same deal
again," Vinnie said. "You got my word. But right now it's the tenth of
November, and if you want another drink you'd better put some more
money on the bar."

Jack slid off the barstool, lit a cigarette, and rummaged through his
pockets. "You know I'm out of cash, Vinnie." He belched. "Look, I
can get you another pumpkin. Free. My brother's still got a whole field
full of 'em. I'll go get one and bring it in—"

Vinnie shook his head. "No more pumpkins."

Jack only paused a second. "Well hey, tell you what, I'll give you my lighter for a drink."

Vinnie rolled his eyes. "I don't want your damn lighter." Several people down the bar laughed quietly.

Jack coughed out a cloud of smoke. "Aw, c'mon, Vinnie, it's only—"

But the bartender's patience had run out. "You need to be running along home. I've got more to do than stand around here arguing with you about lighters and pumpkins. And while we're talking about pumpkins"—he snapped his fingers and the bargirl came over—"Alice, get a tray and gather them things up and take 'em out back to the dumpster."

Alice put her thumb and middle finger through one pumpkin's mouth and eye. "E-e-ew, gross, it's getting squishy."

"Just do it," Vinnie said. "They won't bite you."

Alice, looking disgusted, went around gathering up orange-faced goblins. Jack looked on in dismay. "That's great. That's just great. You people don't appreciate fine art. I'm the best pumpkin carver in this state."

"No argument," Vinnie said, "you probably are. But when them things start getting so ugly they're putting my customers off their feed, they gotta go." Alice was already heading out the alley door with her load, a bizarre pile of malformed heads.

"You know," Jack said, his head really beginning to reel now from the bourbon, "it's a real trick, carving a good jack-o'-lantern. You've got to know exactly how to scoop the insides out right, how to do the eyes—"

Vinnie was starting to look as if his advice about going home wasn't just advice any more. "Time for you to pack it in, pal. I mean it."

Jack put his cigarette out in an ashtray and shuffled toward the back door. "Yeah, all right. I don't know why I even come in here."

"He don't know why he even comes in here," Vinnie said, pointing at Jack with a thumb.

One of the men at the other end of the bar called out, "It's the atmosphere, Vinnie. Classiest atmosphere in town. Nothing but the best for old Jack."

But by now old Jack was through the door and out into the alley, where the lone bulb over the door cast only a wan light over the scene. It was quiet out here, quiet and lonely and depressing. Even the talk back there, people making fun of him, had been better than standing in a dark, dirty alley alone. Well, alone except for the dumpster, which sat there like some squat, silent beast with its huge mouth closed in slumber.

He stood at a loss, trying to think what to do. He could just go home, of course, but it was only a little after midnight and he never went home that early. Something nagged at his mind, and he realized what it was.

"They actually tossed my pumpkins out," he mumbled to himself, feeling resentment rise like a flush to his face. "Tossed 'em right out like they was nothing."

Fishing the cigarette lighter out of his pocket, he opened the dumpster lid with a metallic screech, propped it up, flicked his lighter, and held it down into the throat of the dumpster to try to see by the light of the flame. Ensconced in a jumble of shadows near the bottom, several pumpkin faces, shriveled and discolored, stared back. It was almost touching, the way they seemed to look at him.

And yet—

And yet there was something a little unsettling about it too. And while he was thinking this, he could have sworn that the blur of shadows in the bottom of the bin looked—*restless*—somehow.

He could have sworn, too, that something moved, down there in the gloom, something quiet and furtive.

It had to be rats, of course, but the impression had startled him so much that, holding the lighter down the night-black maw of the dumpster at arm's length, he had jerked his arm and knocked the lighter against the metal, and the flame had gone out.

The darkness down in the bin was deep and disturbing, and he lost no time in flicking the lighter, trying to regain the flame, but he must have had more to drink than he thought, because he dropped the lighter into the darkness.

"Damn." His head was giddy from drinking, and he wished there was more light from the bulb over the door, because he couldn't see a thing down there, or anything clear anyway, just vague suggestions of shapes. The lightbulb didn't help at all, and he had no idea where ex-

actly the lighter was, down among the soggy cardboard boxes and broken bottles and half-rotted pumpkins.

Well, there was only one thing to do. He couldn't afford to give up
a perfectly good cigarette lighter. Hoisting one leg up over the edge of
the dumpster, levering himself over the edge, and pulling the other leg
up, he dropped inside, sprawling amid the trash in the bottom of the
bin.

And from his impact, the lid clanged shut, sealing him in blackness.

This was not good.

It stank in here, for one thing, even when you were used to spending a certain amount of time exploring alleys and picking through
trash. A medley of stale odors rose around him in the dark, and he sin-
cerely wished he was someplace else.

But he was here, lying in a tangle of slimy cardboard and glass
and—

And what was moving around down here, other than himself? He
thought something shifted in the dark, and if it was rats, well, that
might be okay. Rats might be okay.

He fumbled about, running his fingers over the things he could
reach—boxes, bottles, now and then the bare, rusty floor of the bin.
He knicked his fingers a couple of times on jagged glass, cursing in the
darkness, a darkness that seemed now to press too close at his face, as
if there were not enough air to breathe. But finally he closed his grasp
over the lighter, drew it up toward his face, and brought forth a brave
little flame.

And wished he hadn't.

In the wavering light it was hard for him to understand, at first,
what he was seeing. A number of puffy-looking pumpkin faces leered
back at him, which was pretty much to be expected, given the circumstances. What was not to be expected was that they didn't seem to be
just lying there any more, where they had fallen willy-nilly in the bottom of the dumpster.

This is insane, some quaking little corner of his consciousness kept
saying. In the jittery light from the flame, it looked as if some of the
greasy trash in the bin had shambled together to make something
like—what? Angular bodies with pumpkin heads atop them? A bit of

cardboard here, a glass shard there, jumbled angles of shadow and substance, like arms akimbo, like legs stretching to find balance, with leprous pale orange faces nodding in the gloom.

He thought one of the arms had picked up something—a broken bottle?—and was reaching for him, when the flame went out again and the darkness seemed to smash upon him like a palpable presence. In the next instant he was almost too shocked to cry out when a searing pain slashed through his scalp, sending something coppery and warm cascading into his face.

With some desperate access of will, he managed to flick the lighter and bring a flame up to dispel the darkness one more time. Sure enough, a gaunt and jumbled figure leaned over him, with others crowding close, and an unthinkable arm was at work while a vengeful cold light played in the hollows of pulpy orange-black eyes. It was only a fleeting impression, but it would have been enough to drive him mad, had not a new and unthinkable pain come first.

They won't bite you, Vinnie had told the girl, but this was promising to be much worse. Whatever pressed itself close to him had something like a hand, because it held a bent and discarded spoon and was starting its work, in the good tradition, starting on the open head. Nodding over its art.

Scooping out the insides.

The Watcher at the Window

Charlotte wasn't sure that she was happy to see her sister after all. Now that Doris wasn't just a voice on the telephone or a swatch of crabbed inconsequential handwriting on a postcard ("Worked in my garden all week, the petunias aren't taking the heat very well")—now that they were no longer a safe three thousand miles apart—Charlotte was having second thoughts about their reunion here in Larkwood. But then what choice had she had, really?

By the time they had walked halfway down Sycamore Lane, Father's house was swallowed up by a convex blanket of shrubbery, and the street showed only visages of unfamiliar house-fronts, bedecked in Halloween trappings and gazing out at the passersby like rows of blind half-forgotten faces, darkly festive, in a school yearbook. The neighborhood was only a vague, transmuted echo of her childhood memories; the years had altered almost everything.

"Yes, it's all changed," Doris said, as if privy to her thoughts. They turned right onto Bolton Street and walked north between other bland rows of houses. This early in the morning, no one else was about, and the autumn mists of dawn were only now receding like faint gray spiderwebs, and the town seemed cheerless, forlorn almost. Charlotte knew now, glancing sidelong at Doris, what it was that bothered her about seeing her sister again after all these years. Doris's face was too much like a mirror. Seeing the ponderous furrows of time that had settled there, Charlotte knew all too well that she, too, had grown old. Usually she could ignore her own reflection in the mirror, but not *this* mirror. Looking at Doris's gaunt and desiccated form, she thought of a line from William Butler Yeats—"Old clothes upon old sticks to scare a bird"—but she knew the words might just as well describe her own angular and time-ravaged frame.

They crossed Walnut Lane and continued north up Bolton toward Dedham Street, and Charlotte knew what occupied both their thoughts.

"You say it's all changed," she said. "Some things are the same. You see that house?" She indicated a cottage ensconced in bushes. Black-and-orange paper skulls grinned from the windows like strange morning wraiths. "I remember it. The Reverend Patterson used to live there."

Doris glanced at the house and snorted. "Someone's painted it brown," she said as they came to the intersection with Dedham Street. "Not the same at all. Besides, you couldn't care less about the Reverend Patterson's house. I know what's on your mind."

They turned onto Dedham Street and walked west, toward downtown Larkwood. Gradually the placid residential neighborhoods would give way, first to a laundry and antiques shops and a grocery store, and then to the increasingly commercial façades of the business district, such as it was. But before the laundry and the antiques shops and the grocer's, one would see a nondescript stretch of what might once have been outlying little business establishments of one sort or another, now only a depressing assortment of boarded-up windows and collapsed ambitions, sad little store-fronts on whose dirty panes there remained only stuttering remnants of lettering to suggest in a remote fashion what these buildings once were. This area had been called Dedham Square, and Charlotte remembered when most of these bygone stores had been open and thriving. Walking through the area now, she felt, more than ever, the oppressive hand of time.

But there was one building that was different. It was boarded up and empty now, of course, but it had been boarded up and empty back then too, when she and Doris had been children here.

The Place, they had called it.

And here it was now, coming up on their right. The trees lining this part of Dedham Street had always been so thick that one couldn't see the Place until its ugly, unpainted front loomed directly overhead. Indeed, the ramshackle three-story wooden building leaned toward the avenue at so grotesque an angle that it seemed to be over you rather than beside you, and seemed nearly to form an arch with a similar building (the old furniture store, Charlotte recalled) across the way, now long defunct.

The difference, here, was that while the gloomy edifice they called the Place was now just as abandoned and lifeless as its neighbors, it had been so even in the old days, and neither Charlotte nor Doris had ever know what sort of establishment it might once have been. One fancied, sometimes, that it had always been just as it was—purposeless, empty.

But not quite empty?

The thought must have shown on her face, because Doris was regarding her with a knowing smirk that contained no trace of humor. "As I said, I know what's been on your mind," she remarked quietly, almost as though it were a reproach.

As they came closer, the emerging sun cast enough radiance from the east-southeast, behind them, to throw the old building's one remaining window into a confusion of reflected light, and it was probably only this effect that made it seem to Charlotte, for one breathless moment, that a bloated face peered at them from behind the pane. A Halloween face again? No, infinitely less wholesome somehow. The impression passed, with or without Doris's sharing it, she couldn't tell, and in any case they walked beyond the building and continued toward town in silence.

The limited attractions of the business district did little to uplift Charlotte's thoughts, or to make Doris more talkative. As they dawdled over dishes of ice cream, Charlotte remembered more of the old days than she wished to. How distant, yet how unsettlingly clear in the memory, those times—the two sisters, all pigtails and skinned knees and buck teeth, walking past the Place, whispering, shuddering, their childish imaginations running wild.

But how much had been imagination? Even then, the ground floor window had been scarcely less bleary, and one never knew whether it was a caprice of the light or not that made it seem as if a pale, corpulent face stared from behind the grimy glass. The Watcher, they had called him. Or her, or it. They could never see it too clearly, and on occasion not at all, yet more often than not its eerie contours, anticipated on long hushed walks approaching Dedham Square, was at least a suspected presence in the window, and both gawky girls would run past, terrified. Thrilled, too, in an odd way, but still terrified. No imaginable enticement would have moved them to pry their way past the dusty boards and enter the building, or even linger before its spectral window.

What had always been particularly repellent about the glimpsed face of the Watcher was its pasty, unhealthy color. Recalling it, Charlotte pushed her ice cream away, no longer having an appetite for it.

"Remarkable, isn't it?" Doris asked. Charlotte thought that she meant the chalky color or the ice cream, with its dreadful suggestiveness, but Doris only said: "That it took Father's death to bring us both back here at the same time."

On the walk back to the house, Charlotte thought: Yes, I moved fifteen hundred miles west, to California, and she moved fifteen hundred miles east, to Vermont, and decades later Death, the great average-maker, pulled us back to the middle, whether we wanted to come or not.

Charlotte cooked the dinner that night, with the uncomfortable reflection that Death had handed her a house too, or half a house. They would sell it, of course, since neither owned it outright or wanted to live in it, and then they would no doubt revert to their bipolar existence on opposite ends of the country. Charlotte was rather looking forward to returning to her high-rise apartment in Santa Rosa.

Except for one thing.

"You know," she said over dinner, "there's a place in Santa Rosa where I walk sometimes, and there's an abandoned building where I think I see—someone watching me pass by."

Trying to imagine how Doris would react to this remark, she hadn't anticipated the expression that met her from across the table. Doris looked not contemptuous or skeptical, but a little frightened. "Go on," she said.

"Well," Charlotte said, "there isn't much more to tell. Sometimes when I walk by and look, it's there, and sometimes not. The face. When it's there, the disturbing thing about it is that color, a sickly kind of white."

"Like the underside of a toadstool," Doris supplied.

Charlotte, surprised, faltered a moment and then said, "Yes, something like that."

This time, as they walked west on Sycamore, Charlotte didn't glance back toward Father's receding house, nor ahead, in her mind, toward

Dedham Square. She just walked, with Doris beside her, Doris as taci-
turn as ever. Charlotte was grateful for the silence. Her sister looked
thoughtful, and Charlotte wasn't eager to hear her thoughts.

They walked north up Bolton Street again, past the same noncom-
mittal rows of houses as before. Now and then a robed figure (some
priest of the Darkness?—no, a common mortal in a houserobe, and
Charlotte had to get her mind in order)—a robed figure would appear
briefly in a doorway to retrieve the morning paper, or in the shadows of
some yard a stray cat, startled at the approach of strangers, would dart
away into the bushes, gone. The two sisters crossed Walnut Lane,
walked up to Dedham Street, and turned west again, toward downtown.

Gradually the modest houses thinned out and the melancholy
wooden facades of Dedham Square replaced them, frowning upon the
quiet early-morning street with withered faces of decay more somber
than any jack-o'-lantern. And among these ponderous façades—that
unsavory building. The Place.

Involuntarily, both women slowed their pace. Charlotte winced at
the incongruity of this gesture. What good was it to approach the
building more slowly, when what they most needed to do was hurry
past it and get it behind them and over with?

"Don't look," Doris said.

Charlotte was startled. "What?"

Doris elbowed her in the arm. "I said, don't look at it."

But of course Charlotte had to look. This time the bleary windowpanes reflected not a confusion of morning sunlight but only the gray
indeterminacy of an overcast October sky, and it was hard to say
whether this made everything better or worse. It was better, in that
without the dazzle of bright light one could see more clearly through
the dirt-streaked glass. But it was worse, precisely because you *could* see.

And although Charlotte had only the most transient glance at the
pasty white bloated face that seemed to nod and waver behind the
pane, she wished indeed that she had not looked. She couldn't tell
whether Doris had seen it too, and didn't want to ask; they made the
remainder of their journey in silence.

Over lunch, finally, Charlotte asked her: "You said not to look at
it. What did you mean? Not to look at the window, or not to look at
what's behind it?"

Doris took a sip of coffee and dabbed at her mouth with a napkin before replying. "Who said there's anything behind it?"

"You didn't see anything?" Charlotte asked.

Doris sniffed contemptuously. "No."

Charlotte finished her own coffee in a gulp and wanted not to have to say it: "I wish I could believe you."

"Believe whatever you wish," Doris replied.

The day passed in dreary errands, the evening passed at the house, in silence. Finally Doris said, "All right."

Charlotte looked up from a magazine in which she had read the same sentence three times, too preoccupied to concentrate. "What? What's all right?"

Doris sighed and laid her own tattered magazine aside. "I did see it."

Charlotte scarcely knew whether to be relieved or horrified. In any case she wasn't entirely surprised. "What did you see?"

"Don't play games with me," Doris replied. "You know perfectly well. The face. Dear God, that face, too pale, and too large." Her words seemed to be tumbling out now, as if she were anxious to be rid of them. "Too white, and too—"

"Too what?" Charlotte urged, caught up in the words.

"Too much like the other," Doris said.

Both of them needed a few moments of silence, to catch their breath. Finally Charlotte asked, "What other?"

Doris's face in the lamplight was sharp, severe, appallingly frightened. "The one near where I live."

This was too much for Charlotte. She let the words hang in the air and die away, and did not try to reply. Doris at length went on:

"I walk, sometimes, in the evenings, in Brattleboro, when the weather is decent. There's a lonely kind of a road that I turn down, and it winds on and on, nearly out of the city, but before you get out into the country it leads through a cluster of old abandoned buildings, and in one of them—"

"My God," Charlotte whispered.

Doris got up and walked to a window and stood looking out into the night. "I've tried to tell myself it's just a trick of the light. Especially since the face isn't always there. But when it is there—" Her voice trailed off, and no one spoke again that night.

"But why do you have to leave today?" Charlotte asked, hating herself for seeming to whine. "You were going to stay a while longer."

"I just don't think I want to be here," Doris said simply. Somehow, she sounded like the child Doris again, pigtails and scabby knees. But the face in the morning light was ancient.

"Well, I don't want to be here alone," Charlotte protested.

Doris put a hand on her hand, for the first time in uncountably many years. "Don't worry so much. Most of the paperwork is done. The rest we can manage through the mail. I just want to get away. I mean, I just want to get back."

Get away is what she means, Charlotte thought. But all she said was, "You know best."

Alone in the house, she reflected upon the different kinds of silence. When Doris had been here, across the room, silence was a well of uncertainty, of expectation, of knowledge that something, for better or worse, would eventually be said. Now, without her sister, silence was just silence: endless, unpromising, devoid even of the illusion of momentary comfort. She had to get out of the house, if only for an hour.

It had been late afternoon when Doris had left, and by now the sun was down and the western sky was dying like an ember. The lengthening shadows made Bolton Street a tunnel of trees, woody sentries black against the gathering night, forbidding in the intervals between streetlights, where dusky outlines of hedges seemed to change their shapes and small creatures scurried, restless, unseen.

"Scared of cats and trees," Charlotte chided herself aloud, crossing Walnut Lane and continuing northward, but when she turned west onto Dedham Street, the shroud of night had really fallen, and even the wan procession of streetlamps stretching ahead of her seemed unable, or unwilling, to relieve the gloom. Maybe she would see a movie in town. But she knew that there was no need, knew that she could simply turn around and go back to the house. She went on, though, toward Dedham Square.

Toward the Place.

Pausing under a streetlamp goosenecked high in the air above her, she reflected: I don't have to go on *or* go back the way I came. I can turn down the next cross street and that will take me—

But that was the way it was in Santa Rosa, not here. What could she have been thinking?

Walking on, past the last lonely houses before you reached the edge of Dedham Square, she thought: It's not bad enough I forget I'm in Larkwood, I even think I confused it with Santa Rosa, where I've never even been. Heavens, what would Charlotte think?

And this troubled reflection stopped her cold beneath the next streetlamp. I *am* Charlotte, and I *live* in Santa Rosa. Why was I thinking like Doris? Surely the strain of the whole situation—Father's death, putting the house up for sale—but how could she stand here making excuses?

Reluctant to leave the glow of the lamp, she nevertheless felt oddly drawn onward by the darkness, even as the ruined shells of the nearer buildings of Dedham Square began to take form, shapes of darkness against the darker sky. The old furniture store across the street was innocent enough, though sprawling and eaten through with holes like a rotting pumpkin. But the building before her now—the Place—was another matter.

She stood in front of it, fidgeting. Furniture store? But no, it had always been a vacant lot, across the street. In Brattleboro, there had always been a lot of—

Charlotte had never been to Brattleboro, Vermont. This was Larkwood, Indiana. Across the street were the ruins of the old furniture store, pure and simple. But how had she known—

The nearest streetlamp here was some distance away, but cast a familiar glow upon the familiar window. Was that a furtive movement at the glass, a withdrawn face? Perhaps not. In any event, before she knew what she was doing, she had stepped up to the building, pulled a board from across the ancient door, and pushed her way inside.

She stood absolutely still, not even breathing, and listened to the silence around her. This was crazy. There was no reason for her to be here, none at all. Yet here she was.

Outside, the wind came up momentarily and sent a fit of creaking through the dusty boards around her and above her. It probably wasn't even safe to be here; the place might come shuddering down around her at any time, burying her in dirty rubble. She sensed the decaying bulk of the building above her, and it was like being at the bottom of an ocean of rotten wood, gasping for breath. But the groaning timbers gradually grew quiet, settling, settling. She listened.

Nothing. Not a sound.

Or was there just the faintest impression, as if something shifted, unseen, unheard, felt only as a subtle alteration of pressure in the musty air?

Her eyes began to adjust to the darkness, but even so, she could make out only the vaguest outlines of timeless clutter: a half-fallen-down table, perhaps, and some rotted boxes muffled in dust. Charlotte would really be surprised if she could see her now, standing here in the dark like a—

But she *was* Charlotte, wasn't she? Absurdly, she reached up and felt her face in the dark. She should know this face, she had certainly seen it enough times from the window. Right here in Santa Rosa.

No, what was this, what was she thinking? Before she could even wonder, a pallid and puffy face nearly as large as the dirty window out of which it had been looking, turned slowly toward her. Was it she who screamed, or that woman across the shadowy room, the one who had taken down a board from the door and come in? Or was it only an aberration of the light that made it seem as if someone had come in? But it was she who turned—she, Charlotte, who perhaps had never had a sister, and it was Doris, whoever that was, Doris who had perhaps never had a sister, and it was a thousand others, yet it was the Watcher, pale and lonely at a thousand obscure windows, windows like mirrors. Peering across a mirror-maze of lightless rooms, the wan-faced Watcher turned slowly in the murky dark.

It was insane, to be the woman coming down the lane again and again and again, and the other walker and the other and the other, coming down a thousand quiet lanes in a thousand quiet towns, yes, surely it was madness to be all of them and the Watcher too.

But then how could one watch and watch and watch, and *not* be mad?

Desert Dreams

We dwell forever in realms of shadow. Strangely complacent, we wander through our weary days as if we understood the texture of our world; yet in all truth we see with the eye of the worm and hear with the ear of the stone, and comprehend nothing. Our understanding is a skimming water-bug that tastes only the surface of a fathomless black sea, while reality, a frightful abyss of ocean-bottom horror, moves silently and darkly through depths beyond our reach, inscrutable, and mocks our ignorance.

Dreams try to tell us things of which we otherwise would know little, purporting to lend a semblance of clarity to our minds, yet I cannot even say when my own dreams, my strange and ever-recurrent night visions, began. "Dreams," I have said, but these visions, I now realize, have constituted one single pervasive dream running like an insane but oddly persistent thread through my life.

I recall waking in childhood with a sense of some striking impression that I could not quite remember, though when the dream came again and again over time I gradually managed to retain more of what I had seen. There seemed to be a consistent pattern to these dreams, but as the vision slowly gathered form it was not relief I felt at being able to remember, but rather a puzzlement as to what these still elusive fragments might mean. It had to do with some forsaken spot in a vast and sun-baked desert, but beyond that I could not be sure of much.

For a time during my adolescence the dreams became less frequent, and in fact I thought I was outgrowing them, too busy with life to concern myself with insubstantial matters. In time the dreams seemed to cease altogether. Growing to manhood in my native Providence, Rhode Island, I settled into mundane but adequate employment at an insurance company and bought a pleasant old house in Benefit Street, expecting to spend my days in simple contentment. I whiled away my evenings reading Proust and Baudelaire and Shakespeare and sometimes strolling along the ancient streets of the city and thinking quiet thoughts. I was at peace, satisfied with my life.

But then the dreams began anew.

I awoke very late one autumn night and struggled to retain a grasp on the ebbing tide of memory as the dream started to slip away. What had it been? Undeniably, it was essentially the vision of my childhood years, though rather more detailed this time. I remembered now a vista of vast and sprawling desert, where great brittle tumbleweeds, like aimless creatures on some distant planet, careened across the arid sand and spiky yucca leaves and cactus blades pointed skyward in the blinding sun. Behind the scene there seemed to be a kind of subtle rumbling or humming, but I could scarcely be sure; and soon these half-remembered impressions faded, and I fell asleep again.

The next evening the dream was back, and when I woke I lay in the dark thinking about what I had seen. And heard, or almost heard.

Again, the sun-blistered sand had stretched away in all directions, dotted with standing sentries of cholla cactus and great angular yuccas and ragged bunches of mesquite. A warm wind had stirred the yellow earth, and a grumbling suggestion of sound seemed to hover just too low to be heard clearly. But for a moment it had resembled a low-pitched voice, a voice that seemed to be saying something like *"Gwai-ti."* I could recall no more than that.

Unable this time to sleep again, I walked for hours in the silent streets and felt oddly disoriented. The familiar façades of colonial New England houses with their fanlighted doors and small-paned windows only seemed to make me feel more oddly displaced, as if it were unclear which was reality, the well-known sights of Benefit and Jenckes and College Streets or the windswept desertland of my dream landscape.

I had lived in Providence all my life. I had never seen a desert, except occasionally in photographs. What did I know of cholla cactus or yucca plants or mesquite, or of boundless purple skies—the memory of them came back to me—skies unobstructed by city buildings, vast skies overlooking colossal oceans of sand? Yet I did seem to know of these things.

At work I sometimes found myself staring off into space, preoccupied with the enigma of my dream visions. I began to wonder *where* this desertland really was, if indeed it really was anywhere. Then when a work associate returned one day from a vacation in Albuquerque, and when I listened to his accounts of the region, it was suddenly and inexplicably clear to me that the desert vistas of my dreams were real, and were to be found somewhere in New Mexico. I really had no way to know that, yet I felt sure I knew.

As time went on, the setting of my dreams became more focused, but I found that this made the dreams more rather than less disturbing, as I could scarcely imagine how I came to know ever more particular detail about a locale of which I should have been wholly uninformed. I had never traveled any farther west than Columbus, Ohio, and the American Southwest was only patches of color on a map to me; yet these desert visions were unsettlingly familiar in some surreal way.

Under the glare of a dazzling sun I was looking down at my body—a body now surprisingly brown and muscular and clad only in a sort of rough cloth around the middle—and wondering if I were going mad. How could this be me? As I bent forward to see myself better, locks of long, silky, raven-black hair fell across my eyes, and it was only when I brushed these locks from my face that I glanced up to see the unfamiliar yet somehow oddly familiar figure standing near me on the warm, cactus-dotted sand. He was a medicine man, with a wizened face nearly hidden among a nest of lizardlike wrinkles out of which peered two dark eyes that seemed to hold the secrets of centuries. He was puffing at a great long clay pipe, sending jittery little clouds of gray smoke out upon the warm air, and as he puffed the pipe he shook a turtle-shell ceremonial rattle and intoned the words—incomprehensible to me on one level of consciousness, but faintly familiar on some other level— the words of an ancient ritual song. He turned as he chanted, sending the smoke and the cryptic words first in one direction and then another, finally coming all the way back around to face me, and as his timeless face turned again in my direction, the final words of the song took form in my mind: *"Gwai-ti, Gwai-ti."* I awoke with these impressions still fresh in my memory and walked far into the night hours trying either to understand the sounds I had heard or to dispel their memory. I paused among the great black gravestones in St. John's churchyard off Benefit Street and tried to collect my thoughts, finally rousing myself and making my weary way back home with no desire to sleep again. After reading awhile I feel asleep nonetheless, and, so far as I can remember, did not dream.

Taking the next day off from work, I made an appointment to speak with someone who I suspected might possibly be able to tell me something about my mystery: Professor Carlos Armijo at Brown University. His field was the anthropology of the Southwest, and I had heard him lecture once. I doubted that my nocturnal visions would mean anything to him, but it was worth a try.

I found Professor Armijo to be a soft-spoken and pensive-looking man of middle age, comfortably ensconced in a nest of books and professional journals in his office at Brown. Describing the overall nature of my dreams, I felt increasingly foolish having allowed myself to think there might be any real point in taking up his time with my account, and I barely mustered the courage to mention the nonsense syllables that had become part of my nocturnal visions of the desert, so that I was mightily surprised at his response.

"I have heard these syllables before," he said in a soft Spanish accent, "in connections that make them difficult to account for in the dreams of someone unacquainted with the cultures of the Southwest. Even scholars conversant with those cultures would for the most part find the words unknown to them. I only know of them myself because I am a specialist in, let us say, some of the darker aspects of Southwestern lore."

I was intrigued, though in a way unsure how much I really wanted to know about the origins of an expression having arisen for no discernible reason in my dreams; perhaps Carl Jung was right in theorizing that we all possess a Collective Unconscious capable of tapping into profound shared realms of being, archetypal realms, unknown to our conscious mind yet at some level connected to a sort of reality. "Please go on."

Professor Armijo looked out his window for a moment, evidently collecting his thoughts. "For centuries there was a kind of obscure cult among certain Native American shamans of Arizona and New Mexico," he said, "involving what seems to have been the worship of an ancient god unknown in the mainstream of American Indian tradition." He paused, rather dramatically, and not without cause, it seemed to me. "That god was apparently known as Gwai-ti."

I felt my breath catch at this revelation. What did I know of this? What did I really *want* to know of this? Nothing—yet I had undeniably dreamed the name.

"Very little is known," the professor went on, "about this cult or its god, as the whole subject has always been shunned among such few American Indians as have ever even heard of it. Even at places in New Mexico like Nambé Pueblo, where there are very dark and long-standing traditions of Southwest-style witchcraft, in my researches I have found only one shaman who admitted to knowing of the god Gwai-ti, and he spoke of the matter only with reluctance and, I might add, with obvious distaste.

"I gather from his disjointed accounts that Gwai-ti is supposed to have existed from the beginning of time, and to have come to dwell under the earth, showing itself only on rare occasions to hapless souls. There are stories of human sacrifices made from time to time by renegade Indian priests having no standing with the proper spiritual leaders in the region, most of whom, however, regard the supposed activities of the renegade priests as fabrications."

I was struggling to make some sense of all this. "And the name? Frankly, I thought it sounded Chinese."

Professor Armijo nodded. "I have had some interesting discussions with people in comparative linguistics here about the name Gwai-ti. Indeed there are words within the phonology of Chinese that sound like these syllables. I am given to understand that there is a word *gwai* that means something like 'strange' or 'monstrous.' There is a word *ti* that means 'body' or 'form.' And of course ethnologists theorize that Asian peoples migrated in prehistoric times across the Bering Strait into North America, but on the other hand there are virtually no discernible linguistic traces of Asian vocabulary in the languages of Native Americans."

"How do I know the name?" I asked.

The professor shrugged. "Perhaps you have heard it somewhere and have simply forgotten."

I made ready to leave, thanking the man for his time. "You're right, I must have heard the name somewhere."

But of course I knew that I had not. Except in my dreams.

A few nights later the dreams began to take on an even more anomalous character.

One night I seemed to crouch in shadows watching some vile convocation in which a semicircle of strangely painted priests chanted: "*M'warrh Gwai-ti, h'nah m'warrh Gwai-ti, ph'nglui w'gah Gwai-ti.*" Another time I thought I was looking across a great desert plain in a wash of moonlight, with a distant ring of mountains in the background almost beyond the limits of vision, and watching what at first I took to be a swirl of blowing sand. Before long, though, this impression resolved itself into a young Indian girl running, screaming, flailing her arms in terror. In the inconsistent fashion of dreams, my view of her was suddenly closer than before, so close in fact that she filled my entire field of view. Somewhere I could hear a deep thrumming sound, like the bass tones on a pipe organ, and a voice—it was like the old shaman of my earlier visions—a voice that chanted, in some language known to me in the dream: "She was chosen, we had to send her." And in the next instant a great hungry darkness seemed to close around the screaming girl, and she was gone, and the thrumming died away. I awoke drenched in perspiration, and fancied I could still smell the pungent aroma of sagebrush. I was afraid to go back to sleep.

But of course the next night I did have to sleep again, and saw this time a tall, narrow stone in the sand, with ancient petroglyphs carved upon it like runic inscriptions from a bygone age, and I heard again the somber thrumming in the ground, and glimpsed unclear suggestions of movement in the wan moonlight, and only just made out a murmur of the name *Gwai-ti* before the scene grew grainy and faded away altogether.

It was only a matter of time before I could no longer resist the nameless urge actually to visit New Mexico. I must long since have decided, unconsciously, that whatever unthinkable confluence of realities might have brought me into an awareness of that other world so unlike the waking world of my mundane life, I had to see, in objective truth, the setting of my dreams. I had no idea, of course, where exactly in those vast desertlands my visions might have originated.

Nevertheless, I found myself on an airplane one day, landing in Albuquerque with that odd sense of the unreal that one feels upon first visiting a place about which one has only read. Or dreamed.

I rented a four-wheel-drive vehicle at the airport and drove east and then south. While I had no notion where I should be going, I felt no reluctance just to let my instincts guide me. Threading my way through the foothills of the Sandia Mountains and finding my eyes charmed by occasional glimpses of earth-colored adobe walls and coyote fences, I made my way out into open desert, where distant, majestic mesas stood timeless beyond endless plains of waving prairie grass and nodding islands of mesquite and sagebrush and spikes of yucca. Given my motivations for visiting this land so different from my native New England, I had rather expected the desert to be redolent of subtle dread and unease, but I found myself gathering altogether different impressions.

The place was beautiful. There was nothing sinister about the dizzyingly vast expanse of turquoise sky, the stretches of chaparral, the blue-gray mountains in the distance, the great deep arroyos snaking across the land, the tranquil mesas stretched upon the sandy plain like serene grazing beasts. I scarcely knew now what I had expected, but what I had found was a land of enchanting beauty and peace.

As I drove through this desert pageantry, I wondered aloud that I had ever allowed myself to think that there could be anything spectral or bizarre about this region. I felt more at ease than I had felt for quite a long time, and I reflected that I had been foolish to be disturbed by my odd but essentially harmless dreams. Even those nonsense syllables, so coincidentally similar to some name from obscure Southwestern folklore, were surely something about which I had no need to concern myself.

The sun was beginning to go down behind the purple mountain ranges in the west, and I marveled at the beauty of the desert sunset, wherein the sky exploded in a riotous display of color that would surely challenge the brushwork of even the most gifted artist. Somewhere south of Corona I found myself on a smaller, more crudely paved road, and continued to delight in the incredible vistas of cholla cactus and undulating stretches of sandy earth, where the pointed shadows of yucca and mesquite began to splay themselves out upon the plain in the waning light of the sun. I reminded myself that soon it would be getting dark, and I would need either to return to Corona or go on to Roswell or Artesia to find a room for the night.

But first I felt in the mood for some more exploration; there was something addictive about this landscape.

I turned off onto an even smaller road and bounced along in a cloud of dust, feeling, with a certain pleasure, that I was farther from human habitation than I could ever recall having been. After a while the road became a rock-strewn, primitive path where even the rugged vehicle I had chosen found it tricky to proceed. A darkening expanse of chaparral lay all around me, and now for the first time since my arrival I began to feel, in spite of the thrill that the newness of the place imparted to me, a certain suspicion that there could be something a little spectral about this land after all. But still I felt fascinated, and a little disinclined to head back to populated areas just yet.

At length the passable road, at this point merely a vague predominance of rock over cactus and mesquite, played out altogether, and I stopped the car and got out and walked ahead into the twilight, picking my way carefully and once pausing to watch the dusky form of a rattlesnake sidle off into the gloom, its warning rattles reaching me as a paper-dry burring on the evening air. Clearly, one had to be careful here, and the sight of this reptilian reminder was sufficient to suggest to me that indeed it might be time to turn back.

But I thought I saw something in the distance that I wanted to examine at closer range. It was something vaguely familiar, though the light was very uncertain now.

Stepping carefully over snake holes and prickly clusters of cactus, I made my way to a large standing stone that protruded from the sandy soil like a somber finger pointing at the darkening sky.

And I could not believe what I was seeing, in stark actuality now, rather than in the vagaries of dream. This simply could not be, but it was. Its ancient Indian petroglyphs still faintly visible in the dwindling remnants of light, the stone was undeniably the sinister monolith of my dream-visions back in Providence.

Providence, now infinitely far away in another, saner world.

Heaven help me, this was the place of my dreams.

I have no idea how long I stood there, unable to wrest my gaze from the dreadful stone, before my mind registered something else.

A sound. A low, insistent thrumming in the ground, like the bass notes of a great pipe organ.

And then—that other sound.

Two syllables, in some voice of the mind or some real physical vibration, I could not tell which—two syllables upon which I must refuse to dwell.

The impressions that followed are what I must especially resist thinking too steadily upon, if I am to retain what sanity remains to me.

In the uneven light of a chalky moon beginning to spread its radiance from between black, scudding clouds, I thought somehow that the sandy plain on which I stood became—what shall I say?—lower, indented, subtly concave, while the shadowy line of the horizon rose slightly in contrast. Perhaps my unconscious mind understood before my reasoning self could do so, for I broke and ran, hoping that I was headed back toward the car, which was invisible from here. Stumbling and falling headlong, I scarcely felt the cactus and the stony soil rend my clothing as I fell and ran and fell and ran again, trying to block from my ears those reverberant tones that must have been rising in pitch all along, those notes that murmured *"Gwai-ti, Gwai-ti,"* from subterraneous regions of which I dared not allow myself to think.

I had the sensation that a great chasm was opening to receive me, and that in another moment it would be too late, and I would be gone, and no one would ever know what had happened to me. The whole scene seemed to churn itself up into a kaleidoscope of nightmare impressions, a blur of sand and tumbleweed and stone and muttering sound and frowning sky, and I ran and ran, choking on clouds of dust and terrified to look back over my shoulder. It was only when I was driving frantically back up the dusty, rocky road that some corner of my mind registered that I must have reached the car after all, before whatever came for me had time to close upon its prey.

I spent the rest of my trip moodily walking the populous and well-lighted streets of Albuquerque and Santa Fe, and I took an airplane back to Providence.

Now when I walk down Benefit Street and stop to look at a fanlighted doorway or watch a sleek gray cat make its serene way along the ancient brick walkways, I realize that it is possible for consciousnesses beyond the common grasp to reach across unthinkable gulfs of time and space and fasten upon the unwary dreamer. I know now that, whatever some may say of dreams or of imagination or of the fanciful nature of such mythic creatures as the vile cannibal-god Gwai-ti, I came within seconds, one night in the desertlands of New Mexico, of dropping into the primal ravenous mouth of that horror from my dreams.

Grampa Pus

You couldn't tell where his filthy rags left off and his rancid, sallow mountain of flesh began. I'm telling you, honest to God, he was that dirty, hundreds of putrid pounds of him. So repulsively dirty, so given over to living decay that in places, if you looked closely, you got the impression that foetid tatters of clothing were embedded in the dry, sick-looking lizard-folds of his puffy skin, which seemed to have grown around the cloth in groping, pustulent ribbons. He would have made a really, really disappointing blind date. Not that he was likely to play that role, any more; his youth was a faraway, unimaginable fantasy, and in fact it was hard to think that he ever had been young or healthy. Sometimes it was hard to think that he was even human.

The kids I ran with on the streets were fairly used to him, of course, since we saw him just about every day, but even for us, coming upon him suddenly around a corner or in the shadows at the end of an alley was pretty unpleasant, and I'd seen strangers, people who were encountering him for the first time, turn away in disgust. Now, my crowd, considering the uncouth lot we really were, had a certain callousness that kept the disgust at bay, enough, at least, so that we made something of a show of bravado in our dealings with him. But, the solemn and holy truth to tell, there probably wasn't one of us whose flesh didn't crawl a little, just thinking about Grampa Pus.

Yeah, that's what we called him. I have no idea what he called himself. I don't think any of us had ever heard his real name, or cared to. For us, he was just another curiosity of the streets, something else to laugh about, joke about; somebody else to bully and make fun of. We weren't very nice people sometimes, this inner-city social circle of mine. I liked to think I was a little brighter than most of those clowns; I ran with them because they were all I had, and a kid had to have some friends, but they weren't your browse-in-the-library types, believe me, no

afternoons going to museums or listening to Mozart. More like afternoons standing on corners smoking and leering and taunting passersby
and listening to rock on somebody's battered and taped-up old boom-
box. We didn't do terrible things, I mean like robbing and killing people
and pushing dope and stuff, but like a lot of kids who spend most of
their time under a dirty-looking sky instead of under a roof, we weren't
likely to win any prizes for etiquette. And somebody like Grampa Pus
was a natural target when we felt like letting off a little steam. Which,
you understand, was just about any hour of any day, actually.

But the old man made us nervous. Nobody liked to admit it, but
he did have a way of making you feel creepy just by being around.
He'd been around ever since my folks were kids here, and he had been
an old man even then, and that gave me the creeps too. You sensed
that there was something about him, something that bothered you on a
level too deep to be just ordinary revulsion. He was—well, let's say
unwholesome. That's the word that comes to mind. And I'm not talking about infrequent bathing or long-delayed changes of clothing; he
could have scrubbed himself raw and dressed like a fashion magazine
model and it wouldn't have made him pleasant. Not when you knew
what he was really like. Or thought you knew. We thought we knew.
We always thought we knew everything. We had a lot to learn.

One night, some of us learned it.

God, I remember that night, when I was walking back from a
movie uptown with Joel Malensky and Lisa Green, and we were taking
a weird route through a maze of connected alleyways, the sort of place
you really had to know the streets to keep from getting lost in, and we
had gone down a long alley, a dim crevice dotted with occasional windows on each side, a wretched passageway that narrowed down to what
looked like a dead-end. But right where you thought there was nothing
but a blind wall, a little side-passage opened out to the right and led between two grimy brick façades and finally widened out into a half passable alley that ran along for quite a distance between blank and
crumbling walls before you saw any more windows; and even when you
did, they were black and lifeless-looking, like the shattered and shapeless apertures in abandoned and half-fallen-down buildings, only here
there were sounds behind some of the brittle, curled-up windowshades:

faint, hoarse voices, and odd stirrings like things trying to stay out of sight. Under our feet, the greasy pavement was broken in places to reveal ancient cobblestones, and bricks here and there had tumbled down to form forlorn little piles of rubble huddled cobwebbed and dusty against the bases of walls. The air smelled like urine, with a hint of something dead and rotting. Somewhere above us, a sickly moon hung in the sky, but it was able to put only pale tentative fingers down the walls, leaving the alley mostly choked with darkness. It was a damned depressing place. I could see that Joel and Lisa thought so too, even though they wouldn't say anything.

I was beginning to think that I didn't know the neighborhood alleys so well after all, and that we were lost, when I spotted, far up ahead, a pallid wash of light that had to be Eighth Avenue. We were walking toward it when something lurched in front of us from out of the shadows.

At first I had only the impression of an odd assemblage of some kind: stiff tatters of cloth poking out of some shapeless mass that just about blotted out the view of the distant street. It was him, of course.

"Damn, old man," Joel said, laughing a little hollowly.

The crinkled face ran in a confusion of shifting and multiplying wrinkles, in the midst of which a mouth gaped in an obscene grin that revealed long staggering rows of blackened stumps that might once have been teeth. The breath that came out of that mouth was something you wouldn't want to smell twice, and the laugh that came out with it had a tone to it that you knew you'd wake up, some nights, and think about. "Skeer'd ye, did I?" The gurgling voice sounded like bubbles coming slowly up through a murky depth of phlegm, and I reflected on how mercifully seldom any of us had actually heard him speak.

As long as I could remember, he'd always worn the same clothes, or the remains of clothes anyway: on the outside, a shape that only a fairly active imagination could turn into an overcoat, then under that a remnant of a torn and incredibly dirty sweater that might originally have been one color, trailing off into another layer down, something that could have been a coarse shirt of some kind, so tattered and stiff with grime now that pieces of it stuck out like quills. Whether there was yet another garment or not, it was hard to say; half-beneath and mixed up with the shirt, if that's what it was, you could just make out a sort of gray film, like a layer of diseased skin, something that might have been the prehistoric remains of a T-shirt of necessarily enormous proportions. In places, this weird layering of ripped and shifting material blossomed out in ragged holes to offer a disturbing view of what you supposed had to be skin—but if it was, it was the most purulent excuse for skin that ever covered a human frame. A living human frame, anyway. Below the waist he had on a huge, shredded pair of pants stained with so many colors and odors that it could have been an artist's palette in some studio in hell. His bulbous head, surmounted by short, scruffy gray iron filings, sat upon the body itself like something that might have grown and festered there unnaturally, and needed to be lanced. A fat, mangy bird of a man, he leaned on a gnarled wooden cane and stared at us with dark, dark eyes. It was a picture that would stick in the mind, his standing there like that; he made a ponderous figure, and you knew that that cane had its work cut out for it. Since his girth just about filled the alleyway, making me feel all the more uneasy because there really wasn't much room to squeeze around him, I hoped that he would just move aside and let us pass. To say the least, he offended both the nose and the eye. If he had been a billboard, he would have been an advertisement for leprosy.

"What're you doing back here, Grampa Pus?" My words sounded a little silly to me, hanging in the air, reverberating faintly between the smoke-grimed brick walls. What did I mean, what was he doing back here? It seemed that he was always everywhere, always in unaccountable places, like some primordial thing that lived in darkness and made no excuses, offered no explanations. And in fact he offered none now.

This silence was what got Joel going. He leaned a little closer to the man, who stood poised on his cane as if ready to push himself off and shamble away somewhere. "Hey, you old fart, my friend asked you a question."

The old man just stood and stared, and the grin slowly crept back into his face, like a bloated spider returning to its web. He said nothing, and his eyes seemed to dare Joel to do something about it.

Joel was up to the challenge, or so he thought. "I *said*—" He punctuated the word with a little blow to the arm, which shifted the old man a little. But only a little. Joel looked a bit perplexed that the reaction was so slight. "I said my friend Gary here asked you—"

The grin on the wizened face creased out into something several notches more deranged-looking, and the old man dropped his cane, wobbling only a little on his unaided feet, and drew his filth-encrusted clothing open at the chest, widening his eyes and licking his crusty lips.

This gesture drew a curious little squeal from Lisa, who was favoring Grampa Pus with a wide-eyed expression that could easily have passed for frank sexual interest, incredibly enough. You have to understand, though, that I've seen her look at a water buffalo at the zoo pretty much the same way. I swear to God, Lisa could look at a lifeguard or a stack of old newspapers or a puddle of puke and get turned on—some sort of walking universal horniness, I guess. Not that any of us were authorities on the subject, because Lisa was a little older than us, and when it came right down to party time she usually ran with guys her own age. This definitely made me wish my mom had met my dad a little sooner. Yeah, hell, I guess I kind of had the hots for Lisa, as hopeless as I knew it was. A guy can still look, and she was an eyeful, for sure. Standing there in that alley with her lips painted a wet-looking peach and with her jean shorts cut off just about up to her waist and with her tits tied up in a gauzy little bandanna—well, let's put it this way, she didn't exactly look like a monument to virginity. From the look in her eyes, ogling Grampa Pus, she seemed ready to crawl into the sack with him, or crawl into wherever it was that such a creature might sleep in, and that struck me as pretty revolting. I mean, I do try to keep an open mind about things, but damn! There are limits.

Joel just snorted at the old man's exhibitionist antics. "What're you, some kinda *pre*-vert?" But the question tapered down in tone to something without any conviction behind it, because Joel was staring at the opening in the old man's clothes, and so was I.

There was something wrong here, really wrong.

We'd seen him on the streets countless times; we knew that his skin was mottled, unhealthy. But this—this was something else altogether.

Where the mounded meat of a corpulent old man's elephantine chest should have been, I could see only what looked like the surface of some loathsome stew left to crust over and spoil in the pot. In its semiliquid contours, the man's body was a kind of cheesy yellow-gray, like what you'd expect to find cratered in the middle of an ulceration, and as he shifted on his feet, what passed for his flesh seemed in the uncertain light to move like a groggy mudslide of clabber, with a faint, sticky sloshing that made me think of the sound that packing-fat makes in the can when you pull a ham out of it. These visual and aural impressions were so powerful that at first I wasn't conscious of the smell that had come out when the old man had opened his garments. My gag reflex had been aware of it, though, right along, and I had already put my hand to my mouth and squirted parallel jets of vomit between my fingers before I even knew I was doing it. I must instinctively have taken a step or two back, as well.

Joel had a stronger stomach, apparently, and was standing his ground. "All right, old man, now you listen up, I *said*—" For punctuation this time he pushed open-handed at the man's chest, something I wouldn't have thought he would do, all things considered. I think he tried to place his hand somewhere on the tattered cloth of the man's upper clothing, near the chest rather than on it, but he missed, and slammed his hand into that awful flesh, or whatever it was, with a sticky sort of *smack*. Square into the middle of it. The fingers sank right in, and when he pulled his hand back, stringy webs of goo came with it. For a moment, Joel looked like a puppetmaster with a particularly gross and repellent puppet dangling disproportionately at the ends of his jittering strings. But only for a moment, because Joel was off at a sprint then, negotiating the narrow strait between Grampa Pus and the brick wall on the old man's starboard side, and the last I saw of Joel that night was a vague skittering form down at the far end of the alley, making its escape out into the brighter light of the avenue.

That left Lisa and me. And of course Grampa Pus.

Of the three, I was clearly the redundant party. Or I sure hoped I was. Lisa was still looking at Grampa Pus with that we-really-ought-to-get-to-know-each-other kind of look, and Grampa Pus, I think, was giving the look back to her, though his eyes, afloat in that big beefy face, were so unfocused and so far apart that it was hard to tell. In any case he was rotating his body around to face her more squarely, like a hippo coming about in the water, and that's not a bad way to think of it, because the air almost seemed to thicken around him, due to the smell I guess, so that he was more swimming in it than anything else. I was just about ready to heave again, and I thought that maybe before I did that, I'd like to excuse myself from this delightful company and go home. Half of my mind told me that I shouldn't leave Lisa here alone with Grampa Pus, but the other half said: why worry yourself about it, look at her, she loves it, she wants to stay. So, kind of against my better judgment, I slipped around the old man and headed for the avenue, looking back only once to see Lisa and Grampa Pus still just standing there looking at each other. Maybe, I thought, that was all that would happen.

But I was barely back out on the street when my more reliable instincts started kicking in.

What was I thinking, back there? I should have dragged Lisa out of there kicking and screaming if necessary. I looked up and down the avenue, hoping to spot Joel, but he was nowhere to be seen. There wasn't much of anybody on the street at all, in fact.

I would have to go back into the alley alone.

I stood on the sidewalk for a minute thinking about that. Then I decided that I might not *have* a minute.

Or Lisa might not.

I was halfway back down the alley, getting beyond the pale wash of light from the avenue, before I realized that the moon had slipped behind some black, scudding clouds, leaving me to grope my way in near darkness. I put my hands out to feel my way along, running my knuckles into one brick wall or the other from time to time and correcting my course, until finally the moon came back out to cast a pale mushroom-colored radiance part way down the dirty walls, and I found that I had come farther than I thought, and stopped.

Lisa and Grampa Pus were here.

And evidently they had decided not to make do with worshipping each other from afar.

Yeah, astonishingly enough, they were starting to go at it. Lisa couldn't have needed much effort to get out of what little she'd been wearing, and she was on top. Any other arrangement, you understand, would have proven fatal to her. Grampa Pus hadn't bothered to disrobe, other than pulling his clothes a little more agape, and in any event those foul rags were shredded enough to provide plenty of free passage. Lisa, balanced on top of him, looked like a tiny, squirming little doll draped over a beach ball. He had his fat arms clasped around her like link sausages, and he was letting her do all the work. Watching from the shadows, I felt sure that her being more or less impaled on him up there was the only thing that kept her from sliding off and suffering a nasty drop onto the pavement. That the old man could function at all surprised me greatly. That she incited it, appalled me even more greatly. The whole enterprise made my stomach want to take another turn or two, just when it had been settling down. Certainly, any notion I might unconsciously have been nurturing of rescuing Lisa from her fate, of charging in and carrying her to freedom in a rush of youthful valor, was promptly abandoned. Lisa was plainly enjoying what she was doing, and was in no hurry to get rescued. My assessment of her sanity slipped a point or two, I have to confess, and this reflection seemed to add to an already growing sense of guilt—a feeling that I shouldn't be watching this, that it was her private business. Besides, watching it was making me sick, the way those puffy and scrofula-ridden arms were fastened onto her lovely, smooth, healthy flesh. Disgusted, I turned to go.

But stopped, because behind me, something more was happening. Something was changing.

When I looked again at the scene that I had been about to walk away from, it wasn't the same somehow. Grampa Pus, evidently in ecstasy down there on the paving stones, was grunting like a great obscene pig, but I realized that he had been doing that all along. What was different was the way Lisa looked, perched atop him in the visegrip of his pudgy arms, and I must have seen it starting to happen even as I had turned away.

He was pulling her into him.

I mean really *into* him, for Christ's sake.

She was bending, willowlike, under the crush of his armlock in the small of her back, and where the front of her body touched his vast, pustulent chest, she had already sunk in an inch or two. Whimpering now, she tried to pull back, and succeeded in arching up off him for a second, but the mucoid webs of slime that she brought up with her pulled her back down with a nauseating kind of snap, and he pressed her form deeper, deeper into himself, until only her backside was still unsubmerged. Gurgling, she seemed to crumple, then, under the unyielding press of his arms, sinking the rest of the way into him like some poor dumb animal sucked down in quicksand. The indeterminate tatters of his clothing, mixed up with flesh and other organic matter, seemed to part for a moment like weeds in swamp water, with her passage down, and then they rejoined themselves, leaving no trace of her. I must have been pulling at her, then pulling at the foul muck of his body where she had been, but I didn't realize that I had, at least not until I drew my hands back and brought stringy stuff with them.

I guess I ran then, but to this day I don't remember. All I remember is washing and washing and washing later that night in some public toilet, trying to get that feeling and that smell off my hands.

Lisa, naturally, was the talk of the neighborhood for a while, because she was missing, but everybody just assumed, finally, that she had gone off to shack up with some guy or other. I never tried very hard to disabuse anyone of this idea, because it made a much better explanation than the truth would have. I never even told Joel what I had seen happen, back there in the alley.

Grampa Pus was still around, as he always had been. Sometimes we saw him lolling on corners or in alleyways like a great gray slug, bloated and foul-smelling, smiling his unfathomable smile like some fat nightmare Buddha in a dream gone wrong. And one night I was walking through an alley alone and came around a bend in the wall and ran into him, and he pulled his upper garment apart, like that time before, and bared the curdled scum that should have been the meat of his chest, and in the wan light of the moon I saw something there that will haunt me forever.

It was as if the cheesy flesh had thickened and grown subtly darker in one spot, forming a sort of blemish shaped vaguely like the oval of a face.

I knew, of course, whose face it was.

She wasn't the first, for him, I'm sure, and wasn't even special to him in any way, but she was the most recent, and even in its vagueness the suggestion of a face had a terrible, tragic familiarity. About where the mouth would be, I could make out a disheartening suggestion of peach-colored lips, though the color ran and smeared into the surrounding medium, as if being further digested. Maybe this was why, for a moment, the lips seemed to move, seemed to open in a grimace, before dissolving forever in a riot of putrescence as Grampa Pus, wheezing and rolling in layers of heavy fat, waddled on off down the alley, taking her with him.

Gramma Grunt

Like Jason Mitchell's childhood itself, the apartment building was a bygone structure now, a relic, fallen away like a half-forgotten dream. Ah, but only half forgotten. He remembered many things about his far-off early years here, and like his memories, the old building itself was not gone beyond recall. Portions still stood, their ragged outlines marking the night sky like the battlements of some time-lost castle noble even in its ruin. Whether the place had ever really been noble, he couldn't say, but it had been home.

Strange, to be back here, back on the corner of Jespersen Avenue and Third Street, after all these years. Back here old and half-lame and wheezing from the walk across town. How long had it been since he cavorted, all bright young eyes and lusty lungs, with his friends on these streets, in this city? Sixty years? No—longer, oh God, appallingly long ago. The dirty sidewalk was empty now, yet the very air seemed charged with restless ghosts writhing awake in the echoes of his mind, a diaphanous crowd of milling reminiscences.

He'd been a "tough guy" then, an impoverished, streetwise kid feeling all the seasoning of his ten years. The gang that he'd hung out with had never gotten into any serious trouble; they had only presented, to the world, a face of impudence mirrored by kindred faces in ten thousand such bleak streets in a hundred such tired old cities, a collective face of prematurely world-weary urban youth with nothing in life's colorless, seemingly endless span to do.

Well—they did used to have *some* things to do, especially in those sultry days of summer when the schools disgorged them upon the streets. They had managed to keep busy enough.

They had tormented *her,* for one thing. Sometimes mercilessly.

Right down there, in that old alleyway between this building and the next (itself in ruins now too), to the left as you went away from the street corner—that old alleyway whose yawning entrance now the wan light of a rising late-October moon only half-heartedly tried to illumine. The old alley, where now a breath of night wind moaned through the crevices making a sound like a low, lonesome flute-note. In there, that's where she used to sit, a sorry mess of rags on a rotting wooden chair.

Gramma Grunt, they had called her, among themselves, and Gramma Grunt they had often called her, tauntingly, even to her face.

She was a witch.

Or so the smaller children had always said. Of course, the smaller children, younger brothers and sisters of Jason's and Hank's and Billy's and Tommy's and Lester's, would believe anything—that the Tooth Fairy really came in the night, that a grasshopper could spit tobacco in your eye, that if you went all the way up over the bar on the swings in the playground you would come back around turned inside out with all your tubes and shiny-wet organs hanging out for all to see. So no wonder they believed in witches, and believed they knew one. Gramma Grunt—no one knew, no one had ever known, her real name. No one knew where she slept—probably in some dank cellar. She was a rich vein of folklore around the neighborhood, to the little children and to some of the adults alike; seemingly, only Jason's own age-group, stridently all-wise and pubescent, were indifferent, unmoved, skeptical of the things said about the old woman.

Such as Jason's own mother's remark, one night, that she had seen her raise a thunderstorm by elevating her rag-tattered bony old arms and muttering, reaching for the scattered clouds and snorting like a pig and mouthing unintelligible imprecations at the sky. His mother and his Aunt Lucille had really believed that—that Gramma Grunt could raise a storm, and could do heaven only knew what else.

It was because she did grunt like a pig, anyway, that the kids called her Gramma Grunt, sometimes even prancing around her in the grimy alley and chanting *Gramma Grunt, Gramma Grunt, witchy-witchy Gramma Grunt.* Even though this would sound childish in the extreme to a passerby, Jason and his friends had been just big enough to make the shameful ritual a little threatening, something a little more than the cruel but harmless foolishness and caprice of children. When one of them would veer too close to the old woman where she sat in her incredibly filthy jumble of rags, or when one of them would venture to poke her in the arm, she would actually grunt like a wild boar: *Khhhnok! Khhhnok!* Her ancient lizard face, an incomprehensible nest of wrinkles, would contort like some nameless thing disturbed under a rock, and her arms in their mad fluttering tatters would flail like bird wings, and a vile yellow spittle would overflow her mouth, and she would curse the offender in hissing, gurgling syllables that no one could quite understand.

Tommy Fenton, nine years old and quarrelsome, had shoved her down in a puddle of rainwater in the alley one day, and she cursed him, and three days later Tommy Fenton, coming out of Fletcher's Market and dashing across Eighth Street, was run over by a garbage truck. It was a coincidence, of course, Jason knew, but it was the talk of the neighborhood for quite some time, and people didn't quickly forget the old woman's behavior toward the boy, provoked or not. Some heads nodded, some tongues clucked: yes, she *was* a witch.

Jason had had reason to ponder the question of witchcraft, if only to reject it, because shortly after Tommy's death, the boys were hounding Gramma Grunt one day and suddenly decided, like blackbirds taking to flight in unison, to leave her and scamper away on some other errand. Jason had been the last to turn away, and in that instant the old woman's eyes had met his, arresting his gaze with their feverish glow, and she had snorted: *Khhhnok, I'll—khhhnok—I'll get you someday.* That was ages ago, but he had never forgotten; she had clearly meant for him never to forget.

Pulling his coat collar tighter against the chill breeze that had come up, he hobbled now toward the old opening to the alley. Long ago, long ago, those memories, seen through the prism of so many intervening years. His father had gotten a better job and the family had moved away when Jason was barely eleven, and everything had changed: there were new friends, a suburban neighborhood, suburban schools, and later college, graduate school, a family, a career teaching English at the state college, retirement, his wife Nancy's death, the encroachment, on his own fragile being, of illness, purposelessness, and a lonely old age in which he felt, recently, more nearly able to trust his memory of the distant past than his memory, his fumbling grasp, of yesterday or last week. He didn't really have any clear recollection, for example, of getting the sudden urge he must have gotten to come here—here, the old neighborhood, the remembered street corner, the alleyway. What had he been doing when he felt that urge? He couldn't remember.

Over the years he had thought of Gramma Grunt from time to time, but had never, so far as he could recall, wanted to return to the place where he remembered her, and time had replaced his tough ten-year-old bravado, that audacious bravado anxious to repudiate all adult understanding and all folklore of younger sisters and brothers, replaced it with a more worldly and sophisticated skepticism.

In his youth there had been no witches because people younger or older believed there *were;* now there were no witches because—because there just *weren't;* any educated person knew that.

He stepped into the entrance to the alley, where just enough of the surrounding brick walls remained to make it still an alleyway, but where the pallid play of moonlight, though finding a path here and there through the crumbling walls, largely had to give way to a maw of darkness. But just within sight, at the edge of the pale reach of light, he saw—something.

A mound of rags.

And he smelled something in here, in the closer air of the passage, something undefinable but distinctly unpleasant.

He looked at the formless pile of dirty rags, and in some crazy way half expected it to move.

And it did.

It seemed to shudder and shift a little—on its own? Or had the wind subtly touched it?

He stepped closer, peered at the cloth tatters, and began to pull at them, near the top, with his fingers, shredding them away like the layers of an onion, until at length he thought, in the uncertain light, that the rags had begun to look different. He only slowly realized, then, that he was looking at an astonishingly ancient and wrinkled face, whose folds of sickly skin could scarcely be distinguished from the filth-choked tatters in which they were embedded. He thought it must be an illusion, this face, but an illusion would not have opened two baleful yellow eyes to stare at him.

It was unthinkable, preposterous—why, she had been exceedingly old *then,* when he was a boy! As if in sardonic response to this thought, a confusion of wrinkles beneath the eyes widened into a cruel smile, in which a crusty tongue ran snakelike over a staggered row of rotten teeth.

"You!" He was shocked at the horror in his own voice.

The smile creased out wider still. *Khhhnok!* In a way loathsome to see, the whole mass of rags convulsed with the piglike snort. When the voice came out, it was like the dry scuttering of spiders.

"I told you I'd get you someday."

He choked and spluttered, suddenly intensely angry. "You? Get me? I'm not a boy of ten any more, you know."

Khhhnnnnnnok! With the grunt, this time a sickeningly protracted sound from deep in the well of her throat, the creature lifted her arms, bony arms feathered in dirty rags, and in the same instant the sky rumbled with thunder.

"Huh!" He was furious now, though he had the feeling, in some corner of his mind, that his anger was an avoidance of some other emotion. "Don't give me that nonsense about raising a storm. You're not a witch. I never believed you were, even when I was a child."

"Then," the old woman croaked, "you were a fool. And are." She clenched her fingers, thin and angular like talons at the ends of her outstretched arms, and the thunder grumbled in the sky once more, longer and louder this time.

He laughed, though it sounded hollow to his ears. "Save your antics for someone more credulous. You can't raise a storm. You can't raise anything."

She drew her arms back in and glared at him, her face gloating and horrible with a smile that had nothing in it of mirth, and she spoke one more time.

"I raised *you,* didn't I?"

In that awful moment he remembered, he understood everything. He had only a few seconds to reflect, but in those fleeting seconds, with a black veil of clouds drawing across the face of the moon and with thunder reverberating through the alley and a cold rain starting to fall, he remembered the *beginning* of his walk across town, and he also pictured in his mind the scene that the police would find, if they ever entered this forgotten place: they would find an untenanted mound of dirt-encrusted rags and, in front of it, a fallen pile of less accountable debris. He was almost savoring the irony of it, the humor residing in the realization of where it was that she had raised him *from,* when—her spell no doubt having released him—his consciousness faded into grainy dissolution and the very contours of his face and limbs began to slide, amidst an exhalation of steam and an odor like rotten meat, cascading into a nightmare of bone and sinew and grave-sod on the rain-dampened ground.

Sheets

The room was piled waist-high with drifted snow. Or so she thought for a moment, standing at a loss in the gray gloom of the parlor. Why had she come in here? She seldom entered this room. Did she? Strange, that she couldn't remember. The real snow would be at the windows soon enough, with the advent of winter, the brittle-cold death of the year that would bring a muffled quiet too much like the tomb. But for now the drifts of snow, gathered here incongruously in the room with her, were bedsheets: pale lumpy shrouds covering a recumbent host of cadavers.

"Rebecca Hudson Payne," she said to the silence of the room, "you old fool. What in the world do you need in this room?" As if sensing themselves unimplicated in the question, the troupe of hunch-shouldered cadavers made no response.

They were, of course, nothing more than old furniture: a fossil table and chairs, two prehistoric sofas, an antediluvian coffeetable, various endtables predating all memory. Well, predating almost all memory, these ancient, dimly recalled relics from the time when Jonathan was alive.

The evil that men do . . .

It was an unbidden and unwelcome thought, stirring like a grub in her mind. She pushed it away, covered it with more wholesome thoughts, rather like pulling a bedsheet over old furniture that one would prefer no longer to behold. Trailing her faded nightgown, she stepped back across the worn and musty carpet and through the door to her bedroom, still wondering why she had entered the parlor in the first place, when everything about it made her uncomfortable.

The kitchen window over the sink looked out across the leafless remains of the orchard, where gnarled branches of fruit trees clutched purposelessly at a cold Vermont sky the color of slate. From over the horizon, frothy clouds ran up like dirty dishwater, choking out what little suggestion remained of sunlight. She thought she heard something on the roof like tentative first hints of sleet, or was it just the wind, or birds? Her hearing wasn't what it once was, nor was her eyesight. It wasn't fair, this retreating of the senses, at a time in life when one felt one needed them most. Sometimes she felt helpless, a frightened animal in a hole. If it weren't for that delivery boy from the market bringing her her groceries every week, how could she manage? Thank heaven the house was long since paid for. Jonathan, at least, had seen to such things as that, though he'd never missed a chance to remind her of her dependence on him.

Without me, you'd be in the poorhouse, little Miss Hudson. He had loved to call her Miss Hudson, as if the most grindingly belittling thing he could say to her were to deny her the status of being married to him. *I pay all the bills around here,* he would add. That was the good side of him, if one could imagine a good side: he did pay the bills. Faithfully, scrupulously, with a kind of disdain for anyone who would do less.

The evil that men do lives after them; the good is oft interred with their bones. . . .

Odd, that she could remember her Shakespeare when she could no longer remember many more immediate things. Was the house, then, if it represented his interred "good," even more of a tomb than it seemed? She resisted the thought. It might be lonely here, and almost morbidly quiet, but then had living with Jonathan Payne been better than being alone? She scarcely thought so.

I'm afraid of him, Mama. . . .

Madelyn. That was the trouble with children, they never came to see you when they were immersed in their own faraway lives. Madelyn must be—how old now? Rebecca tried to think. Jonathan had been gone eleven years. What year—the calendar on the side of the refrigerator—good heavens, could that be possible, could Madelyn be fifty-two?

Fifty-two and never married.

Unlike her younger brother Michael, who had children of his own in college now. But what good was it for her to have grandchildren, and soon great-grandchildren, no doubt—unimaginably distant little creatures whose faces were indistinct ghosts, misty half-imagined faces never seen.

Somehow, during these ruminations, she had made her slow way across the kitchen and into her bedroom and through the door into the parlor, without realizing where she was going, and once again she stood disoriented among pallid gray-white shapes in the gloomy interior, the eternally chilly room, disused and dead.

The room where Jonathan had died. And where—but no, she wouldn't think about that.

Such a little wash of sunlight made its feeble way in here that until she touched the light switch just inside the door, the humped and shrouded forms around here were things more felt than seen, and when the light came on, a crowd of shadows shuddered and retreated, but did not vanish altogether. Rather, they clustered, conspiratorial, in corners, massing behind white-sheeted shapes, mystery behind mystery. She peered around her at the silent sheets, and heard the wind rise suddenly and sharply, a sad little chorus of moaning at the windowpanes, and she felt the subtle pain again in her right forearm, the little ache she always felt when a cold front came in. It was a sardonic old friend, almost, this pain, still with her at times after all these years, reminding her that if nothing else she was still alive to feel it.

Without warning, the vision sprang before her eyes, the image of his face that night so many years ago, ruddy and belligerent at the door. Even now she could almost fancy she smelled the sour breath of whiskey blown in her face, could almost feel once again the familiar panic clutching her chest as he pushed through the screen door and she scrambled to stay out of his way. His mood would grow uglier as the night wore on, and the rest had been inevitable at some point, she supposed, clutching the forearm now, letting the pain subside. The bone had never set quite right.

She stood for some time in the parlor, until night came on and the cheerless windows admitted only gaping squares of darkness. Later, back in the kitchen, she heated her milk on the stove and tried not to remember.

But coming into the parlor always seemed to make her remember, and now she stood here chiding herself, again, for dwelling upon things that bothered her. At least daylight sometimes made the memories seem more distant, but again today—was it only last night that she was here?—again the day beyond the windowpanes grew sullen with clouds until the sky was like a great iron lid on the world, shutting out the warmth of the sun, and her mood darkened as if it were itself covered by clouds, or shrouded by dusty bedsheets. Maybe the comparison made sense, she thought, maybe my mind has come to be so much old furniture best put to rest.

Nonsense, she retorted: just because that's the way *he* made you feel, like—

Like a roach under my shoe, he snarled from somewhere inside her head. *That's about how much good you are to me most of the time, you know that?* His face would curl up into the usual sneer. *A little roach to step on.*

And he'd done his best to step on her, too, or step on her spirit anyway. The worst was the defiance, hurled like so much foulness at her, after she found out what had been happening. *So you know what you know. Don't do you no good, does it? You tell, and you know what'll happen.* He spoke to her now just as surely as if he stood there in the flesh.

Incredibly, after all these years, a hot tear brimmed over and found a path down her cheek when she thought of the outrage of it all.

I didn't want to do it, Mama. A thirteen-year-old face rose in her mind like a miserable phantom. *He said if I didn't—*

Damn him, damn him to hell, she thought, wiping at her face with the back of her hand and feeling the ache creep back into her arm. And damn the rest of them for never understanding. How many times altogether had he—? She knew what they all must have thought when she turned from his graveside and walked away without tears, without looking back. They thought she was ungrateful, cold, uncaring, unreasonable. People never saw a marriage from the inside, so what did they know? Madelyn knew, oh yes, but she, like Rebecca herself, had been afraid, and for good reason. Madelyn had come home for the funeral and had cried, and it was almost funny to reflect that no one else understood what those tears were really about.

The wind pressed a mouthful of cold breath onto the window-panes; the bedsheets, huddled around her in a clumsy circle, seemed to lift slightly, but it must only have been the uncertain light, for the room was perfectly still now, except for her own ragged breath. It wasn't good for her, being in here, and she wasn't coming in here any more. Ever.

*   *   *

But she did. The next day, or the day after that; it was hard to remember how much time had passed. Or to remember why she had come. She thought it had to do with something she had been thinking about, out in the kitchen, watching the bare branches of the fruit trees in the orchard bend and writhe in the gathering wind, a wind that brought petulant little suggestions of sleet to tap at the windows. Now she remembered.

As much as she had resisted the idea before, she thought now that if she uncovered some of the furniture and looked at it, she might dispel some of the memories that nagged at her, might find that in seeing *his* furniture again for what it was, simply a dusty and half-forgotten collection of old chairs and sofas and tables, she could stop being haunted by him, could dismiss him as easily as she could dismiss his unsightly, tasteless furniture, items that he and he alone had chosen, purchased, brought home. She had to gaze at it all now with the contempt that it deserved, and that he deserved. She had to be rid of the thought of him, because at times his memory reared itself with such force in her mind that she half thought she could feel it, palpable and breathing, in the air about her, as if he had never really left the house altogether. She remembered his habits all too well. In his sick mind he would often lie in wait for her, bide his time until the right moment, and step suddenly up from behind her with some reproach that left her trembling, if not bruised. To this day she cringed when the floorboards creaked by themselves, because she half thought, for a moment, that it was Jonathan. It was as if something of him still lived in the house. That was a tragic thought, and she had to banish it from her mind.

Well, his wretched furniture was what was left of him, for pity's sake, all that was left, and she would lift the sheets and look at it and know, finally, how foolish it all was, how truly dead and gone *he* was.

But when she took the corner of one pale bedsheet in her hand, one sheet covering a long, lumpy surface that could only have been a sofa, she found that she couldn't do it. Somehow, she couldn't lift the corner of the sheet to peer at the sofa, for as she started to do so, a sense of loathing overwhelmed her, and she dropped the sheet from her twitching hand and left the room. It was as if she had been about to look squarely into the face of his evil itself, and she just couldn't bring herself to do that.

The winter came slowly, relentlessly on with its short days gray and somber and devoid of warmth, until spatterings of snow were assaulting the windowpanes and the wind sounded like a dirge. God in heaven, why did no one ever come to see her, to cheer her up? Michael didn't live too far away to come, at least once in a while, but he probably hadn't been here half a dozen times since that day (four or five years ago, it must have been) when he had come in his truck to carry away—whatever it had been, she couldn't remember. Certainly, he had his wife and his children, but one would think that he could find time occasionally. Something about the thought of him disturbed her, now, and not just his failure to come visiting. Something else.

She found herself standing in the parlor again, with the sky growing opaque with snow beyond the windows and the wind playing among the angles of the house like the stops of some strange flute. The only other sound was the distant grumble of the furnace, down in the cellar, a dinosaur pushing its warm breath through the ducts, through the house. What was it that she couldn't quite—but a gust of wind interrupted her thought, and the lights went out.

She stood still in the dark, scarcely breathing, just listening, though she could not have said why. Around her the lightless room was perfectly silent.

And around her, she knew, the sheet-covered furniture stood in the dark like a company of quiet, patient goblins.

A sudden sense of blind panic seized her. Turning toward the door to the bedroom, she ran her arm into the door jamb and a sliver of pain ran through the old wound, and she found herself crying and feeling her way back out of the parlor and into the bedroom and then the kitchen, and fumbled in the cupboard for candles. When she finally had one lit, she sat at the kitchen table in the near-dark and calmed herself and watched the candle in its saucer in the middle of the table casting grotesque, jittering shadows around the room, and she tried to think what to do. The lights, the electricity—a power line was probably down somewhere, and she could do nothing about that. Maybe they'd get it fixed, but sometimes, she knew, it took many hours, or even days.

Meanwhile, the furnace had shut off, she realized now, and she hoped that the house would hold its warmth long enough for the power to come back on. Perhaps she only imagined that it was already getting colder in here, but in any case she got up and started moving about, to keep herself occupied and to keep warm. She fussed over the dishes, taking silverware from the drainer and putting it away in the drawer. She rummaged aimlessly among shadowy piles of papers and old magazines. She looked out the window into the night, where unseen trees must be muffling up in gray, dead snow. And at some point she found herself back in the parlor, holding her candle and looking about at the humpback silhouettes of the bedsheets, which seemed, in a surreal and unsettling way, to waver and shift in the candlelight.

The evil that men do lives after them. . . .

Could some essence of a person still—?

A blast of winter wind shook the windows in their sills, and as if her own frame had been shaken too she suddenly remembered.

Remembered what it was that Michael had carried away, that time, in his truck.

You don't use the stuff, Mama, and it just reminds you of—well, what I mean is, you don't need the stuff, and you don't like having it around, and Jenny and I can use it.

She had offered up no argument to that, but then it meant that nothing had been left on the parlor floor in here but the sheets that had covered Jonathan's furniture. It could only have been the ravages of age, these past years, that confused her enough to make her think that the sofas and chairs and tables were still under there.

And if they weren't, what *was?*

She had, in any event, little time to ponder the question, because now the movement in the room was not just an effect of the flickering candle. Merciful heaven, a man's evil really could live after him, could linger and grow and take shape—many shapes—and the most frightening thing was not that the sheets were beginning to slip aside and down, so that what was under them, emerging, could gather more closely around her. The most frightening thing was not even that the humped and dusky forms, phlegmatic and unyielding, were offering her no way out of the room.

No, the most frightening thing of all was the thought of how very long and how very quietly they had waited.

Up and About

Wade Mullins never intended to become a walking dead man.

Throughout a long, ordinary, and (one might even go so far as to say) prosaic life, Wade Mullins had in fact never given credence to things like the walking dead. It just wasn't part of his tidy, plain-vanilla, unadorned belief system. His was a straightforward world-view in which zombies were the stuff of cheap novels and badly dubbed movies from places like Italy and Mexico and Japan. For a tweedy businessman whose tastes in reading ranged from business journals to other business journals, and whose inclination with regard to motion pictures was to sleep through them as they flickered ghostlike on the television screen at some dreary hour of night—for a man who had outlived three wives and eighty Vermont winters, and all this without burdening his existence with any great excess of imagination, zombies were fantasy, and remarkably uninspired fantasy at that.

Yet here he was now, in a box in the ground, feeling obliged to wonder why the sweet oblivion of death had given over to unaccountable stirrings of consciousness. Simply put, if he was dead, then why the hell was he awake?

Some strange chemistry had gathered him back to the realm of the conscious in slow degrees, as if a nameless hand had fanned the black coals of his death into a dull smoldering of embers. At first he had felt only a vague, blank sentience, like a mirror with nothing to reflect; but gradually his senses, or a grainy parody of them, had come somewhat into focus. Just now he had opened his eyes, what was left of them anyway, upon velvety darkness. And as some crumbling remnant of his brain roused itself into something like life, he idly wondered how long he had been dead. All he knew for certain, at the moment, was that his mouth was full of maggots, and he summoned an access of energy and pursed the rotting contours of his lips and ejected most of the writhing contents of his oral cavity out onto the clean, freshly pressed front of his best suit, and waited.

What he was waiting for, he could scarcely have said. Nothing readily came to mind.

At some point, in any case, the waiting was over, because from infinitely far above, a sort of faint scratching sound made its way down through the soil, and after a few moments the sound grew into a definite impression. Someone up there was digging. Digging in the dirt. Digging him up.

Oddly, he felt no particular emotion. He simply waited, listening, and presently he heard and felt a shovel scraping dirt off the lid of the coffin, and felt himself, box and all, being lifted out of his hole onto level ground. Whoever they were, they sat him down with rather more of a jolt than he would have preferred, and he could hear their two voices whispering, laughing hoarsely.

"Sucker was rich," one of them said. "Gotta have a nice ring or a gold tie pin or something."

And suddenly the casket lid was pried open, and cold night air rushed in. His vision was blurry, but two faces floated into view above him, bobbing like soggy jack-o'-lanterns.

Quite innocent of any thoughts of frightening anyone, he sat up in the coffin and tried to speak, but all that came out was a kind of thick gurgle, and more maggots.

Someone was screaming, and then there were no more faces. There was only the cold, still night, and the ululation of a train whistle somewhere in the distance. Wade Mullins climbed slowly, totteringly out of his coffin and stood beside it, under the icy stars, and tried to think.

The act of standing up had shown him how really changed he was.

It was a bizarre, at first incomprehensible, set of impressions. It felt—his coarsened brain struggled to understand it—it felt as if he were falling. Gradually some corner of his awareness came to know that this was because his tissues were—well, settling. It was as if whatever vile fluids he possessed were shifting downward, smearing, running, puddling into the lower spaces of his cells, cells that must surely slough away in a gray torrent if he moved again. But when he took one unsteady step, then another, then another and another, he left no trail of corruption behind him on the autumn-withered grass. It seemed he was holding together somewhat better than he had thought he might. Whether in truth that was good or not, he was not prepared to decide.

Shuffling along the wan lanes of the graveyard, he suddenly felt that his burial clothes were intolerable to him, and loosening them with scabrous hands, he left them behind. When they fell to the ground, they came down with a kind of gelatinous squish. Now he saw that his corpse-body was not holding together with quite the cellular integrity he had imagined. The clothing had somewhat held him to- gether, apparently, and had kept him from seeing that his flesh, gray and worm-riddled, was slowly falling away in the night air. When the clothes had fallen, parts of himself had fallen with them.

But still he walked, and when he passed under the archway that marked the cemetery's entrance, the irony of the words emblazoned on the arch was not entirely lost on him, even now.

THE DEAD SHALL BE RAISED, it said.

The night was black, moonless, silent. The massive trees on his left and right as he proceeded were ragged shrouds of darkness against the sky, dark outlined against darker dark. Somewhere along the desolate road that wound its way back into the town, his decaying mind began turning over other thoughts, like restless grubs. Where was the farm his two grandsons Chet and Lester ran? It was on the way into town someplace, but he was disoriented, and it was so hopelessly dark that his surroundings weren't helping much. He was going the right way, though, he thought; the river was somewhere off to his right, lost in darkness. Maybe he could make his way to the farm. Of course Chet and Lester had never been too fond of him, even when he was alive, and they weren't going to be particularly glad to see him now, he strongly suspected. But what else could he do? Who else could he go to? At least they were family.

On the way, he remembered something.

Fragments of the memory swam together in his head. It was some- thing having to do with that time when he and Jenny had vacationed in New Orleans. What was it? Somewhere on the outskirts of the city, they had visited a—what was the man, really? A fortuneteller? A voo- doo priest? Jenny had believed in that kind of thing, but Wade thought it was all horsefeathers and nonsense, and had laughed in the man's face, calling him a—what was the word? It was hard now to remember—charlatan. That was it. But the charlatan had only smiled mysteriously and said, "Bless you, my friend. You will live forever."

Was that the truth of the matter, then? Was this what it was to live forever? He would be lucky to make it to the farm with enough of him intact to still be walking. He stopped in the road and stood for a long while, watching the pumpkin-face of a full moon rise above the shadowy trees. In the chalky moonlight now, his body, little more than a shambling, purulent mass of angular sinew, was an amazement to himself. Not a shock, exactly, just a surprise. Somehow he still must have been thinking of himself as looking more or less the way he always had. But how could he? He was dead, had been dead for some time.

Even as his febrile mind entertained this thought, he felt one of his eyes, liquid in its socket, begin to slide. For a few slow minutes the effects on his vision were remarkable, a sick kind of visual cascading sensation that gradually stabilized, more or less, because after a while the one mobile eye was off his face and lying at his feet, covered in dust like some fat, dead insect in the road.

But hobbling farther down the way, he could still see well enough out of the remaining eye to know that he had reached the entrance to the drive that led into his grandsons' farm. Turning here, he shuffled toward the distant farmhouse, not at all sure why he was doing so. He just didn't know what else to do. He hadn't planned on having to think about such things, hadn't planned on having to make any decisions ever again.

He recalled that the house was nearly a mile from the road, and beyond the house, another half mile, the river wound its way across the land. Dimly, he remembered fishing in that river, countless years ago. Now as he plodded up the road toward the house, the moon creeping higher behind him made his gaunt form cast a long, bony shadow out over the unpaved road, and in contemplating this shadow, he felt his senses gather a little more coherently, to the point where he thought he heard, even from here, the flow of the river—until he realized that the sound was the gurgling of his own seeping fluids resounding in his ears. When he shook his head, the gurgling became louder.

Bemused by this, he failed for some moments to notice another sound—the barking of dogs.

He strained to make out where they were, but couldn't see them. From the sound, though, he judged that they were close by, in the direction of the house—which he saw now, but only as a mass of darkness huddled on the dusty ground, lightless and silent.

He thought things over for a moment. Maybe no one was home.

But then the lights were coming on, one by one, as someone moved from room to room, no doubt in response to the snarling dogs, whose racket was now even more frenetic. As the light from the kitchen spilled out over the dooryard, Wade could see the dogs, four of them, tethered near the porch and lunging and barking insanely.

Even in his current state he well understood that his own approach was the cause of the canine turmoil, and he knew that he was in an awkward spot.

Brandishing a shotgun, his grandson Chet burst out through the kitchen door onto the porch. "All right, who's there?"

Even in this condition, Wade remembered that Chet had always had a pretty short fuse, with little tolerance of prowlers, and Wade knew that he had better make it known that despite his somewhat dubious appearance, he was Grandfather Mullins. Clearing a worm-clotted mass of phlegm from his throat, he gurgled, "Gan-wharrh." Damn. He didn't have enough of his lips left now to pronounce it.

Chet was coming down the rickety porch steps, shotgun at the ready, and peering out toward Wade. "What in God's name—?"

Wade tried again, gesticulating with bony, tattered hands. "Guh-HAN-wha-wur."

Chet's eyes were wide with astonishment, and his mouth fell open idiotically. "Holy—" He took a lurch backward, half stumbled on the porch steps, and made a very clumsy job of clambering back up onto the porch, yelling all the while.

"Lester? Lester! Get out here!" From inside the house, female voices were calling out, questioning. "Lester! Where the hell are you? I said get out here!"

Sensing that Chet's attention was divided, and sensing also that his own appearance was the cause of some consternation, Wade began moving past the house, careful to stay out of range of the dogs—who, however, had ceased barking and were howling and whining pitiably. Wade never had gotten along very well with animals. He made his way around to the back of the house and headed toward the river, not at all sure if there was any real purpose in going there. But where else was there to go? His reception at the house would probably have been less than gratifying if he had stayed around to find out. Chet and Lester were bread-and-butter sorts of fellows, very sympathetic toward farming and the good rural life, very little inclined to be understanding, he felt sure, when the walking dead came to call. One had to face the fact that on a well-run farm, zombies were superfluous. And unlike himself at the moment, Chet and Lester had solid backbones. The dogs might be cowed by the sight they had seen, and the nameless smells they had sniffed on the night air, but Chet and Lester, however repelled at first, were going to be up to the task at hand, he was afraid.

Putting distance between himself and the house seemed, to what was left of his cerebral matter, like a better idea as the moments tripped past.

By the time Wade was within sight of the burbling black waters, there were voices and footfalls behind him. Half turning, he made out that both Chet and Lester, dimly silhouetted against the lights from the house, were running through the darkness toward him. Both his grandsons, now, were coming to see Gan-wharrh, and both were carrying shotguns.

He faced them in time to see Lester's face become a mask of revulsion. "Jesus," he said, almost in a whisper, staring at Wade. "Jesus our Lord." The grandsons looked at each other, and some wordless understanding seemed to pass between them.

"Yeah," Chet said, "I don't know where this walking pile of garbage came from, but there ain't going to be no nights like this. Not on the Mullins farm. Not now, not ever."

"Damn straight," Lester said, and both shotguns erupted in a blaze of fire.

At first Wade's sense of what had happened to him was unclear, but in a moment he realized that his head, or what was left of it, had been severed from the rotten bulk of his body, and his body itself had fallen in two separate wriggling pieces. The grandsons, evidently reloading, fired again, and again and again, fragmenting and scattering him. The head fell into the river, but not before it saw the grandsons kicking the rest of the pieces into the water as well. The pieces big enough for them to see in the near-dark, anyway. It took them several tries.

And as he floated down the river, here the head, there the lower right leg, there the ribcage, there and there and there other pieces, and others still, some dim corner of his awareness thought again of the voodoo priest in New Orleans, and of what the holy man had said: "You will live forever."

And indeed Wade knew that he would, after all. Here a scrap of putrescent liver, there a brittle shard of bone, there an ear, there a scrap of fingernail, one piece or another would fetch up among the river-bottom weeds, or wash up on the riverbank, perhaps a tooth to be silted over in the brackish ooze, perhaps a shred of skin to find lodgment in the lining of a bird's nest, perhaps a jellylike wad of flesh to be trodden upon by some fisherman and to stick like gum to the sole of his shoe—here a piece, there another, and by some supernal alchemy, every piece quite aware of every other, just like that eye back there in the road that was blinking its way back to dusty vision even now. And so life would go on, after a fashion.

No doubt about it, though—forever was going to be a long time.

Blessed Event

Catherine Wilkes wondered, at times, whether it was worth it any more, being landlady here. This was a sad contemplation to have to undertake, at her age. It wasn't that she had any complaints about her old and trusted tenants, certainly. But this new one, this Lucy Hutchins—now, that was another matter altogether, and as time went on there would be more and more people like Lucy Hutchins, and she didn't think she could stand that. She felt as if right here in this two-story brownstone-front citadel on the corner of Blackwood Avenue and Ninth Street, her old walls had stood firm against encroachments from that nasty enemy, the outside world. She felt as if she had succeeded, all these many, many years—to some extent anyway—succeeded in stopping time, in letting the mellow past live on, right here among her tenants, her old acquaintances, people whom one could respect, people whom one could even love, unlike those vulgar and incomprehensible young barbarians so rapidly filling up the world out there beyond the walls, out in those squalid streets. No, she wasn't going to be able to stand it, if there were going to be many more like this Lucy Hutchins.

Out in the front hall, the great oaken door had breezed open and slammed shut; here the miserable creature came now. Opening her own door a crack, Catherine watched the young woman start up the stairs, and she felt the same revulsion as before. What was happening to the world? Why were there people like this? Lucy Hutchins had stringy mouse-brown hair that must never have been washed or combed, hair that ran wriggling down her back now like a filthy mop. Her faded jeans were practically in tatters, her oversized sweater sloppy, dirty, repellent; her jacket actually had faint rings of grease about the sleeves. Even a person without much money, Catherine reflected, could keep clean. She was altogether unpleasant to look at. In all fairness to the poor girl, with her flaring horse-face nostrils and her

195

great watery eyes too far apart, she couldn't help being unattractive, of course, but it was more than that; her pallid skin was blotchy, pustulent, decidedly unhealthy-looking, and she was in fact sneezing and snorting as she ascended the dimly lit stairs. Didn't she know, or care, that there were older folks here, people who caught colds easily? Imagine, scattering germs around like that, without a trace of remorse. That was the trouble with people nowadays. No consideration for others.

Mercifully, the girl was soon up the stairwell and gone, out of sight. Catherine sighed and closed her door. It had been so nice and cosy here all these years with her old tenants, all of them well past retirement age, all of them of that bygone era when people were educated and well-mannered and decent—Charles and Helen Ames across the hall here, Sam and Gloria Saunders in the back apartment on the left, Shirley Harris in the back apartment on the right; upstairs, Ronald and Rebecca Blake above Charles and Helen, Gerald Phillips above Sam and Gloria, the Williamson sisters Marcia and Beverly above Shirley Harris.

And, until recently, Elizabeth Tate above Catherine's own apartment.

But poor old Elizabeth was in a nursing home now, and for the first time in over twenty years an apartment in this house had become empty and a cardboard For Rent sign had hung in the front window. And, unhappily enough, Elizabeth's rooms had rented not to some nice retired couple or elderly single woman or quaint old bachelor, but to Lucy Hutchins, whose pouty lips always sprouted foul-smelling cigarettes, and in whose muddled eyes there shone no intelligence, no personality.

Catherine shuddered to think of her most recent encounter with the girl. They had met on the stairs, the girl on the way up, Catherine on the way down, and the girl, as young as she was, had been breathing a little hard from climbing; seeming to sense Catherine's wonder at this, she had flashed a vacuous smile and tossed her dirty hair and said, "I'm going to have a baby, you know." Well, no, Catherine hadn't known. How could she have known? The girl was not visibly pregnant. (Now, there was a word people used cavalierly nowadays; when Catherine was young, the expression would have been that one was "with child.") In any case, the girl had gone on up the stairs, puffing and sniffling, leaving Catherine to reflect that it figured, in this changed world: to be unmarried, to be pregnant, to be unconcerned that one was unmarried and pregnant. Remembering this now, Catherine sighed anew and wondered if she herself belonged in the world any more.

Oh well, yes, the girl had a man of sorts, there was a boyfriend—Catherine had glimpsed him from time to time around the place—but the thought of him imparted little comfort. She refused to dwell on him just now; she drank her glass of warm milk, took her pills, and went to bed.

She had just finished washing her dinner dishes the next evening and switched a lamp on and started to pull the shades down in the front parlor when, looking out across the little yard wedged between the building and the street, she saw the shadowy outline of Lucy Hutchins sitting on one of the lawn chairs there, and someone else sitting beside her on the late-autumn remnants of grass. Even in the uncertain light of a streetlamp trying feebly to come on, it was evident that the girl's companion was the male friend, whom Catherine had heard her address as Jack. There was something indefinably but definitely unsavory about him. At times Catherine thought that he didn't look quite normal—even, however preposterous this was, that he didn't look quite human. He was a squat, shapeless, swarthy sort of fellow with dark, brooding eyes, an oily-looking moustache above a thin line of cruel-looking mouth, a tumble of gray-black unkempt hair; he was obviously quite a bit older than his girlfriend and seemed, in his mannerisms, to treat her with a certain coldness, though she seemed, in her own mannerisms, to be devoted to him. Catherine pulled the shades down, occluding them from view, and somewhat later she could hear the two of them clumping up the stairs to Miss Hutchins's apartment.

Before long, there were obscure sounds filtering down through the ceiling, and Catherine, sitting on her sofa with a volume of Thackeray, drew her legs up under her and tried to concentrate on her reading, but it was no use; try as she might, she couldn't help thinking of what they must be doing up there. Right up there, so brazenly, in her own building, under her own roof!

That was bad enough, but what was worse was that the sounds up there were somehow not normal, not typical. Catherine Anne Wilkes might be seventy-eight years old, a widow of eighteen years, and a proper sort of person, she hoped, but she was not so naïve as to be unacquainted with—with *those* sounds, the sounds people ordinarily made, like the sounds people had made in the next room at that hotel where she had accompanied Henry to the convention the year before he died. But these sounds, these sounds were—different.

It was disquieting, the man grunting in guttural animal sounds, and the girl, the girl all the time sniffing, snuffling, like some diseased waif. Heaven only knew what diseases these people might indeed have. And hadn't the girl said that she was already pregnant? Already pregnant, and the two of them were continuing to—but she didn't want to think about it.

As October shaded off into a gray-domed November and the world began to crawl into its winter shroud, with occasional early snow flurries swirling about under the streetlamps, Lucy Hutchins seemed to be in increasingly wretched health, to the point where Catherine, covertly watching her, wished more and more that she could simply ask her to leave; several of the older tenants were getting coughs and sore throats, and though it might have been just the season, it was more likely the Hutchins girl's fault. Here she came now down the stairs, wheezing and snuffling as if her whole head were congested beyond belief, and sneezing into the air around her without covering her mouth; it was disgusting, it was uncouth. Just as she got to the bottom of the stairs she inhaled mightily, or tried to, through her congestion, and drew out a soiled rag and blew her nose into it with a gurgle that nearly made Catherine sick; the girl looked at the rag and stuffed it away and headed on out the front door, still sniffing and hacking noisily as she disappeared into the night. Later she was back with her peculiar companion Jack, and they went upstairs.

The sounds they made, though indistinct through the ceiling, grew ever worse in their vague abnormality; while the man grunted noxiously, the girl at times seemed to be moaning through the blockage of her head congestion, so that her liquid voice came out thickly muffled, like someone crying out underwater. Every night it was worse, and when the girl and the boyfriend would descend the stairs and Catherine would hazard a sly look through her door, the girl's face would increasingly be bloated, reddened, swollen as if in some terrible allergic trauma; clearly she was not well, but all her actions seemed to be consumed in fawning over the evil-visaged Jack, who treated her more clearly with disdain as time went on. Jack would leave, and Lucy—now Catherine felt almost sorry for the wretched girl in spite of herself, and didn't think of her simply as "Miss Hutchins" any more, though she still felt a certain repugnance toward her—Lucy would turn and climb the stairs, snuffling, coughing her terrible long thick coughs, blowing her nose endlessly as she disappeared up the stairwell. Catherine would hear her up there gasping and gurgling well into the night. She was going to have to say something; the girl was not well, this could not go on.

It was especially unthinkable for her to remain silent when her other tenants were beginning to make inquiries and comments. Old Gerald Phillips from upstairs drew her aside one morning on the staircase, where they were confidential together in a huddled exchange of whispers. Gerald's gaunt face looked downright grave as he leaned close to her and said, "It's getting to be awful, the way those two carry on, and then that girl up all night trying to get her breath; I can hear it all as plain as day, right through the wall. Marcia and Beverly say it keeps them awake, and they're on the opposite corner. You can imagine what it's like for me. What's wrong with her, for God's sakes? She sounds as if she's dying."

Well, that was it. Catherine met Lucy in the hall one morning and let the words flow, before she lost her nerve; the girl's face was becoming sickening to look at, the nostrils torn wide and visibly clogged, the eyes seemingly pushed farther apart by the gray congestion that had swollen and reddened the girl's pallid face. Catherine took all this in with a glance, and spoke up. "I don't mean to pry, Lucy, but I can't help noticing that you seem to be ill. You must have a terrible head cold or—or something. Are you taking any medication?"

It was as if this thought struck the girl as unspeakably funny, but she did not laugh outright, and the look that she gave Catherine was not unkind. She merely swallowed a sort of choked-off sound that might have been a carefree laugh gone awry, and shook her head. "I'll be all right. I just have to clear it all out." Even as she spoke, she was daubing at her nose, where a twin effluvium of gray phlegm was threatening to come forth. She took a deep, raspy breath through her mouth. "Just have to clear it all out."

"But that's what I mean," Catherine persisted. "There are decongestants that would help."

The girl shook her head again, angling away to draw the conversation up short. "It'll be all right." And she climbed the stairs—a bit falteringly, Catherine thought—all the time clearing her throat, hacking, blowing her nose over and over and over. "Oh yes, it will be all right," Catherine said to herself, turning back toward her door. "Well, it doesn't sound all right to me."

As November crawled by, the girl got steadily worse, coughing and spluttering in her rooms, passing through the halls in fits of hacking, blowing and blowing her great swollen nose until her face was a ghastly gray-red and she was moaning in waves of ululant misery, bringing other tenants timidly to their doors to peek out at her. And though the visits from Jack continued, he seemed to be doing nothing, so far as one could see, to help her. Catherine, wondering what kind of brute he was, listened for the old nocturnal sounds, but could now hear only the incessant blowing and sneezing and coughing, all so intensified now that one might actually fear for the poor girl's life; couldn't a person have a heart attack, going on like that all the time? Catherine had a dismal sense that something was going to happen, sooner or later, something most unpleasant.

And it happened, all right, during the first week of December, on a night when the sky was a great iron lid over the city and a light snow was beginning to fall. Catherine had had her dinner, washed up the dishes, and was settling down in a warm cone of lamplight on her sofa to read, when she heard some sort of commotion outside. Not outside the building, but outside her door, in the front hall, or the stairwell. Putting her book aside, she went to the door, opened it, and leaned out into the hall to see what was going on.

The girl's companion Jack was just coming in the front door from the street, sluggishly wiping snow from his hair and face, but that was not where the noise was coming from. It was coming from far up in the stairwell, where now Catherine could hear someone descending. There was no doubt who it was—the poor creature stumbling down the stairs was in a veritable spewing fit of gasping and gurgling, and it was all too clear that she was scarcely able to breathe at all. But through the terrible thickness of her congested head she did send one murky-liquid utterance down the stairs ahead of her:

"Jack? Jack? It's time."

Time? Catherine thought. Time for what? Surely she couldn't mean—

But she had no more time herself to ponder the question, because Lucy had reached the bottom of the stairs and swaggered out into the front hallway, wheezing and spluttering, dragging great agonized breaths in through her mouth and blowing her nose over and over into a large towel. Catherine's mind dimly registered that at Lucy's arrival in the downstairs hall, Jack had smiled strangely and gone back out the door to the street, leaving the door open a crack so that a thin swirl of snow came in on the wind. But Catherine would only later remember noticing any of this, or edging out of her apartment door into the hall. She would only later remember noticing that other tenants were looking on, aghast; Helen Ames was peering out from a crack in her door, and some others—Catherine thought it was Sam Saunders and Shirley Harris from the back apartments—were standing and staring from shadowy recesses down the hall. She would recall these things later, but for right now Catherine's own attention riveted itself upon the hapless girl in the hall before her.

Lucy's bloody nostrils were now so swollen as actually to have torn away the tissue separating them, so that one unthinkable cavity opened like a ghastly crater or ulceration in her bloated face. Gagging, gasping for breath, she blew and blew into the towel, and sucked air in through her mouth, and blew again, and sucked air in, and blew and blew again, her face almost purple by now, and at length she fell heavily to the floor and rolled onto her back, jittering her fingers spasmodically about her face. Some corner of Catherine's mind heard a miserable, keening cry, and didn't know whether it was Lucy's or her own, and didn't bother to try to figure it out, for what was happening now prohibited thinking about anything else at all.

A great clot of some chokingly thick substance was emerging from the one gaping nostril in Lucy's face, a hideous plug of pinkish-gray mucoid matter sliding sluggishly forth, tearing the nostril wider open, almost wider than the face itself that held it. With a sudden lurch and rip, the substance boiled up and came farther out, still hanging partly in, partly out of the face, and Lucy's now strident screaming choked itself off to a thick gurgle, for something was sticking out of her throat, too. Something like a tiny arm.

Catherine, too shocked even to turn away, began to understand. Dear God, was part of that mass hanging out of Lucy's face the other arm, and was that other part, the large part twisting and writhing through its integument of phlegm, supposed to be a head?

But the thing itself answered all these questions, pulling the rest of itself up and out of what was left of Lucy's throat and face. Lucy herself did not move any more, and the little angular pink and gray mass swiveled a sort of face toward Catherine and gave her one inscrutable look out of its dreadful little eyes before loping to the door, nudging it open, and going out to play.

The Cryptogram

Settled comfortably into the worn and faded old chair that so well knew his shape, Alex lit his pipe and glanced quickly over the editorials, the folded his *Cumberland Mirror* back to the amusements page. The pipe smoke eddied in soft gray patterns in the warm cone of yellow light from his lamp, and he felt cosily ensconced there, all the more so with the night wind outside brushing the windowpanes with pattering strokes of chilly rain. The Freudians, he vaguely reflected, would deem his snug comfort an unconscious desire to return to the womb or some such, no doubt; but then who asked them?

Smiling to himself, he let his eyes travel down the familiar layers of comic strip panels. Had any one of the strips been missing or out of order, he would instantly have known; he was, he supposed, very much a creature of habit.

That evidently was some of what Dinah, on the sofa in her own island of lamplight across from him with her magazines, managed to love in him, and certainly some of what he loved in her. Nowadays to have been married thirty-five years to the same spouse was something of a rarity, and you didn't have this kind of marriage, placid and secure, unless you accepted each other for what you both were, finding even in one another's foibles a kind of gentle commonality of spirit. Dinah was in many ways very predictable; at this moment, without looking, he could have told you the names of the half-dozen magazines stacked in her lap, for they would always be the same half-dozen magazines. She was in her own little world with them, as he was in his, and the nice thing was that, even so, they were together, the private little domains subtly intertwined by long-standing knowledge of each other's habits.

As he went through his accustomed pattern with the amusements page, he knew that she knew, in some quiet corner of her mind, just what he was doing, what he always did. The pattern: scan the comic strips, then move on to the crossword puzzle.

But, as always, not without a glance at the cryptogram on the way by. The evening *Mirror* ran one in every issue. He never attempted to solve it, just looked at it and went on. Tonight it had as formidable an appearance as ever:

MBYJY RL TCMBRTE RT MBY QCJHK
MBFM NFTTCM DJCPY MC UY F KCCJ MC
OTSTCQT JYERCTL.

With the usual little explanation of how a cryptogram is formed by substituting letters for other letters: maybe S for A, maybe K for B, et cetera.

It wasn't, he felt, intellectual cowardice that caused him every night to pass over the cryptogram with only a wistful glance, and go on to the crossword puzzle. It was merely a question of what one knew how to do and what one didn't know how to do. If you knew how to swim, you swam; if you didn't, you occupied yourself with something you did know how to do. Now, in the crosswords he would be in his element—he knew his European rivers, his Hebrew letter-names, his "comb. forms" as well as anybody who ever wielded an eraser, by God. But the cryptogram always struck him as an impenetrable barrier; how would one even begin? Passing over the enigma always reminded him of a mysterious old battered wooden door he used to walk past every morning when he was a kid on his way to school. He had always rather tingled to know what was on the other side, but whatever it was, it wasn't for him; it was always locked, and he always walked on.

Shifting his pipe in his mouth, he started to attack the crossword puzzle, but for some reason stopped. If you didn't know how to swim . . .

Maybe you tried to learn.

He looked back at the cryptogram, rather surprised at himself. Well, after all, he wasn't a total idiot, and if they put these things in the paper, it must be possible for people to solve them. Right? More a question of overcoming laziness than anything else.

He stared at the nonsensical tableau of letters, and at first felt helpless, felt as if he were looking at the sort of jumble a child's alphabet blocks might present, spilled on the floor, only there were too many weird letters, J and Q and the like all over the place. But—

There was a one-letter word. Wouldn't that be "a"? Well, maybe "I." His pencil hovered, uncertain. What about the little word MBY—couldn't that possibly be "the"? Well, hell, there must be hundreds of other—but wait, if MBY were "the," wouldn't MBYJY be "there," or "these"?

"Ha!" With a vigorous puff of smoke, he pencilled in "the" over MBY, and "there is" over MBYJY RL.

"Did you say something, dear?" Dinah was looking up at him over her bifocals, a magazine page half turned.

"Ah, no. I mean, did I?"

She smiled indulgently. "Well, I thought you did. The crossword must be an interesting one tonight."

He shook his head, scattering bright swirls of pipe smoke. "No, I'm solving the cryptogram."

"Oh." She looked surprised at this break in the eternal routine. "Well, good luck, dear." She went back to her magazine.

And he to his adventure. If M was "t" and B was "h," then MBFM was—"that." And the one-letter word was "a" after all. The pencil darted like a predator through the cryptogram, filling in the known letters. Outside, the wind heightened, as if in parallel with his own excitement, and dashed more rain against the darkened windows; the sound seemed to enclose him, to wrap him more insularly in his yellow wash of smoky lamplight, where he concentrated on the display of letters before him. It might seem no big thing, he mused, scanning the cryptogram for further clues, but to him—ah. MC had to be "to," and he had another new letter.

Odd, he reflected; this was an opaque barrier to me before, but now—now it's like a thin membrane stretching ever thinner, letting me slip through. RT had to be "in," and the third word TCMBRTE had to be "nothing." He was *doing* it, by damn, getting through the barrier. At some point he thought Dinah had said something to him, but by the time he glanced up she had left the room. The pencil scratched and scribbled faster, filling in new letters; whole new words began to take form. As he stared at the newspaper page, the metaphor of the thinning barrier seemed at moments to become physical fact; it was as if he were literally looking at a membranous portal, and becoming embedded in it, and slipping through. There—now the last of it was clear.

There is nothing in the world—

The wind at the window seemed to muffle itself, to grow distant in his ears.

—that cannot prove to be—

The lamplight grew grainy and dim, and his eyes saw only the words.

—a door—

His senses narrowed to this one sensation, this incredible sensation of passing through.

—to unknown regions.

Dinah sat in the bedroom combing out her hair before the mirror. Dear fragile soul, she thought, smiling. Dear Alex, so excited over a little—but then it wasn't so little a thing, was it? Alex was a man who had his routine, knew his boundaries, and so seldom struck out in any new direction that this must be quite pleasing for him, a veritable triumph. He hadn't even looked up when she said she was going to get ready for bed. But then he was always—

A figure came to fill the doorway in the mirror, and she turned to face him.

"Alex, darling, did you—"

She stopped, comb in hand, staring at him where he stood illumined by the peripheral glow of the bedside lamp. She knew every tiniest detail of him, every slightest nuance of being, right down to that little red birthmark on his finger, that characteristic way he cocked his head before speaking, that funny cowlick behind his left ear.

And in some deep and incomprehensible way, with an icy little clutch of fear beginning to spread up her spine, she knew that this was not her husband, even before he stepped closer and began to speak.

"KRTFB, QBFM'L QJCTE? QBYJY FI R?"

She stared at him wide-eyed, dropping her comb, her mouth open and ready to scream. He gesticulated wildly with his hands, his face bright with his own alarm.

"WCO'JY TCM KRTFB!"

She did scream then, long and loud.

As did that other poor woman, alike faced with a stranger mouthing what was gibberish to her, worlds away on the other side.

Leaves

Furry goblins were rolling down the hill.

Or so Jonathan Wells thought, anyway, until he had walked closer, nosing his cane among the fugitive leaves on the path, scattering them like rodents. Funny, that in all these years he had never ventured this far into the park before. Usually he came only a short way in from the avenue, stopping at the nearer benches with his newspaper. Today, though, with the late October sky the color of slate and the sun only a pale red memory in the west, he had passed up all the usual stopping places, for no particular reason, even though he was very tired and was more than ready to sit down, and he had followed the walk deeper into the park's oak- and maple-guarded reaches, coming now to a gradual rightward bend in the path, which led off, then, to unknown regions.

Just short of the bend, on the left a few feet off the walkway, a solitary park bench squatted with its dull iron feet nestled in the leaves. Behind the bench and a little to the left, a great waist-high mound of earthy-smelling leaves moldered at the base of the long hill that sloped gently down to the pathway, its grassy contour rusty with fallen leaves, its top crowned with trees blasted nearly bare against the darkened sky.

Furry goblins, he had thought, but now he saw that the fur was tatters, and that the tatters were leaves plastered upon the goblins, and that the goblins were children rolling down the hill, squealing, calling to each other, smothering themselves in damp, clinging leaves as they tumbled down. Watching them for only a moment, Jonathan angled off the walk and sat down on the bench and unfolded his paper; there wouldn't be much light left, and he wanted at least to glance at the editorials. Glad to be able to rest, he settled himself, pulling his coat collar snug against his throat and adjusting his glasses. He started to read.

But the boisterous activity behind him was distracting, and after a while he folded his paper back up, fished his pipe out of his coat pocket, tamped tobacco into the bowl and lit it, and turned half around on the bench to watch the children again, not annoyed at their clamorous play so much as simply curious.

There must have been at least ten or twelve of them, maybe more, but they were never nearly enough stationary for him to count them. Down the hill they came in groups, rolling in maple and oak and elm leaves just damp enough to stick to grimy clothes and urchin faces. As some of them descended, others labored back up the hill, panting and shouting hoarsely, only to descend again. Here came one particularly pudgy little form now, rolling and fattening like a snowball, gathering funky leaves to himself as he came whirling down. By the time he lolled on the level ground near Jonathan's bench, the child prickled with leaves like a porcupine fat with quills, and only some of them shook off when he pushed himself up onto his feet and headed back up the slope. But surprisingly, on his way past, he stopped by the park bench and fixed Jonathan with a curious look, two dark eyes peering out from an integument of grime. Gradually the grime opened into a mouth, and the mouth said: "Watch us." And the little figure scampered off to puff and groan its slow way back up the leaf-strewn hill. Now that he thought about it, Jonathan wasn't even sure whether the child was a boy or a girl.

It was odd, this game of rolling down the hill, rolling in the leaves. It was seemingly pointless, but they did it with a kind of avidity that one might have expected from an activity more structured—from a real game, perhaps, a game with rules and with some tangible goal. But then there was often no accounting for the enthusiasms of youth, no rational explanations, and none needed, maybe. Was he so old that he honestly couldn't remember the often formless and purposeless delights of childhood? Sometimes he felt so, but not quite, not entirely. Somewhere in his brittle frame, crusted over with layers of time, faint embers of memory still glowed, and he had not forgotten altogether.

Still, there was something vaguely odd about all this, he thought, watching the evening gather like moss about these children as they tramped up the hill while others came down, or cascaded down the hill while others went struggling up. The scene gave him an unplaceable feeling, somehow, an ineffable sense of strangeness, of the sort that one might feel when looking at an abstract painting and finding it nearly coherent yet elusive, taunting, hard to pin down. It was a scene that wavered between meaning nothing at all and meaning something diffuse and incomprehensible, something too deep, perhaps, for words.

Neglected, his pipe had gone out, and he relit it and sent an eddy of curling gray smoke out on the air, where it capered briefly with the failing light and fled into obscurity. It would be dark very soon, and he really ought to be going home. But home was a cold, empty apartment, and somehow he felt settled here, ensconced on his bench, his coat wrapped tight against the increasing chill, his pipe a warm glow in his hand, his mind bemused by the children, who showed no signs of ceasing their play even in the deepening gloom.

Here came several of them now, plump bundles barreling down the hill, gathering leaves to themselves as they came, sprawling on the ground, writhing, wheezing, regaining their balance, trundling back up the shadowy slope as others came down. But again one of them—the same one? a different one?—stopped in front of the bench and squinted out at him through a moist plastering of leaves that stuck to his face—her face?—like strange aquatic parasites. The covering of leaves was thicker than before, and the eyes, dark and intense, riveted him with a look of entreaty and, as before, the mouth creased open and the hoarse voice croaked out: "Watch us." Then the gnomelike figure was up the hill, following the others.

But this time something seemed to be different. The light was nearly gone and Jonathan couldn't see too clearly, but it appeared to him that his little visitor (scarcely more than a ragged shape) paused on the way past the mound of leaves at the base of the hill and pulled loose a large chunk of leafy compost and dragged it up the slope. But it could only have been the confusion of the failing light that made it seem so, for he saw now, or thought he saw, that what he had supposed to be a thick clump of leaves was really another child, thumping up the hill with its companion as others came rolling down past them.

And now Jonathan's confused impressions reasserted themselves, as two or three of the figures who were starting back up the hill lingered beside the tumulus of leaves long enough to pull armloads of thickly matted leaves off the pile, before ascending the hill once more. But again it seemed to him then that these burdens were really other children, which their playmates pulled along up the slope like grotesque dolls.

More and more, the earthy-smelling mound of leaves grew vague in shape and size, its ragged contours blurred, its details indistinct in the near dark. At times it was more or less its original size, a tenebrous mass huddled to earth like some great torpid beast. But at times it seemed scattered, fragmented, as if pieces of it were adrift, unaccountable, confounding themselves with the childlike shapes that clumped up the hill or tumbled roughly down. At times the mound itself seemed nearly to vanish, its bulk dispersed and wandering. Surely, Jonathan thought, this was a caprice of the vanishing light, an illusion entertained by aging eyes and a tired mind.

But it came to him that there had been something, some strange and unnameable quality, in those eyes that had looked into his own, something not really like a child's eyes at all. And now here it was again, because a leafy ragamuffin, rolling itself up off the ground, had paused in front of him and directed its eyes at him, two orbs that lay deeply receded into a matting of wet leaves and seemed to peer out at him not only from an unnatural depth but with an unnatural fixity. What struck him, upon the instant, was that in their somehow sardonic owlishness the eyes looked—old. Older, perhaps, than any eyes ought to look. Now the sticky webbing of leaves was pulling apart to form a mouth again, and words came out, gravelly and indistinct, though not so indistinct that he couldn't tell that what they said, this time, was: "Join us." And he realized now that it was a chorus of earthy voices that said it, for other dwarfed figures had joined the first, a nodding sea of little heads.

Abruptly, leaf-coated arms were reaching for him, and hands like tattered mittens were closing upon his arms, urging him to his feet. It seemed to him that the gesture was not threatening, but merely insistent. He found himself gently but firmly tugged along, an incongruous playmate among the others, up the hill, and realized that his glasses had fallen off and that he had left his cane behind, but it didn't matter, as the others were pulling him irresistibly to the crest, where, winded and bewildered, he dropped to his hands and knees on the leafy carpet, and then reclined upon the slanting ground and lost his balance altogether and began to roll.

In some corner of his mind he thought that others were coming down the hill around him, but all he could see was a kaleidoscope of blurred impressions, bare treetops against a black night sky, then the pungent wet leaves through which he rolled, then the trees against the sky, then the leaves that clung to him as he descended, then the black sky, then the leaves, in alternation, until at last, aching and dizzy, he had stopped rolling and sprawled inert among the others, half embedded in the mound of leaves.

Even now, pieces of the leafy tumulus seemed to break off and move away in the shadows, back up the hill, but he couldn't be sure, and in his bemusement it even appeared to him that he was fragmented himself, that he merged into the earthy mound of wet leaves but came apart from it to move in curious profusion up the slope, seeing himself and the others through more than one pair of leaf-encrusted eyes. He reflected that in the earthen smell of the leaves there resided something primal, something timeless and fundamental. As if in a dream, he seemed to come back down the hill, or perhaps he was there already. In any event, the aroma of the leaves in their multitudinous presence swelled to fill his senses, and a hundred shapes shifted and a hundred leaf-lined mouths smiled enigmatically at him in the dark.

An odd calm spread over him, focusing him into his own recumbent form again, where he lay among the leaves. Momentarily he felt like getting up on his shaky legs and struggling back up the hill, but he couldn't even feel his legs, and now the soft darkness of the night was closing around him, a mantle that took him into itself, rather like the soft probing of countless leafy hands, and he thought how comfortable, how very comfortable it would be just to lie quiet among the leaves, and move no more.

Pump Jack

It was strange, being back in the desert.

That's what this land was, all right, however stubbornly a half dozen generations of sheep ranchers had struggled to carve a living out of this sandy, mesquite-dotted soil.

Cal Withers pulled his rental car over to the side of the lonely road and got out and sniffed the air. After the clamorous squalor of city life, he wasn't used to all this space, all this quiet, and it tended almost to make him nervous. But the limitless deep blue sky was delectable, no denying that, especially when one was used to cramped city skies stained an ugly gray by skyscrapers.

All these years, back East, he had thought of the desertlands of southeastern New Mexico as a kind of childhood dream. This yellow prairieland had been his home for the first seven years of his life, till his dad, weary of farming, had found a new job and moved them all to the frozen northlands, leaving the old farmhouse in the dubious hands of Uncle Bill and Aunt Clara. Growing up in Boston on the banks of the Charles River, Cal had found it easy just to stay there, settle into life there, grow older there. But now he wondered whether he had made a mistake, never coming back here till now.

Well. He surveyed vastnesses of gently rolling ground, furred over with wheatgrass and spiked with yucca. What would he have done here, anyway, if he had stayed? Would he have had the patience to coax a living out of this ground, tend ragtag herds of sheep, run a ranch, like nearly all his family before him? He wondered. Probably not, the truth to tell; it took a different kind of mentality to live like that.

But damn, this clean, clear sky looked nice, with its regal flotillas of billowy white clouds driven onward by a tempest of sunlight. High above him, a hawk fell across the sky like a meteor, spread its wings, wheeled, and was gone, fluttering into the sun. Somewhere nearby, grasshoppers ratcheted lustily. Even in late October the air was warm and the land bristled with desert life. The place really brought back all the fond old memories.

And yet its pleasantness didn't quite banish the not-so-fond old memories.

The sky seemed to darken almost imperceptibly for a moment, until he realized that it was not the air but his own mood that was slipping into shadow. Funny—he hadn't thought about that other business for years.

And wasn't sure he wanted to think about it now.

He got back in the car and headed farther down the road, toward what the locals called the old Withers place. If he had his bearings straight, the venerable woodframe house wouldn't creep into view for several miles yet, and even then would only barely be visible from the road, a gabled gnome nestled back in a wilderness of chaparral. He would be there in a few minutes, and felt rather curious to see the old place again. But another sight greeted him first.

Here and there, now, at great intervals on both sides of the road, stood the eternal profiles of little oil wells.

There had never been any wells drilled on the Withers property, so far as he had ever heard, but you saw them all over the county, pretty much—here, there, one bundle of hope or another, pumping, pumping, imploring the ground for oil. These were the first wells he had seen in all the years since he was a child here. He stopped the car again, got out, leaned against a jagged post, and watched a nearby pump jack, perhaps only a hundred feet from the road. Somehow he had always found these things lulling, comforting, almost meditative to watch.

Except when he remembered—

But why dwell on that? Inane old stories, the wide-eyed foolishness of infancy. For now, he was content to watch the grasshopperlike head of the pump jack on the end of its long beam, nodding, nodding, nodding to the earth, piercing the desert soil again and again with its drilling rod like the proboscis of some strange hungry insect. Off in the distance, humming among waving seas of chamisa, other insect-heads slowly nodded and nodded, probing the dry earth to their own tune, and the tune of the sighing wind. There was no other sound, no other motion. It was like a scene in a dream, a bit of theater on a stage at the end of the earth.

Rousing himself, he drove on down the road, finally spotting the old two-story house off at the end of a bumpy drive to the right. Arriving in a cloud of yellow dust, he parked beside a rocky ridge near the house and clumped up onto the creaky wooden porch. He had stopped in town for the key, but he needn't have bothered; the door was open. Out here where one measured the distance to one's nearest neighbor in miles, what did it matter? To his push, the door swung inward with an osseous creak, intruding upon shadow. In the window beside the door, the truculent fat face of Uncle Bill hung with a scowl. But no, this was only a crumpled place in the brittle paper shade, an imagined face staring but not seeing, then not even staring. Uncle Bill and Aunt Clara were dead. If there was any certainty in the world, it was that their faces would not be present at dinner. Cal took a breath and stepped inside.

He switched on a light and looked around. It wasn't quite as bad as he'd expected, but bad enough, though there was no way of knowing how much of the general neglect here was due to an aging Bill and Clara's laxness at housekeeping, and how much due to the fact that the house had sat empty for several months. Good thing he had arranged for the power to be on, because the place was morbid enough even in the light. Sea-bottom mantles of dust swam everywhere, undulating, blanketing the furniture, obscuring corners and angles. Old papers, clothes, rags, and nondescript debris cluttered the corners, the floors. The house smelled sour, and Cal pulled up a shade and pried open a window. No question, he had some cleaning up to do, if he was ever going to sell this place. But who would buy it, out here? He cleared a path through the clutter and went down the hall toward the back of the house, to the kitchen.

Amazing, how clearly he remembered where everything was. Nothing much seemed to have changed all these years. The refrigerator was an addition, but the old stove was the same, only more battered-looking now. He hoped the butane tanks weren't empty, as he would have to bring his bag of groceries in from the car and do some cooking tonight.

For now, he had a lot to do, and figured he might as well be about it. Retrieving plastic trash bags from the car, he started making his way through the house, filling the bags, some with trash and some with things to take into Hobbs sometime later to give to charity: clothing, extra sets of dishes, a few books, countless odds and ends. What he was supposed to do with the furniture was a mystery. He didn't want any of this stuff himself; his own life had collected enough barnacle-clinging detritus, without taking on anyone else's. By the time he had made an initial pass through all the downstairs rooms, he had filled several bags, and they stood bulging in a row along the porch now like a strange gaggle of plump children. There were only two bedrooms and a bathroom upstairs, and Cal could see to those tomorrow. It was nearly sundown, and he was getting hungry.

Cooking a meal here wasn't quite the unpleasant chore he had somehow expected it to be, and after washing his dishes he tamped some tobacco into his pipe and strolled outside and down the drive toward the road, and sat on a rock and smoked. He wanted to see the desert sunset.

Its explosion of color didn't disappoint him. In the west, long filaments of lithe cloud glowed red and gold and orange. Behind him, when he looked around, the distant windows of the old house gave the light back like feral pairs of eyes. For a few fleeting moments the effect of the sunset extended to the entire sky, painting wisps of cloud even on the opposite horizon in salmon-pink hues against the deepening blue, like pastel watercolors. Everywhere but in the west, the colors faded quickly to purplish black, but in the west it was another half hour before the crimson oven-glow of the sky paled to a faint memory, then went out like embers.

And then it was night.

Real night. Night in the desert.

It came back to him, now, what that was like. The sky became a great vaulted dome frosted with stars. How *open* it was, how fathomless, an infinite black sea which, one felt, might come crashing down in titanic waves. One felt like an exhibit on black velvet here; the overarching window of heaven was open, and all the universe looked on by starlight.

Not that the stars provided much in the way of light, he thought, getting up and making his way back to the path. Though he was facing the house now, he couldn't make out the faintest outline of it; even the desert terrain immediately around him was the vaguest of ghost-impressions, dark against dark. He rather wished the moon was out. As he started walking, the path somehow seemed rockier than before; in the inky dark his feet collided from time to time with large stones. This in itself was disorienting, and besides, the path must have branched, because by the time he had trudged through stony sand long enough easily to take himself back to the porch steps, he wasn't back there, but was staring out only at more blackness, more night.

Surely this was at least approximately the way back to the house, though he might have been a little confused in the dark. He eased forward, feeling his slow way with his feet on what he hoped was still the path. Even now, when his eyes had had time to adjust to the dark, the chaparral around him loomed only as dim shadows without detail, and it made him uncomfortable to move on without quite being able to tell where he was going. He walked in this fashion for what seemed like a good while, and at length he felt his feet fetch up against a vertical object. This had to be the bottom porch step; he had to be back at the house. He had been mistaken about the moon; it was out, but had been obscured by low-scudding black clouds backlit now in wan yellow light, and as the clouds lifted the gibbous moon shone through, a half-eaten face of chalk. When he looked up he reflected that that angular object beginning to take form in the moonlight could only be a corner of the overhand to the porch.

But it wasn't.

Poised motionless above him, it was a pump jack, its oblong head raised as if contemplating the moon. Had it been pumping at the time, he would no doubt have heard it long before blundering into the edge of the platform on which the structure rested. The odd thing was that in the dark he must have wandered off the Withers property altogether.

But no—now that the light was better, he could see, traced along behind the oil well, a half-collapsed old fence stretching off into the night, rusty wire strands dividing the Withers property from the adjacent land to the west. And the pump jack was on this side of the fence. Did the fence, some yards back, look trampled down? How could it be? He must have been mistaken about the location of the pump jack.

Suddenly the sight of it, that sardonic metal head atop its walking-beam, filled him with nameless panic, and it wasn't until he had backed away from it and sprinted across the chaparral to the house and bounded up the steps, past the procession of trash bags and through the door, and had slammed and latched the door behind him—it wasn't until then that he thought consciously about what it was that was bothering him. Pulling the brittle shades down to shut out the night, he realized now that it must have been bothering him all along, ever since he saw the area again, maybe even before.

It was the old story of Pump Jack, with a capital P and a capital J.

It had never been clear to him, either when he was a child or later, whether this bizarre story was merely a family foible or a folktale of wider acceptance. In any case Uncle Bill and Grandpa Willis used to terrify him with endless accounts of Pump Jack, the wayward oil well that wouldn't keep to its proper place, but tore out of its moorings and moved around at night—seeking, Uncle Bill warned him with great solemnity, seeking someone to punish. Bad little children were its favorite feast. And if it caught you, Grandpa intoned ominously as Aunt Clara fluttered her hands—well, sir, if it caught you, it would pounce upon you with its uprooted metal feet and drive its pumping rod straight into your heart like a giant mosquito and suck your body dry of blood, leaving you lying desiccated upon the sand, dry and dead as a lizard.

Cal snorted, going around and pulling more shades down, though he was not sure why he did so, since no one would be likely to be peering in at him, out here in the middle of nowhere in the dark of night. Pump Jack and his nocturnal feastings—perfectly delightful tales to tell an impressionable child! What in the world was wrong with Grandpa and Uncle Bill and the others? At least his own father had disapproved of such frightful storytelling. His father just might have been one of the few sane people in the family, when you got right down to it.

Not relishing any further reflections on the matter just now, Cal turned in early, choosing the front bedroom upstairs and making the bed over with fresh sheets. When the light was off and he was lying in bed listening to the night in the desert, where the wind made a forlorn moaning sound around the eaves of the old house, he half fancied he heard some furtive creature rooting and nuzzling about outside, somewhere near the house, but he fell asleep before he could worry about it, and apparently dreamed of things strange and vaguely disturbing, though he couldn't quite remember them in the morning.

He rose tired and moody. Breakfast did little to dispel the feeling, and he went about his work more out of duty than desire. By noon he had bagged up more than would even fit in the car. He packed as many bags as he could into the back seat and front passenger seat, and drove the fifty miles into town. The real estate agent was typical of the profession, eager to help in any way possible, blithely confident that the property would sell quickly, don't you worry about a thing, Mr. Withers. Afterward Cal disposed of his trash and his charity items, had lunch at a diner, and spent a good portion of the afternoon just idling about town before he realized that he was making excuses to himself to delay going back out to the ranch.

Preposterous, of course. There was no reason to avoid driving back out, and indeed he should have done so earlier, as there was a good bit of work left to do today, and little of the afternoon left to do it in. He pointed the car back out into the desert and was bumping back up the rocky drive before sunset.

Desert sunsets were incomparable, but he wouldn't go out and watch that spectacular event this evening. Why not? some corner of his mind niggled. Because, his answer was, there is simply no point in it; I saw the sunset last night, and tonight I have more pressing things to do.

But he found himself not doing them. There was indeed a great deal more in the house to bag up, including two closets full of clothes that he hadn't even approached yet, but at dinnertime he hadn't tended to any of it, and after his cheerless meal he felt even less like bothering. There was no particular hurry, he thought, pulling the shades down again and shutting out the encroachment of night that yawned limitless beyond the windows. Why not just grab a good book from his suitcase and settle into the easy chair in the front parlor? He'd been working hard enough, and travel itself had been tiring; he deserved a night off. He eased himself into the chair with the copy of *Bleak House* he'd been promising himself for weeks to start on, and he switched on a lamp and began to read.

. . . *mud in the streets* (he read) *as if the waters had but newly retired from the face of the earth, and it would not be wonderful to meet a Megalosaurus, forty feet long or so, waddling like an elephantine lizard up Holborn Hill.*

With no intended slight to Dickens, Cal's attention had already be-gun to wander, because although he found himself looking away from the page and thinking back over this Dickensian image, or what should have been this image, the passage had changed in some insane way of its own accord. *And it would not be wonderful to meet Pump Jack, twenty feet long, waddling like a bug up the hill from Hobbs,* he reflected, and chided himself the next moment. Balderdash and nonsense. Cretinous drivel. It was a sad comment on something or other, if a man couldn't keep his mind from—

What was that sound?

He sat still, holding his breath, listening.

Nothing. More nonsensical—

No. No, there it was again. Like something bumping and scraping around outside, near the porch. Probably some animal looking for food, he thought, though this evening there were no bags on the porch to tempt any four-legged scavengers. Sighing, he got up to find out what was going on.

When he stepped out onto the porch and switched on the light out there, he could have sworn that something large and of indeterminate shape scuttered away just beyond the reach of the light. Now come on, this was getting to be absurd. If somebody was trying to . . . He had to go out and have a look around.

Getting his jacket, he went down the steps and paced about the area near the house, but saw nothing. At first. Then, off on the horizon, something, he thought. Something moved in the moonlight. He walked in that direction, puzzling it over in his head. What was he so distraught about? Some lunatic folktale designed to scare children into submission? It had nothing to do with him now. Maybe he *had* deserved a bit of censure from time to time when he was a kid—

You don't listen too good, do you, boy? Hey? Late for supper again. Think you'd know better by now. And after dark too. Why, old Pump Jack just loves to hunt 'em down, kids like you.

Yeah, well, put a lid on it, Uncle Bill. Somebody already did put a lid on you, as I recall, and about time too.

Thinking this rather uncharitable thought, he made his way through the mesquite and yucca and cactus, to the spot where he thought he had seen something, but nothing moved here now except crescents of mesquite-beans waving in the wind. Nothing.

Wait—out there, farther off. Something did move, by God. Maybe it was a coyote. But it had given the impression of being bigger than that. He loped across the sandy ground toward it, but when he arrived, again there was nothing to see but the austere moonlit trappings of the desert terrain. Then again, farther out—another glimpse, or imagined glimpse, of movement.

He ran on, determined to find out. Sable clouds drew themselves over the moon like ragged eyelids, and he began to have trouble seeing where he was going. Slowing to a walk, he felt his way tentatively forward, having no desire to blunder into a cluster of prickly pear cactus or sharp-spiked yucca, and no desire to put his foot in a rattlesnake hole. Now and again a bony bit of moon would slip out from behind the cover of cloud, but it was only enough to confuse him more, as things looked different when he caught sight of them in momentary moonlight than he had expected them to look; where the land, he imagined, sloped down, it really sloped up, or where he thought there was an unobstructed way, a ridge of rock jutted in mute defiance.

He kept moving, increasingly wondering why he was out here, what he was doing. Even in the context of that ridiculous childhood legend, what should he have to fear?

He'd done nothing to be punished for.

Had he?

Nothing, except perhaps moving away?

Did the gods of the desert resent one for doing that?

He really *must* be getting daffy, even to entertain such a thought.

He hadn't been paying attention to where he was going, and now, as the moon came back out, he found himself standing in the very shadow of a great pump jack, its motionless head angled above him.

Was this the same one? In the same place? He couldn't tell. There didn't seem to be any fence nearby, and he had only a very uncertain idea as to where he was.

But in any event, the chase was over. Idiotic! Imagine, some animal scavenger makes some noise up near the house, and good old Cal goes running about the desert chasing phantoms, like a madman or a fool. He sat down on a rock near the pumping platform, and heaved a sigh of relief. He looked up at the profile of the pump jack, bizarre and cold-looking in the wan light, but harmless.

"Well, Jack, here's one old boy you're not going to terrorize. The desert may be a strange place sometimes, but it's not *that* damned strange."

He waited. "How's about it, Jack? Aren't you going to say anything?"

The pump jack sat silent, an absurd insectoid shape against a starry sky.

"That's what I thought." Cal slapped his knees and got up off the rock and laughed outright.

The laugh, however, caught in his throat.

Whether it was the sight or the sound, he couldn't have said, but nothing that came afterward, right down to the end, would disturb him any more than that first impression, that first moment.

The moment when the great oblong head, perched atop its neck of steel, bestirred itself with an unthinkable metallic groan and turned, coldly predatory in the pallid moonlight—turned to look at him.

Lujan's Trunk

Nothing would ever be the same again.

True, when Brad Donner moved from Pittsburgh to the little desert town of Corona, New Mexico, he had expected things to be different. He looked out his window now, over a ragged mound of packing boxes, and saw not concrete and glass but sand and cactus and sagebrush, under a turquoise sky too large to be believed. He had expected New Mexico to be another world, certainly, but he could in no way have anticipated what he was really going to find there.

Or what was going to find him.

It was late October, but the sun still cast a bright patina of warmth across the land, imparting pointed little shadows to the spikes of yucca and cholla cactus that stood like sentries over the countryside as far as he could see. He had been lucky to rent this little adobe house "out in the county," as people said around here; most of the adjoining land was pasturage belonging to one sheep rancher or another, and his nearest neighbors were almost a mile away, yet for all this wide open space it was only four miles east into town, when he needed supplies. This was genuine seclusion; the only sounds out here were a distant murmur of farm machinery and the occasional nocturnal howl of a coyote. The local joke was that not only could you set off an A-bomb out in this desert—it had been done, as the Trinity Site was only seventy miles or so to the southwest. Brad had wanted privacy, and he had it. This unperturbed little house was going to be the perfect place to finish writing the new novel. And he had to buckle down and do just that, because the royalties from his last two books were wearing a little thin by now.

On his third day in the house he took a break from unpacking and drove into Corona for some groceries he had forgotten. On the way, he noticed an unobtrusive little woodframe house huddled a hundred yards or so off the road, at the end of an unpaved drive; his eyesight wasn't what it used to be, but he thought he saw someone sitting on the porch, an old man perhaps. There was nothing unusual about this, but something about the sight of the person, whoever it was, seemed to give him an odd little chill, as if some deep and obscure response had awakened within him. It was the accumulation of fatigue from moving across the country, no doubt, and he did his best to disregard it, driving on into town and parking in front of the little market where he would be buying most of his groceries. But first he walked to a familiar establishment a few doors down, went in, drew a stool up to the bar, and ordered a beer. Behind him, two young men, one Anglo and one Hispanic, were playing pool and chatting quietly. Brad had stopped in here once before, the day he moved in, and the bartender remembered him; in a town this small, the bartender probably remembered everybody.

"So how do you like the house?"

Brad took his beer, poured it into the glass, and took a sip. "I think it's going to be just what I needed," he said. "When you're used to living in a big city, there's something almost scary about how quiet it is out there."

"Yeah," the bartender said with a grin. "Don't expect to see no traffic jams around here. You probably can't even see another house from where you are."

"No, I can't, actually," Brad said. "Reminds me, I noticed a little place on the way into town—"

The bartender gave him a knowing look. "Old man sitting on the porch."

Brad blinked. "Yeah. You know him? But I keep forgetting, this isn't the big city, you probably know everybody in town."

"Just about," the bartender said, "but don't nobody really know that old guy. Hispanic, calls hisself Lujan, came into town a couple of years ago and moved into that house. There wasn't much moving in to do, because the house was furnished, and anyhow he only had one big trunk, painted all funny, looked like an old circus trunk or something. He just showed up here one day with it. And nobody knows where he's from."

"You know, I don't know why," Brad said, "but when I saw him sitting there—"

"It gave you the creeps," another man at the bar supplied.

"Well," Brad hesitated, "kind of. I mean—"

"Nothing to feel ashamed of," the bartender said. "I guess pretty much everybody feels the same way."

Brad took a long swallow of beer. "What is it about him—"

"For one thing," the other man at the bar said, "he don't never stir out of that chair. Sits on that porch all day long. Maybe all night too, for all I know. I can't think of anybody that particularly wants to go over there at night."

"But that's no reason—I mean, he's probably just some old fellow who came here to spend his retirement years," Brad said.

"Well, that's not all, though," the bartender said. "He don't ever come into town to buy groceries or anything. As far as anybody knows, he don't even eat."

"Come on," Brad said, "he's got to eat."

"Whatever he eats, he don't buy it here, I can tell you that," the bartender said.

Brad considered this. "Maybe he has somebody come in and buy groceries for him?"

"Naw," the other man at the bar said, "old Mrs. Marney down at the market knows everybody in town. People know other people's business around here, too much if you ask me, but that's the way it is. Mrs. Marney would know. Nobody's buying stuff for Lujan."

"Something else funny too," the bartender said.

"What's that?" Brad asked.

"That old trunk of his. People say when he moved in he just parked it right there next to the chair on that porch, never took it inside, maybe never even unpacked it. It's still sitting right there beside him. And you know what else? People that seen the old man close up when he moved in? They say his skin looks odd."

"Ah well," Brad said, "so he's a little strange. Maybe he's sick or something. Still no reason to feel creepy about him."

"Mostly we just don't think about him too much," the bartender said.

Leaving the bar, Brad wondered if he might get another novel out of all this at some point; you never could tell. In any case, he thought he might just pay old man Lujan a visit sometime.

It took another couple of days to finish unpacking and arrange the house in halfway livable condition, and most of another day to set up the computer and printer and get all his reference books and materials sorted out so that he could get at them. Late that evening, he finally sat down at the computer to work in earnest, starting on the fourth chapter of the novel.

But he found himself staring at a blank screen. *The sun was setting in a sleepy haze on the horizon,* he wrote, and immediately backspaced it out. Where else would the sun set but on the horizon? He stared at the screen for another ten or fifteen minutes before switching the computer off and going to the kitchen for a soda and a handful of pretzels.

What was bothering him?

Somewhere out in the night a coyote howled, long and low and mournful, and Brad drew the shade up and looked out the kitchen window but saw only blackness looking back in at him, so lowered the shade. He sat at the kitchen table and finished his snack before stepping outside and having a look around. A wan yellow gibbous moon was rising like a face of bone over the desert, making strange tendrils of shadow creep out from under clusters of cactus and yucca, and even with the moonlight Brad marveled at the inky depth of the night sky, frosted so thickly with stars that the familiar constellations were difficult to find. It was true what he had heard, then—you really never saw the sky until you saw it in the desert.

But this bucolic reflection was perturbed, at some level in his mind, by something else, something that kept nagging at him. He pushed the less comfortable thought away and went inside and went to bed.

And dreamed of strange faces, strange shapes, and an oddly painted trunk that he felt unaccountably eager not to see opened.

Waking with a headache and a sense of not having rested at all, he resolved to put a stop to what he knew now was bothering him. He would go visit old man Lujan, introduce himself as a neighbor (though the old man's house was over two miles away), and then he'd be able to see for himself what nonsense it all was.

After all, he reflected, driving toward the old man's house, the region was known for its extravagant legendry; he had discovered this much just by reading, before he decided to move here. There were the La Llorona stories, of a ghostly woman who wandered the arroyos at night crying for her lost children. There were the shapeshifter stories, about Indians turning into crows and coyotes and the like. This tendency toward colorful folktales was one of the reasons why he had chosen to come here, because he felt that such an atmosphere would be fruitful for a writer. The local lore about old man Lujan, on the other hand, was no doubt just the usual tendency of any community to be suspicious of anyone who was different, but Brad might well be able to make literary use of these suspicions sooner or later. It was certainly a good work habit to absorb such rumors and to ponder them at leisure.

Turning up the long dusty drive toward the old man's house, he could see him sitting there on the porch as before, and sure enough, an old-fashioned trunk squatted beside him like some dark, sleeping toad. Brad pulled the car up and parked a respectable distance out from the house, and walked up to the porch. As he did so, the old man watched him but didn't move out of the chair; didn't move at all, in fact. Even on so warm a day, he was swathed in a woolen blanket.

"Hello," Brad said, coming halfway up the rickety wooden steps to the porch and leaning on the rail. "I'm Brad Donner. I just moved into the house a couple of miles up that way, and I wanted to introduce myself."

The old man looked at him without any particular feeling that Brad could identify in the face. People were right, his skin did look odd, sort of rubbery, so that the lizardlike countenance, in its coarse folds, seemed not to reflect emotion clearly. The eyes, dark but alert, peered out from a labyrinthine nest of folds and wrinkles; the fellow was evidently older than Brad had imagined. But at length the convolutions of the face swam apart to form a speaking mouth.

"They call me Lujan," the old man said. The voice was rather thick, almost liquid-sounding.

"I'm pleased to meet you," Brad replied, coming the rest of the way up the steps and extending his hand. Lujan was slow to extend his own hand from under the layers of blanket, but did so, and the hand felt the way the face looked, coarse and rubbery and cold. The hand withdrew, then, back under the blanket. All this time, Brad was observing the trunk also, which was indeed painted lurid colors, showing swirls and patterns that seemed almost to stir some latent memory without quite resolving into any identifiable impression. Brad could well understand how the old man's arrival in town with such an object would have aroused a certain amount of curiosity, and would have lingered in the memory of townsfolk.

"They tell me you're new here too," Brad said. "Where are you from?"

Lujan waited so long in replying that Brad at first thought that the old man hadn't understood him, or considered the question impertinent. But at length the answer came. "From very far."

Seeing that he would have to be content with this vague answer, but sensing at the same time that the old man was not altogether disinclined to talk with a stranger, Brad said, "I'm a writer, I'm working on a new book—which is why I came out here, it's so quiet, good place to work. Do you get into town much?"

Lujan was again slow in responding, but finally the liquid voice spoke up again. "I never go."

"Well," Brad said, hoping again not to seem presumptuous, "I'll be going in, once or twice a week probably, so if there's anything I can get for you, just let me know."

"*Gracias,*" Lujan replied, "*pero ya tengo todo lo que necesito.* I have everything I need."

Brad scarcely understood how this could be the case, but decided to let the matter drop for now. "Well, again, let me know if there's anything I can do. Say, that's an interesting trunk you have there. Looks like a real antique."

Lujan's head turned, turtlelike, to regard the trunk, then turned back. "It has been with me always."

Brad again glanced over the peculiar painted swirls and suggestions of pattern that covered the surface of the old trunk, and again he had the disquieting feeling that there was something uncannily familiar, or nearly familiar, about those swirls, almost as if some profound repository of inherited memory should respond to them, should know them for what they were, what they represented on some level perhaps too deep for words. He had to look away, finally, because the sight of the trunk palpably disturbed him.

"Well," he said, "I won't take up any more of your time."

"You're very welcome to visit," Lujan said, surprisingly. "We must talk again."

"I'd like that," Brad replied, and realized that he meant it. As oddly uncomfortable as he felt here on the old man's porch, he also felt drawn here, compelled to plan another visit. "I could call you first."

Lujan seemed to be considering this, almost as if he didn't understand it. "I have no telephone," he said after a moment. "Just come, when you want."

Chapter Four was coming along, after a fashion. Brad found that it seemed to require more effort of him than usual to concentrate, and he drew upon such wells of self-discipline as he possessed to make himself sit at the computer and write. Late in the afternoon of the third day after his visit with the old man, he pushed his chair back and regarded the glowing screen with dissatisfaction. The words, the paragraphs, the pages were coming, but somehow he felt now that his dialogue was unnatural, his characters forced and wooden and unconvincing. Maybe he was just being a little paranoid, a little too self-critical. But maybe not. He closed the file, turned the computer off, and went to the kitchen for something to eat.

Munching a sandwich and washing it down with cold beer, he gazed out the kitchen window and watched the sun begin to descend behind a flotilla of clouds. The sunset turned the whole sky first a crimson blaze of farewell, then a kind of salmon-colored wash of light that lingered on the horizon like a memory. It was beautiful, and it made him glad that he lived in the desert, but it failed to banish altogether that other thought that kept tugging at his mind. He knew, of course, what the other thought was, but it still took overcoming a certain amount of inertia, or a certain amount of some less clear reluctance—mingled with an odd attraction—to make him face the fact that what he needed to do was drive over and visit Lujan again.

By the time he got there it was getting dark, and when he pulled his car up as before and shut the headlights off, the little cloud of dust that he had raised in driving up was barely discernible in the pallid wash of illumination from the porch light, beneath which the old man sat mummified in blankets, beside his ancient trunk. Brad walked up the creaking wooden steps. "Hello again. I thought we might have a chat. Hope I'm not coming at a bad time."

The old man's wrinkled face seemed even more reptilian than before, in the pale yellow light of the single bulb behind him, and again the maze of folds and wrinkles ebbed away to leave a toothless mouth. "There is no bad time, no good time," he said in that half-gurgling voice. "There is just time. Forever and ever."

"Well," Brad said, taken a little aback, "I guess that's so." He cast a glance at the oddly painted trunk. Somehow it looked all the more sinister under the feeble light bulb, which seemed to impart a truly appalling quality to the spectral swirls and patterns that covered its rough surface. But the old man was speaking again.

"No beginning, no end."

Brad strained to see the old man's face in the gloom. "I beg your pardon?"

"The Old Ones were, the Old Ones are, the Old Ones forever shall be," Lujan intoned.

Oh brother, Brad thought, what is this all about? "I, uh, I don't understand. Who are the Old Ones?"

"*Los Antiguos*, the Old Ones," Lujan repeated, raising his head slightly to regard Brad more squarely. There was something a little unsettling in the way the head moved, as if the rubbery quality that one saw in the texture of his skin was imparted even to the quality of movement itself. "In the time before all time, in the days *cuando no había tierra ninguna*, when there was no earth, the Old Ones walked in the Great Silence. *No los vemos*, we do not see Them—They walk unseen among us."

"Is this a story they tell here in New Mexico?" Brad asked, feeling more than a little foolish; he simply didn't know what else to say.

"This is a story always told, everywhere," Lujan replied, "by the few who know. Some know. Some few know of Great Cthulhu, some few know of Azathoth at the center of all chaos, some few know of Yog-Sothoth, the One God."

"Whew," Brad said, shaking his head. "I don't know about all this. Now me, I don't mind, but I get the impression that a lot of people around here are pretty conservative in their religious thinking, Mr. Lujan. I don't think these Sunday-school-going folks—"

"Most people are blind," Lujan stated flatly.

Brad scarcely knew what to say to that. It might have a residuum of truth, but he didn't know what to make of Lujan's reasons for saying it. "What do you call your religion?" he finally asked.

"It is no religion," the old man said, and the eyes, nested within their saurian folds of skin, seemed to grow almost shiny-dark in their intensity. "It is the only truth that there is. The Old Ones are eternal, and one day the gate will open once more to let them in. Yog-Sothoth is the gate."

"I've seen most of the sacred scriptures of the world's major faiths," Brad ventured, "and I can't really say that I recall anything about—"

"Listen to your dreams," Lujan said.

"Sir?"

"Listen to your dreams," the old man repeated, and he appeared disinclined to speak further. After several awkward minutes of waiting in silence, Brad nodded to him and took his leave—but not without receiving one really perplexing impression.

He thought that a sort of shudder had gone through the trunk, making it rattle faintly against the wooden porch on which it rested.

This was just an odd fancy, of course, probably brought on by the weird nature of the old man's talk. But the impression was strong enough to be unsettling, and it was attended by another, vaguer impression, one that wouldn't come clear, one that followed him home and hung like a sable question mark in his mind.

That night he tried again to write, but his thoughts were in turmoil, and he gave it up and tried for a while to read, finding again that his mind kept wandering, wandering back to that peculiar conversation on the old man's porch. The Old Ones? What had that name been—Yog-Sothoth?—he who was "the gate"? What in the world did all this mean? Fatigued both from thinking about it and from trying not to think about it, Brad at length went to bed.

And dreamed a dream of the sky filling with great writhing tentacles as some opening in the very air seemed to gape with horror, showing vistas of restless blackness. He awoke, sweating and trembling, at a little past three o'clock in the morning, and was almost glad that he didn't succeed in going back to sleep right away, because there had been a quality to that dream that profoundly disturbed him. But he did drift back into clouds of slumber, and when he did, his dream was of floating, disembodied and horribly bereft of identity, in a darkness alive with swirling shapes of dread that finally brought him awake again, awake and screaming. It was nearly six in the morning by now, and he got up and took a shower and got dressed and made coffee, and stood in his doorway and watched the sun come up to herald what felt not so much like a new day as a temporary escape from night, and from the horrors of dream.

The novel was not going at all well. The days passed unproductively, the computer screen seemed to glower at him with a terrible sort of irony, as if saying: here you are, privy to some of the most bizarre folk-legendry anyone has ever heard, and you can't seem to write a coherent sentence.

The dreams had grown worse, not in content so much as in intensity. Every night now he seemed to find himself giddily afloat in some restless void where the very darkness writhed with a hideous suggestion of sentience, as if the shadows themselves gathered with purposes of their own, alive and cunning and eloquent of timeless secrets. Some vile name seemed to reverberate in the void, some impression more primal than mere sound, a suggestion of a name older than time. He could almost hear it—

"—oth." The half-sound would linger in his head when he awoke, and would gradually ebb away.

Time passed He stared at the bright screen, wholly at a loss. Outside, darkness grew upon the land as yet another sunset faded like embers. It was no use trying to write any more tonight. He was exhausted, and some corner of his mind kept threatening to dwell on that—other—impression, from that night on the old man's front porch.

He was halfway out to the car before he realized that unconsciously he must have been planning another visit with Lujan for quite some time. But as he started to climb behind the wheel, he chose to follow a different impulse—he suspected that a long walk might do a good deal to clear his mind. The old man's house was only two miles

away, and he was used to longer walks than that. He closed the car
door and pocketed the keys and went down the driveway to the road.

Heading east toward Lujan's house, he found himself quite alone
on the black ribbon of tarmac that stretched across the land before
him, a ribbon of road beneath a bewilderment of icy stars. Parallel lines
of barbed-wire fencing marched into the gloom before him like
strangely insistent heralds. Except for his footfalls, all was utterly quiet
here. There was barely any traffic here even during the day, and none
at night. It felt strange to walk along this road in the dark, in the silence of the night, alone. He had never had any reason to walk on a
highway at night before, and wondered if he indeed had an adequate
reason now. What was this fascination with Lujan?

Was the old man just a peculiar variety of religious fanatic, worshipping some primordial god that no one else had ever heard of? Was
Lujan senile, demented, given to puerile fancies?

Or was he a link to some secret so vast, so chillingly bizarre, that
the mind could scarcely come to terms with it?

Brad kept on along the highway, finding that his vision gradually
adjusted to the dark, though only a faint play of starlight illumined the
landscape, as the moon had not yet risen. As his vision cleared, he noticed that despite the clear night sky above him, a black froth of clouds
had gathered on the eastern horizon ahead, and he thought he heard a
faraway grumble of thunder. As if to corroborate this suspicion, a bolt
of lightning appeared in the distance, where the bank of clouds was
growing more massive. Brad began to wonder if he could make it to
Lujan's house before the storm came on. The lightning flashed again,
showing him vistas of range grass and spindly cholla and furtive clusters of yucca and a field of cotton that looked eerily like snow beyond
the never-ending barbed wire.

He continued on, mulling over some of the old man's remarks
from that time before. *The Old Ones were, the Old Ones are, the Old Ones
forever shall be.* It had a sonorous ring to it, as if it were quoted from
some immemorially ancient tome. *In the time before all time the Old Ones
walked in the Great Silence.* Somehow this didn't sound like merely the
ravings of an offbeat religious fanatic. *Some few,* the old man had de-
clared in that gurgling voice, *know of Yog-Sothoth, the One God.* And the
old man had enjoined him: *Listen to your dreams.*

Brad's dreams, vague as they had been, came alive to him now, here, on the lonely road in the dark, and he remembered the cosmic reverberations of that horrendously timeless name, which the very thunder in the distant night seemed to mutter aloud. And with this access of vividness of his remembered dreams, he suddenly felt that the very sky above him, still crusted with a multitude of stars not yet eclipsed by the impending storm—that this very sky was a bottomless well of blackness into which he might topple and fall, screaming. This onset of unaccountable vertigo subsided after a moment, but left him so dizzy that he stumbled and nearly fell headlong in the road. Preposterous, the notion that one could fall into the sky, like a pebble dropped into a well. Yet if it was so absurd, this feeling, why was he so reluctant to look again at the fathomless black sky over his head? Why was he almost thankful that the gathering storm, whose lightning and thunder rent the heavens again and again now, would soon mercifully conceal that vault of starry night above him? He had to get hold of his nerves. Regaining his balance after stumbling, he set his eyes once again on the cheerless road.

And saw, off in the distance, a faint suggestion of movement on the tarmac, perhaps a hundred yards off.

Was someone walking toward him?

He couldn't be sure, but when the lightning lit up the sky again, bringing a new crash of thunder, he thought that there was indeed someone in the road.

The image, visible in only intermittent flashes in the coming storm, was confusing. One time it appeared to be a tall, thin man, yet the next time it would appear to be a form more squat, more substantial than before. A moaning voice seemed to float upon the air too, and Brad strained to hear it, but a chill wind had come up, howling, driving across the chaparral like a demon, and he could hear nothing over it except an occasional hint of keening, a sound that chilled him more than the wind alone could have done.

And as the enigmatic figure drew closer and another frenzy of lightning filled the air, he suddenly knew why he had been confused, why he had thought the figure first thin, then fat.

It was a tall, thin man after all, and the thickness of the image was not the man himself, but the trunk. It was Lujan in the road, and he was carrying the trunk as if it were weightless. The old man had come to meet him, apparently.

But why would he do so, and why would he bring the peculiarly painted trunk? And if the trunk was weightless—empty—then what kind of ludicrous business was all this, anyway?

But there was nothing ludicrous in the expression on the old man's multitudinously wrinkled face as he drew near, crowned by lightning, wreathed about by thunder, anointed by wind-driven rain. The face was a picture of triumph.

"You have listened to your dreams, and you know," Lujan croaked, leaning loathsomely toward Brad in the wind and the rain and the insane lantern-show of lightning.

"What—what do I know?" Brad tried to say, but his voice, feeble and hoarse, was drowned out by thunder. Nevertheless, the old man seemed to have heard him.

"You know—*this*," Lujan replied, setting the trunk down on the wet tarmac and opening the lid.

A monumental outburst of lightning clove the night, and Brad looked down into the trunk.

It was the end of all that had ever seemed to him to represent order and sanity in the world.

For in the yawning trunk he found not a few feet of space terminating in a bottom, but rather a limitless extent of restive blackness, as if the trunk were a window upon the hideous and unconscionable void of his dreams, a void where the very nighted chambers of space, the very darkness itself, was alive with a lightless gray slime that stirred horribly awake, avid, conscious. What lay within the trunk was the tiniest vestige of this primordial presence, and what lay beneath it—visible as it moved from side to side—was the nothingness of eternity.

There was another revelation too, one that confirmed the thing he had thought he glimpsed before, on the old man's porch, but he would not dare think about it till later, after Lujan had gone.

Recoiling from the old man and his trunk, Brad would remember nothing of the remainder of that night but a mindless, frantic scramble in the rain and the shrieking wind—was it the wind that shrieked, or did he? Somehow he would get home, out of the storm, and would fall into an exhausted sleep, waking around noon and going to his car and driving back down the eastward highway to where he had met the old man. But when he got there, he found, of course, nothing at all.

Lujan was never seen around Corona again, nor was his enigmatic trunk. Brad would wonder, time and again on sleepless nights in his desert home, what new place the old man had gone to, what new porch he perhaps sat upon, beside his eternal trunk. What face would the old man wear next time, what language would he so haltingly speak? Brad wondered who would be next to peer into the trunk and be changed forever. For he thought he understood at least this much: that it was important, somehow, for "some few" (as Lujan had said) to come to know of Yog-Sothoth in the infinite void—especially in light of that *other* awareness that had begun, vaguely, on the old man's porch, and had come to fruition in the madness of the storm that final night.

Brad had thought he saw it in the pale glow of a lightbulb, the night on the porch, and he had seen it all too undeniably the night of the storm, out on the highway.

From within the trunk, pale thin strings of substance had extended, subtly hidden in shadow for the most part, running out like slimy gray tubers to connect with the old man's body.

Lujan had not been some human devotee of the primal and soul-shattering Yog-Sothoth. Blown like glass into a semblance of human form, he had been a vestige and a manifestation, speaking and breathing, of that frightful god Himself.

Wait for the Thunder

The thought had been with him for as long as he could remember. Not always in the forefront of the mind, of course—usually the image crouched in some mental backwater, waiting, like an odd crawling creature lurking in the gloom of an obscure and musty corner, watching with a bright mirror-maze jumble of eyes. And just as a furtive creature might scutter down a hole if you came too close, so too the thought would retreat, coy and tantalizing, when he tried to coax it into the light. And he did sometimes try, in spite of himself.

But more often he was content not to think about it, content to let it lie. What was it, after all, but an insubstantial image in the brain, something of no real consequence? Just a picture in the mind, dim and half lost in shadow. It might as well be the evanescent memory of a face, pale and vague and nameless, seen from a passing train. "A face," Jeff said absently, to no one. The difference was, a face seen from a train would not usually creep slyly back, day after day, month after month, year after year, unbidden. But his special thought stretched like gossamer spider-threads back, back into the mists of childhood, and he seldom had a day, or especially a night, when it didn't impinge on his consciousness, an uninvited visitor come to call.

Jeff stepped out onto the porch, banged the screen door shut behind him with a dry puff of dust, and looked out across the desert, where a faint, hot stir of wind ruffled the prairie grass and the sagebrush like a passing dream. The porch steps, their unpainted boards swollen and cracked with age, protested under him as he made his slow descent. Yes, the house was old, he was old, the thought was old. They were suitable companions, he supposed. He and the house, anyway.

The sun was going down behind him, sending his shadow, a lumbering angular giant, preceding him down the footpath like some gaunt herald feeling its way among the pebbles. He lit a cigar and shuffled on toward the stony foothills where he often walked, where many years

236

ago he and Emma had often walked. That had been another time, another life. Her little shoe prints, birdlike and delicate, were barely a memory now, here in this dust, a thousand times erased by the wind like a half-remembered poem on a blackboard, banished, gone. But the desert vista of chaparral was still the same; the path, the giddy turquoise sky, the frowning foothills were the same as always. Was there anything more unchanging than the desert? Engrossed, he nearly stumbled.

"And what's this?" The culprit was a scrap of wood at the edge of the rocky path. Incongruously in this arid land, it looked like a piece of driftwood cast up from a troubled sea. But of course the sea had subsided here millions of years ago. Bending and picking up the wood, he started to toss it aside, but paused to have another look, and thought that it looked like—well, that was nonsense. Now that he did toss it aside into the sand, though, his sense of distaste stemmed undeniably from the unhappy impression that the twisted piece of wood rather resembled the sinewy neck of a turtle.

Walking on, leaving a shimmering wake of cigar smoke, he remembered his grandmother's words, countless years ago, on the subject of turtles. *Don't you let him bite you, Jeffrey,* she had croaked, rolling her ancient eyes heavenward and fluttering her withered hands apocalyptically. *If he bites you, he won't turn loose till it thunders.*

That was an old Indian legend, actually, but he hadn't found that out till years later. At the age of five he had listened to Grandma Turner's story as one might listen, breathless and wide-eyed, to the solemn pontifications of a sage on a mountaintop. *He won't turn loose till it thunders.* Like grim saurian teeth, the words had penetrated to his bones.

Somewhere in the distance a bird fell screeching across the sky and brought him out of his dark daydream. But proceeding up the incline now, into the foothills, he fell to musing again as the evening came on in soft gradations and his stalking shadow faded passively into the general gloom. There was still a flush of pallid light in the sky, though, enough for him to find his way among the rocks, enough for him to see the petroglyphs, etched into the gray stones a thousand years ago by Indians, strange far-off scribes who scattered their cryptic thoughts across the ages like ponderous fossils.

Circles, spirals, stick-figures, lizards, bulbous-eyed birds covered the rock surfaces—and at one place, crowded among them, beneath a jagged representation of lightning, there sprawled the oval form of a turtle, its scrawny neck and head stretching as if to bite, subtly menacing even in this crude rendering. Jeff remembered Hopi legends about the world being poised upon the shell of the great Turtle Kachina. He was part Indian himself, but he didn't pretend to understand these things.

All his life the image of a turtle's gristled neck, the image of that gaping mouth, had haunted him. As a child he had lain awake through miserable nights, pondering what it would be like to feel that clammy unthinkable mouth closing upon his finger, and what it would be like to lie agonized and helpless, waiting for the thunder, shocked by the gloating mucoid roll of those timeless reptile eyes, appalled by the tenacity of that grasping mouth, waiting. Waiting for the thunder that would perhaps never come. To the Hopi, Thunder was a kachina too, a sacred figure, but it was often elusive.

Jeff sat down upon a stone, finished his cigar, and watched the last riotous afterglow of sunset fade as the frosty stars came out and the white bony face of the moon rose over the prairie. At least he would be able to see as he picked his way back down the path toward home. But he didn't want to go back, not just yet. It felt rather good to sit and think, out here under the limitless sky, even when his thoughts turned to—

I don't know why you let it bother you, Emma had said, more than once. But as profoundly as they had understood each other, she hadn't understood about this. Sadly enough this had always been his to bear alone. How many times, as not a restless child but a restless grown man, slumbering only fitfully but slumbering nonetheless, had he struggled back up the long reverberant well of sleep, struggled toward the distant mercy of wakefulness, as a dream, always the same dream, worried at the depths of his mind? Each time, the turtle's mouth had closed tight upon him, filling him with a nightmare of agony, and as the sky in the dream grew stormy he prayed for the first crack of thunder, the sweet, releasing roll of thunder. But it wouldn't come. Though he waited and prayed, it would *not* come, and eventually he would find himself awake, drenched in sweat, his heart pounding, his memory of the dream lingering, his mind full of that pitiless head poised at the end of that long, twisted neck, drawn and scrawny like the cooked neck of a turkey, that neck thrusting the hungry head close to him. And he would lie awake till dawn, afraid to leave himself vulnerable to the dream-creature again.

It was rank foolishness, of course. One seldom saw a turtle out here, and the chances that—but the image always returned. Sometimes he thought it was as if it were an overarching metaphor for his whole life, an abiding dread of being consumed by forces that he could not control, forces that would only relent, would only leave him in peace if some equally mysterious and improbable force intervened. But no, it really wasn't some abstract symbolic notion that plagued him. It was the stark image of the turtle itself, and quite literally it was only the thunder that could release him, if ever it should happen that—

Absently, he had gotten to his feet to start for home, but he only stood and stared back down the path, where the cold light of the rising moon washed the rocks, the sand, in a wan white glow.

The rocks, the sand, and something else. Something that shouldn't be there, and hadn't been there before. Something moving.

His mind must have gone unhinged somewhere amidst the evening's musings, because certainly that couldn't really be a turtle, about a foot across, waddling up the path. He saw it, though, its shell glistening like some runic mystery in the moonlight, its neck, its groping head angling toward him.

Instinctively he flattened himself against a large rock, drawing his feet against it, spreading his arms flat against it for balance, leaning his head back flush against the stone surface. With his head in this position, he had to strain to look down upon the path, where the turtle was still trundling forward, its mouth agape. As it came up the path, its paddle-feet scrabbling madly and leaving an incomprehensible hiero-glyphic trail in the dust, it seemed to be searching, its knobby head wobbling and lifting, its cold rheumy eyes giving back the moon in bleary little puddles of light. He tried to hold himself absolutely still, tried not even to breathe, but it saw him. He was sure of it. It saw him, all right, and advanced with what seemed to be a heightened sense of purpose, lurching directly toward him. Slowly, maddeningly slowly it came near his feet, and paused, and—

And he came to himself to find only the moonlight upon the path.

How could he have dropped off to sleep? He might have pitched forward and cracked his head. The perils of age. Shuddering at how real the vision had seemed, he stared down the stony path, where there was no trail made by paddling feet, no footprints but his own, and he drew a long breath and listened to his heartbeat until it slowed back down. The dream-vision had been awful enough. But squinting into the moonlight now, he realized that there was only one way such a dream could be worse.

And that was for it not to end when one awoke.

Because far down the path now, there it was again. Only this time he knew he was wide awake, and the turtle was real. It was the creature from his nightmares, all right. From a thousand nightmares.

It edged its slow way up the path, just as in the dream, its liquescent eyes quivering, searching.

Finding.

It moved straight toward him, its cavernous mouth gulping the air, eager, hungry. The eyes, aglow with moonlight, seemed larger than they *could* be, too large for the noxious little head to contain.

Again, as in the dream, he pressed himself flat against the nearest rock, spreading his arms, his legs, keeping his head close to the stone but forcing his gaze downward onto the path, where the turtle clambered ever closer, its jittering head now so close that Jeff could see the black awful surface inside the groping mouth. For a moment he almost thought he could see his own form reflected in the thing's viscous eyes, but then the turtle was too close. He would have had to bring his head up off the stone surface, and he was unwilling to do that. He could hear the creature, though, a soft and terrible movement in the dust at his feet. The turtle came nearer, nearer, and—

Passed him by? Had it passed him by?

Yes. Yes! Now he saw it again, low and beetling in the moonlight. Leaving gently perturbed overlapping patterns of dust in its wake, it continued up the path, and after a while it was out of sight.

Thank heaven. A second reprieve, thank heaven.

There had never been anything to worry about, had there? He had been a fool to worry.

His relief shaded off into other feelings, however, as he discovered, upon trying to lift his head off the stone, that he could not do so.

At first he thought he was just freezing up, just reacting to shock or fright at the proximity of this unwelcome guest, but then it dawned on him what the truth was. Somehow he believed it readily enough, even though he could not accept it, could not accept what it implied.

The sensation around his right forefinger gradually came into focus for him, a vague discomfort metamorphosing into a pain that he understood all too well. He wanted to scream, but the scream lay unreleased in his throat. He remembered the turtle etched in the stone, remembered the sprawling stick-figures. And one stunning fact presented itself to his mind.

Here in the surface of the stone where he was, with his thin arms outspread and his fingers splayed wide, time was frozen—congealed into an unending present moment. Here in the world of the petroglyphs the turtle had found him at last, and they had all the time in the world together. And here in the cold and silent realm of stone, where sleek lizards hung sardonic and unmoving and where baleful birds stared forever with their bloated eyes and where gaunt stick-figures stood mute and unprotesting for eternity, there would be lightning all right, quick and sharp above his head, but there would be no thunder.

Papa Loaty

In a way, it all started in a little bar in Corona, New Mexico, during a sandstorm one afternoon in October.

It started there and then for Chad Sommers, anyway. When and where it all *really* started, heaven only knows.

There were only a few other people in the place that afternoon, most of them talking quietly down at the other end of the bar. Behind them, in a corner of the room illumined only by a small hanging bulb, two young men and a young woman were playing pool, laughing, smoking, chatting softly in Spanish. Trailing cigar smoke, the bartender moved about languidly, wiping glasses, exchanging a few words with the patrons. A small brown dog lay curled on the floor in a corner near the door, asleep. Chad, glad to be off the road for a few minutes' rest, was sitting at the end of the bar nearest the door, sipping his beer, when the rickety door clattered open and the old man came in.

The wind had been building up to a howl out there, and the rusty metal sign overhanging the sidewalk outside (J. LESTER'S PLACE, with the A hanging by a crusty filament) squealed with every new gust. Through the half-closed blinds and the bleary windowglass, one could just make out a large tumbleweed bumbling down the dusty street like some grotesque and insane jaywalker. The metal sign gave a mighty shriek of protest, and when the door to the bar banged open, it was as if the wind itself blew the old man in like a swirl of dry leaves.

He closed the door, and either shutting out the moaning of the wind made it seem quiet in the little room, or the quiet talk at the far side of the bar grew even quieter. The pool players momentarily paused, then went on with their game, making their shots, speaking softly among themselves, and as Chad knew only fragments of Spanish, it was hard for him to tell whether they were talking about the newcomer or not, though he thought he caught the word *loco*. In any case, he noticed, both the patrons down at the far end of the bar and the bartender himself regarded the old man oddly for a few moments before picking up the threads of their conversation. From their expressions, Chad gathered that the others had seen the old man around before but did not particularly rejoice in his arrival.

The old man himself was rather unremarkable except for being uncommonly shabby. Standing there silhouetted against the smoky panes in the door, he looked rather tall, sinewy-thin, with patched multicolor clothes hanging on him like the wildly assorted rags festooning the gaunt and lonely form of a scarecrow. Atop his head perched what in happier days might have been a hat, and the layers of dirty shirtcloth visible through the front of his soiled coat scarcely invited speculation about the cleanliness of the flesh beneath. Chad, anticipating, wished that the old man were not angling toward the stool beside his own at the bar. He was right, on closer proximity; the man smelled.

"Ain't ever seen you here before," he said to Chad as he sat down. The voice had a whining, somehow unpleasant quality.

"Uh, no," Chad replied, "I haven't been here before, I'm just stopping through on my way. Name's Chad. Chad Sommers."

"Where you headed?" the old man asked, shaking Chad's hand.

Christ, Chad thought, he's going to want me to give him a ride, probably looking for a handout too.

"I'm going to a ranch house to work. It's not too much farther. Down toward Roswell. The old Walker place, I guess they call it around here."

Instantly the low hum of voices in the room vanished, and everyone was looking down the bar at him in silence. Even the pool players stopped clacking their cues. He nearly laughed, because the effect immediately reminded him of one of those old horror movies in which someone comes to the inn and announces to the peasant loungers that he's looking for the way to Castle Dracula. In this case, however, the look that he was getting from his fellow customers was more one of distaste than of horror, as if they were asking him, with their eyes: why would you want to take a job there, of all places?

"Yep," the old man was saying, "I know the place. I'm headed down that direction too, maybe you can take me as far as you're goin'."

Chad suppressed a sigh. "Sure. Why not? Uh, want a beer? On me." Damn, he was getting to be a soft touch, at the doddering old age of thirty.

"Don't mind if I do."

"Corona?"

"That'll do 'er. Thankee."

The bartender had drifted to Chad's end of the bar. He eyed the old man with unmistakable displeasure, then looked questioningly at Chad, who said, "A Corona for him. I guess I'll have another one too."

They sipped their beers in silence. Once or twice the old man looked as if he was about to say something to Chad, but he looked down the bar at the others, who were talking among themselves again, more quietly than before, and he seemed to decide not to say anything. For reasons he couldn't pin down, Chad felt relieved, though he had the feeling, somehow, that the old man was going to open up and talk when they got outside. He wished, now, that he had lied about the direction he was traveling. But then maybe the old hitchhiker would still have asked to come along; maybe he didn't really care where he went.

Thirty seconds' drive south from the bar, down the dusty windblown street, past a half dozen store fronts, and you were back out in the desert, where the road ran ribbonlike through huddles of low, cedar-spotted hills. Now and again a long, majestic mesa, furred over with cedar bushes, would appear on the horizon, grazing there like some great languid beast, but after a few miles this hilly terrain gave way to open chaparral country, a desert vista that stretched away endlessly in all directions, sandy plains dotted not with cedar now but with yucca and chamisa and mesquite. In places, standing armies of cholla cactus, their skinny arms lolling in the wind, guarded the plains in eerie monotonous multitudes of grayish green. The wind continued to blow, sending undulations of sand across the land almost like moving waves of water.

Chad loved the openness, the vast turquoise sky, the quiet here—a welcome change from clamor and crowding and dirty city air. But the ragged figure sitting beside him in the car made him nervous. He half wished the old man would say something, and half hoped he wouldn't.

They had driven a good distance down the road to the southeast, through uniform stretches of fenced land punctuated at long intervals by lone houses and the stiffbacked forms of ancient windmills, when the old man turned and said, "So you're going to work for them Walkers. Odd bunch."

Chad's curiosity was piqued. "Odd? How do you mean?"

"Oh," the old man said, as if already changing his mind about elaborating on the point, "you know, just—unpopular, like. People talk, hereabouts. You know how it is. I'm kind of surprised they're hiring somebody to work for them. What're you going to be doing?"

"Just handyman stuff," Chad said. "You know, fixing things around the place, mending fences, whatever. I do a little plumbing, a little electrical, a little carpentry, a little roofing, stuff like that, whatever they need. Probably help with the chores whenever they want me to. They ran an ad in the Albuquerque paper, and I saw it and gave them a call. They hired me right away, over the phone, so I guess they'd had trouble getting anybody from closer by."

"You ain't going to *live* there, too?" the old man asked, making it sound as if that would be a doubtful arrangement.

"Well, yeah, matter of fact," Chad said. "That's part of the deal. Room and board. Sounds like a pretty good deal to me. I mean, to tell you the truth, I don't have anything else I'd rather be doing, or anyplace else I'd rather be, right now."

"Huh," the old man said, turning away to look out the window at the passing landscape.

Fence lines kept stretching ahead on both sides of the road, with occasional tumbleweeds caught up in them, and from time to time one of those somehow spectral-looking old windmills would rear its ragged head on the horizon, far off the road, and would drop away again, like some antediluvian creature returning to its feed. Chad reflected that they hadn't seen more than two or three cars on this road since they'd left Corona.

At length they turned onto another road leading more directly south, where the same sort of desert vistas rushed by them on both sides, an unending world of spiky yucca and gnarled mesquite. Tumbleweeds migrated across the road to fetch up on wire fences. After a while, the old man spoke up again in his high, whiny voice.

"Three brothers."

"What?" Chad asked. It was the sort of thing someone would say whose mind wandered, and for a moment Chad half expected him not to have any coherent continuation. But he did.

"Them Walkers," the old man said. "It's three brothers. Fenton Walker. Joe Tom Walker. Tully Walker."

"They all live there?"

"Yep, and their families," the old man replied, "big old two-story ranch house way off the road. They all live there, all three brothers, and their wives, and some other relatives too. Their old man's still alive, and *his* daddy, old Grandpa Ned. Grandpa Ned, funny in the head, some of 'em say around here."

Sounds like a day at the zoo, Chad thought, but he didn't want to say anything when he was unfamiliar with the locale and its folklore, and couldn't be too sure what relationships and attitudes existed here; he knew from experience that you could crab a job or a friendship or a business deal or a romance with just one unreflective remark made to the wrong person at the wrong time.

"So how many people does that make, living in the house?" he asked, watching another tall wraithlike windmill appear, only to see it slide beneath the horizon on the right.

"Never took the trouble to count," the old hitchhiker said.

Everywhere looked the same out here, and Chad might well have driven right past the turnoff he wanted, if the old man hadn't said: "Old Walker place is up that road to the right, there, where you see that cattleguard. House is maybe a mile off the road."

Chad pulled the car into the turnoff, where an unpaved little road led off farther than he could see, into the chaparral. "Well, I'll have to let you out here. Haven't seen too many cars. Are you sure you'll be able to get another ride?"

The old man shrugged, opening his door. "I'll get along. It's only thirty more miles to Roswell."

"Too far to walk," Chad said. It was already getting to be evening, and the deep blue sky had given itself over to the riotous multicolor frenzy of a desert sunset, with streaks of golden red radiance back-lighting a dark froth of distant scudding clouds, and the horizon all around turning salmon-colored in strangely modified memory of the sun. It was a beautiful sight, but Chad worried now that the old man, on foot on this sparsely traveled roadway, might well not get another ride tonight.

"Don't you worry," the old man said. "I'll get by. Always have. Always will. Thanks for the ride, and—" He closed the car door and stood leaning down to peer in at Chad. "And be careful out here."

"Careful? You mean the machinery—"

"Well, that too," the old man said, looking over his shoulder, toward the Walker property, almost as if he were worried about being overheard, which was preposterous, as there could be no one nearby to hear him but Chad. "I mean—these people. Isabelle, I think she's called, that's Joe Tom's wife, her family, what used to live up in Mesa, is kind of strange, and don't nobody even know anything about Edna Fox Walker, that's Fenton's wife, the one as came from Nambé Pueblo, where they used to have all them Indian witchcraft doings and whatnot. Some of the other wives' folks live there in the house too, I think. I know Susan's dad does, think her name's Susan anyway, the Hispanic woman that's married to Tully. Joe Tom's wife's folks are both still alive as far as I know. I'm pretty sure they both live in the house. Then there's Karen, the daughter, she's one of the most sensible ones of the bunch, at least when that Carl O'Brien ain't hanging around her. You could live here forever and never really get to know some of them people at the Walker house. Folks kind of steer clear of 'em. Some funny stuff has went on out here, so you watch yourself."

"Okay, I will," Chad said, feeling a little dizzy at all this unsolicited detail. He had always been the sort of person who had trouble remembering three names in a row when meeting new people at a party, so at this point he didn't have a very clear idea of the family portrait the old man had just painted for him. He nodded to him in parting. "You take care too, oldtimer."

The old man waved once and started off down the main road, walking south, and Chad pulled the car on through the gate, bumping across the cattleguard, and started down the little unpaved road at a crawl. Any faster, and he would risk breaking an axle.

After five minutes, the main road behind him wasn't visible in the gathering gloom. Neither, yet, was the house.

*   *   *

The two-story frame structure finally popped up at the edge of vision, hugging the darkening westerly horizon like some furtive angular insect in the blowing dust. He could just make out other structures around the house, outbuildings of one sort or another. Beyond these buildings, he thought he saw the gaunt frame of an old windmill nodding into the howling wind. Off to one side of the land there seemed to be a field of unharvested cotton, a grizzled white foam that looked incongruously like snow. He thought he could see sheep grazing off somewhere in the distance too, but it was hard to tell, with the blowing sand.

He drove what felt like a considerable distance farther up the rock-strewn road before the house looked any closer. That was the way distance was, out here in the desert. He remembered times in the past, driving toward mountains for hours at a time without their seeming to get any nearer. But gradually the old house grew larger, its ragged gables prodding the sky and tending to blend into its fathomless darkness as night came on. From what he could see, there were lights on in only one portion of the place, downstairs. The kitchen, probably. It wasn't really very late, only around seven, but he suspected that these ranch families ate dinner and turned in for the night fairly early, to be up early in the morning.

He pulled up in a bare space near the house, turned the engine and the lights off, and sat for a moment in the car. Why was he hesitating? Good heavens, was he really going to let the crazy old hitchhiker's stories bother him? This might well be an odd lot of folks, but he'd met odd folks before, and anyway, this was a living, just when he needed one.

He got out, retrieved his suitcase from the back seat, and headed up the rickety porch steps.

The face that met him at the door was broad, dour, not particularly pleasant-looking, surmounting, as it did, a short squat body that reminded Chad, more than anything else, of some sort of troll. The face, the survivor of perhaps some fifty-five John Deere calendars, didn't seem to know how to smile, but after a moment's hesitation the little man extended a beefy hand.

"Tully Walker."

"Pleased to meet you, Mr. Walker. Chad Sommers."

"C'mon in. And call me Tully. We don't believe in being formal around here. We ain't got time for it."

Chad followed the man along a dimly lit hallway and through a door into a dining room, where a number of people were seated around a long table, finishing supper. It reminded Chad of a mead-hall in an old story about Vikings. Here we go, he thought, with an overwhelming round of introductions, and me incapable of getting names to stick in my head till about the seventeenth repetition.

But the dozen or so people at the table—several men and women apparently in their fifties or sixties, a few people older than that, an attractive near-thirtyish woman, a man of similar age—the people at the table just nodded to him one by one, and Tully Walker said only, "I'll show you up to your room." Chad had just a fleeting impression of the other people; evidently he would get to know them as he went along. In a way he was glad, he reflected, following Tully up the musty stairwell, glad that they didn't stand on formalities around here, as he would prefer meeting the rest of the family one at a time anyway. But he hoped supper wasn't out of the question altogether for tonight, as he was very hungry.

"This here'll be your room," Tully said, opening a door onto a fairly large but sparsely furnished bedroom halfway down the upstairs hall. "Upstairs bathroom's at the end of the hall." In the dim light he couldn't tell how many bedrooms there were up here, but they had passed one other door on the way to this room, and there seemed to be more doors farther along. It was a larger house than its outside appearance had suggested.

Tully waited while Chad put his suitcase on the ancient little brass-frame bed. The wind rattled the windowpanes, moaning under the eaves of the old house. Tully had to raise his voice to talk over it. "When you're ready, come on back downstairs and Susan, that's my wife, she'll fix you up with some supper. We're usually done eating by now. Everybody's to bed by eight. Breakfast is at five."

Supper was the remnants of fried chicken, mashed potatoes, and beans. Remnants or not, it all tasted good, even though it felt odd to sit there at that big table and eat alone.

Not quite alone. Susan, Tully's wife, hovered nearby, between the dining room and kitchen, cleaning up. It made Chad a little uncomfortable, thinking that she must want him to hurry up and get through eating so that she could finish her chores, but she didn't seem impatient. She might have been oddly nervous, perhaps, unless it was his imagination, but in any case not impatient. He looked up at her from time to time. She was Hispanic, dark-haired, dark-eyed, shy-looking, rather attractive, and somewhat younger, he thought, than Tully; she might have been forty.

He was just finishing his meal when an old Hispanic man in baggy pants and a T-shirt appeared in the doorway to the hall. He cast an inscrutable glance at Chad—this might have included a nod, Chad wasn't sure—then directed his watery gaze at Susan.

"Pasa buena noche, mija," he said to her.

"Igualmente, papá," she replied, and he withdrew, glancing at Chad again in a peculiar way, almost as if in some mute sort of concern.

Chad was through with his meal, so Susan began clearing away his dishes. He started to help her, but she motioned with her hand, discouraging his doing so. "The men do not help with dishes," she said.

Huh, Chad thought; not exactly your modern, enlightened household, it would appear. It was an awkward moment, between them, and he filled in the gap by nodding toward the doorway. Susan nodded in response to the unasked question.

"That's my father," she said. "Juan Torres. I did not introduce myself, señor. I am Susan Torres Walker."

"Encantado," he managed to say, retrieving a scrap of Spanish from the whirlpools of his memory. "I'm Chad Sommers."

Susan nodded, withdrew to the kitchen with a load of dirty dishes, then returned, and stopped to fix him with an earnest stare.

""Señor Sommers—"

"Please call me Chad."

"You should—*tenga cuidado*. Take care."

Damn, Chad thought, that's the second time today that somebody has told me that; it could get to be depressing.

"Take care?" he asked.

"At night. In this house, after dark. We stay in our rooms, señor. It is better that way."

He was about to ask her why, but she had slipped out into the hallway, gone.

Upstairs in his bed he lay staring at the dark as if it held something of interest, some cache of answers to his growing questions, but it was only the dark—uncommunicative and unhelpful. The wind had died down now, and he almost missed it in a way; the silence was oppressive. He had to get to sleep; they had breakfast here at five, Tully had said. He wasn't sure he was cut out for this life. The work, yes; the life, maybe not. Then again he'd scarcely given it a chance, and one could get used to almost anything.

He turned over and tried to get comfortable in the old bed, but found himself tensing up.

Listening.

The impression was one of footfalls, but he couldn't tell where. One moment, they seemed to be out in the hall, but hadn't Susan said that people stayed in their rooms at night? The next moment, the footfalls, more felt than heard, didn't seem like someone walking in the hallway at all; they seemed to be outside, in the desert night. Then they were footfalls in the hallway again, where the old boards creaked softly as if someone were passing his door, pausing, going on.

He lay still, listening. Nothing, nothing more to hear.

When he awoke at 4:30 and switched on the bedside lamp, with his travel alarm clock burring softly in his ears, he could hear other people stirring somewhere in the great old house, though it was still quite dark outside. He thought he might have dreamed of someone or something moving about in the dark, tall and mysterious and somehow unthinkable, but he couldn't quite recall his dreams. Maybe, he thought, bestirring himself in the dim lamplight, maybe it's just as well.

"This here," Tully was saying, "is my brother Fenton."

Fenton Walker, who extended a clammy hand dutifully, was rather thin, but short like the plumper Tully. Evidently, for all their variety otherwise, the Walker genes didn't make for tremendous height. Also, nature didn't seem to have provided any ready way for the Walker clan to smile; their faces wore a more or less constant expression of seriousness, as if the tasks at hand were nothing to be merry about.

Fenton, withdrawing his hand, pointed over Chad's shoulder to someone else coming up, a rather muscular man of medium build, short like the others. All three had brown hair quickly going over to gray, and light blue eyes that seemed to look deep into you without letting you look too revealingly into them, as if they were used to keeping their secrets. The third brother introduced himself.

"Joe Tom Walker." Again, Chad shook hands. He hadn't met the other brothers at breakfast, as that meal was apparently a fragmented sort of gathering at the Walker place, with some of the family already out, before sunrise, doing some chores, and others stopping by the table for a cup of coffee and some toast, a few at a time. When Chad had had his own breakfast, only Susan and her father and Tully had eaten with him, nodding good morning but scarcely speaking a word.

"Guess Tully's told you what you'll be doing this morning," Fenton was saying.

"Uh, no," Chad said.

"I was just about to tell him," Tully said, and turned to Chad. "See that toolshed?" Chad looked where Tully was pointing. The sun was just now coming up, and the outbuildings were shadowy forms not yet divested of night. "North side's all dryrotted away. Need you to replace them boards. Some lumber's in the shed."

As the morning advanced, Chad worked alone on repairing the little building. It was so far out in the chaparral that it was more like just being out in the untamed desert somewhere than being on a ranch; the house was barely visible from here. Yellow land stretched away in all directions, spiked with yucca, and somewhere on the horizon a gaunt windmill reared its odd angular head. Although it was mid-October the sun was hot, and he took his shirt off and wiped a trickle of sweat out of his eyes and hung the shirt on a nail.

Tully had been right about the north side of this shed; the old boards had just about crumbled away. The new boards had to be cut to size, so he had set up a sawhorse on the ground nearby. He had power tools in the back of his car, but the shed was too far from the house to run a power cord out, so he had to saw the boards by hand. He was bending over a board, running a pencil line along its width to mark a place for the saw, when a shadow fell across the board.

He looked up to find a young woman, perhaps thirty years old, standing with a pitcher in one hand and a glass in the other. She had straw-blonde hair and frank-looking blue eyes in a face that was pretty in a country sort of way, not like a magazine model, but pretty, the sort of face he really liked. He thought she had been at the table the first time he saw them all there, but that had been only a quick look at a roomful of people. Even so, he did think he remembered her; she'd have been difficult not to notice. She was dressed now in tight-fitting bluejeans and a western shirt, and she looked good in them. Suddenly realizing he'd never spoken with her before, he felt a little self-conscious, a stranger standing naked to the waist in front of her, but she just smiled.

"Mom thought you might be thirsty," she said.

He set his ruler and pencil down. "Well, thanks, I sure could use a drink of water right now." So someone in the family was capable of a smile after all. And it looked very nice, on this lady, as nice as the jeans and western shirt did.

She poured water from the pitcher. "I'm sorry, I should have introduced myself. I'm Karen."

He nodded, sipping the water. "Let me see, you're—"

"Joe Tom Walker's daughter," she said. "It must be a lot of new names to remember."

"Pleased to meet you." He made a mental note of the fact that she was wearing no wedding ring, but maybe women on ranchland didn't wear them, the work being what it was.

Finishing the glass of water, Chad nearly didn't notice that a dark-haired man about his own age was approaching. The newcomer eyed Chad with a hint of distaste, and Chad thought he was about to say something to him, but he spoke to Karen instead.

"Your mom's going to need you back at the house," he said.

Karen gave the man what Chad thought was an uncomfortable glance and nodded, taking the empty glass from Chad and starting back in the direction of the ranch house. A few yards out, she turned back to look at Chad.

"It's nice to meet you," she said. Chad smiled and waved, and she went on her way, leaving him alone with the dark-haired man, who stood in silence for a moment as if overcoming some reluctance to speak. When he did speak up, he introduced himself, after a fashion.

"I'm Carl O'Brien." When Chad offered to shake hands, the man didn't respond, but only gave him a long, cold look. "Let's get something straight right now. You're paid to do your work, not to stand around talking."

"Ah, excuse me, but I was under the impression," Chad said, "that I worked for the Walker brothers."

O'Brien bristled at this. "I'm family, mister, and you'll take orders from me too. I'm a cousin to Isabelle Walker's sister's husband. I live here, have for several years, so you're going to see me around all the time. You just do your work, and we'll have no trouble. And by the way—"

Christ, Chad thought, here it comes, just like in some damn B movie; should I move my lips along with the words?

"—in case you had any ideas, Karen is spoken for."

"I'll remember," Chad said as O'Brien was walking away. "Nice meeting you too." Sometimes it was politic, unfortunately, to be halfway polite even to the assholes of the world, though he had to wonder how much authority this strutting little Caesar actually had.

It was nearly dark, getting on toward dinnertime, and Joe Tom Walker had sent Chad out to roll a length of hose up and store it in one of the sheds nearby. He was just finishing, wiping his hands and walking back to the house, when he looked up to see a Native American woman in his path. She was about the age of the Walker brothers, he guessed, and at the moment was dumping a pan of water to the side of the path and drying her hands one at a time on her apron. Chad tried to remember— hadn't the old hitchhiker said something about an Indian woman?

She nodded to him, stepping aside. He had stepped aside too, at the same time, so that to an observer it must have resembled an odd little dance they were doing. He nodded back to her and said, "I'm Chad Sommers. You must be—"

"Edna Fox Walker," she said. "My husband is Fenton Walker."

Aha. It came rushing back to him now, what the old man out on the road had said. *Fenton's wife, the one as came from Nambé Pueblo, where they used to have all them Indian witchcraft doings and whatnot.* She too, like

Karen, might have been at the dinner table that first night, but he couldn't remember for sure; sometimes he felt as if all these faces melted into one another, even as distinctive as some of them were, but then he had always been awkward at learning names and faces. Nambé Pueblo, Indian witchcraft? It was certainly going to continue to be interesting, getting to know this family.

"Pleased to meet you," he said.

The woman cast a glance back toward the house, almost as if nervous about being seen or overheard talking with him; his imagination, surely. She fixed him with a dark stare that somehow instantly made him uneasy.

"Did Susan tell you," she asked, in that broad-voweled sort of Indian voice that at a more cheerful moment Chad would have loved, "about keeping to your room at night?"

He shrugged. "Uh, well, yes, now that you mention it, I think she did say something like that. I didn't give it much thought. I don't usually get up at night. What's so important about—"

Her expression darkened a bit, and again she looked around at the house as if not wanting to be overheard.

"Watch out," she said.

"For what?"

"For Papa Loaty."

He repressed an inclination to laugh. "Papa who?"

What she said to him then was peculiar in the extreme, and as time passed it would stick in his mind, stirring uneasily from time to time, tantalizing. It was almost as if it half awakened something in his own unconscious mind, something archetypal.

"Him that walks on the wind."

And she turned, in the gathering gloom, and walked away.

Conversation at the dinner table, during Chad's first meal with the whole family, was low-key, and he found himself wondering whether it was partly because he was present, something of a stranger in their midst. But on reflection he thought this unlikely; somehow he suspected that this family had never been one for boisterous chattering and laughing over a meal. There was a curious, almost Puritanical simplicity to their lifestyle, though it was ringed about with an odd, dark quality that he couldn't quite fathom.

In any event, they all ate their evening meal quietly, and it gave him a chance to survey the family, including some people he hadn't met at this point.

The Walker brothers of course were all there—thin and wiry Fenton, muscular and raw-boned Joe Tom, squat and dour-faced Tully. Then there were the wives—Edna Fox Walker, whom he had just met in that strange conversation outside; Susan Torres Walker, whom he had met the previous evening; and the remaining one had to be Isabelle, whom he hadn't actually been introduced to: Joe Tom's wife and Karen's mother. She was fiftyish, rather plump, with light hair like Karen's, and an attractive face. To judge from her general actions, she was rather livelier than some of the others, though he had the impression that her husband and brothers-in-law kept her on short tether, as her manner was somewhat subdued at times.

Isabelle was flanked by an old man and an old woman, whom Chad took to be her parents. Next to them sat Juan Torres, Susan's father, and next to him an old man, short and thin, who rather resembled Fenton; Chad guessed him to be the Walker brothers' father. And farther down he saw an even older man, easily ninety years old; this was the patriarch he had heard about. When the meal was finished and this venerable figure got up, with Tully and Isabelle giving him an assist by a hand on each elbow, Chad noticed that the old man was short like the others, and though the wizened face was too advanced in age to still bear strong family resemblance, Chad theorized that the man indeed might be the Walker brothers' grandfather. The Walker brothers were all in their late fifties to early sixties, Chad estimated, so for them to have a living grandfather was pretty remarkable.

Everyone murmured good night to everyone and dispersed to bedrooms both downstairs and up. By now it was quite dark outside.

Up in his room, Chad lay in the dark and stared at the ceiling, imagining it but not really seeing it, seeing only the luminescent dial of his bedside clock grinning out the hour: ten, then eleven, then quarter to twelve, and Chad still awake. Outside, the wind had come up, touching the windows, the orifices of the house like the stops of some husky flute. Chad listened, and somehow found the sound immensely lonely, depressing.

Why couldn't he fall asleep? Maybe he needed—but the bathroom was down the hall, and he found himself oddly reluctant to get up and pull on a bathrobe and make his way down there in the dark. Could he really, on some unconscious level, be taking those remarks seriously, about the wisdom of staying in one's room at night? It sounded, again, like some hackneyed line from a horror film. This was a ranch in southeast New Mexico, not the Borgo Pass. Surely all this was foolishness, the inane prattle of people too long out of the mainstream of the larger world, people out of touch with reality, with society.

But he had to admit it: he was nervous about going out in the hall.

Nevertheless, he decided to go. There are times, he reflected ironically, when all the philosophizing in the world has to take a back seat to the nagging of one's bladder.

He lay for a few seconds more, listening to the soughing of the wind at the windowpanes, then hoisted himself up on his elbows, rolled over, and got to his feet in the dark. Somehow even though he had decided to take a trip down the hall to the bathroom, he still felt nervous about turning on any lights, though he couldn't have said why. Did he want not to see something? Or not to be seen? Preposterous, he thought, pulling on his bathrobe and heading for the door.

But he had scarcely stepped half out into the dusky hall when he stopped, frozen in his tracks by a barely discernible glimpse of something moving, something unaccountable, moving, out there in the dark somewhere.

The only light was a wan play of moonglow filtering in from the bathroom window at the end of the hall, visible through the half-open bathroom door. And against this backdrop of pallid light, something made a rapid passage across the field of vision, from darkness into darkness. Something tall and thin.

Why did he think *something* instead of *someone*, when evidently the shape moving in the near-dark was a person? But whoever it was, the person passing across the backdrop of moonlight was exceedingly tall and gaunt, very unlike any of the Walkers, unlike anyone who could be in the house, so far as he knew. The glimpse was a fleeting one, but he had the impression that the moving figure, so tall and willowy-thin that it scarcely seemed to have any substance, was surmounted by a head covered with some unthinkable shock of bristly hair, hair that stood out in broad angular bunches like—

It was strange, but in an instant he knew precisely the image he needed—the wildly bristling hair was almost like the blades of a windmill.

In an instant the figure had passed beyond sight somewhere down there in the dark, but it had burned itself onto his mind like a cattle brand.

Aching bladder or no, he turned, slipped back into his room, closed the door, and locked it.

And lay the rest of the night wide awake, except for a brief and unrestful descent into sleep just before it was time to get up. He thought he might have dreamed something, but was rather glad, as before, that he couldn't remember exactly what it was.

It happened that Chad and Joe Tom Walker were working together the next day, far out at the westernmost edge of the property, mending a barbed wire fence. Off to the north, nearly on the horizon, an old wooden windmill raised its angular head, but Chad made it a point not to dwell on what it reminded him of.

They were working on one section of fence that seemed oddly bowed out, as if something large had blundered against it, but so far as Chad knew, there were no large animals here, nothing larger than sheep anyway, and those were kept in pasturage a considerable distance from here.

"Don't see how a fence gets like this," Chad ventured.

Joe Tom only grunted, "Mm." It made Chad feel naïve, the city boy in the country, unable to understand how country matters worked, as if Joe Tom knew perfectly well how fences got the way they were, but was disinclined to talk about it.

They were nearly through with the job when Chad heard a dry burring sound nearby, and noticed that Joe Tom, backing up with a strand of fence wire in his hand and not looking around to see where he was going, was about to back into a rattlesnake not four feet away, coiled and rattling.

"Look out!" was all Chad managed to say.

Joe Tom wheeled around just as the snake pulled its triangular head back to strike. Joe Tom's right foot went up in an instant, presenting the bottom of his heavy boot to the snake. To Chad, time seemed frozen for a moment as the snake darted through the air, making a frenetic zigzag shadow across the sandy ground. When the snake struck, it hit only the sole of Joe Tom's boot. Joe Tom stood on his left foot, his right foot still in the air. The snake withdrew, recoiled, and rattled again, but after a moment it slithered away. They watched till it was nearly out of sight across the chaparral.

"Damn," Joe Tom said.

"Yeah," Chad said. "That was close. You didn't hear it rattling?"

Joe Tom shook his head. "I'm a little hard of hearing. That can be dangerous out here." He leaned against a fencepost and took a rag from his overall pocket and wiped his face. "Listen, Chad, I—well, I just want to say thanks. You saved me from getting a nasty bite. I've been bitten once before, and it's no damn fun." He extended his hand.

Chad shrugged, smiled, shook hands. "Glad I could help."

"You know," Joe Tom said, "frankly, I wasn't sure if I was going to like you, when you came. I mean, life out here is a certain kind of life, and folks who don't live here sometimes don't understand. Most hired hands around here turn out to be about as useful as tits on a bull."

Chad laughed. "Well, I hope I can do better than that. Anyhow, it's good of you to say so, because—well, I don't know if I ought to say this, but even though everybody's basically okay toward me, mostly they don't really—I mean, they don't—"

Joe Tom nodded. "They don't say much. They don't encourage you much. That's just the way my family is, and no, I don't mind you saying it. They're kind of—reserved, I guess you'd say."

Chad thought he might as well take a further risk, now that he essentially seemed to have Joe Tom's confidence and good feelings. "It's almost as if there's something they're afraid of," he said.

Joe Tom shot him a look that at first made him think that he had indeed overshot his bounds. But all the older man said was: "Yeah, well. You and me'll maybe have to talk about that sometime."

They finished up with the fence and started on the long walk back toward the ranch house. As it turned out, the events of the morning had apparently made Joe Tom more talkative than he ordinarily would have been.

"There's a lot of old stories you'll hear around these parts," he said, "and some of 'em you can laugh at, and some of 'em you can't."

"What kind of stories?" Chad asked.

"Oh, one thing and another," Joe Tom said.

"Give me an example."

Joe Tom looked off in the distance before answering. Then he said, "I don't know if you know it, but not too far from here, back in 1947, they say a flying saucer crashed, out in the desert. Down toward Roswell a ways."

Chad did remember. "Yeah. I read a book about that a few years ago. I didn't realize it was near here that it happened. It was all supposed to be a big government cover-up or something."

Joe Tom grunted. "Hmph. Damn government wouldn't tell you the truth if it was the last card in their hand."

"So," Chad said, "now you've got me wondering. What does the flying saucer thing have to do with—"

"With my family? Well, nothing, maybe," Joe Tom said, "except if you believe some of the stories. My father Leland Walker, you saw him at the dinner table, he always said the strangeness in the land really started about the time of that saucer business. My grandpa has said so too, and he's lived out here for the better part of a century. That's old Grandpa Ned you saw at the table. Grandpa Ned says there was already something peculiar going on out here, odd noises, something or somebody moving around at night, but he says that that flying saucer episode kind of—added to it, made it stronger, or something. 'Course, you have to understand, Grandpa Ned says all kinds of things."

What was it, Chad thought, that the old hitchhiker had said? *Grandpa Ned, funny in the head.*

Joe Tom continued talking. "Then again, Isabelle's folks, old Hiram and Mollie Jenkins, tell the same kind of story if you can ever get them to say anything about it at all; they say that except for those sounds at night, in and around the house, things was more or less normal around here till that crash in '47. And Edna, that's Fenton's wife, you know, the Indian woman you met, she says all that business out there kind of"—he seemed to be groping for a way to put it—

"kind of left something. The army, they came out and picked up all the mess, but something stayed."

Chad couldn't have said why, but this choice of words tended almost to make the hair stand up on the back of his neck. It was eerie. From the look on Joe Tom's face, it wasn't as if the man took these old tales too lightly. "What do you mean, something stayed?" Chad asked.

"Don't know what else to tell you," Joe Tom said. "Something stayed on, in the land. Edna agrees with Grandpa Ned, says whatever it was, it kind of breathed new life into the thing that was here already. The thing that walks, she says. Something was here, but something new came, and stayed. And now it walks with a vengeance, to hear some of them tell it. I try not to think about it much, you know, I got my work to do, don't do no good thinking about spooky things, but they all say there's something to it. Don't know what you'd call this thing they talk about. Some—I don't know, Edna would say some spirit, maybe."

"Do you believe in things like that?" Chad asked.

Joe Tom eyed him narrowly. "Probably sounds foolish to you, but let me tell you something, folks out here don't laugh at these stories, if they're smart."

"I'm not laughing," Chad said.

"I know you're not," Joe Tom replied.

At this point they were nearing the outbuildings within sight of the house, and Carl O'Brien came up, smoking a cigarette and lugging a coil of rope over one shoulder. He gave Chad only a glance, addressing himself to Joe Tom. "Fenton needs you to help with something." And with another glance at Chad: "Both of you." Then he strode off, leaving a train of smoke.

Joe Tom spat into the sandy soil. "Don't understand what my daughter Karen sees in that guy. Never did care for the arrogant little shit, myself."

They resumed their walk toward the house. Chad stopped, just far enough out to still be out of earshot of anyone who might be nearby, and Joe Tom stopped too, looking at him questioningly.

"Just one more question," Chad said. "Is there—is there anybody living in the house that I don't know about?"

If Chad could have anticipated the moment of shock on Joe

Tom's sun-brazened face, he might well not have asked. But Joe Tom
recovered quickly, shrugging. "Anybody in the house that you don't
know about." He clapped Chad on the shoulder before turning to go.
"I hope not, Chad. I hope not."

That night after he turned in, Chad lay looking up at the almost palpable dark in his room. This was getting to be a habit; wasn't he ever going to sleep normally, out here?

He couldn't have said what it was, this time, that bothered him. He
didn't hear anything out of the ordinary. Once in a while a little chorus
of wind would gather under the eaves beyond his windowpanes,
moaning, whispering. And somewhere out in the night a coyote
howled, a stark and cold sound. But nothing unusual. Gradually he
must have drifted off to sleep.

Sometime later he awoke. Or was startled awake.

Something was moving around outside, near the house.

A part of his mind protested, sleepily: so what? Desert animals do
come around sometimes, no big deal. Coyotes, foxes, even an occasional antelope; someone had mentioned to him, during the day, that
you might even see a cougar out here at night, if you watched long
enough. People didn't tend to stay up and watch, though, naturally
enough; the work was hard, you needed your sleep.

But these reflections did little to reassure him, because something
was still moving around out there.

Something large and heavy.

What in God's name? He got up, bumbled his feet into his slippers, went to the window, opened the blind a crack, and looked out.

Just in time, he thought, to catch a glimpse of something dim, unclear, moving around the side of the house, out of his range of sight.

He stood there for a moment, looking, but there wasn't anything
else to see, if indeed there had been anything to start with. Maybe he
was still half asleep. In any case he wasn't going exploring; whatever it
was—

Suddenly he thought he felt a kind of shudder in the frame of the
house. It was a crazy thought, but his raw impression was that it was as
if something, something around on the other side, something insubstantial but real, had passed through the walls.

And he had barely formed this thought when something undeniably brushed against the outside of his door.

He froze, listening.

There might have been a sort of breath, a sort of ethereal presence like wind, moving on down the hall for a moment, then another shudder, as if something had passed beyond the old wood frame of the house, back out into the night.

He got back into bed and lay listening but heard nothing more. Felt nothing more. Out of exhaustion more than anything else, he finally succumbed to an uneasy sleep, and awoke tired and confused.

At the breakfast table, people seemed subdued. Old Grandpa Ned was there, for once, but you couldn't read much in his wizened face, a confusion of wrinkles that swarmed into each other and approximated something like a half-smile when you greeted him. Isabelle was there too, looking a little tired herself, Chad thought. And even Karen, who stopped by just for a slice of toast and a cup of coffee, looked a little weary, though she smiled at him and exchanged a few words. Maybe no one had slept well.

After breakfast, out in the dooryard near the back of the house, he noticed that the ground seemed to be roughed up in spots, gouged. Susan Walker was out there with a broom sweeping the sandy soil back into a level state, as if these marks in the ground needed to be expunged. Susan only nodded to Chad as he walked by; she looked as if she would not have welcomed any conversation at the moment. Chad went about his work for the day, trying not to think about things.

But it was pretty hard not to.

That night, in spite of all the weird thoughts crowding and jostling with each other in his mind when he went to bed, Chad slept straight through for once. It was probably just exhaustion; he'd done a lot of heavy work that day, and he hadn't been sleeping very restfully, so his body must have just demanded a decent night's slumber. He awoke barely in time for breakfast, and couldn't even remember having had any dreams.

Anyway, it was Sunday, and it appeared that around the Walker place this was no day for unnecessary work. It wasn't so much that the family was all that religious; unlike many country families he'd known of, the Walkers didn't indulge in prayers before meals, didn't wedge Bible verses into niches in the conversation. They didn't seem outwardly religious in the usual ways, at any rate. Edna Fox Walker, he suspected, had her own spirituality, the faith of her Pueblo, her people, a faith rooted in the land, a faith old before Christianity even existed. In any case, out of physical and emotional necessity if nothing else, the family did seem to keep Sunday as a day of rest, relatively speaking; only the basic chores got done, and no heavy work that could wait till tomorrow. Tully, Fenton, Joe Tom, and a few of the older folks gathered in the kitchen and drank black coffee and listened to a ball game on the radio, and everyone pretty much just lounged around. There was no particular agenda.

So in late morning Chad found himself alone with Grandpa Ned in the living room. Karen, smiling at Chad but clamming up when Carl O'Brien came into the room, settled the old man in a plump chair, gave him some magazines and a cup of coffee, then left with O'Brien. She didn't look terribly enthusiastic about going off with him, but she went. Chad, though not particularly eager to entertain thoughts of any new romantic entanglements, especially in a field of jealous competition, had to admit to himself that he was attracted to Karen, and it gave him a bit of a pang to see her leave with that lout O'Brien, but this was an opportunity to talk to Grandpa Ned alone, and he turned his attention to the old man.

"Did you sleep well, Mister Walker? Do I have your name right?" He thought he had it straight; this was the Walker brothers' father's father.

"Jim Ned Walker," the old man said, starting to rise from his chair. But Chad got up first and leaned across to shake hands. "Yessir, I slept tolerably well. It was a quiet night."

This, Chad thought, might be an opportune reference. "Well," he said, "aren't the nights always pretty quiet out here?"

Grandpa Ned, his expression hard to read in those rheumy eyes afloat in their sea of wrinkles, seemed to consider this for a moment. The wrinkles gathered into a sort of pucker around the nearly toothless mouth. "Well, sir, sometimes they is, and sometimes they ain't."

"Oh?" Chad said. "Why's that?"

"Sometimes he's a-walkin' at night," the old man said.

Jesus, Chad thought, I didn't expect that. "Who's a-walking?" he asked, hoping he didn't sound as if he were mocking the old man's speech.

Oddly, Grandpa Ned seemed to beam at this, as if pleased to respond: "My pappy."

"Your—"

"Yessir. My pappy. Old Lothrop Walker, God rest his rusty old soul, but he don't rest, no, hell. Don't rest much."

Lothrop? Chad thought, making the connection. Hoping he wasn't being altogether too presumptuous, too familiar for an outsider in the midst of the family, he said, "You must mean Papa Loaty."

Grandpa Ned had had his cup of coffee halfway to his face, but froze with it, and set it back down with a clack. "Where'd you hear him called that?"

Sure enough, Chad winced inwardly: I've overstepped my welcome here. He tried to make light of it. "Oh, I don't remember, somebody mentioned him the other day."

This seemed to satisfy Grandpa Ned for the moment, though again it was hard to read his wizened face. He reached for his coffee again, took a sip this time, set it down, sat for a moment in silence, and finally said, enigmatically, "Yep. He's a-walkin' okay. Walkin' tall, walkin' on the wind."

The old man lapsed into silence, and after a few moments he fell asleep in the chair.

Chad slipped out of the room, making his way down the back hall and passing through the kitchen, where those gathered around the tinny radio scarcely seemed to notice him as he opened the door and went outside.

It was a pleasant day for a walk about the place. The sky was a turquoise dome streaked here and there with wisps of white billowy cloud, and a light breeze from the desert plains all around brought rumors of sage to his nostrils. Strolling out without any particular goal in mind, he soon found himself a good distance from the house, whose angular form crouched on the faraway horizon like a drowsy beetle. It was good, for a change, to be alone during the day with his thoughts, unencumbered by work or conversation.

But he wasn't quite alone. Off to the right of the direction in which he was walking, he spotted two figures in the distance, and one waved to him while the other just stood and stared. The one who stood and stared, of course, was Carl O'Brien; the one who waved was Karen. Chad walked toward them across the chaparral.

He wasn't quite within earshot when Karen, smiling, said something to him, but a little gust of wind whirled her words away on the air.

Chad, stepping closer, cupped a hand over one ear and shook his head grinning.

"I said," Karen repeated, "we're going to walk over to the arroyo. Why don't you join us?"

"Thanks—"

"I'm sure he has other things he wants to do," Carl said, his face full of the usual unpleasant presumption.

Chad looked at him for a minute before replying, and when he did reply, it was to Karen. "I was going to say, thanks, I don't mind if I do."

Carl shrugged, looking off over his shoulder somewhere, and Karen nodded. "Good. Let's go. It's a beautiful day for a walk."

"Yes it is," Chad said, falling in beside her. Carl took up the other side, putting an arm around her waist as if to make a bit of a territorial gesture, and they strolled across the chaparral, dodging between clumps of mesquite and sage and chamisa as they went. Here and there, a rattlesnake hole yawned in the sand, but the tenants were nowhere to be seen.

"I had a little chat with Grandpa Ned just before I came out," Chad said, taking off his jacket and swinging it over his shoulder.

"Good old Grandpa Ned," Karen said. "He's pretty amazing. How many people nearly thirty years old still have a great-grandfather living?"

"Yeah," Chad said, "that is amazing. I don't even have any living grandparents."

"Grandpa Ned's a little hard to follow sometimes," Karen said, stepping around a cluster of prickly pear cactus, "but he knows some stories, let me tell you."

"I don't think Chad's interested in the Walker family's stories," Carl said.

"Why not?" Chad replied, deciding to take the bait. "I mean, I don't want to pry or anything—"

"Then don't," Carl said flatly.

"Don't be rude, Carl," Karen said. She angled a little away from him, but the arm stayed around the waist. "What did Grandpa Ned and you talk about, Chad?"

"Well," Chad said, "nothing much. He just mentioned something about his father, Lothrop Walker. Said something kind of strange about him, something like 'He's a-walking tall, walking on the wind.'"

Chad, glancing sideways to study Karen's face, thought she looked rather thoughtful at this. Carl, on the other side of her, just looked grumpy; he clearly resented Chad's being there at all.

At length Karen said, with a sigh: "Yeah, I'll have to tell you about Great-Great-Grandpa Lothrop."

"Papa Loaty," Chad offered, hoping once again that he wasn't presuming upon his welcome here by being so familiar.

Karen looked a little surprised at hearing him use the name, but nodded. "Papa Loaty."

"C'mon, Karen," Carl said, "you shouldn't be telling family stories to this—"

"This what, Carl?" Chad said. "This hired hand?"

"Exactly," Carl said. 'That's exactly what you are."

"Well, so what?" Karen said, slipping out of Carl's hold this time. "So what, if Dad did hire him to work here? You don't have to treat him like that. And that reminds me, Dad told me what you did for him, Chad, and I haven't had a chance to thank you. Dad could've had a bad snakebite, if it hadn't been for you."

"Yeah, big deal," Carl grumbled.

"Well, Carl's right, Karen, it wasn't any big deal, really. I just—"

"You just probably saved my Dad's life, and that means a lot to me," Karen said, casting a cold glance at Carl, who shrugged again and looked out across the plain somewhere to keep from meeting her eyes.

"Anyway," Chad said, figuring he might as well keep the talk rolling in the direction it had been going, "you were going to tell me something about Papa Loaty."

They were approaching an access to a large arroyo, at first only a dry, shallow riverbed, its sandy floors flanked by low rises of terrain on

either side; Chad could see, even from here, that the sides quickly deep-
ened as the length of the arroyo ran on and became a canyonlike maze
of rivercourse dotted up its sides with gnarled clumps of cedar and mesquite. Karen nodded toward it, indicated that they would enter it.

"To tell you the truth, Chad, people in my family don't talk too
much about old Papa Loaty," she said. Carl opened his mouth as if
about to say something, then seemed to change his mind. "He was
born in 1868, I think it was," Karen went on, "and he died in 1939. He
was tall. Very tall, a little over seven feet."

"Wow," Chad said. "That's—" He stopped, a little embarrassed by
what he had been about to say. But Karen second-guessed him.

"That's real different from all the other Walkers since," she supplied for him. "Yeah, it is. You know how short my dad and his brothers are, and their father too, my grandpa, Leland Walker. I don't know
if you've noticed, it's hard to tell because he's kind of bent over now,
but Grandpa Ned is even shorter, the shortest of the bunch. What they
say in the family is—"

"Aw, c'mon, Karen," Carl said, "don't start telling him—"

"Shut up, Carl," Karen snapped. "What they say in the family is
that starting with my grandfather, Leland Walker, all the Walkers'
mothers consciously tried to *will* their sons to be short, so as not to be
like old Papa Loaty."

"Damn," Chad said. "Was he that—"

"That weird? That nasty? So they say. When he first came out here
from Texas in the 1920s and bought this land, he was married to a
woman who didn't like it out here in the desert, it turned out, and Papa
Loaty seemed to thrive on how uncomfortable she was. That was
Becky Anderson Walker, she was Grandpa Ned's mother. They say
Papa Loaty ragged her mercilessly, finally broke her spirit, and she died
young."

"Well," Chad said, "I guess that wasn't all that uncommon a pattern out in the prairie in those days."

"No," Karen said, "but he was a strange one all around, if we can
believe the stories Grandpa Ned tells about him. Old Papa Loaty had a
thing about windmills. Loved them in a weird kind of way, seemed
kind of in awe of them, almost like he was afraid of them, respected
them the way you would respect something that can kill you."

"Really?" Chad said, smiling. "I never thought of windmills as being particularly—"

"No," Karen said, "of course not. But Papa Loaty did. He used to come out at night and stand under the stars, near one windmill or another, and watch them spin, and kind of sing to them. Or with them. Kind of croon to them. Grandpa Ned was in his twenties at the time and he used to go with his dad, and to this day he says it was scary, watching old Papa Loaty, crooning with the windmills. The blades would hum, kind of, you know, the way they do in the wind, and Papa Loaty would hum with them, and tilt his head to one side and the other, and sort of make as if he was spinning with the blades, right where he stood. Like I said, Papa Loaty was tall, and real gangly-thin like, and I guess he fancied he sort of *looked* like a windmill himself. There aren't any good pictures of him, but Grandpa Ned says old Papa Loaty used to kind of wear his hair pulled up all choppy-like, to look like—"

"The blades of a windmill," Chad said, with the uncomfortable feeling that this reference caused some not entirely welcome memory to stir in the back of his mind.

"Yeah," Karen said.

They had gone quite a distance into the arroyo, to a point where the dry rivercourse branched out ahead in a bewildering array of off-shoots, and by unspoken consent they all turned and headed back out. When they came back to the access to the arroyo, where the sandy walls dropped down low again, Karen pointed off toward what Chad thought was the southwest, though after the walk in the arroyo he was a little turned around.

"Off out there—"

"C'mon, Karen," Carl said, "you've told him enough."

"Off out there a few miles," she repeated, pointedly ignoring him, "that's not our land any more, but some of it was, in Papa Loaty's time. I guess you know that they say a flying saucer crashed out there in 1947."

"Yeah," Chad said, "I've read about it. Military people from down in Roswell and other places supposedly came out and picked up all the pieces, and it was all hush-hush after that."

"Well," Karen said, "there's a story Grandpa Ned tells, that people in general don't know about."

"And I think we ought to keep it that way, Karen," Carl said.

"Look, Karen," Chad said, "maybe he's right. If it's something your family—"

"Oh, it's not supposed to be any big secret," Karen said. "It's a secret only because nobody bothers to tell anybody about it, because they don't figure anybody will believe it. You probably won't believe it either."

"Try me," Chad said.

"Okay," Karen said. "This is the way Grandpa Ned told it to me. Back in 1947, in July I think it was, something—a flying saucer, whatever you want to call it—fell out of the sky at night and crashed. Hit by lightning, some people said. The army people came out the next morning and took everything away, but in the meantime there were bodies scattered around out there where the thing crashed. Little bodies. Three or four feet long. Big heads, big dark eyes. Not human."

"Aliens," Chad said. Carl, looking off to one side, sniffed, either out of contempt for the story itself or out of impatience with Karen for telling it.

"Alien bodies," Karen said. "There were supposed to be five of them. Four of them mangled up pretty bad, and dead. The other one was pretty badly hurt—"

"But alive?" Chad asked. It was a sobering thought.

"So they say," Karen said.

"Do you believe these things all happened?" Chad asked.

"I don't know," she said, looking thoughtful. "I think I do. That part of it at least. The crash, the bodies. Anyway, the creature that was alive tried to crawl away from the wreck, but the place was miles and miles away from any roads or houses or anything, and the poor thing only managed to crawl up to a windmill."

Chad wasn't sure he liked the sound of this. It stirred something deep within him, bothered him. "A windmill?" he asked.

"Yes," Karen said. "It crawled up and sort of wrapped itself onto the lower beams in the frame of the windmill, and died there. When the army people came out at sunrise and cordoned the area off and picked everything up, they almost missed that one, the body at the windmill. But they found it, and carried it away. It had bled on the wooden beam where it had lain, and the army had to use all kinds of chemical cleaners or solvents or something to clean it off. But—"

Chad felt a little chilly suddenly, and slipped his jacket back on. "But what?"

"But Grandpa Ned says something was left."

"How do you mean?" Chad asked.

"Something—remained," she said. "Some—I don't know. Essence. Spirit. Something."

"Something—"

"In the windmill," Karen said.

Silence fell among them. They stood, heads down, not speaking for some moments. Finally it was Carl who broke the silence.

"Well, Karen, now that you've hung all the dirty laundry out for everybody to see—"

Something about the tone of Carl's voice, on top of what he had said, brought Chad's blood to a boil.

"All right, Carl, damn it, now you listen, one more snide remark like that from you—"

That was as far as Chad got, when Carl swung his fist and connected with Chad's jaw, sending him reeling back. Chad had seen the blow coming at the last split second and had begun to move back, but a little too late. Putting a foot back to get his balance in the sand, he shook his head and tasted blood in his mouth. Karen was looking on with a pained kind of expression, and started to say something. But Chad spat to one side and stepped back up close to Carl.

"What's your problem, Carl? What the hell did you do that for?"

Carl's face broadened into a sneer. "Well, what's the matter, city boy? Can't take it? I thought it was about time somebody—"

And that was as far as he got, when Chad decked him. It made his hand hurt, clobbering somebody in the face like that; he hadn't done it since high school. Carl went down in the sand like a bag of rocks.

Karen was shaking her head, looking from one to the other of them. "Honestly. Like a couple of children." She turned on her heel and started walking back in the direction they had come. Leaving Carl sitting in the sand nursing his jaw, Chad caught up with Karen, who cast him a sidelong glance.

"I guess he's been asking for that," she said, looking a little sheepish. "I still think it's foolish to fight."

"Well, hell," Chad said, "so do I."

"Now you're going to say he started it," Karen said, looking as if she were trying not to laugh.

"No," Chad said, pacing along side her through the chaparral, "I don't intend to regress quite that far back into my infancy. Two steps removed from thumb-sucking."

Now Karen did laugh outright. Over his shoulder, Chad could see Carl now, huffing and puffing some distance behind, though apparently in no great hurry to catch up.

"Well, I guess this'll cost me my job," Chad said to Karen.

She shrugged. "I wouldn't think so. I don't think my dad is too fond of Carl."

Why not go for it, Chad thought. "And how about you?"

Karen visibly colored at this, but didn't look displeased. She only said: "Contrary to popular opinion, Carl doesn't have me in a cage." Carl was catching up to them. "Do you, Carl?"

"Do I what?" he asked, breathing heavily.

"Nothing," Karen said. And they walked on back to the house.

That night a gusty wind came up out of the desert, howling under the eaves, rattling the rickety doors of distant outbuildings, moaning at the windowpanes like some fretting beast wanting to be fed. Chad lay awake listening, then trying not to listen. Trying to get to sleep.

But he couldn't sleep, and after a while he opened his eyes to the palpable darkness of the room and stared, unseeing, at the ceiling. From time to time the wind would rattle the windowpanes in their ancient frames, and he began to be annoyed with the sound of the wind and the rattling windows, because he realized, suddenly, that he had been trying to listen for some altogether different sound.

Outside, somewhere in the windblown night, a thudding kind of impression registered just beneath the wind, just too low to make it out, just too noticeable to ignore.

Maybe, after the day's wild stories, he was imagining things. He didn't seem to hear anything now except the ululating wind at the windows.

No. No, there it was again.

A deep, heavy sound. A sound nearly too subtle to hear. *Thud.* *Thud.* Then, unless he imagined it, a sort of scraping, then: *thud, thud.*

Like something ponderous, something heavy, walking.

Was it growing louder? He couldn't tell for sure, but he thought it was. Yes, there, outside now, surely not far from the side of the house, the sound again, like something striding up nearly to the very boards.

Maybe he ought to go out and have a look.

Rising in the dark, he pulled a pair of jeans on and slid his feet into his slippers, and went to his door and slid the bolt open, and pushed at the door.

Out in the hall, all was dark, quiet. Now that he thought about it, it was quiet altogether now, because the thudding sound from outside seemed to have ceased, and even the wind had died down to an occasional gust. He took a couple of steps out into the hall, stopped, waited. Watched. Listened.

What happened next, though he had had a hint of the impression at least once before, made prickles of hair stand on end on the back of his neck.

Whether it was the wind that came swooping back up all of a sudden, or just some similar effect, a rushing access of sound seemed to press itself against the outside of the house, on the side where the hall terminated farther down in front of him, and he could have sworn that something—something insubstantial but real—passed through the very wallboards at the end of the hall, and came into the house.

But he could see nothing. Fumbling with shaking hands in his jean pockets, he came up with a package of paper matches, and struck one to dispel the darkness. And out in front of him, near the end of the hall, something moved.

Something tall, something gaunt. In the wavering light from the match, he could see only a vague outline, but its head, if it was a head, terminated in a wildness of hair that resembled—

But the thing was down the stairwell and gone. The match burned his fingertips and went out.

He ran to the top of the stairs, struck another match, and tried to see down the inky maw of the stairwell, but the flaring of the match revealed only a jittering nest of shadows down there, shading off into unrelieved blackness. He had a momentary impression of something moving around, down in the parlor, then a kind of experience like the one moments before, but in reverse: it was as if a vacuum gathered, slowly filling back in with air—something gathered itself, passed silently through the walls, and was gone. The feeling was as if for a moment everything stopped, imploded, collapsed to unquiet silence; it was like the stopping of one's heart.

He leaned for a moment against the door frame, half in the hall and half in the parlor, catching his breath, because it was as if the thing had taken the very air out of his lungs in seeping back out through the walls. At first he took the thudding in his ears to be the beating of his heart, which did seem to thrum in his ears, but he soon realized that it was more than that. Outside, moving off away from the house, something thudded on the ground in muffled cycles, almost like a gargantuan kind of swaggering walk.

He pushed himself out of the door frame, crossed the room, opened the front door, and stepped out on the porch, where the boards creaked so loud under his weight that he had to stop and listen now, for the thudding sound was receding into the distance, growing faint. The wind was coming back up a little, and it made it difficult to hear.

He went down the steps and rounded the corner of the house at a sprint, straining to see his way in the dark. Steering clear of the vague bulk of an outbuilding, he ran out into the chaparral, following the sound. There were black billows of wind-driven cloud overhead, and as the moon peeked from behind them he could just make out the ground around him, an endless plain of sand and chamisa and sage, with spikes of yucca here and there, sending their pointy shadows fingering out over the dry ground. He ran on in the direction of the sound, pausing from time to time to listen.

He half thought that it was no good, there was nothing left to hear, to see, to follow, half thought that he had imagined the whole thing, but suddenly up ahead in the near-dark somewhere, a shape moved. He ran on toward it, noticing as he went that the ground seemed scuffed, furrowed, beneath his feet. He went another hundred yards, maybe, before he was so winded that he had to stop and double over and catch his breath. A cloud of dust, whether stirred by the wind or by his own footfalls or by the recent passage of something else, swirled in the air, and he coughed and wiped sand from his eyes.

And when his vision cleared a little, he got one glimpse of it, off in the dark.

The moon had retreated behind clouds again, so it was hard to be sure, but he thought the thing was spindly and tall, twenty or thirty feet maybe, and shifting and angular at the top. Just as the last of the moonlight ebbed away, the thing seemed to take on a new burst of speed, moving hastily away from him, out into the desert, into the night, beyond view.

And he could have sworn that in that last instant before it moved away, it turned, stiffly and consciously, to look at him.

In the morning, people came through the kitchen a few at a time for breakfast as always. Carl O'Brien, his face bruised bright purple on one side, was just leaving, and gave Chad only a sullen glance on the way out. While Chad was at the table, the Walker brothers' father Leland Walker took his toast and coffee, as did Joe Tom and Isabelle, and, a few minutes later, Karen. Susan Walker and Grandpa Ned were just coming in as Chad got up to leave, with Tully behind them. Everyone looked tired, unrested, jumpy. Karen caught up with Chad just outside the house.

"Did you sleep well?" she said, and something in her face said that the question was rhetorical.

Chad just shrugged. He felt, in fact, nearly ill with fatigue, as he hadn't gotten to sleep till three o'clock or later, after walking back to the house in the dark with a head full of equally dark thoughts.

"Me neither," Karen said, evidently seeing his expression and drawing her own conclusions. "Where are you going?"

Chad had started to move around to the side of the house, and Karen followed him. "I just want to see something," he said.

They stopped at a point several yards out from the house, and Chad pointed at the sandy ground. "That's what I thought. Look."

The ground was gouged, furrowed, scuffed, at intervals with distances of several yards between, in a pattern that seemed to lead off beyond the outbuildings, into the chaparral. "What do you make of that?"

Karen looked uneasy. "I've seen it before," was all she said.

"I imagine you have," Chad replied, a little dryly. "Look, I know I'm just a handyman around here and nobody owes me any explanations about what's going on—"

Karen stopped him, shaking her head. "I'm not trying to be mysterious," she said, "and I wish you wouldn't say you're just a handyman."

"Well, what would you call me?"

She looked at the ground for a moment, then back up at him. "What's the matter with 'friend'?"

He shrugged, smiled. "Not a thing." Something caught his eye, and he pointed back toward the house. "Here we go again," he said, as Karen turned to look.

Susan was out in the dooryard again with a rake, smoothing over the ground where it had been scuffed, working her way slowly outward where they stood. Edna, Fenton's wife, was coming out with a broom to help her. Karen glanced back at Chad, and back at Susan and Edna in the distance, and back at Chad. "Like I said, I'm not trying to be mysterious. I'd tell you what's going on if I was sure I knew. I don't think anybody really knows for certain."

"But you have some ideas," he ventured.

She seemed to consider this for a moment. "Yes, I do."

"You want to talk some more about it?"

She nodded. "Yes, I would. You know, I never really got to talk to anybody before you came. Not about anything important."

"When can we talk?" he asked.

She took his hand for just a second. "Soon."

That afternoon, Chad was working in the yard, repairing shingles on one of the storage shed roofs, when Fenton came up to him and asked, "You ever do any plumbing?"

"Oh, a little," Chad said. "I've got some good pipe wrenches in the back of my car. I used to help out with my uncle's plumbing business in Bernalillo, back when he was getting started. What do you need me to do?"

"Nothing major," Fenton said, nodding toward the back of the house. "I could take care of it, except I'm going to be busy, and Tully and Joe Tom are both in the field. Like I said, it's no big deal. Some washers need changing out, I think, in the kitchen. That ought to stop the tap from dripping. But under the sink there's a trap needs cleaning out too, and I think while you're at it there's a section of pipe and some fittings under there that need replacing. Here's a list of what you'll need." He handed Chad a scrap of paper. "I called the hardware store down in Roswell and priced everything, so here's a check to pay for it." He handed it over. "You mind taking your own car?"

"No, no," Chad said, 'that's fine. I'm not familiar with Roswell, though. Where's—"

"I'll ride in with him and show him where the hardware store is, Uncle Fenton." It was Karen, who had come up behind them. "I need to stop and pick up some things at Walgreen's anyway."

An odd kind of look appeared in Fenton's eyes for a second, though not a disapproving one exactly. He shrugged. "Yeah, okay. You two better get going, then, if you're going to be back by suppertime. You can work on the plumbing tomorrow, it'll keep till then. And you can finish these shingles anytime. Don't matter anyway unless it rains."

Chad and Karen walked back to the house. "I just need to get my purse," she said, and he waited for her beside the car.

When they had bumped their way back out to the main road and headed south toward Roswell, Chad turned to her and said, "Now we can talk." He was always wondering how freely he could speak without being presumptuous, and hoped what he'd just said didn't sound as if he were suggesting that her family members would have been eaves-dropping on their conversation if they were still back at the ranch. But he thought she understood that he meant Carl primarily.

Anyway, she only looked out over the desert as it flashed by and shook her head and said, "I don't know, it's almost too nice a day to talk about anything unpleasant."

"You're right," he said, smiling at her, though in fact he was going to be disappointed if this didn't work out to be a chance to learn more about what was going on. But any conversation with her, he realized, was welcome. He was beginning to admit to himself that the way he felt about her wasn't exactly casual. Here we go again, he thought; how many times before have I thought I'd met Miss Right? But why dwell on the pessimistic side? He was fishing around in his head for the right thing to say, when she beat him to it.

"How do you like working here?"

"Oh, I like it. Chance to be outdoors a good deal, chance to do a lot of different kinds of things. Like this plumbing your uncle wants me to do. Can't remember when I did anything like that, but I don't think it'll be difficult."

"What I really mean," Karen said, "is how do you like being around the Walkers? My family?"

"Well—"

She laughed, a lighthearted, lilting sound. To him, a beautiful sound. "Be honest now."

"Well, they're okay. No, I mean it. I know some people say they're a little strange—"

"Where did you hear that?" she asked, and for the umpteenth time he wondered if he'd spoken in too familiar a way for an outsider, if that was what he still was. But she didn't sound offended, just curious.

"Oh, you know, remarks you hear. Actually this was from an old hitchhiker I ran into in a bar in Corona."

Karen looked thoughtful, nodding. "I think I know who you mean. But no, don't look like that, it's okay—I know people do say the Walkers are a little odd. Now that you've been here for a while, do you think so too?"

Chad glanced out over the desertlands to his left and shook his head. "Not exactly."

"You can say what you feel," she said.

"No, really, I don't think they're strange, exactly. But—but there's something about the whole deal. Something strange." He glanced at her to try to read her expression, but he couldn't see anything in particular in her face except pensiveness. He looked out the rearview mirror and saw an old pickup far behind them. From time to time a car would rush past in the other lane, but there was very little traffic out here, refreshingly different from the city.

"Are you sure my stories aren't just spooking you?" she asked.

"Well," he said, "I might have thought so, yeah, I might have thought that my mind was just playing tricks on me, you know, the old subconscious taking your stories and weaving some even weirder stuff out of them, but I don't think I'm given to out-and-out hallucinations. I think I've experienced something real." He looked at her again. "And I bet you have too."

She looked out the car window and was silent for quite a while, but finally said, "You don't live out at the Walker ranch without seeing and hearing some unaccountable things. It's just the way it is."

"And you think it's because of—"

"I think it's something we can't even begin to understand," she said. "I guess this is going to sound peculiar to you, since you're from the city, but the desert is a strange place. Weird things happen in the desert. Things that don't happen anywhere else. They just do."

"I can believe it," he said. "I mean, I've heard stories about shapeshifters, for example. Spirits that are crows sometimes, and then coyotes, and then lizards or whatever. I used to think it was all just folklore—"

"It is folklore," she said, "but folklore can be based on truth. My Aunt Edna could tell you some stuff that would make your hair stand on end."

"I don't doubt it," he said. "Hey, we're getting into town."

The northern fringe of Roswell had appeared around them—the Roswell Mall, then clusters of service stations, branch banks, fast-food places, antiques shops, grocery stores. Karen directed him through the streets of the town to a sizable hardware store, where they stopped.

Inside the store it didn't take Chad very long to round up the items on Fenton's list, and as he and Karen were walking back across the parking lot to the car, they ran into Carl O'Brien.

"That your buggy over there?" he asked, nodding toward Chad's car. "Looks to me like you got a flat."

The three of them walked the rest of the way to the car. Carl's pickup was parked a few yards away; Chad was pretty sure it was the one he'd glimpsed on the road behind them. Sure enough, the car's right rear tire was flat.

"Must of run into a nail," Carl said. There was an unmistakable hint of a sneer on his face, where a purplish bruise still shone like an odd blossom. "Ought to watch where you're going."

Chad tried to stare him down, but the other man's face was a mask of insolence that didn't change. "I'll put the spare on and go get the tire fixed," he said, and turned to Karen. "You mind waiting around a bit?"

She started to shake her head, but Carl intercepted her, saying: "She's going back with me."

"Oh really," Chad said. "And why's that?"

"'Cause her dad wants her home," Carl said. "There's work to be done, and she ain't hanging around here all day while you get a tire fixed."

"I'm going to stay and wait," Karen said.

"No, you're not," Carl said, "unless you want your dad and your uncles mad at you. They want you home right now. You better get in the truck."

Karen looked archly at him. "If I find out you're not telling me the truth—"

"You questioning my word?" Carl asked.

"God, no," Chad put in, "heaven forbid anybody'd ever question your word, Carl. I'm sure it's as good as gold."

Carl cast only a scowling glance at him. "You stay out of our business. C'mon, Karen, we're going to be late for supper."

Karen gave Chad a sort of what-can-one-do look and followed Carl to the pickup. "I'm sorry," she said over her shoulder. "There's a station back up the road here, we passed it on the way in, where you can get the tire fixed."

"He's a big boy," Carl mumbled. "He can take care of it."

"That's not all I can take care of," Chad said. "Hey, thanks, Karen. See you when I get back."

"Don't count on it," Carl said as they were getting into the pickup. Karen looked sourly annoyed, but didn't say anything. Evidently for all her spunk she was afraid of this strutting little psycho. In a moment, the pickup was gone.

"Damn," Chad said, looking at the flat tire again. "Ran into a nail, my ass."

He took out the spare and the jack and the lug wrench, hoisted the car up on the jack, removed the tire, replaced it with the spare, tightened the lug nuts, and stored the tire in the back of the car. By now he was really annoyed, but by the time he drove back up to the service station on the north end of town and was standing around watching them take care of the tire, he was feeling a little more philosophical about the whole thing. Let the cretinous little weasel have his fun, he'd pay for it in the end, by God.

"Ain't no nail or anything in here," the boy working on the tire said. "Looks like somebody just stuck a pencil or something down the valve stem."

"I kind of thought so," Chad replied. Of course, maybe that let Carl out as a suspect; only people who knew how to read and write carried pencils.

"All it needs is air," the boy said. "Got to charge you for the labor anyway, though."

"I know, that's okay," Chad said. "What the hell, it's only money."

The kid grinned. "Ain't that the truth."

It was a dreary drive back up to the ranch alone, and it was something of a revelation to him, how little he brooded about Carl and how much he missed having Karen in the car beside him.

He arrived back at the ranch too late for dinner, but Susan had set aside a plate of roast beef and potatoes and black-eyed peas for him, which he ate in solitude at the table. Carl was nowhere to be seen, and neither was Karen. Old Leland Walker and his father Grandpa Ned were sitting in the parlor smoking cigars, and everyone else had apparently gone to their rooms.

While he was finishing his meal, Chad amused himself by trying to see if he knew where everybody's room was, running over them in his mind. This big rambling old house actually had four bedrooms downstairs and four bedrooms up; Chad was pretty sure some of these were the result of fairly recent subdivisions, new sections of wall put in to chop the available space up into more rooms. Joe Tom and Isabelle's room was downstairs, as were Tully and Susan's room, Karen's room, and Carl's room at the back. Upstairs, besides his own room, there were Fenton and Edna's, and the room shared by Leland Walker and Grandpa Ned, and finally the room of Isabelle's parents, Hiram and Mollie Jenkins he thought their names were. Not that it really mattered, he guessed. Maybe he was only trying to divert his thoughts from less pleasant things.

After he finished eating he went upstairs, washed up, came back downstairs, and headed out the back door. Up in his room he had stopped to pick up his pipe, which he didn't smoke very often and in fact hadn't smoked since he came here, and a pouch of tobacco and some matches. He was intending to walk out into the desert a little way and find a rock and just sit for a while, but when he came out onto the back porch, although it was almost dark now, Edna Fox Walker was sitting there shucking a bushel of corn under the pale porchlight. She looked up and nodded to him, and he sat down on the porch railing and started filling his pipe.

"Hi, Edna. I'm just out for a breath of air."

"And to do some thinking," she said.

This startled him a bit. There was always something a little inscrutable in Edna. He remembered, again, her origins in Nambé Pueblo, famous for Southwestern Indian-style witchcraft. Edna wasn't a witch, he thought, but she had her dark side. "Well—yes, as a matter of fact. How did you know?"

She shrugged, continuing to shuck corn. "There's always a lot to think about."

"Even out here," he said.

"Especially out here," she said.

They let silence well up around them for several minutes. Edna was halfway through the bushel of corn when Chad got up the nerve to ask: "Do you believe in shapeshifting?"

She gave him a glance that was hard to read any particular expression in, then looked back down and continued her work. "Everybody believes in shapeshifting."

He laughed. "I don't know, Edna, I wouldn't say that. Back in the city they think—"

"This isn't the city," Edna said. "Out here, this is the real world. The desert."

"And things happen in the desert that don't happen anywhere else," he offered, echoing Karen's recent remark to him.

"Yes," Edna said. "There's spirits in the land, out here."

"Good spirits?" Chad asked.

"Spirits," Edna said. Her hands worked through the corn like small intent creatures, peeling, peeling.

"Somebody told me one time," Chad said, "a friend in Albuquerque, that he was out in the desert, and a coyote came running up close. My friend was kind of scared and turned to run, and glanced back, and it wasn't a coyote at all then, but a crow. Can a coyote really turn into a crow?"

"Did your friend believe it did?" Edna asked.

"Yes."

"Then it can," she said.

He finished tamping tobacco into the bowl, struck a match, and lit his pipe, sending an eddy of gray smoke out onto the evening air. "I think I believe in things like that," he said.

"I know you do," she said. "You have to."

"Why do I have to?"

"Because the spirit world is very close sometimes. You've seen things. You know."

"I'm not sure what I know at this point," he said.

"You know," she repeated.

He couldn't think of anything else to say, except, finally: "I'm going to take a little walk."

Leaving her to her work, he went down the porch steps, across the dooryard, and out into the dark land, past the nearer outbuildings, where he did find a good broad rock, as he had hoped, and sat down on it, puffing his pipe.

It felt good just to sit and think. Or maybe not think. It was really dark now, the way it can be only in the desert, away from electric lights, away from houses and cars. The sky was a limitless black void overhead, frosted incredibly thickly with stars. Off on the horizon, the waning gibbous moon was just rising, a half-gnawed-away yellow face surveying a dark kingdom. Somewhere in the distance an owl hooted forlornly, the only sound in an infinite sea of silence.

Smoking his pipe, he realized that in some corner of his mind he was here for a reason. He was here to see if anything extraordinary would happen tonight. If anything would come.

Maybe, he thought, it was all foolishness. Karen was certainly someone he trusted, and respected, and more, but she was only repeating family stories that might or might not have any basis in fact. All such families probably had their stories, one as outlandish as the next. Certainly the flying saucer crash, out there in the desert night, was something that really happened, he had little doubt. He didn't know how he felt about the story of the surviving alien, the little creature that crawled to a windmill and wrapped itself around the wooden frame and bled to death. He didn't know how he felt about the idea that something then remained, a sort of presence, in the windmill. Who could say, some of this might just have been inspired by the older family members' odd but perfectly mundane recollections of old Lothrop Walker, old Papa Loaty, with his simpering fascination with windmills, standing and inclining his head and humming along with them. Tall, gaunt old Papa Loaty, whom the women in the family remembered with such distaste that they supposedly willed their own children, his descendents, to be short of stature, in order that they should be unlike him. What did any of it mean, in the end?

His pipe went out and he knocked the dottle out on the side of the rock and refilled the pipe and lit it again. Maybe the Indians were right, maybe a pipe helped you sort out your relation to what Edna would call the spirit world, or whatever.

Of course here he had been, tonight, thinking prosaic and skeptical thoughts, so was he really being honest? Was he coming any closer to the spirit world?

Was it coming closer to him?

He puffed a billowing cloud of smoke out onto the air, where it hung illumined only by starlight and by the pallid glow of the low-grazing moon. He listened.

Listened, half expecting to hear—what? Whatever he had heard, those times, from his room upstairs in the house.

And he had indeed heard things there. He had possibly even seen something. So maybe Edna was right. Maybe he had to believe. Had to believe that unaccountable things happened in the desert.

But whatever the truth of the matter, things were not happening tonight, unaccountably or otherwise.

Or were they?

Off on the horizon, across opposite from the moon, something was moving.

He sat very still, very quiet, and listened, and watched.

There. In the distance, just above the horizon, something shifted from left to right, something as black as the sky behind it. He strained to see.

Where was it now? Peering into the near-dark, he thought he could almost make it out. There. There. It was moving again. And it was—

A low ridge of black cloud, scuttering across the sky ahead of the wind.

Sighing with a complex of emotions that he had to admit included an element of relief, he sat for a while longer and smoked his pipe down to ash again, and headed back toward the house, whose dark, gaunt frame gathered itself spectrally on the horizon in the wan moonlight.

At least there were no other tall, gaunt things abroad tonight. Back at the house, he climbed the stairs to his room and actually had a restful sleep.

The next morning after breakfast and after the rest of the men had scattered to their various tasks, Chad settled into the plumbing work that needed doing in the kitchen. The women came and went as their own work demanded, exchanging remarks with him and with each other. Karen came through the kitchen on her way outside, and stopped to chat with him.

"Sorry about yesterday," she said. "I had to come back with him. And you know something? My dad and my uncles hadn't said a word about hurrying up and getting back."

Chad paused in the act of replacing a pitted washer at the sink, and grinned ruefully at her. "Now why doesn't that surprise me in the least?"

Karen shook her head, evidently less inclined than he to have a sense of humor about the thing. "Carl really ticks me off sometimes. I think I've about had it with him."

"Watch out," Chad said, tapping the washer down into its seat. "Men are scarce out on the prairie."

"Oh, I don't know about that," she said, and gave him a playful poke in the arm and ran out the door.

He finished with the washers and tested the faucet to be sure it didn't still drip, then gathered his materials to work on the pipes and fittings in the cabinet beneath the sink. While he was getting started, Isabelle's parents came downstairs and sat at the table, and Susan served them coffee and muffins.

"Morning, Chad," the old man said.

"Morning, Mr. Jenkins. Mrs. Jenkins."

The mother smiled and nodded. "Good morning, Chad."

"Did you sleep well?" Chad asked them.

"Oh, yes," Mr. Jenkins said. "Very quiet night."

"Quieter than it is sometimes," Chad ventured. "I mean, it's usually pretty quiet out here, but—"

"But sometimes not," Mrs. Jenkins said. "Sometimes—well, sometimes things are uneasy."

Chad, half lying on the linoleum to get at the plumbing, gave his wrench a turn at the pipe and looked over his shoulder and asked, "Uneasy? How do you mean?"

The father looked at his wife as if to say: maybe you'd better not say too much, the young man doesn't want to listen to silly stories. But she replied, interestingly enough, "Things that ought to be at rest. Sometimes they aren't."

"What sorts of things?" Chad asked, tapping the pipe to loosen it.

Mrs. Jenkins looked at him curiously, as if he ought to know, as if he shouldn't have to ask. "Things that have woke up."

"Too early in the morning for this talk," Susan said, refilling Mrs. Jenkins's coffee cup.

Chad honestly didn't know what next to ask her, but he was saved the trouble of puzzling over it, because Susan's father, old Juan Torres, came in and sat down at the table across from Isabelle's mother and father and said to Susan, *"Buenos días, mija. ¿Y cómo amaneciste?"*

"Bien, papá," she replied, kissing him on the cheek. "How about a cup of coffee and a muffin?"

"Claro," her father said. *"¿Dónde está Tully esta mañana?"*

Chad was following the conversation only in bits and pieces, and beginning to realize that his Spanish needed some work. But he did understand that the old man had asked Susan where Tully was this morning.

"En el campo," Susan said. *"Está trabajando cerca del papalote."*

This last remark gave Chad a start, but continuing with his task he waited till everyone at the table had finished and left the room, before he turned to Susan, who was stacking some dishes at the sink, and asked her: "Did you say something about Papa Loaty?"

She looked at him quizzically. "Yes. I said Tully was working out in the field near the *papalote*," she said. "It means windmill."

That afternoon Chad finished the job on the roof shingles for the storage shed. It took another three hours of work and another half hour cleaning up the mess, and it was good to be busy. Being busy kept the mind from wandering over into dark areas where it might not be healthy to linger.

Dinner with the family was quiet, uneventful; nobody seemed to have much to say, including Carl, who sat several places away from Chad at the table and ate desultorily. Karen sat next to Carl, as she usually did, since people didn't tend to change the overall seating arrangement, but she seemed to pay her erstwhile boyfriend scant attention. From time to time her eyes met Chad's with a kind of wistful half-smile. He looked for her after dinner, but she must have gone to her room early. He went upstairs and made ready to turn in early himself; it had been a busy day, even though it was all routine, and he was pretty tired.

It must have been a little after eleven when he heard the soft rustling of something moving out in the hall beyond his door. He lay still in bed and listened in the dark.

Maybe he had imagined it. No—there it was again. Definitely, unmistakably, some movement out there, close to his door.

He got out of bed, crept to the door, stood in the dark, listened.

Someone or something was standing just outside the door. He was sure of it.

Rather than give himself time to think, time maybe to lose his courage, he seized the doorknob, twisted the lock, and yanked the door open. And sure enough, someone was standing there.

It was Karen.

"Jesus—"

"Ssssh," she said, putting a finger to her lips. She stepped into the room, and he closed the door behind her.

"Damn, you scared the living hell out of me," he said, modulating his voice down to a whisper as he went.

"I'm sorry," she said, snickering, "I was going to knock, but you didn't give me a chance. You've got good ears."

"It comes from sleeping in this house," he said. "I find myself listening a lot at night."

"I know," she said. "I guess you're wondering why I'm here."

"Now that you mention it," he said.

She looked at him ironically and shook her head. "I didn't think anybody was *that* naïve." And her arms were around him.

Afterward, they lay together in bed, listening to the night. At length she reached over and nudged him.

"Let's go outside. Look at the stars."

He nodded, a useless gesture in the dark. "Okay."

"Be quiet, though," she said. "I really don't think we ought to wake up the whole family."

"No, that might not be a good idea."

He switched on the bedside reading lamp, and they got dressed. Switching the lamp off again, he leaned to her in the lightless room and kissed her, and they headed out the door and down the stairs and out the back door of the house.

They didn't stop walking till they were nearly at the arroyo where they had gone before. Everything looked different here at night; the moon was well up, and its radiance cast long shadows of yucca and mesquite shapes out onto the dry ground, but the light was a surreal ivory glow that made spatial relationships less clear, rather than more. They stopped near the entrance to the arroyo, and he drew her to him, kissed her, held her close. After a while they walked a little farther, found some flat rocks, and sat down.

"I never dreamed I'd be here with you tonight," he said.

"It came upon me kind of suddenly," she said, "wanting to go up to your room. Not that I hadn't thought about it before," she added, smiling mischievously, then growing serious of expression again. "But tonight I just decided I needed to be with you. And I think you needed to be with me."

"Was it that obvious?" he asked.

"Just a feeling I had," she said. "But I've seen how you look at me. And I like it."

They became silent, looking at the universe of icy stars yawning above them. It made Chad think, once again, of the story of the flying saucer, and he drew Karen a little closer to him, as much to enjoy her warmth as to give her his. She put her arm around him.

"In the city you never see the stars like this," he said. "It's enough to—"

"Ssssh," she said. At first he thought she meant that what he was going to say went without saying, or that they shouldn't spoil the peace of the desert night with talk, but he quickly saw in her face, pale but lovely in the moonlight, that she meant for him to be quiet so that they could listen.

They sat perfectly still, and for a few moments Chad heard nothing. A little before, he had thought he heard something distant, muffled, unclear, but had dismissed the thought. Now something in the back of his mind whispered to him: yeah, and the problem is, you hear nothing at all now. Shouldn't there be the usual little night sounds? The owl cries, the insect scurryings? There was nothing.

Nothing, now, except a dull thud on the ground behind them.

They jumped to their feet, wheeled around together.

And there it stood, not fifteen feet away, tall and spindly in the night, its wooden blades whirling and creaking overhead.

He would never have thought the sight of a windmill could be so deeply, devastatingly terrifying.

It couldn't be standing here, couldn't be standing here now, but it was, and some frenzied voice in his mind said: Look. He did look, and it seemed to his disturbed senses that a drool of some thick liquid extended from the windmill blades nearly to the ground, a trail of thick fluid that whipped and shifted as the blades turned, *whirr whirr whirr whirr*. He grabbed Karen by the arm, seeing, as they turned to run, that her eyes were starting almost out of her face with terror. They broke and ran into the chaparral. He had no idea where they were going. They just ran.

After a kaleidoscopic nightmare of running, they somehow arrived back at the house. He must have been unconsciously letting Karen guide them all along, because he never could have found his way back, given the state his mind was in. He had only a jumbled memory now of moonlit desert scenes—standing armies of cholla cactus, stretches of sandy land dotted with sagebrush and chamisa and spiky extrusions of yucca and prickly pear cactus and mesquite—and always somewhere behind them, the suggestion of a tall, gaunt presence following. But when they reached the back porch steps, it seemed that nothing had followed them after all. The night was quiet, a silent stage-set that stretched away into limitless space.

Karen opened the back door and he followed her in. She gestured to him to be quiet. Panting with exhaustion, she held him close for a minute, then motioned toward the stairs. He could feel that she was trembling, either with fear or fatigue from running, or both. They crept upstairs, down the hall, into his room. He held her in the dark for a long time before turning on the light.

"My God, Karen," he said, alarmed at how hollow his voice sounded. "We didn't see that. We didn't see it. Did we?"

She pressed her face to his chest for a moment, then looked up at him. "Yes we did."

He fumbled for something to say. Finally he asked, "Are we going to tell anybody?"

Trying to catch her breath, she shook her head. "I don't think so. Not right away. There isn't any point."

He considered this. "Maybe you're right. Nobody would believe it, I guess."

"I don't know, they might or might not believe it," she said, regaining her breath and her composure somewhat, "but either way, there's no point. It wouldn't do any good."

He put a hand on each of her shoulders and looked squarely into her face. "I want you to tell me what you know about this thing."

"By now you probably know almost as much as I do," she said.

"It's alive, isn't it?"

"Yeah," she said, swallowing. "Unless things that aren't alive can move around."

"And it's alive because of Lothrop Walker. Papa Loaty."

"Or," she said, looking very solemn now, "*he's* alive again because of *it*. Take your pick."

It was nearly one o'clock. They went to bed, but neither of them slept particularly well.

*   *   *

The irony was, Chad thought, at dawn, that they had to be more concerned with discretion than with the horror of what they had seen, at least for now. The irony of the situation had no doubt occurred to Karen as well, because as she slipped from his room and hurried to get downstairs before the rest of the family was up, she looked almost as if she wanted to laugh, in spite of everything. She made it to her own room, anyway; unless he was mistaken, no one knew that she had spent the night in his room. All things considered, he thought it best that they not know, for the time being.

He was glad that breakfast around here wasn't a family affair, because he didn't want to face everybody just yet, thinking the thoughts he was thinking, remembering what he remembered from last night. Was it memory or hallucination? He would have been delighted to think it was the latter, but then the problem with that was obvious: Karen had seen it too. She knew this land, knew that there wasn't supposed to be a windmill where they had seen one. Even he knew that much by now, working on the land for the time that he had been here.

It was better to try not to think about it too much. Happily, the day ahead was filled with work, and his tasks consumed his time altogether. He had only a glimpse of Karen, who waved to him from across the way as she and the rest of the women carried rugs out for beating. The sight of her reminded him that not all their memories of last night were dark ones; somehow he felt that she was thinking the same thing. Good old Chad, he thought, ruminating upon his feelings; you come out to work for a ranch family and you fall in love with the daughter. It sounded like a B-movie. But, he reflected, one could do worse than fall in love. Much worse.

He also caught sight of Carl at some point during the afternoon, mercifully at a distance. It was clear that he and Chad had nothing in particular to say to each other. Carl just gave him a smug kind of look, and otherwise ignored him, which was fine with Chad, certainly.

At supper that evening the conversation seemed even more subdued than usual; Chad thought that people seemed uncommonly tired—from the work of the day, or were he and Karen not the only ones who had had a less than restful night's sleep last night? Perhaps both. Everyone soon started going to their rooms, in any case; it would be another early dawn tomorrow. Chad, under the disapproving glare of Carl, said good night to Karen and went upstairs.

Momentarily, getting undressed and climbing into bed, he wondered if this would be a quiet night for once, but he was too tired to worry about it, and soon after switching the lamp off he was asleep.

And sometime after that, he was awake again.

Oh God, now what?

Out in the hall, the faint whisper of footsteps.

He slipped quietly out of bed, pulled his jeans on, and crept to the door. And listened.

Whatever it had been—but no, there it was again, a faint whisper of movement.

Then silence.

He waited.

Silence.

And all of a sudden he realized what was happening, and broke into a chuckle. It was Karen, of course, and she was hesitant to knock for fear of waking some of the others. Feeling a real warmth at the prospect of seeing her now, he unlocked the door and swung it open.

And was utterly unprepared for what was standing there.

It was gaunt and tall and dressed in nondescript rags, and it stood so close to the door jamb that at first he couldn't see its head. But bending its bony knees, it stooped to bring its face into view.

It was as if he couldn't quite focus on what he was seeing, couldn't quite understand it. Beneath an impression of choppy hair, the front of the head was a face of sorts, though it seemed oddly angular, as if caved in at some spots and projected at others. Either the thing rolled its head on its scrawny neck, or parts of the face actually shifted, rotated. It took Chad a moment to realize that the thing was crooning a demented sort of song under its breath, and that a long, sour-smelling river of ropy-looking drool trailed from the mouth nearly to the floor. As the thing's feverish eyes met Chad's its wormy face seemed to grow more lively, the diseased suggestion of a mouth widened, the mindless crooning grew more strident, and the ejection of drool became a torrent of liquid filth. The thing leaned close to him, projecting itself into the room, spraying his face with spittle, then withdrawing back into the hall and straightening up again to an appalling height.

It took Chad some time to realize that by some unreasoning reaction, he had followed the thing out into the hall, or that the screaming in the dank air of the hallway was his own. He was dimly aware that other bedroom doors were opening, alarmed faces were peering out. Mainly he was aware that the tall apparition, its jagged head nearly scraping the ceiling, had dropped like some deranged puppet down the stairwell.

Driven by an impulse that he could not have named, he ran down the hall to the top of the stairwell and started to descend, and found Karen on the second or third step down. She was pressed against the handrail, clutching it, her face chalky-white, her eyes big and terrified. Evidently the thing had passed by her on the stairs. Somewhere in the turmoil above and behind, in the hall, he thought Fenton and Edna were there, but all he could think of was the horror that had just passed through.

Grabbing Karen's arm, he pulled her along with him as he headed farther down the stairs. Halfway down, he had that uncanny sensation again, as if something had seeped back out through the walls of the house, leaving a sort of psychic vacuum that seemed almost to stop one's heart. But he had only a second to think about it, because at the bottom of the stairs he and Karen collided with someone starting to come up. Everyone screamed at the same time.

The party they had collided with was a clearly flustered Carl, who eyed both of them with a roiling kind of anger in his face. "Well, now, Karen, this is cute," he snapped. "You want to tell me what you're doing upstairs with him in the middle of the night?"

Chad pushed him out of the way. "For Christ's sake, Carl, is that all you can think about? Didn't you see what just came through here?" He pulled at Karen's arm again, and the two of them ran toward the front door. Carl was muttering something like "All I see is a couple of losers" behind them, but it was hard to hear over the general babble, because by now the entire household was up. Not pausing to attempt any explanations, Chad and Karen ran out onto the porch. A gust of wind rose around them the moment they emerged from the house, and Chad saw Karen clutch at herself for warmth, as she was wearing only a thin nightgown and slippers. He felt the cold himself, as he had put his jeans and slippers on but no shirt, but the overarching impression was that this wasn't just normal wind they felt, but something else, something stirred by the presence that was still moving around out there in the night. Chad could hear, could almost feel, the thudding in the ground somewhere close. Somehow he still felt compelled to follow it, to see, to try to understand something that couldn't be understood. Evidently Karen had the same feeling, for it was she this time who pulled him, urging them both down the porch steps and away from the house.

A layer of dark clouds had gathered, and only a dim periphery of moonlight filtered through, so there was little that they could see in the night air before them. They had scarcely started peering into the gloom to try to make out what was there, when Chad felt a flat-handed slap between his shoulderblades, and turned around to encounter, again, a seethingly angry Carl.

"I'm only going to ask you one more time, scumbag. What were you and Karen—"

Chad thrust an arm out and grabbed him by the throat. "Listen, you imbecile, don't you see anything going on around you? Don't you know why we're out here?" With a little shove backwards, he released the man's throat and pointed off in the direction they had been looking. But it was Karen who spoke.

"Don't you know what's walking around out there?" She glared at Carl and shook her head at him in frustration. "Don't you know what has always walked around out there?"

Carl sniffed contemptuously. "All I hear is a lot of halfwit rumors, family fairy tales that don't amount to diddly-squat. And all I see is you standing out here in your nightgown that a person can see right through, and all I remember is you coming down the stairs with this lowlife stable-boy."

Karen, who had half turned back around to stare out into the night, snapped back around to face him. "Yeah, well, you'd better learn to see something more than that. You don't think there's anything here, you walk out there and find out." She pointed off into the dark.

Carl laughed, a nasty, barking sound. "Sure, babes. Whatever you say. Just to show you I'm not as loony as the rest of you." He stalked off into the gloom and was almost immediately lost from view.

Chad started after him. "Carl, wait up. I don't think you understand." He could see Carl dimly outlined in what little light there was, maybe twenty or thirty feet away.

Carl's voice came back oddly muffled in the distance. "I understand all right—" But whatever else he had been going to say was cut off by a sort of gurgle of surprise, or shock, or fright. Then: "God in heaven—"

"Carl?" Chad ran forward as well as he could manage in the dark. He sensed that Karen was close behind him. "Carl!"

Then the moon came partly out from behind the clouds, casting a sickly and all too revealing radiance over the land.

Carl was there, all right, and had turned around, facing Chad and Karen, as if he wanted to run back in the direction he had come, but behind him stood the windmill. No windmill could have been there, of course, but there it was.

It happened fast, and Chad scarcely trusted his senses, but what he thought he saw was the windmill pivot on one wooden foot, lean its creaking form down, nearly to the ground, and press its spinning blades onto Carl, who howled with rage and pain as the blades pummeled him. Then the thing straightened back up, teetered on its footing, and moved off into the night, gone.

The whole family gathered around at first, long enough to see Edna bandage Carl's wounds, and then Karen, Chad, Isabelle, Edna, and Susan sat up watching over him. He lay on the parlor sofa where Chad, after carrying him back to the house, had placed him. Carl was conscious, moaning, evidently in considerable pain. There had been some bleeding about his face and shoulders and back. He was missing several teeth as well, and his whole face was swollen, to the point where one puffy eye was nearly shut. They made him as comfortable as possible on the sofa.

When things seemed fairly well under control, Chad and Karen stepped back out onto the front porch and stood looking out at the dark.

Chad turned to Karen. "What does it want? What does he want?"

She shook her head, and said something that he would never forget. "Maybe it doesn't want anything, really. Maybe it just wants to be here."

After a while Chad asked: "What was Carl's crime? You saw what it did to him. I mean, I know he's a jerk, but what did he do to deserve—"

Edna Fox Walker had slipped the screen door open and come up behind them, and answered the question. "He didn't believe."

"How can anyone believe in something like this?" Chad asked.

Edna looked long and thoughtfully at him. "How can we not?" she said.

Just before breakfast Chad saw Carl heading out to one of the cars, and he was carrying a couple of suitcases. By six o'clock in the morning he was gone.

No one talked very much. There didn't seem to be any need.

Around ten in the morning, when Chad was working out in the field, Joe Tom Walker came up to him and clapped him on the back. "You must think we're a pretty strange lot," he said. "Couldn't blame you if you didn't want to have anything more to do with this family."

"On the contrary," Chad said, "I'd like to be part of it. I'd like to stay."

"Oh?" Joe Tom said, a faint suggestion of a smile showing on his face. "Well, I can't say I'm entirely surprised."

A few weeks later, Chad and Karen were driving to Roswell on a very special errand. Things had been quiet around the Walker place, but Chad knew that there would be other events, other presences, other unaccountable stirrings in the night. He didn't mind, because Karen would be with him, and because he really didn't think of Papa Loaty as a menace any more, though some corner of his mind still whispered to him how uncanny, how unearthly it all was—right down to the towering old man's very name, chosen through channels of mystery that cut across time, space, and logic in a way not to be imagined. But in the end he was just a lonely old man who wanted to be with his family.

Halfway to town they saw a ragged hitchhiker, whom Chad recognized, after a moment, as the one he had met in the bar in Corona. Chad pulled over, leaned back and opened the rear door and let the man in, and drove on.

"How's life been treating you, out to the Walker place?" the old man asked.

"Tolerably well, I'd say," Chad replied, nodding toward Karen. "We're going into town to see about a marriage license."

"Well, now, congratulations to you both," the hitchhiker said.

"Thank you," Karen said.

"Who's going to be best man?" the hitchhiker asked.

Chad gave him a grin in the rearview mirror. "You want the job?"

"Naw, listen, I ain't no good at that kind of thing," the old man said with a chuckle. After a moment he added a cryptic comment: "It tested you, didn't it?"

Chad eyed him curiously in the rearview mirror. "Beg your pardon?"

"It tested you," the old man repeated.

"Did it?" Chad asked.

The old man nodded in the mirror. "Yep."

"How did I come out?" Chad asked.

"Are you stayin' on?" the old man asked in return.

"Yes," Chad replied, "you know I am."

"There's your answer," the hitchhiker said.

When they got to the outskirts of town, he tapped Chad on the shoulder. "You can let me off here. Much thanks for the ride."

When the old man was climbing out of the car, Chad turned to look at him. "We'll invite you to the wedding."

"Thanks anyhow," the man replied, "but that's for family. Walkers have got a lot of family."

"Yes, we do," Karen said, waving goodbye to him and turning then to Chad. "Don't we? A lot of family."

Pulling the car out onto the road again, Chad glanced back for a last look at the old hitchhiker, but there was no sign of him. A large crow sat on a fencepost nearby. It flapped its ragged black wings once, rose like a kite against the desert sky, and was gone like a dream beyond recall. The wind rose, husky and ethereal like the sighing of some strange chorus of Indian flutes, fleeing down arroyos, lost, down timeless abysses where the mind could scarcely follow, a wind, a song older than time, and redolent of all the magic that the desert holds. After a time, the night grew still, the cries of coyotes ceased, and there shone down upon the silent scene an icy field of stars.

It was over—he could go home now. Or maybe, he reflected, looking out into the limitless night, he was home already.

Because, now that he thought of it, home was a different concept to different people. To some, home was the mystery of the desert—inscrutable, capable of killing you if you slipped, even for a moment, in respecting it. It had, in fact, a million ways of killing you, and maybe that was the beauty, the fascination of it, that it could outlast you, survive you. In the desert there was a kind of beauty even in death.

But today the thing to celebrate was life.

Acknowledgments

"Blessed Event" first appeared in *Wicked Mystic* (Fall/Winter 1994).

"Country Living" first appeared in *Bare Bone* #7 (2005).

"Crayons" first appeared in *Black Petals Magazine* (Autumn 1999).

"The Cryptogram" first appeared in *Twilight Zone Magazine* (December 1986).

"Desert Dreams" first appeared in *Black Wings: New Tales of Loveraftian Horror,* edited by S. T. Joshi (PS Publishing, 2009).

"Down in the Mouth" first appeared in Burleson, *Beyond the Lamplight* (Jack O'Lantern Press, 1994).

"Fwoo" has not appeared previously.

"Gramma Grunt" first appeared in *100 Wicked Little Witch Stories,* edited by Stefan Dziemianowicz, Robert Weinberg, and Martin H. Greenberg (Barnes & Noble, 1995).

"Grampa Pus" first appeared in *Wicked Mystic* (Spring 1996).

"Hopscotch" first appeared in *Terminal Fright* (Spring 1996).

"Jack O'Lantern Jack" has not appeared previously.

"Jigsaw" first appeared in *Deathrealm* (Spring 1996).

"Leaves" first appeared in *Terminal Fright* (Fall 1996).

"Lujan's Trunk" first appeared in *The Disciples of Cthulhu II,* edited by Edward P. Berglund (Chaosium, 2003).

"One-Night Strand" first appeared in Burleson, *Four Shadowings* (Necronomicon Press, 1994).

"Papa Loaty" first appeared in *Poe's Progeny,* edited by Gary Fry (Gray Friar Press, 2005).

"Pump Jack" first appeared in *Bare Bone* #1 (2001).

"Sheep-Eye" first appeared in *Weird Trails,* edited by Michael Szymanski (Triad Entertainments, 2002).

"Sheets" first appeared in the *Roswell Literary Review* (March/April 1997).

"Spider Willie" first appeared in *Bare Bone* #3 (2002).

"A Student of Geometry" first appeared in Burleson, *Four Shadowings* (Necronomicon Press, 1994).

"Tumbleweeds" first appeared in *Dark Terrors 4,* edited by Stephen Jones and David Sutton (Victor Gollancz, 1998).

"Tummerwunky" first appeared in *Inhuman Magazine* #1 (July 2004).

"Up and About" first appeared in *Fusing Horizons* #5 (n.d.).

"Wait for the Thunder" first appeared in *Cemetery Dance* #46 (2003).

"The Watcher at the Window" first appeared in *Gathering the Bones,* edited by Dennis Etchison, Ramsey Campbell, and Jack Dann (Tor, 2003).

"The Weeping Woman of White Crow" has previously appeared only in Spanish translation as "La llorona de cuervo blanco" in the Mexican anthology *Frontera de Espejos Rotos* (Roca, 1994).

Lightning Source UK Ltd.
Milton Keynes UK
14 April 2010